# REST HARROW

# REST HARROW

## Janice Kulyk Keefer

HarperCollins*Publishers*Ltd

*The author would like to thank the Canada Council for its continuing support.*

*This is a work of fiction; the characters and settings found within are imaginary composites and do not refer to actual persons or places.*

First Edition

Canadian Cataloguing in Publication Data

Keefer, Janice Kulyk, 1953-
  Rest harrow

ISBN 0-00-223993-0

I. Title.

PS8571.E435R43 1992   C813'.54   C92-094490-6
PR9199.3.K434R43 1992     74803

92 93 94 95 96 97 98 99 ❖ RRD 9 8 7 6 5 4 3 2 1

For Jan and Antony Cleminson

**Rest-Harrow:** medium erect undershrub, stickily hairy. Leaves trefoil or oval. Flowers in leafy stalked spikes, sometimes with soft spines. Dry grassy and waste places.
—*Wild Flowers of the British Isles*

**Harrow:**
1. A heavy frame of timber (or iron) set with iron teeth or tines, which is dragged over ploughed land to break clods, pulverise and stir the soil, root up weeds or cover in the seed.
2. A cry of distress or alarm; a call for succour.
3. To draw a harrow over; to plough; to tear, lacerate, wound.
—*Shorter Oxford English Dictionary*

The child is with her mother, at a cottage by a lake. Is not with her mother, for her mother sits on the porch, reading. She has been reading all the afternoon while her daughter slept; she is still reading when the child calls through the screen-window, "Can I wake up yet?"

"Not just yet," her mother says. She doesn't look up, she doesn't look anywhere but at the page on which the child sees only black swimmers in a stiff, white sea.

The child wants her mother, wants to be the book on her mother's lap, the covers she holds as if they were the edges of a cracked bowl, a broken bowl that will mend itself if you can only hold its pieces tight enough, long enough together. The child returns to her bed, closes her eyes but cannot sleep. She thinks of swimmers doing backward somer-saults off the dock at evening, falling into water so still, so clear it seems to be the sky prisoned in a mirror. Flies crawl up and down the screen, the only sounds their fat, black buzz, and wind brushing the trees the way her mother brushes her long, long hair. Leaves lifting, spinning, telling stories in a language she will never learn. All walls are white, here; even the mirror in its bleached wicker frame is the white of an eye; when she stands on the corner of her bed, she finds her face lodged in the glass like a splinter, an eyelash to be blinked away. And all around the mirror, leaf shadows swimming into light.

Your mother is reading. She doesn't see you stealing past the porch, down the steps, along the path between the trees. You tread carefully, heel to toe to heel along a trail of powdery dirt. You've been warned about poison ivy: three-leaved clusters, berries even birds won't touch. You've been warned, too, about the lake. *Never, ever go down to the lake alone. It isn't safe. One day when you've learned to swim you can go on your own, as far as you like. No. You're too young to learn. No. Perhaps next summer.* Always next summer; never yes, never now.

Sand scorches your feet; in the mild, washed-out air you smell the toast your mother burned this morning; burned because she was reading a book when she should have been watching. *Watch    look out    how many times do I have to tell    you're all I've got    you're my responsibility.* Your feet are matches as they strike the ground but you can't call out, if she hears she'll run after you, put you back inside the small white cedar-smelling room, make you lie all afternoon listening to flies drag themselves across the screen, searching for holes in the webbing.

Quiet. Careful. You reach the place where sand gives out and blue begins, water and sky and hills beyond all blue, like the lakes in your mother's eyes, blue you can't ever touch the way she sometimes lets you stroke the swansdown powder puff, the china nosegay of forget-me-nots. You can put your feet in the water, you can't get into trouble for doing that. She didn't say anything about the water, only the lake, don't go down to the lake alone.

No one else is here: the boy with a squint, who threw a stone at you, the old man with a dog small, quick as a butterfly. And all the families: fathers with mothers; children who make fun of you for not knowing how to swim, for not knowing. Your mother reading on a blanket in the sand *I'll play with you later    later    time to myself    why don't you play with the others?* Who keep asking where your father is, your brothers and sisters, asking and knowing in spite of your saying nothing as you turn away. Pretending you can't hear them any more, the other children, their questions, the questions she asks that you can never answer. *What's wrong? How can I help if you won't tell me? What is it that you want?*

Now there is nobody here but you. The others are all reading books or taking naps, doing what they're told, not what they want. You want, you are always wanting everything you cannot have. You've been forbidden the lake, but you want the lake. Here, now, grabbing your feet: water so clear and still you can see every ridge of sand, each stone poking its snout up. Not water, but something denser, richer, like the mirror Alice walks through into looking-glass land. Look, your feet are turning into fish, they flicker away from you, far away to the middle of the lake where the water is bluest, deepest. Your hands nibble free from your wrists, chase after your feet as water licks through your shorts and the brown skin across your belly. Soaking your halter top and now the tips of your braids where they prickle your shoulders. Water that opens and shuts, opens and shuts like the window at which you sat and watched your mother, reading.

Buzzing. The last thing she hears is a fly, not black but silver, high over water that's brimming her chin, spilling into the small curve under her lip, over her lips and up, up. Tilting back her head so only her eyes and nose touch air, the small silver scar above her. *What do you want? Why can't you tell me?* She wants to vanish through the screen and the glass and the water into a hiding place which only he can find. Buzzing. Not black but a small, silver scratch across the planet of her eye, always hurting and thus always with her: the only thing she has of him this never having. The plane passes over her, its wings spread wide as her arms. Till her eyes cannot bear to see what she does not hold; like her feet, like her hands, they swim far away, leaving what's left of her invisible as light and falling, turning, into the water's cold transparency.

# I

# IN TRANSIT

Half an hour before the plane was due to depart, Anna reached into her handbag for a pen and came up with her finger gushing fat, red tears. Quickly she pulled a Kleenex from her pocket, winding it round and round the gash, trying to hide the damage, make it go away. The woman beside her in the no-smoking lounge tapped away on her lap-top computer, oblivious to what was happening to Anna. The Kleenex bred crimson dots: poppies unfurling under time-lapse photography. "Septicaemia, gangrene, amputation," whispered Anna, falling helpless prey to the imagination of disaster.

Up to now her departure had gone with the finesse, the exactitude of a royal tour. They'd be boarding any minute—what if the plane took off before she could find a Band-aid? Was this a portent, a signal? Hadn't she seen, didn't someone once tell her of that episode from "The Twilight Zone"? On the eve of a journey, a woman dreams of being wheeled down a hospital corridor, not to the operating theatre but to the morgue instead. When she boards her plane the next day, who should greet her but the morgue attendants of her dream dressed up as pilot, stewardess? And because this is "The Twilight Zone," she's able to scream, racing back down the ramp into the departure lounge as the plane takes off without her. Shortly after, it explodes, one great metallic firework.

Anna wasn't the sort to scream under any circumstance at all. She merely clutched the Kleenex tighter round her finger while attempting to secure her handbag, author of this freak disaster. A nasty, no, a vicious cut—she had no idea how to deal with it. After all, she wasn't the sort of person to whom emergencies occurred. Disasters, emergencies—what on earth was she thinking? Ridiculous to get so upset over a minor accident, not even an accident, an inconvenience. Except that it was her right hand, her writing hand. And it was bleeding such a lot.

Waiting in the line-up at the Information Desk, trying to smile and straining her ears to catch boarding announcements made by

someone with a cleft palate speaking Finnish, Anna resolved to take
control of the situation. She did so in the manner most natural to her:
by creating a fiction. "The art of living," she has heard it said, "is the
art of concealing from yourself everything you know to be true.
What's true, of course, being everything you'd rather not know." Has
heard it said by Luke, who was the real author of this accident, Luke
and not her handbag. If he hadn't insisted on spending the night with
her, he would never have left his razor behind, and she would never
have swept it into her handbag along with all the other bathroom
effluvia—toothbrush, dental floss, Qtips—in that last panic before
the taxi arrived.

"It's not an omen," she kept repeating to herself. There was only
one person ahead of her now, a man asking for detailed information
about car rentals at Heathrow. "Not an omen but a propitiation of the
gods. Remember hubris, the sin of pride, Allah frowning upon perfection. Good then, I've made my sacrifice, I've offered up my fingertip to
pain's necessary tether. Humour is always concealed pain, therefore
pain must always be concealed humour, or at least, the sunny expecta-
tion that you'll sail through everything exactly as you've planned." Not
quoting Luke this time, but herself, Anna English, Dr. English, B.A.,
M.A., Ph.D.—

"Yes?"

Anna jumped. "I'm sorry." Why was she apologizing? And to
whom? This bubble-gum blonde, pop-eyed and fuschia-fingernailed?

"You're bleeding," observed the girl at Information. "We'd better
take a look at that in First Aid."

Why, Anna wondered, was she so grateful for the attentions of this
most professional woman who was leading the way to what looked like
a temporary fall-out shelter? Was it simply the manner in which she
splashed peroxide over Anna's hand, the tone in which she sympa-
thized—"That's quite a cut you've got there—" soothing the invisible
child within, the one who has never stopped weeping over the scraped
knee or name-calling she still suffers in some long-demolished schoolyard? And how long had it been since she'd allowed anyone to take
care of her like this? She was perfectly capable of looking after herself,
that was the whole point of this excursion. But why was it taking so
long to get the bandage? If the girl didn't hurry she'd miss her flight,
and then—

By the time Anna returned to the departure lounge, they had finished boarding passengers requiring special assistance. It was the end of July, so she hadn't the excuse of gloves to hide the comically excessive wrapping on her finger. She joined the rest of the passengers tramping aboard, sheep-like, somnambulistic, obsessed with matching themselves to their predestined seat numbers. It became something of a feat for Anna to control raincoat, handbag, briefcase with her one unlacerated hand. But she managed, wishing that Luke could see her braving out the consequences of his act of sabotage, the razor booby trap, last straw of a desperate man. Who hadn't challenged her insistence that she get herself to the airport on her own. And why shouldn't she? It wasn't as though she were going off to the wars or into an eternity of exile in a desperately foreign land. She did, after all, speak the language; she had, in a sense, already been there.

The man who squeezed into the seat beside her offered to stow Anna's raincoat in the overhead compartment. She could barely make out his words—the air conditioners were on, along with classical music, something Haydnesque, calculated to soothe tempers and temper brooding on the odds of survival in an age of Semtex, defective auxiliary engines, improperly fastened cargo doors. Anna secured a book from her briefcase, strapped herself in (rather clumsily, due to her bandaged finger) and started marking passages of a text she would immediately forget when and if the plane should land. Stoicism seemed the best course, given she was doomed to spend the next six hours in a shark-shaped, metal projectile buoyed up by a law of aerodynamics far more fictive to her than anything in *Bleak House* or *Barchester Towers*.

The pilot announced an indefinite delay while they lined up for runway space; the stewards plied the aisles with every conceivable kind of doll-sized container for what was referred to as "alcoholic beverages," but which everyone was calling "booze." Anna never drank: one glass of wine and she'd be sleepy; an inch of brandy made her comatose. "Cheap date," Luke always said, though she made a point of paying her own way. She liked to be in control: alert, cautious, with her cloak of invulnerability wrapped tight around her. And besides, if the plane were to explode mid-Atlantic, she would want to know what was happening. *"Why?" "What for?"* Luke's refrain, ringing the whorls of her ears, tapping at her breastbone: *I told you so, I told you so* as the cargo doors burst open, sucking her out into something dark and foreign, viscous as a plucked eye—

"Cushions? Would you like an extra blanket?" The stewardess was being especially attentive, Anna observed. This must have been due to the passenger on her left, the man who'd helped her with her raincoat. He was handsome in a Robert Redford sort of way. Anna may have been the only one of her entire generation who knew Robert Redford from *Out of Africa* rather than *Butch Cassidy and the Sundance Kid*. She'd seen *Out of Africa* only because one of her students wrote a paper comparing the film and textual versions; on the whole, it had confirmed Anna's prejudice against the cinema, and technology in general. She had no television, rode a bicycle to campus except in winter gales, owned neither a dishwasher nor a microwave, and did all her laundry by hand. Her one apostasy was her user-friendly computer, travelling in the hold, plastered with fragile stickers and wedged between a Burmese cat and a Kerry blue. The computer, however, was Luke's doing; he had shamed her into giving up the antique Remington she'd inherited from her mother. Giving up, but not away—she had it still, in a corner of a closet where she knew he'd never look.

Anna waved away the offer of a *Globe and Mail*. Newspapers frightened her; they were too immediate, too insistent, the way the print refused to stay fixed, bleeding all over her hands. The stewardess shrugged, moving on to the next row of seats; Robert Redford fiddled with the settings on his ultradigital watch, and Anna returned to her book. She was grateful he didn't seem to be a talker. Though she was definitely not the type to draw forth banter from strange men, offers of drinks or requests for telephone numbers, she'd been consigned by fate to the role of confidante, good listener. Students, colleagues, even supermarket strangers would drape their lives across her ears as if she were the aural equivalent of a dressmaker's dummy. It came, she'd decided, from being so visibly unattached—no children tugging at her skirts, no wedding band lodged on her finger. It came from being as good as invisible.

Who, then, did the stewardess see in seat K11? Anna imagined herself in a navy blue uniform with crimson maple leaves attached; set down her observations as though she were Jane Eyre constructing the self-portrait that would fascinate a certain Edward Rochester.

*Item.* A woman somewhere in between the crest of "young" and trough of "older." Average height, average weight, neither buxom nor anorexic. Her clothes understated, but not without a certain style. (She favoured dark shades; she'd grown up believing it was dangerous to draw attention to yourself.) Hair and eyes a shade of brown you could call chestnut, if you were of a poetic turn of mind. A face so pleasantly indistinct that people always thought her a good ten years younger than she really was—hadn't Luke mistaken her for a student the first time he'd seen her? But otherwise perfectly ordinary, as her passport declared: no distinguishing marks whatsoever.

At last the plane began to taxi down the runway. Anna's finger burned; she wondered if she should loosen the bandage, but envisioned blood spurting over her new biography of Virginia Woolf. Haydn gave way to a voice-over from the screen that slid down before them; passengers were being counselled to watch a video about safety procedures. Anna reached instead for the plastic-coated booklet in the pouch in front of her. If she needed to know how to fasten a life jacket or the correct method of attaching an oxygen mask, she would rather learn from paper than from film. Unlike the images on the screen, the figures in the booklet were cartoonlike, vestigial as they slid, shoeless and minus eyeglasses, down a rubber chute into the Platonic idea of a lifeboat.

A sweet, rough pressure at the back of Anna's throat; underneath the safety booklet was the flight sickness bag, but how could she use it even before the plane took off? She was being absurd, this wasn't at all like her, this was just like her. She flipped the pages of her biography, trying to resist the plane's rising up, the blur of lights outside her window as the city fell away, roads and houses prudent enough to obey the laws of gravity. None of her fellow passengers looked anything more than tired, anything less than confident that the plane would gain the upper air and wing it blithely all the way to England. All Anna could think of was the woman from "The Twilight Zone"; the plane blooming into fire.

But now the *No Smoking* and *Fasten Seatbelts* signs switched off and people were actually laughing. A small girl sucking on a stretchy hairband peeped round the side of the seat ahead, giving a smile so open and trusting that Anna couldn't help herself. She smiled back as if she, too, had no knowledge of the need for life preservers, oxygen masks, crash landing procedures.

"What's your name?" the child asked.

What could Anna do but tell her?

"That's almost the same as mine. I'm Emma. We're going to visit my Dad. He lives in Norwich now." She pronounced the name correctly, to rhyme with porridge; otherwise she sounded perfectly Canadian.

"Shush, Emma." The child's face disappeared—there was murmuring from the seats ahead, and Anna overheard the phrase, "Mustn't talk to strangers." She would say the same thing were she Emma's mother. But she wasn't, and she felt a blind, sudden bond with the child. She'd like to tell her that when she'd been her age, long ago when she'd been with her mother at a cottage up north, she had walked right into a lake, though she hadn't had an inkling of how to swim. Tell how she remembered the peculiar stillness of the water; how calmly she'd put her head under.

Anna forgot all about Emma and Emma's mother. She was walking into memory as if it were that very lake, walking out into the cold, still water, as much at home as if she were one of the minnows nibbling her toes. Anna remembered everything in the smallest detail: the way her head was forced up, the sounds of glass shattering as she began to breathe again. And her mother holding her so tight she had bruises for weeks after. It had become the master narrative of her childhood, more familiar, far more consequential than *Hansel and Gretel* or *Cinderella*: her mother telling how, on running down to the lake to look for her, she'd glimpsed the ruffled bottom of a child's bathing suit sticking up through the water like a Portuguese man-of-war.

It took a moment before Anna registered Emma's head over the seat—the smile she cocked before her mother tugged her down; the slap. Anna winced and returned to her book. She had brought this child nothing but trouble, she had never been good with children, even when she was a child herself. She couldn't imagine raising a child; she couldn't fathom how her own mother had managed to do so singlehandedly. She'd said as much to Luke the first time they'd slept together. Running his hand across her breasts, tracing the branches of her ribs, he'd asked her whether she'd ever wanted to have a baby. When she'd answered, he'd kissed her; she had tasted his relief as though it were a peppermint she'd bitten. For it turned out that, at his ex-wife's insistence, Luke had had a vasectomy. He'd presented it as an argument in his favour—now Anna needn't mess about with pills or coils or diaphragms.

The woman from the seat ahead manoeuvred herself into the aisle, ordered her daughter to behave, then joined the line-up for the toilets. *Queue, Anna, not line-up. Biscuit, not cookie; don't say undies: knickers.*

As soon as her mother had disappeared, Emma darted round again. "Are you going to Norwich?"

*The Man in the moon*
*came down too soon*
*and asked his way to—*

Anna knew she should say nothing, that she'd only get the child into trouble again, but Emma was staring into her face, daring her to answer. "No." It came out far more sharply than she'd intended. Then, since the child showed no sign of losing interest Anna relented. "I'm going to Sussex. That's on the south coast."

"Norwich is way better. We're staying for two weeks. How long are you going for?"

"A year."

"I wish I could. I've got to go back to school. What grade are you in?"

Emma's mother bore down the aisle; Anna shook her head in warning, but the child kept asking questions. Her mother arrived, glared at Anna, then ordered Emma into the middle seat. The child complained, began to cry as the mother threatened something and Anna buried herself in her book once more.

*He went by the south*
*And burnt his mouth*
*With eating cold plum porridge.*

Attendants passed up and down the aisle, proffering drinks, headsets for the movie, dinner trays. Anna attempted to read through the meal but the combination of her bandaged finger and suddenly loquacious neighbour made this quite impossible. While she toyed with a pallid lump of chicken he confided to her the various allergies of his children, the perfections of his wife, and the rewards and hazards of his line of work. At last, to Anna's dutifully disguised relief, he excused himself, treading on her feet on his way to the toilet. *Loo.*

Anna took advantage of his absence to examine her right hand. The gauze was sticky with blood, rusty-brown blood. Gingerly, she flexed her finger, felt a slight jab and gave a prayer of thanksgiving. She had recurrent nightmares of losing her sight or the use of her hands while going deaf and dumb. To lose power over language: this was her definition of true calamity, beside which annihilation in a jumbo jet would be a mere misfortune.

Another stewardess came by to collect the trays. The person next to the window had been asleep or dead ever since the plane took off; Robert Redford seemed in no great hurry to return. Anna could hear nothing from the seats ahead of her. Presumably the little girl had fallen asleep, and was dreaming of monsters to whom she was forbidden to speak, strangers who pursued her down dark alleys, pelting her with candy. At any rate, Anna was alone at last, in lovely limbo. She tilted back her seat and shut her eyes. Instead of counting sheep, she repeated to herself a letter she had memorized months ago:

Dear Dr. English,

I'm delighted you've agreed to take the cottage—to tell the truth, I'd given up all hope of renting it. I really don't understand why you'd want to come to this country in the first place. If you had any sense you'd stay right where you are—most of us would rather be anywhere else these days than the Septic Isle.

The cottage is all yours for the year, as long as you pay the rent and don't kill off the garden. You'll need a car, of course, though Pyeford's close enough to the univerity. I'm afraid the university's not what it used to be, thanks to the present government. But I suppose that won't stop you, either.

The cottage, I should warn you, is fairly primitive—no telly and no phone. But the neighbours are all right. It's called Rest Harrow and it's near the end of Pyeford High Street. Sorry I won't be there to meet you but I'll be somewhere in Bulgaria the day you arrive, and shan't return till the end of September.

I'll leave the key with Simon Jeffries (Chantry Cottage, up the lane, round the churchyard, to your left.) I've asked him to look in on you, see that you get properly settled. I assume you're coming on your own, though there's room for two. Just sign the lease and pop it back by return post and deposit the cheques with Lloyds in town.

Best of luck with your work. Why not ring up sometime when you're in London? Give my best to your Dr. Sleeman, though I really can't remember ever having met her. Good of her to have given you my name. I should think you'll hate it here.

Rosalind Oliver.

Anna shut her eyes, but it wasn't any help. The letter kept printing itself onto the page of what she supposed she should call her mind, though she was increasingly unsure whether she could be said to have one. *Idiot, imbecile, what are you doing, renting a house from someone capable of writing a letter like that? And at such an extortionate price—no wonder you were the only taker.* She knew exactly what Dr. Oliver would look like, she'd met her time and again in the novels her mother had always been reading: a regulation English eccentric, small and fat, with wild white hair and biscuit crumbs clinging to her whiskered mouth. Off on a bus tour to Bulgaria, of all places. Imagine the fun Luke would have with that. She hadn't dared show him the letter; he'd been so opposed to her going in the first place.

"You'll have to fill out a landing card."

Anna sat staring at the cardboard square the stewardess had given her as though it were a pocket mirror refusing to return her reflection. *Reason for Travelling to the U.K.* What should she write, what would ring true? *Family*—a promise given, a debt long overdue. The English Country Calendar on the kitchen wall, every Christmas a new one and always the same, her mother crossing off the dates until the next brief summer holiday at a northern lake, pretending it was the Lake District, pretending that one year they would go off together to Gad's Hill, Bateman's, Haworth, Abbotsford.

*Erotic Entanglements*: would that sound more convincing? Hadn't she resisted Luke's concerted campaign to come to England with her, and then, even more valiantly, his plan to exchange his cramped apartment for the freedom of her house during her year away? Eventually they'd struck a compromise: Anna would rent out her house to a pair of graduate students, but would appoint Luke as caretaker should pipes burst or rads leak. He would write periodically to tell her that the house was still standing; she would invite him to spend Christmas with her in England. And after that?

*Reason for Travelling to the United Kingdom.* That she had a book to write, a book for which she would need to plunder the Woolf papers at that red brick university where she would have studied, had it not been for her mother catching what turned out to be her death, some fifteen years ago. That her job depended on her book, for Dr. Sleeman had made it clear that even at small, Ruritanian universities, those who do not publish surely perish.

*Business*, Anna finally scribbled in the blank space on her landing card. She tucked the card into her passport, then searched in vain for the book that had somehow slipped off her lap. For a screen was descending two feet in front of her; overhead lights were being dimmed. Helplessly, Anna lifted up her eyes. In the middle of a teeming freeway, Caucasians in Asian dress were performing a bewildering variety of martial arts. She couldn't make head or tail of the dialogue, whether she tuned into the French or the English version. Shutting her eyes tight, Anna pretended she was Virginia Woolf at a showing of *Storm over Asia* in a Berlin cinema, circa 1929.

*       *       *

Only after the film was over, just as the stewardesses were reapplying their lipstick, erasing the smudged mascara from their cheeks, switching on lights and preparatory-to-landing Muzak, did Anna fall into sleep deep enough for dreams. Literally fell, since the trapeze from which she was swinging splintered in her hands. For one clear, still moment she hung, then dropped. Not somersaulting to a safety net; not floating like a wayward feather, but smashing so fast her body telescoped, head screeching through ribcage, gut and birth canal. With a shudder violent enough to shake the plane apart, she woke to a stewardess pushing a breakfast tray towards her. Woke and instantly forgot her dream.

Anna wasn't the least bit hungry, yet she finished the egg staring up from her plate like a one-eyed desperado. The person in the window seat grunted, twitched—Anna was as startled as if she were witnessing a resurrection, not a mere awakening. She checked her watch, and deciding she could put it off no longer, shoved her tray onto the empty seat beside her and queued up for the loo.

Once locked inside, Anna removed the bandage from her finger. It didn't throb anymore—the slashed skin let through no meaty blood, not even pale pink tears. Carefully, she disposed of the bandage, then brushed her skirt and turned to go, without even checking her reflection in the mirror screwed above the sink.

Regaining her seat, she nodded at her neighbour by the window, who looked as though she were going to be sick. Buckling herself into the aisle seat, clutching the safety precautions booklet to her, eardrums popping like champagne corks, Anna forced herself to keep swallowing. They made a perfect landing into Heathrow, Anna sighing her thanks to the God of Travellers. She was safe and as good as sound—her finger was fine, everything would go exactly as planned. But as she reached for her coat in the overhead compartment, there was a sharp, painful tug at her arm. It was the little girl who'd been forbidden to speak to her— Emily? Emma? She was standing on her seat, holding on to Anna, holding for dear life. Anna tried to smile and make a joke of the whole thing, but the child's eyes were as easy to read as the clutch of her hand. *Stay with me. Help me. I need you.*

"Come *on*, Emma, none of *that*." The mother didn't even look at Anna as she pried her daughter's fingers loose. The child didn't cry, or make any further show of resistance as far as Anna could tell. For Anna was crouched down, staring under the seat, following the stewardess's instructions to make sure she hadn't left any cabin baggage behind, that she had all her belongings with her. By the time she allowed herself to look up again, the child and her mother had vanished.

# II

# PYEFORD

Despite her computer and printer, her bulging suitcases with their **Warning, Heavy Baggage** stickers, Anna sailed through customs. They seemed to be stopping only Africans and Asians for luggage checks and examining their passports as though they were prophecies. Anna hadn't time to think about any of this; the car she'd arranged to lease for the year was already waiting for her and she was onto the motorway headed for Sussex less than an hour after landing.

It required no great effort to drive on the left; what proved far more difficult was finding the BBC. Her fumbling produced nothing better than a talk-show program which, except for the accents, could have been broadcast from Moosonee or Iowa City. People were phoning in to comment on the condition of Britain's youth. Lager louts. Yobbos. Football hooligans. The terms puzzled Anna, whose students back home were invariably polite, well groomed and industrious. Then a commercial came on, in which a mock Texan hectored his unseen audience on the necessity of purchasing air conditioning for those dog-gone days when the mercury soars to 70 degrees.

Anna laughed out loud and switched off the radio. Cars clogged the motorway but she didn't care. She felt a pure, rambunctious joy at being released from the airport, loosed upon a world as new, yet as familiar as morning. Once off the motorway, an enchantment seemed to enclose her and the car and the road itself, suspending them like bees in amber. Nothing was named or marked at all: she seemed to be driving past the same stretch of hedgerows over and over again; identical cottages and fields. She rolled down her window, but refused to pull over to consult the map—what did it matter if she took a wrong turning? Reckless, that's how she felt—reckless, abandoned, free. Hadn't she the whole day in which to make her way to Pyeford? Who was there to sit in wait for her, or call her to account?

The car pushed through ever-narrowing lanes, releasing pungent, heat-soaked scents. "Cow-parsley," Anna called out. "Vetch. Moon carrot. Bladderwort." And then, at the top of her lungs, "Stinking hen-bane!" Names streaming past like the scenery: names her mother had taught her years ago out of imported field guides to the English country-side. Anna's fingers tightened round the wheel; she felt as if strangers were dancing wildly in her heart, knocking down walls and crashing the furniture. How could the names of wildflowers hurt her, any more than the sun honeying the leaves of oak and beech? The day, the place itself was made for her—she would feed off the year ahead like a wasp hollowing a pear, hollowing and hoarding until she had the whole of it locked sweet and safe inside her.

"Oh," cried Anna, in a voice one might use to call out to a lover: not so much a word as a sound that could barely be shaped into letters. Yet it wasn't a lover turning to meet her, here where leaves gave way to sky. It was the Downs, the low, green hills Virginia Woolf had walked, suddenly a real and not a printed passage. The car swerved, nearly ploughing through a hedge; Anna jammed on the brakes, her heart racketing against her ribs. It was all right, there'd been no one there to see her. Shakily, she opened the glove compartment, searching out the map of England that came with the car. Hopeless, of course—Sussex was nothing but a road-raddled inch of green. Meticulously she folded up the map, then chucked it out the window, driving on until she came at last to a petrol station.

To get to Pyeford you turned off the A onto a B road, then surren-dered to a leaf-tunnelled lane, winding round and about till you found yourself on a narrow street labelled, logically if unimaginatively, The Street. All perfectly straightforward and simple and unsignposted. Past the pub: bulging, crooked, *echt* Tudor, with a picture of a magpie swing-ing from the post. And then a row of cottages, some stuccoed white, others lapped with burnt-orange tiles. A new-looking village hall, and something very grand behind a high flint wall and iron gate. More cot-tages. One of them had a wooden sign with the letters partially erased: it took her some time to spell out Rest Harrow. There was no drive and no garage, so Anna parked in front, rolled down the window and ven-tured a closer look.

It wasn't the wreck she'd expected. She stepped out of the car and made her way up the front walk. Small, leaded windows over a border of yellow snapdragons and crimson dahlias. Everywhere, roses like gigantic bowls of clotted cream. Gold slashes of rest harrow, a plant she'd seen only in wildflower guides before. A bright blue door with a device rather less welcoming than a lion or dolphin: a woman's head, her long, thick, almost seething hair gathered up and fastened to the hinge of the knocker. To discourage visitors, or perhaps to encourage only the right kind? Anna looked it straight in the eyes.

"I'm not afraid of you," she whispered. Stepping right up she grasped the ring of the knocker firmly in her hand and brought it down hard between the lips of the Medusa. The knocks were cannon shots in the hazy stillness of the afternoon, but the creamy roses, the small convoluted suns of rest harrow didn't so much as quiver. Anna dropped the knocker, stumbling back. Imbecile—knocking on the door of an empty house.

*I'll leave the key with Simon Jeffries.* Anna sank back against the car. She was exhausted; tears pricked the corners of her eyes. How could she have permitted such casual arrangements—having to get the key from a perfect stranger? What if he were out? Would he even know it was today she was coming? What would she do if she couldn't find him? Curl up to sleep in the car? Hardly—the computer was in the passenger seat and two enormous suitcases crammed the back.

She would not break down, she would not admit defeat. Repeating Dr. Oliver's directions from memory, Anna proceeded further down The Street, but found no church, only an ash glade and a wire fence with a shaky stile over it. Why couldn't her landlady get her own directions right? Or had she misread, mis-memorized them? Where was the letter? In the bottom of her briefcase which she'd slid behind the suitcases, and which she couldn't bear to think of excavating now.

Anna walked back to Rest Harrow in what was becoming intolerable heat. She propped herself against the car and looked helplessly round. Opposite was a paddock, and then a barn, and then empty fields. Next door to her was a severe white cottage from which someone seemed to have removed any trace of flowers or vines. On the other side of Rest Harrow lay a thick beech hedge, finishing in a flint wall with a wrought iron gate. Peering between the bars, Anna made out a rambling stone house fronted by a prodigal garden and a lichen-splotched nymph guarding a lily pond. On the gateposts pelicans pierced their breasts with long, wind-chiselled beaks. The name *Fortuna House* appeared not on

some coy porcelain plaque with pastel flowers, but in slate, the letters
chiselled in Gill Sans. Dr. Oliver hadn't mentioned that she had the
local squire for a neighbour. In fact, her letter hadn't mentioned anything of any conceivable use. She'd been taken in, deceived, just as
Luke had warned. What was the use of a seventeenth-century cottage in
an idyllic Sussex village if she couldn't get into the place, if her way was
barred by a Medusa head who'd bite off her fingers, her already wounded
finger, when she lifted the knocker?

"The thing to do," Anna lectured herself and whoever else cared to
listen, "is to knock on someone's door and find out where Chantry Cottage is." In her sweat-drenched blouse, with her glistening face and
wilted hair, she did not feel like approaching the lord of the manor. She
would try the plain cottage next to Rest Harrow, instead. There was no
knocker, just a white, plastic circle, a blanked-out eye. Anna pressed it
without so much as denting its silence. She pressed again, and suddenly
the door opened: a black gap in the glare of the afternoon.

Not a face, but a mask—not a mouth, but a gouge. Eyes streaming,
flooding: tears or blood seeping from swollen lids? A woman's voice—it
would have been shouting if she weren't so hoarse: "I don't want you.
I'm not going. You know that. I don't go out, I don't take anything."

And slammed the door.

Anna shook herself and lurched back to Rest Harrow. Ignoring
the Medusa face, she grasped the handle of the door, twisting it
sharply in the hope that it might somehow have unlocked itself.
Nothing gave. "Fine, I'll try round the back," she cried, and dragged
herself along until she found a kitchen door, bolted shut. There was a
cat flap at the bottom. She crouched and pushed open the flap with
her right hand, the wounded one. What if this were the wrong house?
What if there were a hulking Tom ready to scratch or, worse, bite the
proffered hand? Or an Alsatian, a pit bull? But the only thing to meet
Anna's fingers was a long bolt at the edge of the door. She pulled it
free, straightened up, glanced over her shoulder, then tried the
handle. It gave. It gave! The first thing she'd do once she got inside
would be to board up the cat door. Nothing had been said about a cat.
Perhaps it *was* the wrong house?

On wobbly legs Anna found her way to the front hall, opened the
door, and, propping it wide with her handbag, made heroic sallies back
and forth from car to cottage, dumping her suitcases just inside the

threshold but carrying in her computer, printer and crate of diskettes as though they were the Host Itself. She put them in the study, a close, dark-curtained room at the very back of the cottage, but didn't stay to look around her. Retrieving her handbag, Anna let the front door swing shut, dragged herself to the parlour and fell into the sofa's soft, plush arms as if she were a bomb tearing through a cloud.

\*       \*       \*

For a moment after waking, Anna could recall her dream in perfect order and detail .

She was still a child; it was her birthday and she was going on a long journey to a city whose name she didn't know. Her mother and she wore matching dresses, white with blue lines, like fresh pages torn from a scribbler. They went to a house dark with heavy furniture. The darkness smelled of lemon polish; she was warned that lemon polish was poison; should she lick her fingers after trailing them across a sideboard or table here, she would die, die horribly. The house belonged to an old woman she had never seen before. The woman didn't smile, but put a hand like a heavy bracelet round her wrist; led her into a room in which a man was sitting by a window. She noticed the windows because they were covered with white curtains that tossed across the glass—they were the only things in the whole house that spoke of light and air and summer.

She was put in the middle, between her mother and the man. She looked back and forth, from her mother to the man, the man to her mother. The man was in a dark suit; he had a dark hat on his head. There were no hands at the end of his sleeves. He had no face. There was nothing but air between the brim of the hat and the white collar that gleamed in the dark like something smiling. Anna turned round and looked at her mother, who did not hold out her arms or make any sign for her to come to her. "Go on, then," said the old woman, whose house this was. "Go and say hello." But the child could not move, either forwards or backwards: her mother and the man kept silence, a silence that made Anna think of how, one winter, she had licked a metal fence and torn her tongue, trying to get free.

And then, as quickly as it had come to her, Anna lost the dream. All but the feel of metal in her mouth, the aftertaste of fantasy, or

memory, or some unstable mix of both. It didn't matter, Anna told herself: it was perfectly natural to have anxiety dreams your first night in a
strange house. What did matter was that it was six in the morning. She
was ravenous. Rummaging in the kitchen she chanced upon a packet of
Bath Olivers, a jar of capers, and a package of UHT whipping cream,
all of which she devoured while standing at the counter, using a tarnished silver spoon she found in the sink and which, she later realized,
must have been used to feed the cat. If cat there was, for she certainly
hadn't caught a trace of any living thing other than herself and a
colony of woodlice installed in a window sill.

Anna rubbed her hands over her face. She needed a bath: her body
felt as though it had been sunk all night in cold porridge. Upstairs she
found a murky closet into which a toilet and sink had been jammed.
And then a long, narrow room with a chipped enamel tub and a blank
medicine cabinet. Shivering, Anna undressed and ran the bath, waiting
for huge clouds of steam to billow forth. Testing the water, she could
feel nothing but icy ribbons. The whole cottage shook as she wrenched
the tap shut, as if the beams were about to snap. Counting to ten, she
stepped into the bath, imagining foundries, molten lava, the black hole
of Calcutta; encountering ice storms, polar caps, Ungava Bay. Taking a
deep breath, she slid under, surfaced, then washed her hair with a lump
of soap she'd found congealed to the side of the sink. She got out of the
bath much colder than she'd gone in, and with no impression of being
any cleaner.

Naked, shuddering, she reached for a towel, only to discover that
there weren't any. Presumably, they would be in the linen cupboard,
though where that was, Anna hadn't the least idea. The hallway was a
maze of doors; she started turning handles into bedroom after bedroom,
but found nothing to her purpose. She'd simply have to go downstairs,
all naked as she was, pry open a suitcase and pull on something warm.

She was in the hallway, fiddling with her purse, looking for the suitcase keys when the front door opened. The man stared at her for a
moment, and she stared back at him. And then, before she could think
to run upstairs or even to crouch behind her cases, the man made a half
bow and backed out of the cottage, closing the door so gently behind
him that the Medusa's teeth barely rattled. Anna simply stood there, as
if she were some strange flower that had sprung up from the transient
soil of her suitcase. When she finally moved to go back upstairs, it was

as if someone had reached out and gently turned her by the shoulders, a quarter turn, so that she saw, through the archway to the parlour, a large dark stain on the wall across from her. At first she thought it was a curtain, or even the entrance to a cave, but finally she recognized the huge mirror over the mantel, tarnished and spotted, the silvering gone in places so that all it gave you were shadows instead of a reflection.

Half an hour later, dressed in the first things she'd found in her suitcase—a long tweed skirt, a sweatshirt, woollen socks and running shoes—Anna reasoned that it must have been a peeping Tom. How on earth could she have left the front door unlocked? To have been found out, standing there naked for all the world to see. . . . What if he weren't a peeping Tom, but a burglar out on a break-and-enter? Except that burglars didn't usually come in through the front door. And she was so sure she'd locked up the night before. Perhaps the lock was defective—yet hadn't it shut her out the other day? She should go to the police, of course. But what could she say that wouldn't make her look a perfect fool, or worse, an exhibitionist? She comforted herself, at last, by dismissing the whole episode as a hallucination. What had just happened was quite impossible—therefore, it couldn't have happened. All the same, she wasted a good half hour looking about the house for a trusty poker. There wasn't one. Her landlady had had gas fires installed—she didn't seem to believe in self-defence.

*     *     *

In the garden of The Magpie, Anna sat at a decaying wooden table. She was surrounded by languid couples, overheated children and their catabatic parents, pint glasses of Harvey's ale and wooden platters heaped with bread and cheese, anaemic tomatoes and Branston pickle. She poked at the treacle-coloured pickle with her fork, remembering Luke's comments when she'd opened a jar during their first meal together at her house.

"What? You mean they actually import that stuff? It looks like the inside of a baby's diaper, a diarrhoeaic baby."

She had laughed then, but now she couldn't muster the strength to smile. She felt like sagging into the mess of cheese and pickle, hugging the platter like a pillow, and never waking up again. The incident with the intruder had unsettled her more than she cared to admit. To distract herself, she'd spent the entire morning unpacking, stowing clothes and shoes and boots, discovering that the linen cupboard was in the study, and that most of the sheets and all of the towels had holes in them, some large as an open mouth. Next, she'd rearranged the furniture in the biggest bedroom, moving the vanity with its triptych mirror away from the window and into a corner; closing the mirror's wings so that no glass showed at all. On the marred surface of the vanity she'd put a picture of Luke, one he'd given her years ago, and which she'd kept in a drawer until now, never having found a use for it. Resisting the temptation to pick the photo up, she'd gone downstairs and, studiously avoiding the tarnished mirror, straightened the prints on the parlour wall—images of what she knew to be houses, trees, animals, but which she somehow couldn't connect to their names. She wasn't seeing straight—she hadn't caught up on her sleep. Yet, knowing she ought to try and eat something, she'd dug out her last five-pound note and forced herself down to the pub.

Anna pushed away her plate and watched a sparrow pecking at a pat of butter. Its feathers were intricately shaded, its feet a dry, tense pink. Hadn't Keats said something once about sparrows, about happiness and watching a sparrow on a window ledge? It took Anna a moment to realize that she'd been speaking out loud, addressing an imaginary Luke or rather, a real Luke, unimaginably distant. Frightened by the sound of her voice, the sparrow flew to another table; Anna consoled herself by examining the wound on her finger. It was healing nicely—nothing to worry over *there* at least. And elsewhere? She couldn't imagine getting through the next twelve hours, never mind the next twelve months, shut up in Rest Harrow.

But to think like this was to admit defeat before she'd even begun. And defeat would mean that Luke had been right after all. There'd been no need for her to come to England—all the really important Woolf papers were in the States, even Luke knew that. Luke used to be a historian and was now a middle-level administrator at Anna's university—though she hadn't fallen in with him because of any power of the keys that he possessed. It was his being a lapsed Rhodes scholar; his having, despite his Australian birth, an ineradicable tinge of Englishness that had won her at the last. The way her mother had been won by a man she may have married purely for his name. Antony English, born, if Anna's papers were correct, in Minneapolis, Minnesota, and now a native of no place anyone knew. Her mother, born to a remittance man and his transplanted English rose; her mother, dreaming always of the "home" to which her daughter had at last returned.

Walking slowly back, Anna filled her eyes with the green of the Downs rising softly up, undulant flanks pocked here and there by a thornbush, a splash of gorse, a cow or sheep. At the gate of Rest Harrow, she paused for a moment and looked about her. Fortuna House seemed sunk in an enchantment—not a whisper, not a flicker of movement from inside its walls. And at the white cottage, where she'd rung the day before, all the curtains were drawn. Though someone had left a light burning over the porch, in the middle of a sunstruck afternoon.

# III

# SIMON

The next day Anna took hold of herself, deciding to go into the traffic-clogged county capital some four miles away. After visiting the bank, which had grudgingly agreed to take her money, she made her way to the new supermarket at the bottom of the High Street, passing whole rows of expensive shops offering Spanish scarves and German brollies, designer kitchen ware and undergarments for the Larger Lady; refusing the blandishments of small greengrocers and quality butchers—they cost too much, and besides, she'd never cared for plastic parsley.

Hard by the supermarket doors she ran a gauntlet of some half a dozen different groups leafletting, holding demonstrations, rattling tins for charity. Helplessly, Anna accepted two pamphlets. One urged her to repent of her sins before the Second Coming, upon which, if only she Believed, she would be rapt up into the Seventh Heaven. The other leaflet, mimeographed on pale green paper, was put out by the local Citizens' Coalition. Ban the bomb, nuclear power, aerosol sprays, factory farming, apartheid. Save the whales, the Amazonian rainforests, the greenbelt, the National Health Service. Anna hadn't time to do more than skim the second leaflet, but she didn't throw it into the bin thoughtfully provided just inside the supermarket's doors. For she'd liked the face of the woman doing the leafletting, a face that reminded her, absurdly enough, of her mother's. Absurdly, for this woman's eyes were brown, not blue, and her skin was coffee-coloured under a bell of greying hair.

Anna wandered down the aisles, not knowing where anything was, unable to decode what was piled before her. Where she lived in Nova Scotia, bean sprouts and kiwi fruit were the only exotica. Here, however, were all manner of succulent temptations: papayas, guavas, starfruit, breadfruit, persimmons, pomegranates. Even the green beans came from Kenya. She fended off the lures to decadence, picking pears from Kent, local leeks. Remembering the leaflet-lady, Anna turned a cold eye on mounds of South African grapes, "White-fleshed and seed-less for your eating convenience."

Despite the list in her hand she bought impulsively, crazily: Bath Olivers but no cheese, cereal and no milk, margarine without bread. Somehow she ended up with a dozen soup-mix packages, all of them Scotch broth, the one sort she couldn't abide. Even the coffee was a failure, decaffeinated as she discovered hours later when brewing up a cup at home. Despairingly, Anna set out for the village shop to pur-chase, at exorbitant prices, the essentials she'd forgotten. Half the eggs were cracked or smashed by the time she lugged them home. And to crown it all, the soup she'd put on to simmer before leaving had caused a conflagration. She'd entered Rest Harrow to find the fire alarm bleep-ing, the kitchen full of smoke, the soup pot a mess of blistered metal. Plunging it into the basin, she'd opened the tap only to unleash new billows of foul, black smoke. Trying not to inhale, suspecting she'd appreciably shortened her life expectancy, Anna hurled the pot into the garden, where it decapitated a rosebush. She ran into the study, seized a sheet of paper, and wrote in a trembling hand:

THINGS TO REPLACE
1) one small saucepan
2) one rosebush

She opened all the windows, but the smell of burning seemed to have impregnated the curtains, the carpets, the very paint on the walls. At last she unplugged the stove and slammed the front door behind her. When things reached this impossible pitch, the only rea-sonable thing to do was to run away. She couldn't go very far, since she hadn't the energy to climb up the Downs, and since Pyeford seemed to consist of nothing more than eighteen houses on a dead-end street.

Down this street she dawdled, pulling her cardigan tighter round her. After the extraordinary heat of her first few days in Pyeford, the weather had turned seasonably cold—apparently the British had had summer during the bank-holiday weekend in May. She stopped for a moment before the cottage that belonged to the Weeping Woman. That was how Anna thought of her, not as a Mrs. Smith or Jones, but as some personification of grief itself, like the shrouded figures carved between urns and willows on antique gravestones. Anna rebuked herself for being morbid. After all, the woman could have been weeping at some trauma on the day's soaps. Certainly there was no black cloud hanging over the house, no ravens croaking; on its lawn the grass grew green under a lace of small daisies.

Anna decided that she couldn't walk up and down The Street forever. She would have to go in—but not to Rest Harrow and the stench of burnt saucepan. She decided to try The Magpie again; she had to establish her credentials as a villager. It was quiet enough inside. Brass gleamed, varnish glinted; the help all looked like students or local youths, if there was such a thing any more. They were sloppily dressed, scraggy and unsmiling and not, to Anna's vast relief, in Tudor costume. She bought her drink and sat down at an empty table by the fireplace, only to be interrupted moments later.

"Miss English? Simon Jeffries, a friend of Rosalind Oliver's. May I join you?"

Anna couldn't see that there was much she could do to stop him. She wished she had the conviction, the assurance to counter with "It's not 'Miss' but 'Doctor,' and you'd better bugger off before I call the constable." For this man sitting down at, and nearly overturning the small oak table, this Simon-Jeffries-friend-of-Rosalind-Oliver's was her hallucination, peeping Tom himself.

Simon neither blushed nor smirked, but merely gazed at her through dust-furred spectacles. Anna had a sudden, comforting thought: he probably hadn't seen very much of her at all—it must have been years since he'd last cleaned his glasses. His hair was grey, lank, and badly needed cutting; his collar was frayed, and he'd tucked his mothy tie into his shirt pocket, presumably to keep it from falling into his beer. Awkwardly, he cleared his throat, then asked if she were settling in all right. After a moment's hesitation, Anna replied. Since she'd had to surrender her own fiction that this man had never barged into her house, she might as well seize onto his—that they had never met before. Strictly speaking, they hadn't. That impromptu morning call had been more in the nature of an incident than a meeting.

"You've enough hot water?"

"Yes, I figured out the time switches."

"Any trouble from the boiler?"

"No."

There was a long silence during which someone at the counter held forth on the dangers of budget surpluses and trading deficits. Anna finished her drink and stood up to go. She was nodding goodbye to Simon Jeffries when he sprang to his feet. His pint of Armada sloshed stickily over the table as he assailed her in frantic shorthand.

"Come to dinner? Sunday night? Six o'clock? Past the churchyard—on your left. Flint-walled cottage. Garden impenetrable. Do come. Lovely—"

And it was he, not Anna, who rushed out of the pub, his face on fire.

Anna didn't dare to look round her, convinced that Simon had been shouting at the top of his lungs, that everyone would be staring at her, leering or joking. But the conversation continued just as it had before—they were onto interest rates now—and the dart players were still bonded to the board. She couldn't have been more grateful had she been saved from drowning. On this her third day in the village it was far too early to be generating gossip. Of course she wouldn't think of having dinner with this purblind peeping Tom, this joyless Mr. Jingle. She had plenty of excuses—she needn't even offer excuses, she wasn't bound by any lease to accept the hospitality of a man who'd barged into her house without so much as knocking. And who, before he'd left the pub, had reached out and squeezed her hand so hard that she could still read the imprint of his fingers on her palm.

*     *     *

Not till Saturday morning, after endless hours of laying in provisions, stacking books on shelves, fiddling with adaptors for the computer, sorting out files and changing lightbulbs, did Anna allow herself the luxury of the terrace at the back of the house. Large enough for a few deck chairs, and a round, marble-topped table, it was sheltered by a japonica hedge, so that on good days you could actually lie out without an eiderdown, or your pages blowing halfway up the Downs. The study doors led out to the garden; over those doors was a placid corrective to the Medusa knocker, a medallion in the style of della Robbia. It contained a madonna and child. The figures were not so much white as blank, the background the blue of a Tiepolo sky. Wisteria flooded over the study wall, parting round the medallion so that mother and child smiled out of a sea of leaves, over a door offering entry into a house of gentleness and peace.

Resisting the temptation to fall asleep in the arms of her chaise longue, Anna began her letter.

*Dear Luke,*

But that was far too tepid a salutation. What then? "Dearest" seemed uncomfortably assertive and particular. Anna realized that she'd never written anything to Luke before but memos: To— From—. All you had to do was fill in the names; emotion simply didn't enter into it. But this letter involved more than emotion: it would be read as a statement of intent. Lavishness, she finally decided. Excess and over-flow, but so positioned as to be almost an afterthought.

*Luke, darling,*

*I arrived safely, and what's more, so did the computer. And the printer, thank God. The cottage is*

Should she be truthful?

*appallingly uncomfortable: damp, dreary, dingy. I have even found the skeleton of a cat buried under the weigelia.*

And have him say I told you so? Have him refuse to come out at Christmas? Wouldn't that be introducing more distance than she desired into their affairs?

*The cottage is charming, and I've more or less settled in. I've already met several of the villagers—they seem like an inoffensive bunch.*

She would not mention Simon Jeffries's dinner invitation, nor the events which had preceded it.

*I hope everything's well at home. I needn't tell you how much I miss you. Please make sure Emma and her friend don't overload the laundry line—I forgot to tell them how delicate it is.*

*I haven't met the famous Dr. Oliver yet. I think she's on a mystery tour of the trans-Caucasian Alps by now. Amazing how game some of these aged English spinsters are. Plucky, is that the word? I don't expect I'll actually meet up with her at all this year—thank Heavens!*

It had taken Anna five minutes to scribble this far; half an hour later she still hadn't settled on a signature phrase. The essence of their relationship was, as far as she construed it, indeterminacy, incomple-tion. *Love, Anna.* How prescriptive, how closed that sounded. Or worse, dictatorial: *Love Anna!* How would she ever finish this letter without seeming to alter the house they'd built between them, a house in which they had rooms of their own, monogrammed bedsheets and personally encoded coffee mugs, a *His and Hers* forever distanced from the mush of Ours? How could she write "love" when she'd never said it? Besides, she still felt cross at him about the razor. In the end she settled for *As always, Anna.*

Sealing the envelope, she looked round the garden. Really, the house wasn't so very bad, and even if it were much worse, the garden would make up for it. From the terrace there were steps up to a stretch of grass that had been mowed the way a three-year-old might give itself a haircut—Anna detected Simon Jeffries's hand. On either side of the terrace were pots of geraniums: white, crimson, candy pink. At the end of the lawn came huge rosemary bushes and dead-white roses; beyond that, the Downs.

Anna put the letter into a book for safekeeping and walked down the garden. She broke off a sprig of rosemary and rubbed it between her fingers. All the while she was looking up at the green, sleepy hills, so close and so tame you could stretch out your hand to stroke them. Even the sound of them was idyllic: cows lowing, the occasional bleat of a sheep. Only gradually did she admit a human sound as well, a low voice, nicked by a note of panic. "Maeve? Maeve?" Anna couldn't tell from what direction it was coming. Whomever the voice was calling didn't answer. After a while the sound stopped, as suddenly as it had started. Then Anna heard a door slam, and a silence she hadn't known was there.

# IV

# CAKES AND ALE

Before sitting down at her computer and plotting out the text that would carry her through the next eleven months, Anna set out to claim a different kind of territory. Sunday morning, just after dawn, she let herself out through the back garden, hopping the low flint wall and crossing a meadow which took her to a chalk road winding up the Downs. It was cool out; clear and windless. The road stayed dry and white underfoot—the Downs were made of chalk and flint, a synthesis of crushable and crusher. On one side of her lay ripened wheat; on the other, a field with three horses: a bay, a chestnut and a roan. It was so quiet she could hear them tearing off sweet, drenched blades of grass.

The path wasn't especially steep, but midway, she was panting. If she hadn't been afraid that once down she'd never get back up again, she'd have collapsed into a slope of wildflowers. This wasn't, she reflected, the sort of exertion for which a life of tapping at keyboards, lecturing at podiums, or hunching over student essays had prepared her. Anna pressed on, remembering Virginia Woolf's indefatigable walks across the Downs, through Richmond Park and in and out of half of London. Were they all great walkers, the English Lady Novelists? Charlotte Brontë catching her death during a moorland expedition to a waterfall; housebound Jane Austen. . . . *Remember what happened to Louisa Musgrave jumping the steps at the Cobb!* The voice was so strong behind her that Anna whirled round, only to find a small grey bird on a thorn bush. And yet she'd heard it all the same, that entry from her mother's catalogue of cautionary tales, drawn not from newspaper columns (*Children Killed Tobogganning. Boy Paralysed in Skiing Accident. Girl Drowns at Supervised Beach*) but from bookshelves. *You can get everything you need out of life from books, Anna. Read The Mill on the Floss and you'll see what happens to those who go on unsupervised boating expeditions; read The Return of the Native and you'll find out* what happens to women who go walking alone at night. Read the last journal of Virginia Woolf. . . .

But her mother never would, wanting only the Victorians: rich, weighty worlds she'd consume like endless Christmas cakes. Anna's embrace of Bloomsbury had been the only revolt she'd ever mustered, except for that last one, the one she'd promised herself never to think about again. She stopped, pressing her hand against her floating rib, feeling air scrape her lungs, convinced she was exhaling blood.

Desperately, Anna willed herself to make it to the top of the hill. Just when her lungs were bursting, the crest of the Downs thrust up before her, and a sudden wind whirled her about. Anna pulled herself a good yard further and fell, first to her knees, then on her belly. She hugged the ground for a long, dizzy moment, then looked back to find her reward spread out below: three dark dots in a meadow the size of an eraser, a thin white line, like a length of exposed bone, and even farther away, a hodge-podge of roofs and walls that had to be Pyeford. Behind the flint tower and conical spire of the church lay a cottage which must belong to Simon Jeffries. She could make out other houses, too: Rest Harrow, the village shop, the cottage of the Weeping Woman.

Above and beyond them all she sat, God surveying Creation. Suddenly she felt just as she had those first few hours in England: free and whole and open to anything. She jumped up and ran the next hundred feet, frightening a lark from the long grass. Its song rained sharply sweet, slashing her ears—language direct and undecodable, never to be learned, reduced to meaning. Spreading out her arms, refusing to care what anyone might think, knowing there was nobody here to say or see anything, Anna spun herself round and around, shouting, laughing—

A couple came riding by, too quickly for Anna to drop her arms in time. They nodded to her as they passed, but she made no response. "Fool, *fool*, it serves you right." That made twice in the last three days she'd exposed herself to strangers. Scowling, Anna followed the track along which the horses were still cantering, though they were far ahead of her by now. Sheep coughed at her approach, lifting yellow eyes, then shook themselves and hobbled off, gazing back at her, savagely suspicious. How starved their legs and faces were: scraps of skin over knobbled bone. And how filthy their fleece, ending in stiff, dung-smeared driblets.

The path led on along the ridge, with views of villages and farms on one side, and on the other, a stretch of empty valleys, looking like

green-gloved knuckles, interlocked. Anna halted at a signpost with
eroded lettering, walked down the slope a few paces, and stood staring at
endless parallel grooves along the flanks of the Downs. Generations of
browsing sheep and cattle had made these shallow terraces. Butterflies
sunned themselves on splats of cow dung, and on the slopes where the
ground was left fallow, scabious and coltsfoot bloomed. Bending between
dung and flowers was someone Anna hadn't seen in the pub or on the village street, or even in town: a woman with a basket on her arm, searching
for something—keys or a bracelet, perhaps—in the feathery grass.

When she stood up to stretch Anna could see that she was slender,
no longer young; her dull hair blew every which way in the wind, and
she wore a shabby, drooping dress. Anna kept waiting for a glimpse of
her face, but the woman's back was turned to her. Suddenly Anna
guessed who she must be: her landlady, the eccentric, absent-minded
Dr. Oliver. Who wasn't out of the country at all, but hovering close by,
getting Simon Jeffries to spy on her, hiding the secrets of weeping
neighbours and boilers and burners so that she'd nearly burned the
whole cottage down. "Serves you right," Anna shouted, "serves you
bloody well right—" But the woman kept on moving between clumps
of tall grass, while Anna climbed back up the ridge, hacking her feet
into the turf with every step. Once at the top she looked below, but the
woman had vanished.

On she walked, on and on, though she took no pleasure any longer
in the sun and wind, and the very air seemed to be sighing round her,
leaking from some sad balloon. She picnicked in a grove of pines
behind someone's hilltop villa, and then set off again, determined to
reach the place she'd marked on the map the night before; the place
that had marked itself on her mind or heart, whatever serves as paper
for desire's pen. Desire, obsession: which was the right word for the co-
ordinates to which she was hurrying now, pushing blistered feet along a
path trod bare by cattle? She was about to perform an act of magic, or
at the very least, transubstantiation. She was about to turn black marks
on a white page, one of a hundred thousand entries in *A Reader's Guide
to Literary Britain*, into wood and brick and grass. Monk's House, Virginia Woolf's house, which she knew by heart already, from its Omega
tiles to its garden hut.

Under the signpost to Rodmell, a widened rut turned into a gravel
path twisting round the hill. Under the signpost Anna stood for a

moment, a quarter of an hour, forever, as if she were perched on a cliff, as though to put one foot in front of the other would be to take a running leap over the edge. She wanted to shut her eyes and find herself instantly translated to the garden of Monk's House, clutching the hand of a stone nymph to steady herself. All she had to do was follow the path; she had risked everything to come this far and yet now she couldn't move so much as her hand. *To want, and want, and not to have.* But she could have, that was the whole point. The book had dropped from her hands and the world had risen up beneath her feet, yet she could do nothing but stand here, afraid to go past wanting, terrified of having.

She ran. Wheeling round, pitching herself along the path as the sky began to darken, the way a blow turns into a bruise. She told herself it was rain soaking her shirt, her hair; told herself it would have been a disaster to go down to a Monk's House swarming with tourists looking for semen stains on the sofa, ghosts raving in the garden—in Greek, no less. It would hurt far more to stop than to keep going, and so she lunged ahead blindly, shoving her way through the same flock of sheep she'd met on her way up, finding at last the path which would take her back to Pyeford.

And it did, but not in the way she'd expected. Instead of the chalk road, the footpath veered into a sheep track bordered by waist-high thistles blowing into ghosts of themselves. Why was it so much harder going down? She was afraid of falling on the slick path, breaking an ankle or arm, but couldn't keep herself from galloping past different fields than those she'd passed on the chalk road coming up. For instead of three dark horses, here was only one: pure white, a violent white, signalling something irreplaceable that had been lost or stolen, something it was standing in for. She turned her eyes back to the path in front of her, hoping the horse would disappear with the next turning. And it did—she was suddenly in a wood, all brambles and ivy and slippery earth, roots like ropes to snag her feet. Groping, falling, Anna pushed her way at last into a clearing and slumped against a high wooden wall. "Thank you, thank you," she panted, gripping the wall, digging her fingers into a surface ridged and rough as elephant skin. For if there was a wall, there would be a house; if there was a house, there would be a road; if there was a road then she could find her way home.

She had perhaps three full minutes of grace before she realized she wasn't leaning against a wall, but rather, a tree, an enormous tree heaved onto its side, exposing mazy, withered roots. In fact, what she'd taken to be a clearing was nothing but a battlefield with trees for corpses. Everywhere she looked she found the same thing: huge, toppled trees and great holes where they'd been blasted from the earth. Her mouth felt dry, contorted, as if she had put back her head and howled. But she hadn't—she could feel silence filling her mouth with stones. The air had gone glassy, green, as though she were underwater, being held underwater by the sheer weight of the toppled trees all round her. And then, just as the silence began to grow deeper and greener and fuller, she heard a dog barking—a large dog, much too near, and footsteps, someone hurtling, crashing through the bushes. *Men drag women into bushes, terrible things can happen in bushes.* Bloodhounds baying: machetes slashing at the undergrowth, clubs beating her down—

*          *          *

"Sherry?"

"I'm afraid I don't drink." Anna hated making this admission—people always assumed she was just out of Alcoholics Anonymous.

"So sorry. I mean, I think it's admirable—"

"I'm allergic to alcohol."

"Quite. Could I offer you—"

"Perrier will be fine. You don't have Perrier? Well, then, some fruit juice. No fruit juice. Water, then. Yes, out of the tap. No, I certainly don't need ice, not in this weather. Actually, I'm dying for a cup of tea."

A lie, but it would buy her time. Not nearly as much as she needed, but it was a start. Why, oh why had she come down that particular path? And why did Simon Jeffries have to be out walking his dog just then—an unusually witless terrier which had jumped all over her, making it necessary for Simon to get out a grimy pocket handkerchief, more hole than cloth, and rub the muck more firmly into Anna's trouser legs. Why did he have to find her, rescue her, lead her out of the woods into Chantry Cottage which, if she'd only had her wits about her, she'd have known to be next to the white horse's field? Why hadn't she been quicker on her feet, feigning illness, sunstroke, a death in the family, anything to get her out of this man's clutches? For it was, of course, Sunday, the very day of the dinner invitation Anna had determined to ignore.

Anna was in a strange condition: gone gothic, gone grotesque during that ridiculous first moment in the bushes. She was struggling to maintain composure, praying to appear no more than a little flushed, a little tongue-tied. *Calm down, get a hold of yourself, relax: that cup of tea should help, though it would be far easier if you'd accept a twin of the tumblerful of sherry Simon's pouring for himself.* But Anna was not the most self-possessed of subjects, and certainly far from reliable in her perceptions. For one thing, there'd been no dog barking back in the ash glade—or at least, no dog connected with Simon, who did not appear to be the doggy sort at all. She must have fallen—that's how she got the mud on her knees; Simon had simply helped her clean herself off. And look what she made of poor Simon as he calmly sipped his sherry, having apparently forgotten all about her cup of tea. As far as Anna was concerned, he was just some Dickensian sub-species, a character remembered from one of her mother's books, a book left lying out in the rain.

He seemed no taller than she, for his shoulders stooped under his tatty jersey—a hopelessly skewed argyle pattern, knit by someone going progressively blind. His trousers were too short: you could see an inch of hairy skin between cuffs and mustard-coloured socks inside shoes that resembled nothing so much as heaps of dead mice. Why did he live alone? If for the usual reason, why ask her over here for dinner? And why couldn't men who lived on their own ever manage to do it properly, without sending out distress signals in every direction? She guessed that he lived off a diet of beans on toast, chips and tea; from the dust that blurred the books and papers strewn about the room, he got a char in once a month to deal with the mess before it turned foetid.

"That cup of tea?" Anna inquired, instantly regretting it as her host sprang up from his chair and rushed off to the kitchen, where he began making banging sounds with pot lids. For tea now would only delay supper, and after supper there'd be a token conversation to get through before she could decently head home. At the very least it would mean two hours of his company—time enough to establish a perfectly polite distance between them. For not to stay to dinner, she'd realized, would be to revoke the fiction Simon had created at the pub—tantamount to admitting discomfort, even shame, and worst of all, complicity at what had happened in her front hallway the day after her arrival. Having accepted Simon's invitation this once, she could refuse all subsequent ones. It seemed perfectly logical to her, and efficacious: the undoing of a spell, a necessary recantation.

She wished he would hurry up. She had already examined his bookshelves, gathering ammunition for their table talk. Chesterbelloc, C.S. Lewis, T.S. Eliot, the whole High Anglican Mafia. An entire bookcase was devoted to ecclesiastical architecture; all the prints on the wall were drawings, severely technical, of the floor plans of English cathedrals. Next to the *Illustrated Glossary of Architecture*, Anna found an outsize book, an art book full of reproductions. The lettering on the spine was worn—she couldn't tell what the title was, but she pulled out the book and began leafing through it. Landscapes, dockyard scenes, a most peculiar St. Francis Preaching to the Birds.

And over the page, a nude. A blonde woman lying stretched out on a bed, breasts huge and slack, her hip bones alarmingly tilted. But what disturbed Anna in this picture was the man inside it, or at least, the head and shoulders of a bespectacled man, his face the same purplish hue as the woman's nipples, his skin below his twisting neck as white and rumpled as the bedsheets on which the woman lay. The walls, sprigged with small pink and white flowers; the man looking neither at the wallpaper, nor at the woman, but at some point just beyond her head. Not looking at, Anna decided, but for something, something whose absence obviously caused him the greatest pain.

"Here you are. I'm afraid I couldn't find the tea things—I seem to have fallen rather behind with the shopping and washing-up. I'm terribly sorry—"

Anna shoved the book back onto the shelf, and held out a mildly shaking hand. Simon pressed into it a water-filled jam jar with evidence of its former contents ringing the bottom.

"Could I interest you in a tour round the garden, Miss English? It's not anything special, of course, but I thought you might like a change of air."

"It's not *Miss* English, it's—Anna. And I'd *love* to see the garden." Her nerve had failed her at the last minute: to have him using her academic title would seem as pretentious as having him call her "Your Grace." And anything would be better than staying here, where naked men and women seemed to be projected onto the walls, sprawled over the cathedral floor plans. Simon poured himself another tumblerful of sherry before leading Anna out the back door into a bed of lilies.

It was much better outside: almost soothing. Anna let Simon lead her here and there, surreptitiously pouring water into the phlox, but imbibing all sorts of information on greenfly and black spot, the hardier species of rose and the difficulty of cultivating fritillaries. How, she wondered, could someone so fussy about plants be so careless about himself? She knew there was a long and honourable tradition in England of equating the height of one's intellect with the depth of dirt grained into one's cuffs and collar; that the more slovenly one's appearance, the more genuine one's scholarship was thought to be. And Simon was an academic of sorts—at least, he taught the upper forms in the local infant school. "Never had the proper qualities to become headmaster," he confessed to her. "To tell the truth I'm not terribly good with children. I'm told I don't know how to keep them in line— though why one needs to in the first place I don't quite know. Do you think it has something to do with rulers?"

"I—it's not my field," Anna managed. She'd been thinking of Luke's children, who'd gone off to British Columbia with their mother long before Anna had even met their father. He visited them twice a year, and kept their photographs on his office wall, old ones from when they'd still been at primary school. He'd begun to talk of taking Anna with him out west on one of his visits; once he'd suggested the two of them start looking for jobs in Vancouver, though she'd never for a moment believed he was serious. And yet there was something in the way Simon was standing with her now, hands in his pockets, staring mournfully down at a dying begonia that reminded Anna of Luke when he got onto the subject of his children.

The church clock struck seven; Anna's stomach began to rumble. Sacrificing her principles, she asked Simon whether he'd like some help setting the table for supper.

"Good heavens, I'd quite forgotten. How awfully kind of you. I'm afraid it's going to be a very humble meal. Usually I get Mrs. Morton in to do the cooking when I've got guests, but right now she's on holiday in Crete. I believe these package deals are far cheaper than a trip to Blackpool, nowadays."

"Right, then—where shall we start?" Anna had seized the initiative, walking back into the cottage and looking purposefully about her.

Simon swept the Everest of books, pens, paper, biscuits and Marmite jars off the dining table into a laundry basket. He blushed. "Sorry for the mess. But it's my book, you see. On tracery."

"Tracery?" Anna spread a cloth over the table's scarred surface. The cloth looked clean enough, but was full of holes and frayed threads which stuck up like eyelashes.

"Tracery—sorry, the salt shaker's been empty for months now, I really ought—napkins? Oh yes, of course—perhaps in that drawer over there? Tracery, you see, is the ornamental work formed by—butter? Haven't a clue, I'm afraid—the branching of mullions in the upper parts of Gothic windows. There are five basic kinds: geometrical, 'y' tracery, intersected, and, of course, plate—"

"The plates?" Anna interrupted. "To eat off. Everything else is ready."

"Of course. I do apologize, I really shouldn't ride my hobbyhorse quite so hard. It comes with living alone, I'm afraid—there's no one to stop you from talking a blue streak." Simon disappeared into the kitchen and came back with crockery and cutlery. "I should think I'm boring you stiff—"

"Oh, no," lied Anna. "Shall we sit down?"

"Right then. Ah, of course—the food. I thought there was something missing."

Simon re-entered with a tray of dishes from which rose not the slightest sniff of steam. Since sausages, tinned peas and chipped potatoes were being served, this was a serious omission. The meal must have been cooked hours ago; no doubt it had been left on the counter to tempt flies and heaven knew what else all afternoon. Anna sat down opposite Simon, tried to unfold her napkin and, seeing that it was stuck together with something like syrup, let it fall off her lap. Simon smiled at her and removed his glasses, perhaps to keep them from getting splotched with gravy. He seemed to believe that the object of a meal was to consume whatever had been heaped on one's plate at the greatest possible speed. All of which made Anna's toying with peas and chips the more conspicuous. Simon, however, didn't notice.

The instant he'd finished, Anna rose, taking his plate and cramming it down on her untouched meal. "There's more," he called out as she sped into the kitchen. She returned bearing another tray with two small plastic containers on it: "Choc'o'Bloc, a Whole New Concept in Dessert Technology." Anna managed two spoonfuls of what tasted like chalk and twiggy bits. Simon quite happily devoured his, and looked as though, given half a chance, he'd polish off Anna's, too. At last he pushed away his plate, retrieved his glasses, and suggested they find some more comfortable chairs.

The walk must have been more tiring than she'd realized, for Anna fell asleep in the depths of a cracked leather armchair while Simon was explaining the difference between rectilinear and drop tracery. She woke with a start, in a darkened room, to hear him inquiring as to whether it were Sunday.

"Yes, of course." Surely she hadn't managed to sleep right through and into Monday?

"That will be lovely."

Anna glanced at her watch. It was nearly eleven. Refusing his offer of an escort home, she did agree to the loan of a torch, remembering that it was a flashlight Simon was offering her, and not a flaming brand. Picking her way past the church and its crooked gravestones, she quickly reached The Street. Everything was dark except for one window of the Weeping Woman's cottage, making a great white glare. Hurrying, Anna let herself into Rest Harrow, making sure this time that the door was firmly locked behind her.

# V

# MAIL AND MESSENGERS

Anna woke much too late the next day, as though she'd a night of debauchery to sleep off instead of a duty call to an officious neighbour. Her head ached; her stomach heaved. Simon had poisoned her with that slop he'd served up—of which she hadn't had more than a forkful. But then, a forkful could easily be enough—look what a handful of pomegranate seeds had done to Persephone.

When a bath and weak tea and another bath hadn't restored her, Anna decided on a walk. After all, she had Luke's letter still to post. She'd just go the length of The Street (leg muscles screeching from yesterday's climb) then turn round and make her way to the village shop. Simon had told her—it was the one useful piece of information he'd managed to impart last night—that you could buy stamps there.

A few people were out, mostly retired couples with baskets on their arms and shelties on retractable leads. Anna smiled at them as she went past, feeling oddly guilty, like a trespasser or fifth column. She didn't want to stop and talk to anyone and so she found herself walking rather faster and farther than she'd intended; found herself, in fact, going down a narrowing lane, hopping a stile and stumbling into the very glade from which Simon had rescued her the day before.

She was careful to get her bearings, making sure she knew exactly how to get out again. It was hot; the sun boiled through eye-shaped leaves sprouting from the fractured trunks. Beech trees, she noted; perhaps two or three centuries old before they'd been hurled up out of the earth. But who or what had done this? She ought to have asked Simon last night. She ought never to have gone to Simon's. She ought to be home, starting in on her book. Except that she felt so much better here, now, her head clear, her stomach calm, as if she were lying on her back and floating in a shallow, sunny pool. She walked over to a root mass thrusting high over her head. It made a sort of cave: you could imagine children crawling in, building a fort or hide-out there. And she had a steep, sudden craving to burrow inside and live there like a wild child where no one could ever find her, as far away from books and studies of Virginia Woolf as these bruised roots and rotting bark were from that nun-white paper on which she'd penned her letter to Luke.

Her hand tightened round the envelope, crumpling the address she'd so carefully printed in indelible ink. She ought to have sent it off long ago. *Admit it, Anna, you're delaying, you're afraid. Of what? Of sending signals, of putting your foot in it, of opening up that gash on your finger that's healing so well you hardly notice it's there at all.* But Anna didn't admit anything; she merely sighed, rubbing the scar on her finger with her thumb, not even noticing as Luke's letter fluttered to the ground.

"Luke and Anna," she said out loud. "Leonard and Virginia." But it didn't sound quite the same. She had spent whole evenings explaining to Luke the perfection of the Woolfs' relationship (she hadn't said anything so suggestive as "marriage"). During lunches and dinners and brunches and tea, she had ventured her theory that for any truly equal partnership to last, the partners concerned would need a great deal of space around their roots; indeed, would thrive on slightly acid soil. "Like Simon's rhododendrons," Anna thought, recalling the other bit of useful knowledge she'd gleaned from the night before. She walked back to the fallen trunk and leaned against it, shutting her eyes and pulling in the sun through every pore of her skin. Simon, she decided, was infinitely easier to deal with than Luke. Because he was so impossible. No one in any kind of mind at all could possibly fall in love with Simon, whereas with Luke—

He had asked her to marry him. The night before her flight he'd walked smack into the middle of her packing with a sheaf of irises, a bottle of Moët and a box of Belgian chocolate. "Don't go. Change your plans. Stay with me instead. You need a honeymoon, not a sabbatical." She'd gone on packing. It was only for a year, she'd said. Time to get things sorted out in their heads. Priorities; promises.

She hadn't said yes, she hadn't said no. They'd drunk the wine and eaten half the chocolates; he'd shaved in her bathroom while she took off her clothes, folding them neatly, so they wouldn't be creased when she stepped back into them. They'd gone to bed, and all the time they were making love Anna had kept worrying that she'd got the day wrong, that her plane would already have arrived in England without her.

When she was quite sure he'd fallen asleep she'd got up, showered, dressed and resumed packing. She could remember every detail, including the long moment before she'd woken Luke, when she'd stood looking down at him, thinking that though running off to England might be the safest thing she could do with her life just then, it was probably the stupidest. And how, when the taxi had come, she'd bundled Luke inside it, then called another to take her to the airport.

He'd be angry, still—she knew it. And the funny thing was that here, several thousand miles away, she didn't want him to be angry or aloof but tender, regretful, eager to restore things to their former footing. That was why the letter had to be in perfect pitch, why she was dithering so about sending it. But she still couldn't think of a better way of saying what she had; surely any signal would be better than none? She closed her eyes for a moment, conjuring up bits of Luke, the whorls of dark hair on his belly and the backs of his hands, the shaving scars on his chin, the way his collarbone jutted up against her cheek when he pulled her to him. For a moment he was there in the clearing with her, those parts of him she had by heart phosphorescent against the rest. And then he disappeared, bit by bit, till only hair and chin and collarbone were left, and then even they dropped from the air.

The letter—where was the letter? Frantically, Anna felt her pockets, coming up with only a balled, discoloured tissue. She bent down and searched the grass, stinging her hands on a lush crop of nettles. But just as she was about to give up, she froze. A scratching noise was coming from inside the very log against which she had been leaning. A scratching noise too loud to be a shrew or vole, or even a fox. And then a sound, a hooting, howling sound that turned abruptly to laughter. Anna hung back only for a moment, then ran round to the maze of tree roots. There was her letter, lying right on the lip of the cave. She was afraid to pick it up, she was afraid of what might come scrabbling out from the tree roots. For a long moment she crouched there, her hand frozen halfway to the letter.

And then something seemed to push her—she was falling forward, closing her hand round the letter and snatching it up. She backed out of the clearing, as cautiously as if she were playing Mother May I. It was only when she'd backed into the stile that she turned and ran all the way to the village shop, not looking once behind her.

* * *

The sign read OPEN in Gothic script, and Anna took it at its word. Purposefully, she passed by shelves of crisps and biscuits and Jaffa cakes, then lost her nerve and lingered over a box of puckered oranges.

"Can I help you?" It was interrogation rather than an interrogative, and came from the woman who ran the store, a Mrs. Higley whom Anna wanted instinctively to address as Major. Her hair was white, her eyes the colour of shrapnel. And her bosom, sheathed in starched cotton and a sombre cardigan, was quite simply prodigious. Not soft and pillowing, but something more like a continental shelf or the prow of an icebreaker.

"I'd like to post a letter, please—" Anna faltered, all too aware of the blush mottling her face, and the grubby state of the envelope.

"Only one?"

"Yes. For now, that is. To Canada."

"I see." Mrs. Higley grasped the letter Anna had slid under the glass screen as if it were some common garden pest that had to be eliminated. Indeed, it looked ten times as crumpled as it had in the clearing. Anna put her hands in her pockets, where their trembling wouldn't be noticed, as Mrs. Higley weighed the letter on her brass scales and announced the price in disapproving tones. "I suppose you want an airmail sticker?"

"If it's no trouble."

Mrs. Higley surveyed her customer as if she were a good deal less intelligent than the flies clustered on the sweating rounds of Stilton. As the postmistress detached the stamp and sticker from her booklet, Anna made conversation in a blurting sort of way.

"Whatever happened to the trees?"

"What on earth do you mean? Of which trees are you speaking?"

"The trees in that little clearing—I mean glade, or really, it's both. At the end of the street. Where the path to the Downs goes up?"

"*Those* trees." Mrs Higley ladled immeasurable scorn into her words. "They came down, of course, in the hurricane."

"Hurricane?"

"Last October." Mrs. Higley pushed the stamp towards Anna. "We were lucky in Pyeford—it more or less passed us by. Though anyone who wasn't blind would see there's been considerable damage to the churchyard. They say it's all this global warming. That's the second hurricane we've had in three years, and after the first they said it wouldn't happen again for another three hundred. It's all quite unnecessary, as far as I can see."

"Unnecessary—yes, of course, it's hardly necessary, I mean—" As if to make up for the utter failure of her faculties, Anna hammered the stamp onto the envelope, and shoved the letter under the grille. Mrs. Higley shoved it back, shaking her head with as much scorn as severity. "The postbox is outside the shop. It is affixed to the wall. You may give me packages that will not fit inside the mail slot, otherwise, you are expected to post your letters yourself. It is all written down in the regulations booklet. *Should* you care to look."

"No thank you. I mean, I *do* see, of course. Good day."

But Mrs. Higley wasn't finished with her yet. As Anna was making her way to the door, she heard another stentorian command:

"Stop! You cannot post that letter."

Anna turned and retraced her steps, clutching the edge of the counter as she confronted Mrs Higley. "Why ever not?"

"Because you haven't provided a return address. Should the person to whom you have addressed your letter refuse or be unable to accept it, the post office would be obliged to open the envelope to ascertain the sender's whereabouts."

By this time Anna had decided—given all the letters which would flow between Pyeford and Nova Scotia—that the local postmistress was someone who ought not, under any circumstance, to be offended. She capitulated. "I'm sorry. I forgot. Could I have a pen, please?"

"A pen? This is a post office, not a stationer's shop. We do not supply pens for the use of the general public."

"But all post offices supply pens. Pens chained to little plastic stands, so members of the general public won't carry them off."

"Ah—" and here Mrs. Higley drew herself up behind the glass, her hair looking as stiff and crested as her bosom. "Ah, they may very well do that where you come from. But in English post offices affixed to village shops, we are not obliged to." She stared triumphantly down at Anna; then, victor to vanquished, made a show of mercy. "I will make an exception in this one case, since you are a foreigner." And she pushed a Biro to Anna, who scribbled her name and address so vengefully that the pen scored through the paper.

Posting the letter outside, her face red as the pillar box embed-
ded in a wall hardly more flinty than Mrs. Higley's adherence to the
regulations booklet, Anna vowed she'd never use the village shop
again, would cheerfully walk the four miles into the nearest town, and
brave the queues at the central post office all for the sake of avoiding,
no, eradicating Mrs. Higley. For on her way out the door she had spied
the sign reading If You Want It—Use It! Save Your Village Shop!

                            *        *        *

Lodged in a chaise longue, a pot of tea and package of chocolate diges-
tives at her side, Anna was trying to get through a recent collection of
essays on Virginia Woolf. She was not making any appreciable progress.
There were pieces using *Mrs. Dalloway* or *To the Lighthouse* to deny the
possibility of definition and excoriate essence, to dismiss the whole
concept of gender as so much metaphysical fool's gold. One critic pursued the ramifications, in *The Waves*, of the feminine/female libidinal
economy vis à vis Jinny's Lacanian Imaginary. Anna had struggled
halfway through a brilliantly impenetrable paper situating *The Voyage
Out* within the fluid motility of Woolf's semiotic *chora* when the distraction occurred. A high, clear, perfectly assured voice called out to
her—"You're from Australia."
    Anna dropped her book. Standing not six feet away was a small girl,
most peculiarly got up in a long, dark, dowdy dress and black stockings.
She was holding something cupped in her hands, a ball perhaps, and
though Anna could see with exaggerated distinctness the tucks in her
dress, the laces of her scuffed leather shoes, the child's face was oddly
blurred. Except for her eyes—they were black splashes on the small white
face: ineradicable, like India ink. But the child herself seemed to have
materialized out of nowhere—Anna hadn't heard footsteps on the paving
stones which led round the side of the cottage, and she certainly hadn't
seen anyone moving across the terrace. Yet there the child stood, waiting.
    "You *are* Australian," she said again, making it clear this was a
statement, not a question.
    Anna remained seated, but took off her sunglasses before replying.
"I'm Canadian. From Canada," she added, feeling a sudden need to be
emphatic.
    "Mrs. Higley says that you're Australian."

"Mrs. Higley is mistaken," Anna said with considerable satisfaction. But the child did not appear convinced.

Anna folded her arms, trying to wield as much authority as she could from the depths of a chaise longue. How did one go about banishing a child from one's garden, particularly a child as self-possessed and yet as insubstantial as this one? "What's your name?" Anna asked, too sweetly, since the child became suspicious and refused to answer. Yet she took a step forward and, imitating Anna, crossed her arms before she spoke again.

"What's *yours?*" Her tone was so peremptory that the answer came spilling out: "Anna. Anna English."

The child considered for a moment, carefully turning the ball she held up in her hands. At last she said, "I'm Maeve."

"And where do you live?"

"Next door, of course." She pointed not to the manor house but to the bare white cottage where the Weeping Woman lived. This child, in her elaborate, awful costume, was that woman's daughter. Anna looked more closely at her, as if to find a reflection of the mother's aggressive melancholy in her daughter's face, but the child's face remained unclear, like a badly focussed photograph.

"Do you want me to go?"

"I didn't mean—"

"You have to say please."

But before Anna could say a word the child took a step back, lowered her arms and pitched the cricket ball straight towards her. As it rolled across the grass it became brighter and brighter, developing stripes that started to whirr and swing, as though they were the rings of Saturn. Her attention was fixed on them and so she did not see the child disappear through a gap in the hedge, leaving the garden perfectly still and empty.

Anna waited for several moments, then got up from her chair and crouched down at the place where the ball had stopped rolling. She picked it up and examined it. A cricket ball, quite plain and very scuffed. She lobbed it over the hedge, then walked with a conspicuous show of calm into the house. Where she spent the rest of the evening making notes, grimly copious notes, on *Post-Modernist Approaches to Virginia Woolf.*

# VI

# FIONA

$A$nna, seated at her study desk by the French doors. Chin in hand, eyes fixed on a cloud or branch or far-off field—except for the fact that the brocade curtains (once crimson, now faded to flesh colour) were drawn as tight across the glass as sagging curtain rods allowed. Eyes fixed upon, bombarded by countless ions from her computer screen, in a pattern Luke had devised: hearts and narrow zigzags, like daggers. All she had to do was to click twice on the icon called *Anna's Book* and she could finally begin. Instead, she dragged the mouse in figure eights across the screen, then folded her hands in her lap, looking at the totems she'd ranged around her.

A reproduction of a photograph of Mrs. Leslie Stephen and Adeline Virginia, slipped into an ornate frame she'd found in a curio shop next to the shoe repair. It was a photo that troubled Anna when she took the time to look at it: the black ground out of which the figures loomed, more light than flesh, the child's face open and the mother's shut. As troubling in its way as the other photo in its matching frame, the one she'd set at the other edge of her desk. Sir Leslie Stephen, KCB, with shark's-fin profile. His frail hair and beard were traced with punishing exactitude, while the face of his daughter was blurred, almost dissolved, as if long submerged.

Anna's reverie was interrupted by a bird flying against the French doors, thumping its wings again and again upon the glass. Jumping up from her desk, tugging the curtains open, Anna uncovered a small axe, with a slice of flint for a blade, and a handle fashioned from a large, split twig. The handle was attached to an illustrator's idea of a Red Indian: that is, a child in what would pass for Native dress only in an English country garden.

Even with the curtains shut the rapping went on, more insistent than before. The next time, Anna opened the curtains only by a fraction. The small face was still there, or at least, what she could see of it under the red and green and yellow streaks meant for warpaint. The child had a couple of rooks' feathers in her hair, and a string of glass beads round her neck. Anna forced a smile that was meant to say "Yes, I see you; lovely, now go off and play." But the child kept hammering the French doors with her flint axe till Anna finally gave in and slid them open.

"You're to come to tea. Mummy wants you."

Whatever Anna had been expecting, it wasn't this. "Tea? Now?"

For answer, the child pointed with her axe in the direction of the Weeping Woman's cottage. "She's expecting you. I'll run back and tell her you're coming. You have to hurry, you *have* to."

Anna tried to call out after her, but the child had already vanished through the hedge.

Sliding the doors shut, drawing the curtains tight, Anna sat down at her desk once more. But she couldn't work—she couldn't even bring her hands to the keyboard. As for the text propped up beside the screen, her beautifully bound and gilt doctoral thesis, which she was to transform alchemically into the theorist's stone, it seemed to be written in an utterly foreign language—she couldn't recognize the letters, never mind the words. She reached out and shut the book, then closed down the machine as abruptly as if she'd given it a slap.

Anna straightened the photographs on her desk and then the books on her shelves. And then, when she could delay things no longer she slipped out the French doors into the garden. Ignoring the gap in the hedge through which the child had disappeared, she walked all the way round to the front door of the white cottage, ringing the bell as confidently as she could. This time she noticed a tarnished brass plate with the name *Gibson* barely visible. No one seemed to be coming. She rang again, almost angrily, and immediately the door opened.

This time the woman wasn't weeping. She still looked overexposed, like a photograph in black and white; she was no more talkative than a photograph, either. The woman stared at her as if demanding an explanation, but Anna couldn't think of a thing to say until the child appeared, still in costume and holding a large, struggling cat in her arms. The cat sprang at Anna, scratching her arm before it fled down the steps. "You'd better come in," the woman said at last. Her voice startled Anna. It wasn't furious or forlorn at all, but soft, warm, like honey dripping off a spoon. So soft and warm and sweet that Anna followed her inside, down a corridor of closed doors and into the kitchen.

She was given a cloth moistened with antiseptic to press against her scratch, and then a bandage—a plaster, the woman called it: "Go and fetch a plaster, Maeve." Anna didn't understand what was going on; it was as if the cat had drawn her wits, not her blood. After she'd bandaged her arm—it was the merest scratch, but what else could she do?—Anna stood awkwardly on one side of the kitchen table while the woman stood just as helplessly on the other. Until the child—Maeve—said, "Don't you think you should give her some tea?" And then Anna guessed that Maeve must have trumped up the whole occasion on her own—that her mother must be as surprised, perhaps as resentful as Anna at the interruption of her afternoon. Yet she could think of nothing to say that wouldn't betray the child who was pulling her mother's arm around her, pressing her face into her mother's shirt. The woman gently disengaged herself, told Anna and Maeve both to sit down, and went to put on the kettle.

Anna didn't trust herself to look at Maeve, and so she watched the child's mother instead. She was rather beautiful despite her extreme paleness and the savage cut of her hair, so blond it looked white. She was dressed entirely in black, and her body was so slender she could have been a line drawn on the bare sheet of the kitchen walls. Silence exaggerated the emptiness of the room, so that the sounds of the kettle coming to a boil and Maeve kicking her feet against her chair seemed like an intrusion, a trespass. At last Anna had to speak.

"Look, Mrs.—Mrs. Gibson, I didn't mean—"

"That's not who I am."

It came out as a shout. And then, quietly, as though to erase her show of anger: "My name's Fiona."

"I'm—"

"I know who you are. You're a friend of Rosalind Oliver's."

"I'm Dr. Oliver's tenant," Anna said, as though defending both her landlady and herself against an accusation. Fiona said nothing, but poured out the tea.

It was Maeve who spoke next. "She's from Australia."

"I'm from Canada," Anna blurted out, tears suddenly pricking at her eyes. "My name's Anna, I'm from Canada, and I've never even met Dr. Oliver. And I've no idea at all what I'm doing here."

For the first time something moved in Fiona's face, as if the strings holding a mask in place had come untied. She hunched forward in her chair, her tea untouched, and abruptly started asking questions about Canada. "We're thinking of emigrating," she said. And suddenly Anna knew, just from the way Fiona's shoulder bones pitched up through her cotton shirt, and from the way she hugged her elbows, that "we" meant only mother and daughter; knew at last what felt so familiar about this house. It was the lack of any trace of husband or father; the curious complicity between Fiona and Maeve, as though they were sisters instead of parent and child. *You're all I've got, you're my responsibility.*

Feverishly, Anna started talking—about the number of provinces, the various forms of government, the range of landscape and weather and social services in Canada. Maeve sat sipping milk, staring at Anna out of eyes that were quick and keen and undeceived. She interrupted once, to ask about wild animals and looked aggrieved when Anna confessed to never having seen grizzlies or wolves, even in a zoo. And when Anna went on to insist that most Canadians lived in cities, where they went to the same kind of stores and wore the same sort of clothes as did the English, Maeve's disgust was complete. Fiona didn't say a word through Anna's recitation, but stared instead at the tabletop, as though she were reading some invisible graffiti carved there. But when, after a few moments' silence, Anna stood up to go, Fiona pressed her to come by for Sunday lunch. Pressed her so that Anna felt the invitation like a bruise all that evening and the next day, a mark of coercion. Yet how could she have refused?

She returned to the Gibsons' two days later with a bottle of wine and a packet of sweets for Maeve. She'd meant to be perfectly polite; to make it clear that the visit was a formality, no more to be repeated than her dinner at Simon Jeffries's house. Yet when she rang at the door, Fiona greeted her as though she were a friend of ten years' standing, and Maeve grabbed her hand and tugged her inside, Maeve dressed up as a gypsy tonight, with golden hoops screwed into her ears, and an emerald turban.

It had been a little like playing house, helping Maeve to set the table while Fiona stirred and seasoned various things that were simmering in a pot. White shirt, black trousers: Fiona dressed as severely as a nun—perhaps she, too, was in costume? Her movements, as she pushed her cropped hair back from her face, or reached for a plate, had the

assurance of a somnambulist's. Like her daughter's, her face was astonishingly pale—not the dead-white of chalk, but pearly, glimmering.

Over dinner they talked about the weather and the shops in
town—or rather, Anna talked and Maeve interrupted with stories
about her school, and her cat, and how she was going to dress up as a
Knight Templar for Guy Fawkes. Later, when Anna was helping Fiona
with the washing up, she looked across to find Maeve drawing at the
kitchen table; not scribbling, as Anna had at first supposed, but producing lightning sketches of the cat and one of Anna in a chaise longue,
sleeping with a book in her arms. Astonished, Anna stood and watched
her for a while, then returned to Fiona.

"She's got a wonderful gift—is she taking lessons?"

Fiona pushed a scouring pad round and round the bottom of a pot,
as if there were something burned on that she couldn't scrape clean.
Finally she spoke:

"It's the only gift he ever gave her." Another pause, and then:
"Those are his, on the wall over there."

Anna put her dishcloth down and walked over to the room Fiona
had gestured to, a dining room off the kitchen. It didn't look or smell as
if it had ever been used. Where everything else in the house seemed
picked and bare, the walls here were burdened. Landscapes in which
each hump and curve of the Downs had been transcribed with luminous exactitude. Portraits in chalk pastels, slightly blurred as if to protect the sitter from the viewer. A baby, who must once have been
Maeve. A fair-haired woman sitting by a window in half-light, her face
so suffused with tenderness that it hurt to look at her. Anna turned
away and saw Fiona, who had followed her into the room. She was
drying a glass, pushing a teacloth round and round inside it.

"They're—wonderful," Anna repeated.

Fiona was crouching down, picking up bits of the glass which had
quietly exploded in her hands. Anna understood, again: Fiona's husband had run off, perhaps with a student, abandoning his resident
madonna and child. She wanted to make some consoling gesture, to
reach out and stroke Fiona's hair that did not fall in waves and tendrils,
like the picture-woman's, but made a jagged halo round her face. But
then she remembered Luke's wife and the children she had never seen,
and all she could do was pick up the dishcloth Fiona had left lying on
the rug, then follow her back to the kitchen.

From that point on it became a law, like that of gravity or inertia, for Anna to spend Sunday evenings at Fiona's house. Sometimes she'd read to Maeve, while the child did her drawings and Fiona sewed costumes, cutting up brightly-coloured silks and cotton prints she must once have worn. Anna never saw her in anything but black or muddy brown, with sometimes a white scarf or shirt to disrupt the appearance of mourning. They still spoke very little together, but their silences were becoming more and more comfortable. Sometimes it seemed to Anna that Fiona invited her only to keep herself from losing the trick of being able to talk with or be around anyone other than Maeve. For if Anna was verging on becoming a recluse, Fiona was veering into agoraphobia, leaving her house only to take her daughter to and from school, or to do minimal shopping in town. Yet there were also times when it seemed that Fiona wanted her only because Maeve, for whatever reason, had taken a liking to her. The child would talk to Anna in the same quick, concentrated way she drew, describing her teacher and classroom, taking her out to the garden to inspect the fortress she'd constructed, showing off the dancer's or devil's costume her mother had made her. And after Maeve had gone upstairs, scrubbing off her face paint but refusing to change from her costume into her pyjamas, it was Anna from whom she'd beg a story—Anna, who couldn't tell whether it was more her attachment to the child or her concern for its mother which made her keep on with the visits.

For there was a part of the Sunday ritual which Anna didn't like at all, the part for which Fiona seemed most to need her. After Maeve had had her story, Anna would come down the stairs into the parlour, to find Fiona sitting on the sofa, watching telly. Not a sitcom or an American movie, but the news. Anna, who had never in her life owned a set and who felt hopelessly debauched after one commercial, only got through these broadcasts by treating them as global narrative, a technological advance on the serial novels that had hooked a similar audience a century before. Every night another crisis: a war or a coup, a bombing or flooding or famine—anything to keep the plot going. There was an obscene element of anticipation about it all: she caught herself hoping, each time Fiona gestured for her to sit down beside her, that something startling would have happened, something more important than what went on the week before—something apocalyptic, elemental.

This night the broadcast she watched with Fiona featured an Italian plague ship carrying an illegal cargo of toxic waste. The ship was in British waters, cruising the coast, being turned away from port after port. One reporter gave a history of illegal dumpings of poisonous substances in third world countries; footage was shown of children playing alongside leaking barrels of radioactive waste. A leading environmentalist came on the screen, her face collapsed, soft, like a plant that needed watering. She feared that if the ship was refused permission to dock it would discharge its cargo into the sea; she was even more afraid about what would happen if the waste were allowed into England. Anna decided she'd had enough—she was about to make a joke about being sick to death of bad news when she caught a glimpse of Fiona's face. It was the mask she'd first seen her wear: eye-holes, mouth-holes, and something black, bitter pouring out—something you couldn't stop or clean away.

"Fiona?"

There was no reply, nobody home.

"I'll make some coffee," Anna said, brisk and cheerful and false. For she was sick at having sat through it all, furious at Fiona for feeding on disaster all night long, night after night. If she had to watch why couldn't she do so the way everyone else did, erasing one story as you moved on to the next, then shutting the whole thing off for the night. But Fiona wanted to remember everything, to store up catastrophe upon catastrophe inside. She was like those unfortunates in a theatre audience who can't distinguish between fiction and truth; who try to rush on stage to prevent Hamlet from accepting Laertes' challenge, Romeo from drinking poison. Except of course, that this wasn't supposed to be fiction.

Before Anna finished making the coffee, Fiona joined her in the kitchen. She no longer seemed unusual in any way, except, perhaps, for a composure and quietness that began to weigh on Anna like the sound of a clock ticking in an empty room. Anna took a sip of her coffee before trying to excuse herself: she had to be up early the next morning; she had to get back to her book. But Fiona wanted to talk—or rather, to be talked to. She kept on at Anna, asking about her work as if it really mattered, as if everything Anna could tell her about Woolf and modernism and the novel was some coded answer to a set of questions too important to be asked. "What is she saying, why is she saying it? And to whom, Anna? Tell me."

Anna shifted on her chair, avoiding the sight of her reflection in the black circle of her coffee. Anna without blackboard or overhead projector, without lecture notes or supporting texts, without a row of faces looking up at her, attesting to her authority, her knowledge, her undisputed power over them. She started pulling at her fingers, feeling with her thumb for the small ridge of scar tissue left by the bite of a razor, unable to come up with a response to what had been asked of her. Afraid that if she were to acknowledge this—to hold out her hands to Fiona, palms up, apart, and empty—that silence itself might answer.

Anna did what she'd been trained to do. She paused for just a moment, the way an actress might pause before going on stage, her face averted from the audience, her ears turned inward, as if waiting to hear something click and catch. And when it did she made her entrance and never once looked back. She held the floor, summoning up everything she knew, everything she had read, willing herself to speak down the silence in the room. She had spent the last few weeks reading and re-reading her doctoral thesis; making notes, anticipating arguments, plotting out ways to make what she wanted to say the only thing that could be said. She quoted whole paragraphs of her doctoral dissertation.

*The reality of death, of chaos and fragmentation at the heart of life; the vision of a fin in a waste of waters. . . . Nothing but a strip of pavement over an abyss, scraps which can never coalesce into any lasting whole. . . . In death alone our partial, momentary selves are joined to the immense and unseen part of us. . . . Woolf walking into the river, weighing her pockets down with stones, not surrendering to death or disintegration but preserving the integrity, the purity of the self at last speaking to the self; reaching, at last the centre. . . .*

"The centre," was all Fiona said. She didn't go on to ask, "The centre of what?" to Anna's vast relief. Not that she'd admit she didn't know. She would say: transcendence—the larger vision—the unknown. She wouldn't say anything, except what she did now:

"Sorry—you really shouldn't have got me started on the divine Virginia. I'm afraid I've kept you up, Fiona; you'll be dead tomorrow morning—"

Fiona smiled. "But I hate going to sleep, Anna. Because then I have to wake up. When I wake it's as though someone's shoving my head under water. She was right, you know."

Her voice was perfectly clear and light as she said this: what she wasn't saying rattled Anna even more. It was as though a student had stood up at the end of a lecture with a question which undid everything Anna had said, or fatally misconstrued it. What had Fiona taken from her about Virginia Woolf? Submersion instead of transcendence; extinction rather than completion? It was terribly important that she correct this, that she go on to tell Fiona she was misreading Woolf, that there was a passionate delight in life as well, sixty years of it before she put those stones into her pockets. Why was it that she couldn't summon the proper phrases now, when she'd been so eloquent before?

Fiona had already collected the coffee mugs and rinsed them at the sink. She was saying good night quite cheerfully, asking Anna to let herself out. And Anna did so—she'd been given the run of the house it seemed, the power to walk in and out at her discretion. This pleased her; it made her feel a kind of family tie. This distressed her; it made her feel somehow responsible.

That night Anna walked for a while in the garden of Rest Harrow under a sky that made her think of an endless bolt of black crepe. She wandered down the neat rows of the garden, rows of round white flowers, each on a stalk as thick and fleshy as a throat. Each flower a full moon, a blank face that the night inscribed in its own speech. Anna's hair fizzing like a sparkler as she bent and cupped each flower in her hand, and then, with a sharp upward movement of her wrist, broke off each round and empty face. Walking down the rows and picking faces, a willow basket full of faces. Until she reached a stalk with two faces growing from it, and no matter how hard she pulled and tugged, so that sap began to gush down her wrists, and her nails rent the stalk, opening but not breaking it, she could not free them.

When Anna woke from this dream which had taken only a mouthful of her sleep, but seemed to have left behind nothing but bones, she made herself go to the window. She opened it wide and pushed the dream outside. A small, black wind carried it in the direction of Fiona's house. There, all the windows screamed with light, except for one, the room in which Maeve, still in her silks and scarves, and with the cat trapped between her arms, lay fast asleep.

# VII

# THE LORD OF THE MANOR

Anna was trying to find a whole week's notes which her computer appeared to have eaten when a knock came at the door. Not a timid, but a forceful knock, from someone who was not at all intimidated by the Medusa head—perhaps a police inspector, a customs officer? Undoing the latch, Anna braved herself for a request to see her passport, an inquiry into the legality of her having imported computer equipment into the U.K. without a licence, a recital of the thousand different crimes she might have committed in fact or omission since leaving Canada.

But it was an old lady with forget-me-not eyes and a tremulous smile which made you want to gather her up as if she were a newborn lamb. She was wearing a skirt and sweater that reminded Anna of a pair of tea cosies minus the pots—that must be why she ended by inviting Miss Molesworth in and offering her a cup of tea. It took fifteen minutes for Miss Molesworth to exclaim sufficiently over the soundness of the plaster-work in the hall, by which time Anna had carried the tea things into the parlour. They talked of the weather—quite remarkably fine, more like summer than anything we've had since April, Anna's guest declared. The postcard from Bulgaria was admired, since Miss Molesworth had asked whether anything had been heard from dear Miss Oliver. Admiration was expressed at Miss Oliver's visiting a place so very foreign and so far away. But only after her curiosity had been satisifed as to whether Winnipeg were the capital of New Brunswick or Newfoundland did Miss Molesworth finally dig into her crocheted carry-all and introduce the purpose of her visit: a book of tickets to the Annual Village Wine and Cheese. After earnest admonitions that Anna needn't feel obliged to purchase anything—but it was a wonderful chance to get to know the other villagers, though naturally they would understand, as she was here only for a year, yet no less welcome for that, it was always such a pleasure to see a new face, and by any chance was she an alto, they were terribly short of them in the church choir, and while she thought of it, she would ask the Women's Institute to add Miss English's name (such a lovely coincidence wasn't it, Miss *English,* visiting *England*) to its mailing list—Miss Molesworth gratefully received Anna's two pounds and issued her with a ticket.

The day after Miss Molesworth's visit, a letter slid through the mail slot—not from Luke but Simon, saying he'd be honoured to escort her to the wine and cheese. Anna scribbled a card back to him, saying she'd be away in London all that weekend. Desiring no further acquaintance with Mrs. Higley than was absolutely necessary, Anna waited till Simon had raced to school the next morning before slipping up the path past the church and sliding her own note under his door. Damn Dr. Oliver for asking him to look out for her in the first place. But damn her most of all for the timing of the missive which had arrived in the same post as Simon's letter, summoning her to spend the weekend with her at her house in London—the weekend *after* the wine and cheese.

She wasn't altogether sure she approved of it, this overture on the part of a perfect stranger. How should she interpret Dr. Oliver's invitation? Generosity? Curiosity—although a little on the tardy side? Condescension, interference? Was it loyalty to Fiona, a memory of the scratch of her accusation—"You're a friend of Rosalind Oliver's"—that made Anna tear up the letter from London and toss it into the waste basket, along with Simon's innocently courtly note? And what kind of afterthoughts made her bend, some fifteen minutes later, over the wastepaper basket and retrieve the pieces of the letter, stuffing them all into the envelope, and the envelope into her *A to Z?*

Anna got ready on the night of the wine and cheese by settling down with cocoa and the copy of *The Luck of the Woosters* she'd discovered in the spare room. She ignored the first few knocks at the door, but on the seventh rap, when it had become obvious that the Medusa head wouldn't scare her visitor away, Anna hauled herself up and answered the summons.

It was Miss Molesworth, her iron fists swathed in lavender gloves. "I'm so glad you haven't gone on—I thought you might like some company going down to the Hall, it's sometimes a little difficult, isn't it, making friends in a strange place? Oh, dear, you hadn't forgotten? How lucky I decided to come by! Everyone's longing to meet you. I've told

Mrs. Pendergast—she's the head of our W.I.—all about you. No, of course not, take all the time you need. Why, we've the whole evening ahead of us."

As they left Rest Harrow, Anna looked back in the direction of Fiona's cottage. Tonight only the parlour lights were on, seeping through shut curtains. She felt guilty, still, about her last visit there, when she'd been stupid enough to go on and on about Death and Virginia Woolf. Now she stopped, quite suddenly, nearly tripping Miss Molesworth, who'd taken her arm as they'd crossed the green. It had just occurred to Anna that Fiona might keep so close to home not because she was ago-raphobic, but for the simple reason that she couldn't get a baby-sitter, child-minder, whatever the right word was. Someone by whom Maeve would want to be minded. Why, then, shouldn't she offer to baby-sit Maeve one evening a week so that Fiona could get out of that oppressive cottage? She must have someone with whom she could see a film or have dinner: she could go to evening lectures, yoga classes—attend the Women's Institute. Delighted with herself, hardly knowing what she was doing, Anna shook off her companion and embarked energetically in the wrong direction, down an unfamiliar lane.

No moon, not even the evening star; just a yellow patch of light. Anna pressed on towards it, despite Miss Molesworth's murmurings behind her. But by now there was no Miss Molesworth; she had disap-peared like a minor character in a novel, a lady's maid or an elderly vicar's aunt. By now there was only the criss-cross of a leaded window, through which Anna could just make out the figure of a woman writing at a desk. Her back was turned, but Anna recognized the pattern of her dress. It was the woman she'd seen on her first walk over the Downs. Cigarette smoke wreathing her head; hunched shoulders, terribly thin. And the steady movement of an arm across a page, the elbow swaying back and forth like the bar of a metronome.

Anna could have stayed and looked forever—she was pressing her face into the glass as if the warmth of her skin could melt it. But Miss Molesworth called out through the dark, her voice plaintive, fretful. "You've gone the wrong way. Dear, dear—we've got to go back the way we came. There's only one way down the street. Do come, they'll be wait-ing for us." And as soon as Miss Molesworth spoke, the woman lifted her arm to turn out the light, so that the glass became the same unyielding darkness as the strips of lead, and Anna had at last to turn away.

They weren't the first ones in the Hall, but they did arrive uncomfortably early. It was a no-nonsense, rectangular room with notices on the wall about playgroup sessions, bake-a-thons and a lecture series on *The Role of the Volunteer in Today's Community*. Women were bustling in the kitchen, setting out row after row of plastic glasses. The wine was in cartoned polythene bags, and there seemed to be something wrong with the spigot—a man had been called in to set it to rights. It was, observed Anna, something one of the women could easily have done, but they seemed to want to make a show of bringing a man in, congratulating him on his cleverness as if he were a small boy needing to bolster his self-esteem. The women were heaping plates with Cheddar and Danish blue, and here and there a sliver of Stilton, lavishly trimmed with real, not plastic parsley. Bowls and bowls of apples; grapes looking suspiciously like the South African variety Anna had boycotted at the supermarket, and enough crackers to girdle the globe.

Anna didn't know what to do. She had no inclination to tie on an apron and join the servers as Miss Molesworth had done, and she could scarcely stand at the door collecting tickets. Instead, she bought herself a glass of Ribena and walked up to a trio of fiftyish men who seemed to be having an animated conversation. They nodded, a little startled at her boldness, then ignored her entirely.

"I tell you it will be the end of Pyeford."

"But people have to have houses—you can't have prosperity without people. And one's got to house them somewhere."

"But if that plan goes through we'll end up clapped onto Pelham. There won't be a Pyeford anymore, just one great dormitory town. There won't be any green space left at all."

"Why not build a brand new village from scratch, somewhere more convenient for them—closer to the rail links? What's the good of swamping Pyeford with cheap, nasty bungalows?"

"And the cheap and nasty people who go with them?"

Anna hadn't realized she'd spoken until the men all turned to stare at her. She smiled uncertainly and walked away. A woman was coming up to her, a woman in a pink blouse with a pussy-cat bow, and a pleated flannel skirt. Her shoes were the sensible sort; her hair was short and grey and permed. Anna's heart sank: this could only be the president of the Women's Institute.

And so it was. Mrs. Pendergast took her firmly by the arm and began walking her round the room, introducing her to the little clumps of pleasantly smiling, uniformly gracious villagers who were entering the Hall. They all had some relative or acquaintance in Canada, or failing that, New Zealand; they all imagined she'd find the winters here something of a letdown after all the ice and snow which she was used to. She didn't bother explaining that a Nova Scotia winter was not the sort to burst tires or paralyse transport systems. Everyone asked her how long she would be staying. They were such agreeable people, so hearty in their wishes that she would enjoy herself, so earnest in their assurances that they'd had a lovely holiday visiting their cousin/sister/son in Saskatoon/Victoria/Calgary. And they seemed so disappointed when she'd had to admit that she'd never been to any of those places.

In between introductions—Anna forgetting each new name as soon as it was proffered—Mrs. Pendergast informed her about the role and function of the W.I., the new image it was attempting to cultivate in order to accommodate today's dynamic, professional woman. And how much they regretted Rosalind Oliver's absence from the village. "We know she's terribly busy—one sees her everywhere these days. On the television, radio. . . . Not that we always agree with the things she says. I'm afraid she's been rather rude in her remarks about the Home Secretary on 'Question Time.' But she's still one of us—she's more than welcome in Pyeford. I *do* wish she'd give up living in London. There are just so many—foreigners there. The Blacks, of course, and the Arabs, and now all these people from Hong Kong. . . ." Anna excused herself to get another glass of juice, but not before she'd promised to attend a meeting in a fortnight's time. She may even have committed herself to giving a lecture on the role of the woman writer in a world of shifting— or was it shifty?—moral values.

By now there were enough people cutting hunks of cheese and crumbling crackers that Anna could dive behind a palisade of stacked chairs, count to a hundred, and decide she'd better leave before Simon showed up. She was sneaking out along the corridor, behind the stage and through the emergency exit door; she was almost home free when the local squire caught her out.

Or at least, he had the look of a local squire in the pose of a Buddha. He was sitting cross-legged in the wings of the stage, beckoning to her from the edge of the curtain. She couldn't ignore him—he was obviously someone who wouldn't put up with being ignored, and so she turned towards him. Equally obviously, he held village wine and cheese in low esteem, as he was pouring Chambolle Musigny into a crystal glass he seemed to have brought along for the occasion. He held the glass out to her with a perfectly steady hand, and greeted her with an odd, piratical smile.

"*Skol, prost, l'chaim, na zdarovlya, santé*—which do you prefer?"

Anna shook her head, unable to think of a thing to say.

"Let me guess—no, don't tell me. You're under an evil enchant-ment, and until you've sewn seven shirts out of thistles you won't be able to squeeze out so much as a syllable."

And as if she were indeed bewitched, Anna continued to stare. She couldn't place the man at all—characters from her mother's favourite books went whirling through her head: Grandcourt? Willoughby? D'Urberville? The man put down his glass and leaned back against the wall, his hands clasped behind his head. A combination of indifference and self-interest seemed to well from the fullness of his clean-shaven face, from the beginnings of a bulge over his belt—too great a fondness for pheasant and smoked trout, never mind the burgundy he was belting back. He must have just returned from holiday in some place expen-sively south, for his skin was the colour of dried oak leaves. She didn't like the blue of his eyes—it reminded her of the skim milk she'd had to drink as a child. Even less did she like the way he was keeping her here against her will, as if he had some kind of claim upon her. And yet what most disturbed her was the way his accent collided with his words, as though a stage cockney were reading a Speech from the Throne.

"I heard all about you when we got back last week. Meant to drop in and say hello, but somehow I just haven't had the time. It's really very bad of Rosie—she might at least have warned me. *Lèse-majesté*—what can one do about that kind of thing these days? And of course she enjoys being bolshy about renting the cottage—she's always picking students for tenants, yobbos who bounce their empty lager tins into our grounds. I've had to give them a good talking to more than once. I don't suppose we'll have that sort of trouble from you, love?" He reached into the briefcase beside him and drew out another bottle.

"I don't know you, I don't understand a word you've said, and whether or not you'll excuse me, I'm leaving this instant," was what Anna should have said. Instead, she merely managed "Who—?"

"Ah—I beg your pardon, I ought to have bowed low and properly introduced myself, if only to keep up appearances. She never thinks of that; she probably didn't even tell you—but that's Rosie all over, absolutely all over, and I can tell you I'm an authority on that. Pryce-Jones. Nicholas. Your next-door neighbour, at Fortuna House. We must have you round for supper one of these days."

"We—?" For one wild moment Anna had put two and two together to get the impossible sum of Nicholas Pryce-Jones as Rosalind Oliver's son.

"My wife, of course, Iseult of the White Hands, Lady Bountiful herself, a.k.a. the Woman in White." And he gestured over the stage to a far corner of the hall.

Anna could just make out a tall, black-haired woman dressed in what looked like Miss Havisham's bridal finery. The woman seemed to be looking back in her direction—Anna blushed furiously, as if she'd been caught up a ladder staring into someone's bathroom window. What in the world was she doing in this place, and in such company? She was turning to go when the man reached forward and put his hand on her arm. She tried to shake it off, but he pressed all the harder.

"Good night, Mr. Jones—"

"Pryce-Jones. Nicholas Pryce-Jones. It was my publicist's idea, though it's all perfectly authentic. Pryce was my mother's maiden name." For a moment he sounded contrite, abashed; he let go of her arm, but she stood there as if she were still in his grasp. She was, in fact, remembering a display of books she'd noticed in one of the town shops, books with a glossily arresting cover—a demi-tasse of coffee surrounded by after-dinner mints which turned out, on closer inspection, to be a cup of blood upon a plate of condoms. "You mean you're the Nicholas Pryce-Jones who's written—"

"Shit, mostly. But it seems to go down well. Better than this dung they call cheese. Cressy insists we come to these affairs—she wants to be part of everyday village life, you see."

"I see—" Anna couldn't help herself—she craned her head forward to catch another glimpse of Lady Bountiful in the crowded room below. Though tall enough, Mrs. Pryce-Jones was distinctly fat. Looking closer, watching as Cressy detached herself from one group of women and pushed her way over to another, Anna could see that she wasn't fat, just heavily pregnant.

"Twins, no less," her husband drawled. "Bringing the total up to a round nine. All girls. These will be, too. Please don't mistake me—I don't at all mind the sex. I'd hate to have boys: brutish, vengeful. I should know, I was one myself. And they're not eyesores, by any means, though God knows what they've got in the way of grey matter. You'll have to call round and give me your opinion. Not on the girls, but on my novel. It's at the stage of viscous, pulsing, pre-birth. D'you know, there's a theory that most British novels are conceived and brought to birth in garden sheds? I'm no exception. Except that mine's more of a coach house—renovated, of course. Centrally heated. I have a bed and cooker and fridge and loo. And a whirlpool, with unlimited hot water. Thanks to *Pig Sticking*. I wrote the screenplay, as well—that's where the money is, of course. You sure you won't have even half a glass? What, running off and leaving me to finish the bottle on my own? Won't even stay and chat, tell me all about wherever it is you come from—Brisbane, is it? Auckland? I've got it—don't tell me—Fox Jaw?"

"Moose Jaw."

"I knew it—"

"Look, I don't come from Moose Jaw, and I don't particularly want to carry on this conversation." It was time, Anna decided, definitely time to go home. If Mr. Pryce-Jones wouldn't let her past him and out the back door of the hall, she'd simply retrace her steps and make a public exit. But just as she was turning to walk away, he grabbed her arm again.

"Hallo—who have we here? Why, it's Simple Simon, straight from a meeting of the Fellowship of the Lamb. Bunch of rubbery farts—no wonder his wife ran off. The wonder is she waited as long as she did."

Helplessly, Anna watched Simon making his way through the hall, looking all too obviously for someone who wasn't there. She was done for—and since there was no help for it, she submitted to this stranger's grasp. "Simon's married?" She almost shouted it.

"He was. I see you know our local Gimpel? Can it be that he's developing a romantic interest in the tenant of Rest Harrow? I'd advise you to watch out, dear girl. When a celibate unzips his fly—but I'd have thought it was the Fair Fiona he was after. You know, Pyeford's resident Cassandra and Tragic Muse. Rosie's other neighbour."

This time she didn't even try to resist. "Why tragic? What happened to Fiona?"

"What happened to her? Principally, her husband—not an alto-gether superior specimen, I'm afraid. Brainless bugger, he went back to see his dear old mum, who had the stupidity to live in Belfast. And on the way to one of the local beauty spots—he fancied himself a painter, you see, flogging pretty little house-and-garden pictures to the people who'd bought up the houses and gardens in question. You know the kind of thing—'View from Colonel Pootle's Sunken Rose Arbour.' 'Mrs. Ashcombe-Vole's Lily Pond, Sunset.' Anyway, on his way to Par-nassus he happened to wander into a road block. All very quick and rel-atively painless—and, what's more important, profitable. Nothing like an early death for boosting one's reputation. His dealer must have made a mint off it, even if his wife wouldn't do her bit. God knows she's well rid of him. Frankly, he was the worst bore I ever had to suffer at my dinner table."

"But what about—" Anna caught herself reaching out to grab his sleeve. For he'd breezily let go of her to pack the empty bottles into his briefcase.

"Sorry, love, but I really do have to push off. I'll see what I can do about dinner. I'll have to win Cressy round first, of course. I'm afraid she looks down on colonials, but not to worry—it's a congenital defect in people of her class, and certainly not catching. Oh—by the way—give my love to Rosie when you see her, will you?"

Anna watched him jump off the stage into the crowded hall and join his wife, putting an arm round her shoulder and hugging his brief-case tightly to his side. She waited to see if he would glance or point in her direction; only when it seemed as if he'd entirely forgotten her did she turn and run through the exit doors.

Once on The Street, she stopped to take in a good, long breath of air free of smoke and wine-soured breath. It was amazingly clear and bright—the sky looked as if someone had smashed a million glasses against it. She hugged herself and threw back her head, looking up as if the stars could crowd out of her head everything she'd heard over the last half hour. The man must have mistaken her for somebody else—better still, she must have made him up, him and all the stories he had to tell her about Fiona and Fiona's husband, about Simon—

"Anna, how lovely! I thought you were stuck in London for the weekend. I don't blame you for coming back early—it's a terrible place these days." Simon had seized her hand and was shaking it so hard Anna thought it would break off at the wrist. She freed herself as soon as she could, mumbling something about being tired, needing to get home.

"I'll see you to your door—no, of course not—how could it be any trouble, it's right on the way. What luck running into you like this. We must set another time for that church crawl I promised you—"

"Church crawl?"

"Yes, we settled it the night you came to dinner. I'm afraid I'm tied up tomorrow, but how about next week? I thought we might try and look out some Curvilinear. Actually, there's a splendid example in our own parish church."

"Really?" It came out with an exasperation that Simon mistook for enthusiasm.

"How about next Saturday? We can start off at ten, say, and I'll have us back for tea. Are you any good with a tripod?"

They had reached Rest Harrow—Anna was desperate to get inside and shut the door on the whole disastrous evening. "No, Simon. Not next Saturday—I don't know when, not—oh, for God's sake, good night."

Anna slammed the door so hard that the knocker rattled for a full minute. Simon waited until the noise had stopped completely. Then he put his hands in his pockets, and, whistling far too jauntily, set off for home. Anna kept hearing him long after he must have turned his key in the latch and shut himself inside.

# VIII

# ROSALIND

Once settled into the carriage—not a sealed compartment, a woman had been stabbed to death in one of those the week before—Anna closed her eyes, breathed deeply, and waited for the whistle. There was still time, she told herself, time to jump out of this train and hop aboard another going to Chichester or Canterbury: anywhere but London. Or else to climb into her car and drive back to Pyeford, back to the four walls of her study, the drawn curtains behind which no one could find her, not Simon, not even Maeve or Fiona. Or the Lord of the Manor. She hadn't wanted him to tell her those stories; she hadn't wanted to know about Fiona's husband's death—she wouldn't know how not to show that she knew. He'd spoiled it all for her, Mr. Nicholas Pryce-Jones, whose love she was bearing to the famous Dr. Oliver, whom Anna pictured now as a woman in her late fifties, a hetaera with dyed, dark hair, dizzying cleavage and a throaty voice inflected like the cuts in a crystal vase. What on earth would she do with such a woman—what would such a woman do with her? She needn't stay more than ten minutes, Anna told herself. She needn't do more than look up at the woman's house and decide from the very façade whether or not she'd step inside. She could book herself into a hotel, she could spend the entire weekend in the British Library, she could send post-cards to everyone she knew proving that she'd been to England, been to London, done what was expected of her. The carriage gave a shud-der, the engines thrummed wildly and Anna's eyes clacked open, exactly as if she were a doll, violently up-ended.

It was no distraction to look out the window at the scenery gliding past: too many trees had been blown down, or else were gesturing from field or hedgerow like giant amputees. The England her mother had read into her, printing Platonic forms of meadows, copses, brooks—she couldn't find it here at all. So many houses, so little open country left. Everywhere were red brick villas—the kind Virginia Woolf had so

detested—and the bungalows she hadn't lived to see go up. Anna
shook her head as if there were hornets buzzing between her ears. What
had she expected? What had she wanted? Her mother's book-built England, or the one she herself had conjured out of a lighthouse, a florist's
shop on Bond Street, an inn near Hampton Court? Not even these
places, but the words that drew them out of blanks of paper. Luke,
telling her it was a mistake to come, that all reality can do is to evict
you, evict you—

Anna hung her coat on a hook over the window, blanking out the
view and the roll of Luke's words in the wheels of the train. She opened
her overnight case and, with a deliberate flourish, produced the notebook in which she'd drawn together all the ideas she'd hatched for her
book over the last few weeks. She felt vastly better with the notebook
in her hands—what she was holding onto wasn't paper but her very
self, Anna English, someone no amount of accidental meetings, no disruptive summons could negate.

When they reached Hayward's Heath (another deception, for there
wasn't even a handsbreadth of turf to be seen) three louts—she
couldn't think of any other word for them—burst into the compartment. Squeezing into a seat meant for two they pulled out tins of lager
from a paper bag; drank, belched and shared a copy of the *Sun*. An
older woman in a powder-blue raincoat made a great show of leaving
her seat across from them for another at the opposite end of the car.
Though there was a large No Smoking sign above their heads, they
pulled out a pack of cigarettes and started to puff away. Anna glared
across at them, only to have a pair of pumpkins lobbed at her: Today's
Sunshine Girl, hands clasped behind her back and pigtails bouncing.

It's no worse than it would be in Toronto or New York, Anna told
herself. At least they didn't shout obscenities when the powder-blue
raincoat huffed away, but merely put up their black-booted feet into the
empty space provided. If Anna were to draw their attention to the No
Smoking sign, what would she achieve? A slightly diminished possibility of contracting lung cancer; a greater probability of being told to fuck
herself. She looked surreptitiously for an empty place in the coach—all
seats were packed tight. So she settled for taking out her annotated
copy of *To the Lighthouse* and facing-off against the Sunshine Girl.

It wasn't any use—she couldn't read. Though she told herself she
wasn't the least bit like the powder-blue lady, she wished the louts in

the next compartment, or preferably, bounced off the train into a gravel siding. She couldn't iron out their accents, she couldn't read them right. Even their laughter seemed to be in a foreign language. She clutched her book tighter and found herself wishing Luke were with her, wishing she'd brought his last letter along so she could brandish it in front of them. *See, I'm not alone, I have someone of my own, and if he could hear the way you're sniggering at me he'd crumple you exactly like those lager tins.* Furling her contempt, aiming it like the steel tip of an umbrella, Anna dropped her book and glared at the men across from her. One of them smiled, almost wistfully, and then lifted his hands, making a circle with his thumb and forefinger, pushing it up and down over his index finger.

Anna jumped up, grabbed her overnight bag and staggered across the jolting carriage to the door. Several compartments on she found herself in the seclusion of first class. The two gentlemen inside the car rustled their copies of *The Financial Times* as she sank down onto an empty seat, resting her head against the clean linen pinned there, she supposed, to ward off hair oil and head lice. She counted to a hundred, by which time her heart had stopped rattling like dice in a cup, then reached into her bag for her notebook. It wasn't there.

By the time she'd dragged herself back along the wildly jolting corridors to where she'd started from, the louts were gone. So were her books. She asked a woman in the seat ahead whether she'd seen any-thing, but the woman, who was wearing a sari under a drab wool coat, could only gesture apologetically. By this time the train was slowing into Victoria. Anna slumped into a seat, clutching her overnight bag on her lap. This was hardly the way to begin her *vita nuova.* All she could think of was the notebook that had been stolen from her, the four weeks' work she'd been too dilatory, too superstitious, even, to copy into her computer. How could she ever retrieve what she'd written there? A whole month's work, and they'd toss it in the nearest rubbish bin, or worse, keep it. She imagined them defacing the few empty pages that remained, scribbling the crudest of anatomical drawings, writing four-letter words, mis-spelled, of course.

Once off the train Anna rushed to the Lost Property office, hoping that some principled person had seen her leave the books behind; had collected and handed them in, just moments ahead of her. But once she walked up to the counter and looked over the attendant's shoulder at the racks of overcoats, the shelves of briefcases, the crates of umbrellas, she knew her notebook was lost forever. How could mere ink on paper count as property, either lost or found? When the man asked if he could help she shook her head and then surrendered herself to the stream of passengers flooding in what turned out to be the direction of the Tube.

Poor Anna. Or stupid Anna, hapless, inept, absurdly incompetent. Certainly she was nothing like those heroines her mother had brought her up to admire: Dorothea Brooke, Becky Sharp, Elizabeth Bennett, Esther Summerhouse: women fixed and solid and capable as bookends or doorstops. And yet, as she fumbled at the automated ticket vendor, half of which was out of order, as she jammed whatever change she had into the slot and came up with a plethora of destinations, none of which matched the address printed on a scrap of letter buried in the bottom of her bag, this woman who avoided mirrors out of the fear that the various parts of her face would drift out of the frame and never return to her, whose very name was a tunnel through which everything passed and nothing remained, still accomplished the impossible. In a state of helplessness bordering on fury, and fury exploding into helplessness, legs shaking, heart flapping like a sheet in the wind, she lurched to the right platform, squeezed herself into a train with a hundred other hot, ill-tempered and unsmiling passengers, and managed to shove herself out at Camden Town.

Her arms ached from humping the overnight case up the escalator and through the mob in the entrance of the station. A trio of buskers, no, beggars barred her way out: men who looked as worn as their clothes. One had a wine bottle in his hand; another, a tin of cat food. They were staggering and singing, singing and staggering—she didn't stop to try and make out the words of the song, if there were any words and not just sobs and wheezing. One of the men held out his hand to her—blood grinned from a gash over his knuckles. She clutched her bag tighter against her, butted her way out of the station and collapsed into a cab.

She was let off in a crescent of Regency houses blackened by coal fires and car exhaust. A stand of sickly chestnut trees screened a cement wall behind which trains were shunting. Tubs of geraniums fronted the door, and Anna almost wept at the sight of them. Not roses or orchids, but blistered geraniums, and yet they were flowers, after all. She was beginning to think that nothing but dirt and diesel fumes could take root in London. Stretching out her hand to touch a leaf she found sooty traces on her fingers. Not bothering to wipe them off, she raised her hand and pushed the bell.

The door flew open, and a woman with her hair on fire leaped out. She grabbed both of Anna's arms, looked at her for a long moment, as if she could will Anna's face into whatever shape she'd been expecting, and then released her.

"Who on earth are you?"

Anna was registering too much—that the woman's hair wasn't on fire, but simply an explosive shade of red; that she was nearly six feet tall and wore an emerald body stocking and a black skirt so brief you couldn't have dried your hands on it, that she was beautiful enough to produce the effect of static electricity: short, sharp illuminating shocks—to be able to answer.

"Ah—you must be my tenant. Come in, come in—all the way up to the top floor. I rent out the bottom two, you see. They're lovely people, hardly ever here. An archaeologist couple, gay, and boringly monogamous. They send me postcards from equatorial Africa. Mind the carpet, it's coming loose there."

Ten minutes later Anna was sitting, sipping champagne, on a small, carved sofa across from Rosalind Oliver. And however blatant Rosalind might be with her flamy hair and brilliant clothes, everything else in the room spoke in the richest of whispers. A rosewood spinnet, a small Sisley of poplars over a pond full of leaping, golden fish. Bookshelves the full length of the walls, ancient bindings and raggedy paperbacks cheek by jowl. Carvings of fruit and flowers framed the doorway, on either side of which a life-size cherub perched, one with a palm leaf in its arms, the other hoisting—

"A wooden spoon?"

"The palm leaf was the only thing that got damaged at the house-warming party—exactly how, I'm not quite sure. We decided that kitchen utensils would do nicely as a martyr's emblem."

Anna looked round again, as if to find some clue as to who the "we" might be, but the place had the familiar feel of solitariness: a silence and control you could read like the grain in a piece of wood. She couldn't put this place together with Nicholas Pryce-Jones, pouring out wine and gossip, holding her far too tightly by the arm. Or, for that matter, with Simon. Yet both of them knew Rosalind—Anna had already begun to call her that. As for Rosalind, she had started in by calling her Annie, and Anna didn't dream of correcting her.

Rosalind was drinking her third glass of champagne, sitting cross-legged in a huge armchair, Jacobean, and not reproduction. Anna knew because she'd asked—she couldn't think of anything else to say. Rosalind wasn't explaining—explanations, you felt, were something she'd never feel any need for—but saying there'd been a change of plans. Annie was still quite welcome—she could even stay the night, if she chose—though she'd find it horribly noisy.

"I'm having a gathering here tonight—and I do mean a gathering, not a party. But that's not for ages yet. You must be starving—I've made the most awful lunch, why don't we eat?"

Lunch turned out to be a perfect *boeuf en daube* but Rosalind's performance was even better: scandalous anecdotes about academics whom Anna knew only by reputation, descriptions of the state of state toilets in Bulgaria, an account of an American-initiated plan to turn Stonehenge into a Disney theme park. The amazing thing was how Rosalind seemed to surround her listener, making her one of the chosen and initiated, so that Anna quite forgot to be suspicious or angry or even bewildered. It wasn't just the champagne, which she'd had to drink to be polite—or the burgundy which had followed. When, halfway through the meal, Anna mentioned Rest Harrow, Rosalind had laughed and shaken her head, making it seem that Rest Harrow were a mere pretext for meeting Annie. By the time they got on to pudding and liqueurs, Anna felt as though she were floating in a warm, scented bath with petals drifting down on her, and lutes and viols playing. It was nothing short of enchantment, a singing-round of spells. She was in Rosalind's house—she was Rosalind's Annie.

After showing her how to take her spoon and draw swirls of double cream over the surface of her coffee, Rosalind sprang up from her chair. "Come on, Annie—you've five minutes to pee or brush your teeth or whatever you need to do. I've got tickets for the ballet and we've less than an hour to get there. We'll have to take a cab—the Tube is perfectly useless, it breaks down every ten minutes these days."

Once in the cab, Rosalind instantly fell asleep, her head flung back on the upholstery, perfect as a marble portrait bust. Anna, however, was wide awake: she forced herself not to stare at Rosalind, turning instead to the crowded streets through which the car careened.

Not rubbish-strewn this time; not so much as a flick of graffiti over the walls which hemmed in crescents and terraces of Palladian design. *A splendid achievement in its own way, after all, London; the season; civiliza-tion.* High windows, plush curtains, long and gleaming cars pulled up below—the heraldic devices of those who never need set foot in the Tube, or dodge a lager tin lobbed by the new young men carbuncular. But this was churlish, mean-minded. Why should she accuse those who lived in Cumberland Terrace? Of what? Not knowing—or not having to know?

"We'll get out here." Rosalind, waking as if by magic, paid the cabbie and led the way over Charing Cross Bridge, across to the South Bank. "It's *L'Enfant et les Sortilèges*. You can eat licorice allsorts in the lobby if it gets to be too much for you. I adore dance, I wanted once to have been Pavlova before I found out she'd been turned into a dessert. Why does that only happen with women—Pêche Melba—"

"Cherries Jubilee?" Anna sang out, but Rosalind couldn't hear her. On legs long as the Nile, Rosalind galloped along while Anna worked her own like eggbeaters just to keep up. Off the bridge, and down the steps to the National Theatre—they were in a rush, yet Rosalind stopped dead in front of two kids sitting in a corner of the stairwell, nothing but a layer of denim between the concrete and their skin. They were chatting to one another, a girl and a boy, perhaps eighteen, seventeen. Rosalind reached into her pocket and fished out two pound coins—dropped them between them. The boy nodded thanks, but kept on listening to what the girl was saying. Anna stiffened—what was she expected to do? The kids looked genuinely miserable, but wouldn't they just spend the money on a pint between them at the nearest local? And what if they did? Weren't they free to beg, just as she was free not to put her hand in her pocket? Though she did at the last, letting go the coins a moment too late, so that they rolled in the wrong direction. She had to stoop to pick them up and couldn't bring herself to offer them again.

"Come on, Annie—you're making us late." Both of them running along the embankment now, over concrete that flowed up into the the-atre itself, one endless snot-grey sea.

They dived into their seats—front row—just as the houselights dimmed. Anna spent much of the performance watching Rosalind, who was sitting hunched forward in her seat, arms crossed, a hand grasping each shoulder, elbows digging into her knees as if she were both prompting and restraining herself; as if otherwise she would have leapt onstage to join the dancers. She seemed oblivious to what was distracting Anna's attention—a man in the row behind them, fishing crisps, one by one, from a cellophane bag. It took him the whole first act to finish the package. But once the curtain came down on the teapots, chalkboards and toy soldiers, Rosalind sprang up from her seat, grabbed the empty cellophane bag from the man's lap, ripped it in two, and crinkled the pieces right in his ears. Three whole rows burst into loud applause.

Afterwards they went onto the balcony and looked out over the Thames. It was late afternoon, now: mist scarved the rooftops and boats and the divested branches of the trees. Anna felt like a helium balloon, afraid to say a word lest she cut the string tying her to Rosalind's hand. She had forgotten everything else about the day—the theft of her papers, the lager louts, the beggars in the Tube—everything except being here with Rosalind. All around them people were laughing and talking, some in Swedish or Russian or Spanish. Diplomats: the thought made Anna absurdly happy. "I am in London," she kept saying to herself. "I am at the very centre of the world. I am here in London with Rosalind Oliver; I am a thousand bees swarming to the hive, a hundred birds rushing to the arms of one great tree." She wanted to throw back her head and laugh louder than the orchestra—she wanted to make a hoop of her arms and jump inside them, over and over, hearing the smash of paper each time she burst through. When Rosalind went off to get them each a glass of wine, Anna turned her back to the river, leaning hard against the railing so that it punched her spine, telling her she was awake, that this was real, that Rosalind would come back and she would have a whole two days of this extraordinary buoyancy. She looked into the crowd, trying to see Rosalind flaming overhead—she wished she had worn something far finer today: silks rather than wool; ribbons in her hair.

When Rosalind returned, Anna downed her wine so quickly that she almost choked. All through the second half of the ballet she could feel her mouth fizzing and glowing; she felt like the women in watch factories who had licked radium-coated brushes, whose tongues and lips burned like green moths in the night. Like Rosalind, she sat forward in her seat, music strumming her legs and arms, making her want to hurl herself onto the stage and dance. She shut her eyes as though to distance the music, until Rosalind pressed her arm—this was the part of the dance she simply had to see.

Anna opened her eyes onto a roly-poly doll in an enormous hoop skirt. Suddenly doll and skirt vanished to reveal the cage beneath the silks, a cage in which another dancer was trapped, running wildly this way and that, pushing the huge contraption round and round until the veins in her long, delicate arms rose up like whips. Within the iron confines of her cage she was able to perform the most astonishing steps, yet always she had to shove the cage in front of her, as if to clear room for the very breath she drew.

Anna wasn't ready for how painful it was to watch this—painful as a bird beating against the unyielding transparency of glass. She wanted to be the child dancing beside the woman, holding her hands through the bars. She wanted to take an axe and chop right through them, set the caged dancer free. But there was no help for her, no hope. Anna shut her eyes again, and would not open them till she heard the music change, till she knew that cage and dancer both had vanished.

On the way out of the theatre, Rosalind slid her arm through Anna's, pulling her gently along and out the lobby doors. Arm in arm the women walked back up the concrete steps to the bridge. A train hurtled behind them—Anna felt the updraught singe her skin. She wanted to stop for a moment and look at the river, as if to recapture that buoyancy she'd felt during the interval, on the balcony, but Rosalind had started to run—she was leaping aboard a bus, holding out an arm and pulling Anna up, in. Somehow they found two seats together, and while all Anna could do was fight to catch her breath, Rosalind spilled over with words.

"Terror and delight, Annie—remember? What one's expected to feel before a great work of art. Delight in the making, and a recoil from the revelation. Resistance—that's the viewer's part. Resonant, responsible resistance. Not surrender, like all those sods at the National Gallery, melting in front of Monet, a little bow of fealty before the Wilton Diptych. Or van Gogh. If you really saw what there was to see in his cornfield you'd run screaming, right past the Gallery Shop with its Old Master tea towels and laminated carrier bags. You'd throw yourself under the nearest bus, except that it wouldn't do you any damage— traffic round Trafalgar Square is always at a standstill."

It was to Trafalgar Square that they were heading, Anna realized. Night was closing in already—it was nearly six o'clock. "I thought you were having friends in?"

"Not friends. A gathering. Come on, this is our stop."

Anna grabbed at Rosalind's arm as they pushed their way up the road through an enormous crowd holding signs and handing out leaflets. She was terrified they would be separated—she'd left her purse at Rosalind's, she had no map should she get lost, no money to get home. Rosalind stopped dead in the thickest part of the crowd. It shifted slightly, and Anna jumped as an antelope reared in front of them. Rosalind shouted something at her, reaching once more into her pocket, finding a couple of coins for the pot displayed prominently on the kerb, signing a petition asking her to end apartheid forever. A lorry screeched by and left them choking at the fumes.

"Now you've had your daily dose of lead, Annie. Don't worry, we're here now—watch your footing on the steps."

They were in the crypt of St. Martin's-in-the-Fields. It had been turned into a restaurant-cum-bookshop: you could do your bit for London's homeless by eating fairly well and somewhat reasonably here, under the screech and blurt of traffic, while tourists did brass rubbings and the spiritually inclined looked for new editions of *Imitatio Christi*. Rosalind and Anna lined up at the counter, choosing ratatouille and chicken breast, Old Peculier ale, and at Rosalind's insistence, bread pudding slathered in custard. "Comforting," she observed to Anna, as they settled down in rickety chairs. "Nursery slop. Just the thing after aesthetic disturbances. Eat up and I'll tell you about tonight. They're not coming till ten—we have plenty of time." And with her eyes narrowed to grass blades, her mouth masked by her hand, she looked to Anna exactly like a conspirator.

*       *       *

"When you've got a government which defines dissent as subversion, what else can you expect?"

Rosalind had bottles of Scotch, sherry, red and white wine on hand, as well as limitless supplies of coffee. Anna was filling up the cups, passing round the bottles, tossing away empties. She had chosen the task as a means of circulating without awkwardness or the tedium of having to introduce herself, produce an opinion, have her ear bent. There must have been fifty people in Rosalind's sitting room and hallway and kitchen—academics, writers, publishers, actors, journalists. No politicians of whatever stripe, as far as she could tell; after the first wave of people had arrived, Rosalind had given up on introductions.

Anna had expected the evening to have some definite shape: an hour or so of informal drifting about and talking, then everyone somehow finding a chair and listening to speeches. She felt out of place and anxious—she kept thinking back to her lost notebook, wondering whether she should have phoned British Rail to see if someone had turned it in. To distract herself from the probability that someone hadn't, Anna kept on fetching, carrying, refilling. Once Rosalind broke off a conversation to call out, "Annie! Stop the slavey business, will you?" but Anna kept right on.

"What do you mean, 'What they're *doing* to Education'? It seems to me it's already been *done in*. What the government is aiming for is not the decline but the actual death of research into the social sciences. If they carry through this plan for first- and second-class institutions—"

"Coffee?"

"Yes, thanks. Any cream? Marvellous. I really shouldn't, but would you happen to know if Roz has got some sugar stashed away? White sugar?"

Roz? This balding, tub-shaped man in a sweater with the elbows unravelling called Rosalind Oliver "Roz"?

"Lovely. Thanks so much. As I was saying, public transport has been overburdened to beyond the point of containing, never mind preventing major accidents. We all know how many King's Crosses could have happened in the last ten years. And as for the rail system, there'll be disaster after disaster if we don't invest in proper signalling and safety devices. Not to speak of paying maintenance people a living wage—"

"Can I refill your glass?"

"Fascism with a friendly face doesn't begin to describe it. If this Official Secrets Act becomes law—and there's nothing to stop it, everything, in fact, to push it into the statute books—then our last pretence at being a democracy disappears. Thin air? Bloody starved, famine-stricken. Now listen hard, because this is the point to get across: if people aren't allowed to know what mistakes their elected representatives have made—or to what illegalities they've resorted just to keep in power—how can they be expected to vote them out of office and preserve what we are so rash as to call 'the democratic process'? White, please."

"Rubbish. They don't need an Official Secrets Act, they've got the *Sun*. As long as they get their tits and bums they're happy enough to believe whatever the bastards tell them."

"Let's not get into 'them' and 'us,' shall we? Sixty percent of 'us' voted against her. It's your faithful readers of the *Times* you should be shitting on. Got any whiskey, love?"

"But that's the whole point. Abolish the principle of tenure and you ensure a *trahison des clercs*."

"Health Service? Of course they're going to trash it. What's the charming phrase—devolution? Giving back choice to the people. So if you've got cancer you can spend the little life left to you shopping round for treatment. The consumer consumed. Or take abortion—can't you just see us briskly doing the rounds, looking for the very best deal, as if we were trying to get rid of a useless fridge or cooker?"

Anna went to the sideboard to pour someone a whiskey, but stopped abruptly with her hand on the decanter. She felt dizzy: sick — she should never have drunk as much as she had today. Turning her head she looked round the room for Rosalind. She needed badly to see her—not to speak but just to exchange glances, prove to herself that this person with her hand on the decanter lid, about to pour out whiskey for a perfect stranger really was Anna English. Rosalind was the only one here who even knew her name; it was Rosalind who had singled her out, invited her alone of all these people to stay with her, to be her chosen guest.

It wasn't that Rosalind wasn't there—the trouble was that she was everywhere at once, making introductions, bringing together the oddest people, controlling the burst of questions and exclamations and ideas which seemed to flow from her and return to her after making a thousand loops and zigzags through the room. *All with the most perfect ease and air of a creature floating in its element.* Anna felt exhausted just watching her. Exhausted and dispersed, like a blob of mercury that had broken loose from a thermometer and fallen into endless rolling bits of silver. She loosened her grip on the decanter top, and, keeping her eyes fixed on the cherub with the wooden spoon, walked away from them all, away and up the stairs. Light leaked out from under the bathroom door at the top of the landing. She ignored it, finding her way to what she thought was the guest room, but which turned out to be Rosalind's.

It wasn't really an intrusion—everyone's coats were piled high on the bed and the desk light was on in case someone wanted to sit somewhere quiet and look through a brief or petition. Anna's only interest in the desk lay in the photographs she didn't find there. It would appear that Rosalind had no family, and no domestic ties—no husband, lover, child. The closest thing in the room to a portrait was the mirror over the mantel; otherwise the walls were bare, except for a small, heavily framed painting over the bed. When Anna went to look at it, clambering onto the pile of coats to get as close as possible to the canvas, she saw that it was a portrait of sorts. The artist's attention had been given over, almost entirely, to the meticulous reproduction of a screen window, a perfect geometrical grid, behind which you could just make out the shape of a woman's face—shape or shadow, Anna couldn't tell. She only guessed that it was a woman because of the way the hair stood up around the head, like little licks of flame, or the points of stars—spider stars, the kind that children draw.

Thinking she heard someone coming up the stairs, Anna ran from Rosalind's room and into her own. The latch wouldn't close properly; she couldn't lock herself in. Too tired even to open her nightcase, she lay down on the bed, thinking she'd rest for a moment before getting undressed. Her head was buzzing with the wine she'd drunk, the people downstairs, the dancers she'd seen that afternoon. A woman locked inside the cage of her own skirts, her steps a choreography of panic—

Voices drifting up the stairwell; laughter and outrage and endless argument; a man pounding against a locked door. "Give me a hand, for God's sake." Her door thrust open, light splashing in, a cold bath of light. "For Christ's sake, can't you see I need help?" The bathroom door off its hinges, a woman lying face down and arms outstretched, trailing crimson scarves over the small white tiles. Anna must have cried out, for the man was hissing at her as he grabbed a towel and started binding up the blood and skin, "Shut up. Go and fetch Rosalind. Don't tell anyone else. For Christ's sake, run."

# IX

# DUCKS AND DRAKES

"Tea." It wasn't a question, but a fact. Rosalind, in apricot silk pyjamas, holding out a cup. In this morning's light she looked thin as the porcelain, as though her bones had grown too large for her skin. A skin no longer perfect but marred round the eyes and mouth, the way a tabletop can be marked by someone writing a letter on it, pressing too hard with the pen. And yet this clock Anna could hear ticking through Rosalind's skin gave her a different kind of beauty: poignant; far more dangerous. Anna wriggled under the blankets—they were much too tight. And then she realized there were no blankets; she was wearing her clothes from the night before. Unsteadily, she held out her hand for the cup, took it, and drank.

"What time is it?"

Rosalind shrugged. "Around eleven."

"Eleven? I can't have slept in till eleven."

"You have. You're probably sickening for something." Rosalind took back the empty cup and pressed her hand against Anna's forehead. "No temperature, thank God. I'd never have forgiven you if you'd brought me a bout of 'flu this weekend. One case of slashed wrists is quite enough."

"What—who? It did happen, then? She really did—?"

"No, she didn't, largely because Henry had to relieve himself. Thank God for unlimited quantities of cheap red wine. It doesn't matter who it was. It could have been any one of us—God knows I've felt like slitting my wrists over what's happening to this—you'll pardon the pun—bloody country. She's all right—it needn't concern you, Annie. And if you're going to feel sorry, let it be for the fact that you missed the formal baptism of the most significant protest movement to emerge in this country since, oh, the ban on killing baby seals. Go and wash and I'll tell you all about it."

Over coffee and toast downstairs, Rosalind explained that the people she'd had over last night were all intent on pressing the government for a charter of rights. "Rights set down in law, not assumed by virtue of some fine-sounding notion of tradition. Tradition in this country is about as substantial as a waxwork figure; turn up the political temperature and there's nothing left but a puddle. Not that anyone will notice. They'll be too busy watching the Olympics or laying bets as to what sex the next royal baby's going to be. Are you listening, Annie?"

"Yes, of course I am." But she'd been staring out the window at a yellowing chestnut leaf. A blackbird was singing. It was singing the tune to which the hoop-woman had danced, to which that other woman had razored her wrists.

"You'd listen if you had to live here. You don't have any idea what's going on in this country, do you? Well, it's becoming what is commonly referred to as an elective dictatorship. Rule by extermination of opposition; rule by silencing anyone who finds out the truth and wants to tell it. It's the great British tradition: whisper, don't scream. Christ, don't even whisper, *keep mum*. Even when screaming is the only sane response to a situation, the only way to get help. It simply isn't *done* here, Annie. But some of us have settled for the visual equivalent of a scream, or at least a smallish shout. We're taking out full-page ads in all the major papers, declaring the need for a charter guaranteeing civil liberties. You've seen them, I suppose?"

"I don't read the papers," Anna confessed.

"But that's—that's *criminal*, Annie. How on earth do you find out what's going on?"

"I don't have to. I just assume everything's happening for the worst. Every day a new disaster, isn't that how it goes? Besides, I hear all I need to on the radio."

"No television, no newspapers—not even a colour supplement on Sundays? Scandalous." Rosalind, however, didn't look the least outraged—she was teasing Anna the way you would an old friend. Rosalind reached forward, tweaking a strand of hair that had fallen into Anna's face. "What can you expect from someone who spends all her time on Virginia Woolf. Katherine Mansfield's life is far more interesting—even Virginia conceded that. Camping in the outback, flings with Maori princesses and Polish mountebanks; German pensions and cow byres at Fontainebleau. What does your Virginia have to compare with that? Bread baking at Monk's House and a schoolgirl's flirtation with blue-blooded, mustachioed Vita."

Before Anna could answer, Rosalind had walked over to the window, which she opened wide. "Look, it's turned into a perfect day— why don't we get out into the sun? We can walk in the park and cheer ourselves up by looking at all the animals in their cages."

Outside, no trains were shunting. Instead, there were pools of Sunday quiet everywhere. Rosalind led Anna past streets of terraced houses, some still dilapidated, others gentrified with rooftop gardens and pots of geraniums no different from the ones in front of Rosalind's own door. Past an imitation castle, down a flight of stairs and suddenly, along the canal. Neither woman spoke a word. They passed graffiti blooming pink, violet, chartreuse over blackened walls, in alphabets Anna couldn't decipher. Willows grew laggardly from the bank—rank weeds, a mess of shrubs and bushes: not so much greenbelt or parkland as the perfect venue for rape or murder. Running up a flight of stairs, they found themselves across the road from Regent's Park. Hopeless to wait until the traffic thinned and so they dashed across, arms tightly linked, making a magic circle against hurtling cars and buses.

Once inside the park they drew apart, Rosalind striding ahead, then stopping for Anna to catch up. All around them men played football, couples strolled, dogs bounded. Rosalind led the way to a bridge over a pond, where children were feeding buns to a flock of ducks. She leaned her elbows on the railing. Anna copied her. They were silent, watching the ducks peck idly at the dirty water, and then Rosalind spoke, as much to the ducks as to Anna.

"Everything's all right? In Pyeford, I mean. You've met—"

"Simon introduced himself, yes." Anna turned so that her back was against the railing. She'd remembered the Lord of the Manor's charge—*give Rosie my love.*

"He's a darling. Harmless as—I don't know what is, nowadays. As a disaffected church."

"He does go on about churches, Rosalind—at least about church windows."

Rosalind laughed. "Mind you don't break his heart, Annie."

Anna stiffened—she could feel her face suffused with blood, the blushes she'd never learned how to control. "What on earth are you talking about? As if I'd—as if I weren't already—"

"Otherwise occupied? Is that it? How lovely for you. As for me, I'm something of a vacant lot, these days."

She laughed as she said this, making a sound like a knife scraping a plate. Anna turned, trying to catch a glimpse of her face, but all she could see was the fiery blur of Rosalind's hair; her hand shielding her eyes as she leant against the railing, looking down at the ducks. Anna's face was still hot—she couldn't bear for Rosalind to think of her and Simon like that—she didn't know why Rosalind's thinking it, even joking about it, made the idea so much worse. But she knew that she wanted to right the balance somehow, and so she delivered Nicholas's greeting, after all.

If she'd been expecting some kind of jump or jolt on Rosalind's part, Anna was disappointed. "Muscovy," was all Rosalind said at first, waving her hand in the direction of a singular-looking duck at the far edge of the pond. And then she went on. "I suppose I ought to have warned you about Nick; Pyeford's pride, the Hugh Walpole of our times. Though he fancies himself our Dickens, I shouldn't wonder, with all those children he's producing."

"He seemed to know you quite well—"

"We knew each other once—a long, long time ago. At university; we were both involved in student politics. Mr. Jones—sorry, Pryce-Jones—and I don't get on terribly well these days. He's shifted somewhat in his views, you see. He's a self-made man, Annie, a perfect example of the enterprise revolution. Though his father wasn't a barrow boy, or even a trapeze artist. I think he was something quite respectable—a tile installer."

Rosalind clapped her hands, then rubbed them together. "It's not as warm as I thought. Let's move on."

They started along a path towards the lake. From behind the trees outlines of buildings rose up: lavish Regency terraces, a minaret topped by a crescent moon. For a moment Anna tried to supply the sight she couldn't see—the spire she'd expected. She pointed to the minaret, asking, "What on earth?" and Rosalind shot back, "A mosque. Haven't you ever seen one before? Don't they grow in your part of the world?" Anna shook her head. "In Nova Scotia? No. I don't think so. We do have a lot of Buddhists, though. From Boulder, Colorado."

They both laughed and walked on, Rosalind slipping her arm through Anna's.

"What do you think they talked about together, Woolf and Mansfield? You're writing on Woolf, you must have some ideas. I did my thesis on Mansfield—I once thought I'd write her biography until I got sidetracked, frontally assaulted, whatever you like to call it, by Cultural Politics and What-is-to-be-Done. At any rate, the Mansfield book's redundant now, but still, I'd love to know what went on between them."

"Woolf said Mansfield stank like a civet cat."

"And what did *she* stink of, the estimable Mrs. Woolf—chloral? Intellectual and other less permissible forms of snobbery? That's not what's important, Annie, the scratches they left on each other's skin. It's only because we don't know what they said together that we keep on reciting the same stupid gossip we *do* know.

"Picture it, Annie: two rivals desperately in love with the same thing—not a man, but an art. Think of their long conversations in twilit rooms, those two extraordinary women, one mad and anorexic, the other syphilitic and tubercular; both of them living only for fiction. If I were writing a book, that's what I'd do—not yet another tome on semiotica in early Woolf, but a reconstruction of the siren's song. What they talked about together all through the afternoon, the light failing, their words becoming incandescent. So that they have no need for the lamps the servants bring in, and least of all for Middleton Murry galumphing in to demand his tea. Think of two women talking passionately, in the dark, about writing—"

Anna did think about it, or rather, the thought came lunging at her. She felt a blow, as though she'd been knocked down; there was a roaring in her ears—yellow bloomed at the back of her eyes. Lost words between two dead women: the only book that needed to be written, that no one could ever write. Her doctoral thesis and the plans she'd scribbled in her notebook; every article and book she'd read on Woolf—what were they all but babble, chatter, simulacra? She felt loathing, a sudden deep nausea at the very thought of them. For what was there, after all, but Virginia Woolf's own books, and against them Woolf's silence, her willed absence—no longer mere abstractions, but things real, unyielding as stones, and far too large for any critic to carry. Anna leaned against Rosalind, so hard that Rosalind stopped and put her arms around her, Anna breathing in the scent that clung to Rosalind's hair and clothes and skin.

"Are you all right, Annie, do you want to sit down?"

Shaking her head, shaking herself free, Anna managed a laugh that was more like a wail. "Sorry—I think it must be 'flu after all. I'll have to get back home—I'd better leave right now."

Rosalind wanted to call a cab, but Anna insisted she'd prefer to walk. They returned home, Anna hopelessly embarrassed at having collapsed like that against Rosalind. She was careful to keep a little distance between them as they walked; to keep silence, too. Along one dismal stretch of canal, they passed an old man playing a concertina, pleating sweet, strange sounds into the air. This time Anna moved before Rosalind could. She reached into her pocket and drew up a fistful of coins. But if the man saw her toss them into his hat he gave no sign. He went on and on, playing his delicate, joyous music with a face as grey as the cement under his feet. And then, aiming at a spot no more than an inch or two from her feet, he spat, his fingers never leaving the keyboard.

# X

# PICTURES

Anna was late—she arrived at the Gibsons' full of apologies, but Fiona had not seemed troubled. In fact, she was reluctant to leave the house, and Anna had to half cajole, half bully her out the door. Maeve was in a nightgown so beribboned and lace-encrusted that it might as well have been a costume: the Victorian Child at Bedtime. She was lying on the sofa downstairs with the cat heaped on her stomach, while an American sitcom brayed from the telly. Canned laughter reached right to the end of the hallway, where Fiona was giving Anna last-minute instructions. "The telephone numbers are on the bulletin board—police, ambulance, fire department, doctor."

"Fine. But I won't need them, Fiona. Everything's going to be dull as ditchwater round here. There's no need to worry—just go, go on, goodbye."

When Fiona had finally left the house Anna joined Maeve, who was stroking the cat and frowning at the screen. For a moment, Anna was panic-stricken at the thought of what she'd let herself in for—what did she know about taking care of children? What if Maeve took against her, demanded her mother, wouldn't be comforted? Anna forced herself to speak up over the soundtrack: "Shall I look for something else? Maybe there's a children's show on?" There was a performance of Britten's *War Requiem*, a documentary on the activities of various neo-fascist groups in Britain, and *Miami Vice*. Anna switched off the set and sat down beside Maeve. "Would you like me to read you a story?"

"Not a fairy story."

"What then?"

"*The Wizard of Oz.*"

"Can you go and get the book for me?"

Maeve didn't reply, but kept on stroking the cat—too hard, because it jumped off her lap and pelted into the kitchen. Finally she spoke. "It's in Mummy's room. She was fixing it—the cover came unstuck."

"Can you go and bring it to me?"

"No. You come with me, Anna. Please."

Maeve was tugging her hand, insisting that she follow her. But instead of taking Anna upstairs, Maeve led her down the hall to a door Anna had assumed to lead into a laundry or storage room. "It's here," Maeve whispered. Feeling a little like Bluebeard's wife, Anna turned the handle and walked in.

At first her impression was of a peculiarly drab, yet cluttered wall-paper. It was only when she walked up close to the walls that she understood. They were photographs clipped from newspapers, scraps of articles, headlines. "Here it is," Maeve shouted, picking up *The Wizard of Oz* from a work table on which copies of *The Times*, *The Guardian*, *The Independent*, *The Observer* lay heaped, their pages interleaving. Anna was still looking at the walls when Maeve snapped off the light.

"Come on, Anna. You promised to read to me. You promised."

Back in the parlour, sitting on the over-padded rocker, the gas fire showing mauve and apricot and whistling faintly, Anna read to Maeve, who'd crawled onto her lap. Afterwards Anna couldn't recall what chapter she'd gone through or what had happened to which characters, though she must have read with some animation, for Maeve did not wriggle or complain. After she'd finished, Anna let the child look at the pictures. She rested her cheek lightly on Maeve's hair, inhaling its bread-and-butter scent. *Haven't you ever wanted to have a child?* The cradle Virginia Woolf had been given as a wedding gift. Katherine Mansfield's baby, vanishing into the trunk she'd lifted to the top of a cupboard in her German pension; Mansfield lying on the white-tiled floor just like Rosalind's guest, but wearing her blood in different places.

Anna wanted to put her arms round Maeve and hug her tight, hold onto her, as if it were not her lap on which the child were sitting, but some treacherous, shifting ground. But you couldn't hold her—she always twisted free. Even when she held out her face to be kissed, or ran up to you to be embraced, what you held wasn't her, but her imminent absence from your arms. Holding her now, not holding her, but being the branch on which she settled for a moment, Anna was astonished at the tenderness she felt.

"I want to go up to bed. Will you tuck me in?" Maeve had jumped off Anna's lap and was hovering at the door. Anna followed as Maeve leaped up the stairs, two at a time. "Keep the hall light on," she called, as Anna turned off the bedside lamp, then pulled the covers straight, turning them back so that Maeve would have the sheet and not the wool of the blanket next to her face. She wanted to lean over and kiss her good night, but hesitated: Maeve had not asked to be kissed. So Anna just looked down at her, and the child looked up.

"Good night, Maeve."

"Good night, Anna." And then, just as Anna reached the door, Maeve called out to her again.

"What happens to your body when you die?"

"Why on earth do you want to know that?"

"Because."

"It's not what happens to your body," Anna began, summoning up from some long-forgotten hiding place what her own mother had told her, once. "It's your soul that counts. Your soul's like a bird, a white bird that flies—"

"I know what happens to your soul. What about your body, your arms and legs?"

"Your body turns back into—it becomes like a special sort of—earth."

"Do worms eat you? Sally says they do."

"Who's Sally?"

"*Do* they, Anna?"

"No." Her answer was absolute. "Now good night."

Maeve didn't respond, except to hug the cat, which she'd lured in under the blankets.

Downstairs again, Anna made a point of sitting at the kitchen table and opening the notebook she'd bought to replace her stolen one. But its pages remained blank—try as she might she could not unthink the revelation she had had about the impossibility of her ever starting, never mind completing, the book she'd come to write. And the longer she stared at the empty page, the more she thought of the pictures in Fiona's room.

\*     \*     \*

There wasn't an inch of wall space that wasn't covered. Anna walked slowly round, scanning headlines, images, passages of texts: *Children murdered in bloodiest fighting yet. UN observer reports whole villages gassed.* In some places photographs were fastened one over the other, a fan of images over the first one, yellowing and brittle, taped flat against the wall.

Two policemen on white horses, bringing batons down on the heads of marchers: young people, students, perhaps—she could make out Westminster in the distance. A child clutching an older child whose arms were a trapeze of bones, whose eyes seemed swollen shut: *An emaciated child screams with hunger in Mozambique where 3,500 people are known to have starved to death during a six week period this year.* A bashful teenager and a man who looked like a Scout leader, flanking a portrait of Hitler; above them a swastika's twisted daggers. A bird with its beak taped shut, its oil-smeared wings being stretched out, scrubbed in a wash basin. An Action Aid ad showing that it cost twice as much to keep a cat alive and well in Britain as a child in any third world country. From a local paper: *Babies at risk from nitrates in water.* White-gloved African doctors and nurses attending an emaciated child believed to be dying from AIDS. Tibetan Monks and women throwing stones at a police station in Lhasa, smoke and dust obscuring the middle ground, the woman's long black braids tangling as she ran. A Palestinian child shot by Israeli soldiers, teenagers, who have been sent to maintain order in the Gaza Strip. Swiss civilians draped in polythene shrouds and gas masks, taking part in exercises to protect them against chemical and nuclear attacks. Three marble arches, beautifully rounded, giving onto a lake into which fell shadows of pines, oaks and a country house; the pillars between the arches bearing letters two feet high: "Fuck your Granny," "CND is a Load of Bolocks."

And the last image—not that there were no others, but that after seeing this, Anna couldn't take in anything else.

An overexposed shot, slightly blurred; dark figures on a white ground. The edges of the figures eaten away, as if the air around them were corrosive. One figure definitely male, holding a long black cyclinder, holding a gun aimed at someone an arm's reach away from him. A woman. Her back turned; her hair and skirt cocooning round her. She held something in her arms, a package, a piece of luggage. And then Anna saw the legs, dangling. Everything blurred, dark, but she could make out that the woman was holding a child—not a baby but a small child, a little younger than Maeve. Holding the child so it didn't see the soldier, his ballooning trousers, his peaked cap. And the rifle poised, the child already falling through the helpless circle of the woman's arms—

"What are you doing here?"

The question wasn't an angry one, but calm, simple, a request for information. Anna couldn't bring herself to face the person who'd compiled this book, this story that wasn't a narrative at all, but a sustained explosion of images.

"What are you doing here?"

Anna turned slowly round. "I was looking for some Sellotape," she began. "To mend Maeve's book. You're home early—you're not supposed to be back for another hour yet."

Fiona pulled off her scarf and gloves; sat down by the table on which scissors and newspaper clippings were scattered. "The lecture was on 'Preparing Your Children for the Future.' Making them competitive. Forward-looking. I asked what there was for them to look forward to, and the speaker began about vast increases in leisure time, upward leaps in the standard of living. I said I didn't think there was going to be a future. I said it was just like the cartoons Maeve likes to watch—the ones in which Coyote chases Road Runner out along a cliff. He's running so hard and fast he doesn't realize the ground has vanished from under his feet. I told her that I look down and see nothing under us, nothing except the fact of our not knowing it—not wanting to know. I told her that, as far as I could tell, the only direction was down. She said it was an interesting point of view, and asked for another question. Someone wanted to know which computer games were best for young children. I decided not to stay for the coffee and biscuits. It was kind of you to offer to sit for me, Anna, but I don't think I'll be going out again."

"Fiona?" Anna gestured to the walls.

"Is Maeve all right?"

"She's fine. Look, Fiona—" And Anna blurted out the first thing that came to her, a text she'd memorized long ago. "Look, Fiona, I know the world is in a horrible mess. All these pictures, all the headlines. . . . I know it's obscene, unspeakable. But we have to believe that things will get better."

"Is it right to believe something that isn't true?"

"We have to try and make things get better."

"I can't. Do you?"

"Fiona, what I mean is—in a democratic—one can vote against, one can bring pressure to bear. Send money—"

"Alun and I adopted a child in Guatemala. Instead of a hamster."

"Don't belittle what you've done, Fiona. It's a wonderful thing—"

"We would have done better to adopt the child's whole family. The village itself. The neighbouring village. The whole country, the conti-nent. I'm tired, Anna."

"Of course you are—it's late, you must be exhausted. But listen, Fiona, please, please listen to me. You mustn't—"

"I'm tired, Anna. I'm so tired of running and running on air."

"Of course you are. Let me make you some cocoa."

Anna went across to Fiona, helping her up from her chair. She led her out of the room, then switched off the light, shutting the door firmly behind them. She took Fiona's coat and hung it up in the closet; she sat her down at the kitchen table and put on the milk to warm, chattering all the while, describing the deficiencies of the cooker at Rest Harrow, confessing her accident with the soup pot the first week she'd moved in, how the stench of burning still clung to the curtains even after she'd washed them twice.

"Baking soda," Fiona said, accepting the mug of cocoa. "Large open boxes of baking soda. It absorbs every kind of smell."

Anna watched as Fiona sipped from the mug, slowly, cautiously. She couldn't tell. Did Fiona want to talk it all out: her husband's murder, the shock, her emptiness? Had she ever had anyone to talk with—to listen? Anna wanted to say, "If there's anything I can do to help, if I can lend an ear, a shoulder—" but it sounded so patronising. She was supposed to have all the words at hand, and she could come up with nothing better than this? She should go over to where Fiona sat, reach out her arms, hug her, let her cry or laugh or whatever it was she had to do to unknot herself, to open.

But Fiona was sitting nursing her mug of cocoa; there was a wall, a frame around her as if she were back inside the portrait her husband had made of her, the pastel sketch on the dining room wall. If she had to immure herself, why not choose the room of lovely, gentle paintings, instead of those horrors across the hall? Anna sat staring at her hands, at the small scar Luke's razor had kissed into her fingertip. It looked exactly like a new moon. She covered it with her thumb. If only she could come to Fiona's one day when no one was home; bring a knife, a scraper—unburden the walls. It wasn't good for Fiona, it wasn't right for Maeve to live with that. Should she tell someone, call Fiona's doctor? Who was her doctor, how would she find out without snooping and prying?

Fiona was rubbing her eyes, a slow, deliberate gesture, rotating her knuckles like gears against the soft, large lids. Suddenly she stopped, as if she'd just remembered Anna was with her; pulled her shoulders back and clasped her hands in front of her, exactly as if she were a child greeting a teacher at school. "Thanks for sitting, Anna."

"Any time at all."

They both walked to the door, and though it was raining, Fiona stood in the porch, under the light, watching as Anna walked up the path. Anna turned back to wave goodbye, but Fiona just stood there watching, waiting for Anna to disappear.

*         *         *

Anna had made up her mind before she'd even bolted shut the door to Rest Harrow. At nine the next morning she snatched her mac off the peg and hurried down the street. Fine rain beaded her hair, soaking her face as she marched up to the entrance of St. Pancras Church of England School. She allowed herself not a moment's hesitation before walking inside—to hesitate would be to give herself the time to run away. What she had to do was clear. An interview, strictly professional, with the head master: "I'm alarmed—no, I'm disturbed"— but that was worse. "Concerned"—yes—"I'm concerned that perhaps Fiona Gibson might be a little—unbalanced. By grief, you know. Concerned that it might be having an effect on her child."

But there was no one in the office, neither the Head nor his secretary. Immediately, Anna felt uncertain as to whom she should approach and whether she had any rightful reason to be at the school at all. What she had been planning to say sounded preposterous to her, offensive. They would laugh at her—or lecture her. How could she, a mere visitor, presume to judge Fiona Gibson? Confused, Anna walked a little way down the hall, trying to distract herself by looking at the paintings tacked up on the wall—seaside scenes, starfish, buckets and spades.

There was a particularly jaunty picture of a mermaid on a deck chair. It was signed Maeve, and Anna felt instant, immense relief: it was all right, she needn't have come at all. A mermaid on a deck chair—this was what Maeve associated with pictures, not the appalling images her mother had glued to her study walls.

As she looked closer at Maeve's drawing, noting the mermaid's rainbow sunglasses, the finned cat asleep in her lap, Anna heard a familiar voice coming from behind a closed door. Positioning herself so that she could not be seen, she peered through a small glass panel. Simon was lifting his hands, conducting a group of children in a song. They sat in a semi-circle round him, looking up with concentration that was a form of worship. He'd insisted that he didn't really like children—had that been a bit of tracery, hiding the hurt that he had no children of his own?

Anna crept out of the school and returned home greatly relieved, as though she'd prevented a massacre, or single-handedly lifted a siege. She was still smiling to herself as she hung up her coat, fussed with the kettle, and switched on the radio to keep her company.

It was the news. There'd been a collision of two commuter trains at Clapham Junction. Eighty people were feared dead. A hundred had been taken to hospital. Many would have perished standing, since there would never have been seats enough for everyone to die in relative comfort. The prime minister was reported to have left already to show sympathy to the afflicted.

"Photo op," Anna found herself saying. No, that was what Rosalind would say. And now she stopped short, clutching a jug of milk in her hands. Where was Rosalind? What if she were on one of those trains? A thousand to one that she wasn't; a million to one, but Anna had no use for the laws of probability; knew that the worst could and did happen. Not even stopping to grab her coat, she rushed back out into the rain and ran to the call box at the top of the street. She dialled Rosalind's number, letting it ring five, ten, twenty times. Mouth parched, hands clenched, rain soaking her to the skin as the telephone rang and rang, telling her that no one was home, not telling her why she felt her tongue turning to a stone in her mouth, her teeth breaking against the stone choking her, when finally Rosalind picked up the receiver.

"Hello?" Her voice still creased with sleep. "Hello—who is this, who's calling?"

Anna couldn't say a word.

"Hello? Please answer. Are you there—" And then she spoke a name, a name which wasn't Annie.

Anna hung up.

# XI

# VARTI

The next day was Saturday. And although Anna could have bought all the groceries she needed from the village shop, she drove straight into town, to the supermarket where she knew she'd find the leaflet lady. She couldn't explain to herself why it was so important that she see her—she only knew that as soon as the woman had smiled at her and handed her a piece of paper, everything would fall back into its accustomed place. For the coffee-skinned woman with her unjudging eyes had become a talisman of sorts. She had nothing to do with Rosalind or Luke or Virginia Woolf; she didn't worry her as Fiona did; she made no demands on her at all, but just dispensed her leaflets and her smiles in lieu of blessings.

When Anna arrived before the supermarket doors, she found an embarrassed young man who didn't seem able to get rid of any pamphlets at all. She ignored his outstretched hand; in fact she lost her head altogether and started shouting: "Where is she—what have you done with her?"

"Whom do you mean?"

"The woman who's usually here handing out leaflets. The—the Indian woman."

"Indian? Oh, you mean Varti. She's organizing things for the lecture this afternoon—at the Meeting House. Two o'clock—why don't you come along?"

Anna shrugged and turned away. Trapped, betrayed—what else could she do but hang about town, waiting for the meeting to begin? For she had to see the woman—Varti, he'd called her. Luke would laugh at her if he knew. But Luke didn't know what had happened to her here, what wouldn't stop happening. She needed to see Varti, just see her, that was all—they needn't even say hello to one another.

She had a few hours to kill. At a corner shop she bought an indigestible chicken pie, feeding most of it to a stray cat in the public gardens. She climbed up into what was left of the castle, trying not to notice the reek of urine coming from the moat and bailey. And she wandered up and down the narrow streets below, peering into walled gardens where birds sang in the crippled trees and apples were sleepily reddening. At a quarter to two she felt her stomach flopping against her ribs, then creeping up into her throat. Nervousness, that was all—not nervousness but panic, the same panic she'd felt listening to Rosalind's phone ringing and ringing the morning before.

The Meeting House turned out to be a disaffected church. Varti was setting out cups and saucers on a plywood table when Anna walked in; she smiled at her as though she hadn't for a moment doubted Anna would be coming. And just as Anna had succumbed to Rosalind the week before, so now she did to Varti, though hers was a different kind of magic. Walking into the church and finding Varti there had been like going after school to the library where her mother had worked; finding her still there behind the counter, stamping books, waiting for her. *Still there. . .* People were beginning to gather: a man came over to take charge of the coffee, and Varti led Anna inside the hall, where the pews would once have been. They sat down on stiff wooden chairs, waiting for the lecture to begin.

It was easy to talk, for they were perfect strangers with everything in the world to tell each other, and nothing to lose by doing so. Anna explained that she was over from Canada for the year.

"I have a son in Edmonton," Varti replied. Her accent was no different than any of the others Anna heard around her. She blushed again. What had she been expecting—a Gujarati singsong? "He's working for one of the big oil companies," Varti added. "But he's a lovely man, in spite of it." They laughed, and Varti went on to tell Anna something about herself. She'd been born in England—her father had emigrated from Calcutta between the wars. He'd run a successful import business in London; on the proceeds, she'd studied medicine.

"And then I married, and left my practice. You did in those days. My husband was an Englishman, a real, that is a white Englishman. He was a professor of fine art, his specialty was the Mughal period. He never seemed to notice the looks we sometimes got, walking down the street together. His real shock was reserved for the fact that I knew nothing whatsoever about Mughal painting. And that I had no desire to go to India. He ended up doing quite a lot of travelling on his own. Are you here with your husband?"

"No—he's in Canada, he couldn't get away. But he's coming over to visit me—he's coming for Christmas."

"How lovely for you. Though I have to tell you—I've been widowed for eight years now, and in many ways I'm just as glad to be on my own. Heaven knows I see enough people through my practice. Nothing fancy, I'm just a GP. My oldest girl is about to make me a grandmother. I shall like that, having a baby at hand to cuddle and play with and hand right back when I've got to rush off to an appointment, or a film I want to see. Do you have children?"

Anna drew back a little. "No. No, I don't."

Varti smiled, a little sadly. "I only ask because most people who attend our meetings come out of anxiety for their children—they want there to be an earth left for them to inherit, you see."

"Of course." But she didn't see. She felt a sudden need to defend herself, as though Varti had been accusing her of some unpardonable selfishness. "I'm an only child. My parents are dead. I'm alone, and I—" She trailed off, her face burning. Stupid, stupid—why was she going on like this? What did she expect from the woman? Did she want her to adopt her? But as she looked at Varti's fine, calm face, she realized that yes, this was exactly what she wanted. To be somebody's child again— to be taken care of, looked out for, enfolded. Anna leaned back in her seat and turned her face away. Varti said nothing for a moment, then whispered, "It's going to start, at last. I think you'll find what she has to say quite interesting."

The speaker was a woman in her fifties, stylishly dressed, and with all the right letters after her name.

"Fatalism," she began, "is fatal." And as she continued in her clear, unimpassioned voice, the audience strained forward, not so much to catch her words, Anna thought, as to demonstrate their attention. Nothing of what the woman said sounded particularly dramatic. Anna, who'd never attended a lecture like this before, and who habitually tossed out reams of unsolicited mail bearing the logos of fifty different peace or environmental groups, was mildly astonished. Everything the woman said made such perfect sense. She nodded as the speaker touched upon the proper use of the world's resources and the logic of planetary survival. If she'd had the speaker's text under her eyes, could she have taken it apart, exposed its contradictions, traced at least the outline of the ambiguities it would be sure to contain? And yet Anna believed the woman to be telling the truth. Not a truth, but the truth. One of those unparalleled syllogisms every schoolchild learns: All men are mortal, John is a man. Therefore, John is mortal.

The speaker went on to concede the enormous difficulties that lay ahead. "But politics, economics," she declared, "are not obstacles to peace and to restoring the health of the planet—they are tools to be used in achieving these goals." She spoke about the psychological effects of getting involved—of how easy it was to fall into exhaustion, disillusionment, despair. And she gave examples of people who'd lived with the knowledge that their work would be done only to be ignored or misconceived. "But not undone: there can be no erasure of the efforts you and I have made—and will continue to make—for the survival of life itself."

A short silence, followed by sober applause. The Chair asked for questions, but Anna found it impossible either to ask or to listen. She was thinking about Virginia Woolf, about the things that make one stuff stones in one's pockets and calmly walk out into the water. And then Fiona came to mind: Fiona's husband. Murder is fatal, too—what would the speaker say to that? And Maeve? Had Maeve ever asked about her father—did she even remember him? What did she, Anna, know of her own father, about whom she'd never dared to ask? Because to ask was to hurt, and to risk being hurt, and if she only kept silent and good her mother would never walk away and leave her.

People were starting to file out. Anna pressed closer to Varti in the crowd. She didn't want to be on her own just then—she badly wanted company, and she had no one else to whom to turn. She invited Varti to have an early dinner with her someplace in town; they found a café on Station Street and ended up staying till the place closed for the night. Over bread and soup, Varti asked her what she'd thought of the lecture. At first, Anna didn't know how to reply, and then she settled on a quarter-truth. "It was so sensible and straightforward. The only problem is that everyone in that audience agreed with her. She should be talking to the politicians and industrialists—she should be on television and radio, instead of just preaching to the converted. I'm sorry, I don't mean to sound hostile, it's just that the whole thing seems so hopeless—"

"And fatalism is fatal. But what about you, Anna? You're a teacher; you write books. Does what you heard tonight touch in any way on what you teach or write? I don't mean to be hostile, either, but just to ask the question. The pastoral tradition—I was taught that it was the backbone of English literature. How do pesticides and the pastoral go together? And when the woods decay and fall due to acid rain, what happens then?" Varti's voice was gentle but insistent.

Anna toyed with her spoon, looking at her reflection there: distorted, yet drawn-in, contained. And then she smiled at Varti, a perfectly honest smile. "I'm afraid I don't know. I've never thought about it in that way."

"There's been quite a lot of research done here about children living round nuclear power stations. They're at a much higher risk of leukaemia than children in other areas. Is that true in Canada as well?"

Anna let her spoon fall back into her soup, and pushed the bowl away from her. "I'm sorry, Varti. I just don't know."

"All right, then—change of subject, change of scene. Tell me about the book you're writing."

"It's—oh, I'd really rather not."

"Ah, you're superstitious. Well, then—what do you want to talk about? Because you do want to talk—and I'd like to listen. Really." Varti smiled and gently touched Anna's hand, then leaned back, sipping at her wine while Anna launched in.

About her mother, though she couldn't begin to explain why. Or yes, she could—because Varti was a doctor, and would understand the details of her mother's illness: how, having gradually lost the ability to walk or even sit in a chair, she'd been confined to her bed for the last eight months of her life. And how Anna had taken the year off university, had stayed home and done the one thing she could to help her mother, who was rapidly becoming blind. She had sat and read aloud what her mother had wanted to hear: *The Newcomes. Daniel Deronda. Wives and Daughters. The Egoist.* And all of Jane Austen, until the very last month, when her mother was in too much pain even to listen, when it had become a matter of palliative care and visiting hours, and finally a cot by her mother's hospital room.

"She was dying, nothing could change that, but they wouldn't leave me alone with her. The nurses kept coming in, fussing with tubes and needles. They kept saying I'd be better off in the lounge, that I needed a little break, a cup of coffee or an hour's TV. I couldn't tell them why I had to stay. When I was a child the only thing I ever wanted was to have her all to myself. My father, my grandparents—they all died before I was born, you see—she was the only family I had. She was a passionate reader, and I used to be horribly jealous of her books. She said she found me once, sitting on the kitchen floor, tearing out pages. She didn't punish me—she simply sat down next to me and taught me to read. I learned in order to please her; it was years before I understood that I could read to please myself. It became a kind of consolation for the fact that people and things in books were more real to her, more important than I could ever be. It was only when she was dying that I could be with her, without anything else—even a page in a book—coming between us."

A waitress came with the bill, which Anna grabbed. "Please, Varti, let me pay for it. You've been wonderful, hearing me out all evening. I've never talked about this with anyone before—I'm always the listener, you see. But I meant to ask you about the lecture, there are things I don't understand."

"Then we'll have to have dinner together again. Next time I'll take you out. And Anna—you can talk about whatever you please. I promise you."

Anna didn't trust herself to look up at Varti—instead, she reached for her purse, and tore off a bit of paper from the back of her chequebook. "Here's my address. I haven't got a phone, but you can always ring me at the neighbour's—she won't mind."

Varti scribbled something on a page she'd ripped from a small notebook. "You can reach me here if I'm not in the clinic. And by the way, if you ever come down with anything I'll do the best I can for you. Good night, Anna. Thanks for dinner."

Hours later, Anna lay awake in her bed, curled up in confusion. Why should a talk about the future of the planet make her turn in towards her past? What was it about Varti that she needed so? The sheer safety of her company; the certainty that she'd never turn her away or refuse to listen to her? That only when she was with Varti could she be herself? *When the self calls to the self, who answers?* How many Annas were there—her mother's, and then Luke's; Fiona and Maeve's Anna; Simon's, however accidentally, and now Rosalind's Annie. She pressed her arms down tight on either side of her, so that the sheet looked like a shroud around her. Having been with Rosalind just for those two days had been like standing in a sudden fall of light from a stained glass window, taking on heat and colour right through the skin. . . .

It had been a mistake to go to London, just as it had been a mistake to go to Simon's and even Fiona's. To have gone back into Fiona's room, to have sat reading aloud to a child whose hair and skin smelled of bread and butter and honey—

She fell asleep at last, saying over her errors instead of her prayers, errors irretrievable as figures carved into a blackboard. Not just the people she should never have met, but the book she should never have promised to write, the husband she should never have refused. And over all the errors, all the faulty sums scratched into the blackboard rose a face, whether her mother's or Varti's or that of a perfect stranger she couldn't tell. A face luminous and empty as a full moon.

# XII

# SOLITARY

It was Michaelmas, half-term, and for the first time since coming to England, Anna found herself entirely alone. Fiona had taken Maeve to see her grandparents in Shrewsbury. Varti had gone off to Greenham Common for a vigil and Simon was spending the holiday in London, scouring the streets for examples of snecked rubble and scagliola. Rosalind was attending a conference in Copenhagen—*Greetings from the Tivoli Gardens* sat on Anna's mantelpiece next to *The Splendour of Peggy's Cove*—Luke's confirmation that he'd booked them in for two weeks at a resort on the Ivory Coast, starting Boxing Day. The Pryce-Jones, thank heavens, had never issued that dinner invitation she'd been threatened with. Even Miss Molesworth was keeping her distance—perhaps because Anna had cancelled, at the very last moment, her promised address to the W.I. And though she'd walked down the village's every footpath and branching lane, she could find no trace at all of the woman she'd glimpsed at her writing desk the night of the wine and cheese.

It was no longer weather for walking. The trees looked arthritic, sprouting black, bare, swollen twigs. Lichen glowed phosphorescent on rocks and stumps; ivy stabbed between bricks and battened on wood that simply submitted, the way the female of the species, ewe or nanny goat or bitch, submits to a mounting. Everything was slurred, soaked, except for the blackbirds' yellow beaks, disruptive as exclamation marks in the stillness of the garden.

Anna was in a bad way, though she wouldn't admit it to herself. Time seemed to have stopped, or rather, to have become as insistent as a leaking tap. And if time had expanded, space had contracted, till she felt the cottage walls like an exoskeleton around her; stepping out the front door became as impossible as stepping out of her skin. She was incapable of the merest exertion: a day-trip to London to walk through

Bloomsbury or trace Mrs. Dalloway's progress along Bond Street had become as unthinkable as a swim down the Amazon.

On her first day entirely alone Anna didn't drag herself out of bed till dusk. Then she shuffled downstairs and switched on the radio. But the only thing she could bear to listen to was the shipping forecast. *Rockall, Land's End, Farroes. Valencia, Malin Head. Continuous slight drizzle, falling slowly, east by north 3, haze 4 miles, 1023 and falling slowly.*

It wasn't just the poetry of naming, but the certainty of judgement the report supplied: visibility fair or poor, bad or good. No ambiguities or relativity in this world without people, a world composed only of names and elements. Anna sat in her nightgown, listening, letting the words wash over and soothe her, as if they had nothing to do with ships at sea, but were simply a litany, easing day into night.

The next morning she pulled herself out of bed in time to catch the ten minutes set aside for the nation's moral guidance by the Governors of the BBC: Thought for the Day. Today's broadcast addressed the subject of teenage beggars sleeping rough in London. It wasn't the subject that kept Anna listening, but the speaker's conviction that justice, honesty, compassion were things solid and incontrovertible as Rockall or Malin Head. For ten minutes every day, God spoke by the grace of the BBC. It was as close as Anna could get to all being right with the world. As close, and about as long.

And so the pattern was set for the rest of the week. In between Thought for the Day, and the shipping forecast Anna drank endless cups of tea chased by instant coffee, ironed pillowcases, straightened pictures and rearranged bookshelves everywhere but in the study. One day she sat cross-legged by the gas fire, looking at every scrap of paper sent her by Luke. Photographs of her house by the sea; the pine woods, her scraggly garden. Her tenants, Emma and Frank, reading on the verandah, looking for all the world as though they owned the place. And one they must have taken of Luke, looking different from how she remembered him: stranger, handsomer. Luke sitting on the porch steps, a cat on his lap. Whose cat? Anna turned the photos face down and picked up the letters. She paid special attention to the openings and closings, gauging their warmth, sifting their sincerity; trying to sniff out what the spaces between the lines were saying.

Then threw them down, disgusted with herself. She had no reason to doubt Luke. Fidelity. The word made her think of yapping little dogs, lapdogs. She stuffed the letters back into her dresser drawer, and proceeded to something far more constructive—cleaning closets, rereading *The Luck of the Woosters*, and sleeping.

The only interesting things that happened to Anna in this week of confinement occurred in her dreams, although immediately on waking her head would turn into a colander, all images streaming away with no hope of retrieval. Except for one dream which she had recurrently, that she'd jotted down into a notebook, though in principle she despised people who did that sort of thing. She would like to be able to tell this dream to Varti, to see what she would make of it.

*I am at a concert with Rosalind; we are sitting in the best seats, so near to the orchestra we can see the sweat pour from the musicians' faces, and the cracks on the conductor's baton. Suddenly a voice shouts from the balcony: "Tirez dans la foule!" But there is no crowd: there is only Rosalind and me, and someone up in the gods cocking a pistol at us. Rosalind rushes out—I grab onto her skirt, holding on for dear life, and am swept along with her into the lobby.*

*And now Rosalind vanishes—I look for her everywhere, but the only person I can find is a cloakroom attendant. Walking towards her, I see that the attendant is really my mother. At first I think how well she looks, as though she'd completely recovered from her illness. And then I see how gaunt and white her face is—how her thick, gleaming hair is only a wig she's struggling to keep in place.*

*She speaks so bitterly to me, saying she knows she has only a week to live. She points to her belly; she is heavily pregnant. Either she will die before the child can be born, or else the child will surface just as she drowns. I stare at her—I cannot say a single word. My mother turns away from me, she turns away and disappears.*

\*     \*     \*

On the last morning of her solitude, Anna woke from this dream to rain slashing at her window. She was still tunnelled under the blankets when the knocking started, getting louder, louder, cracking her ears wide open. She didn't know whom she wanted it to be—Varti, Rosalind, even Simon—but she tore down the stairs, nearly tripping head over heels, only to arrive to total silence. Still, she pushed the door open and ran down the steps. A woman was hurrying along the road, the woman she'd glimpsed once on the Downs and once through a lighted window. Anna called out to her, though she didn't even know her name. But the woman had her back to her, and the rain was drowning Anna's cries, soaking her as she stood in the doorway, clutching her nightdress.

# XIII

# FIRE AND LIGHT

It was Varti who'd given her the idea. She'd asked Anna for supper the day after her return from Greenham Common; towards the end of the evening the conversation had veered to Guy Fawkes.

"I find it curious," Varti was saying, "that people can spend an entire year sewing costumes and planning parades for one night's carnival, yet have no time at all for what the Greenham women are doing. The burning of effigies rather than burning causes—that's what most attracts us, I'm afraid. Well, this year at least I shan't have to go through another night of torches and broken glass—I'm spending the weekend with my daughter in Leeds. Why don't you come along, Anna—the baby isn't due for another two months yet, there's lots of room. You really can't spend your whole time in England crammed into a pocket of Sussex. Come with me, it will do you good—you look as though you could use a break."

"But I've just had a break, I took a whole week off work when you were all away. And besides—" Anna broke off, staring down at her empty plate. How could she explain to Varti that she didn't want to share her with anyone, certainly not with a daughter, and a pregnant daughter at that.

"Anna?" Varti reached across the table, gently raising Anna's chin until her eyes were level with her own. Anna shut her eyes. It was the same gesture her mother would use when she knew Anna was hiding something from her, something that hurt. When Varti took her hand away, Anna felt abandoned. She wanted to grab Varti's hand, prison it in her own; her whole body wanted to curl into a shape that could be held in two hands and given into the keeping of this woman. But Anna smiled, instead; she could feel her whole self stiffening into the smile she gave Varti, and the words she made up to fill the space between them.

"Besides—I've promised to take my neighbour's little girl into town for Guy Fawkes. My neighbour—haven't I told you about Fiona? She's a bit of a recluse—her husband died a short while ago, and she isn't up to crowds yet. Maeve—that's her daughter—wants to see the parade. She's at the age when that kind of thing seems more important than anything—torches, bonfires, fireworks. . ."

What Anna didn't admit was that after a week locked inside Rest Harrow with the book she couldn't write and the dream she couldn't shake, it was she, not Maeve, who was hungering after spectacle and self-indulgence. And so she'd found herself, a few days later, guilty of the worst kind of manipulations. She knew she ought to have spoken first to Fiona, given her the chance to refuse; that to barge into the Gibsons' kitchen and tell Maeve her plan for Guy Fawkes was a breach of the laws of friendship. Fiona seemed perfectly aware of this—she stood silent, her face paler than ever as Anna wheedled—there was no other word for it—and Maeve, who was being fitted for a costume for the school play, tugged loose from her mother's hands. She jumped up and down, her raggedy sleeves fluttering. "Please, please, I want to go, and you promised, you promised." Still, Fiona stood there, her mouth full of pins and her eyes fixed on Anna with a look of exhaustion and defeat.

This is the point, Anna knew, where she ought to be picked up by the scruff of her neck and pitched out of these people's lives. For though she could deceive herself as to the nature of her misdeed (she wasn't lying to Fiona, but making good her lie to Varti) she understood that somehow everything was changing, in ways she couldn't predict or control. But what Anna knew did not move her. She stayed where she was as Fiona took the pins out of her mouth, one by one, and said, "Go on. Take her then," and Maeve hugged first her mother, then Anna in a burst of affection that ended by almost smothering the cat.

On the eve of November fifth, Anna fetched Maeve, who had been far too excited to eat her tea, and who was dressed in her beggar's costume, her face made up with paints so that her eyes shone out of a mass of bruises and scars. Anna was horrified—she wanted to take a cloth and wipe the child's face clean, but Fiona was standing there, watching them, silently laying down the rules which included, it would seem, Maeve's battered appearence. "Historical accuracy," she said, as Maeve darted out of the room to put on an extra pair of socks. "Of course the costume's all wrong—too bright, too clean; it smells of soap instead of pus and shit—"

"Fiona, if you'd rather I didn't—"

"It's too late for that, Anna. She'll die of disappointment if you let her down tonight. Come along, Maeve—Anna's waiting for you." And when Maeve came clattering down the stairs, Fiona pushed both her and Anna out the front door, locking it behind them.

\*     \*     \*

It's black and cold outside; Anna's car has a funny heater, right down the middle; one side of you is hot, the other cold, as if a line's been drawn dividing the two sides of you: red/blue; fire/ice. Anna's unhappy; Anna's worried, but not like Mummy; Anna's worry is like a pocket handkerchief balled in a pocket, something she can squeeze and squeeze and throw away when she's done with it. You fold your arms tight across your chest the better to see the beautiful flamy tatters of your sleeves; you push them up and down and begin to chant:

*Remember, remember*
*The fifth of November*

"Do you know it, Anna?"

Anna shakes her head and keeps driving, gripping the steering wheel so tight her knuckles look as though they'll pop straight through her skin. There's already lots of traffic going into town; when Anna says she doesn't know where on earth she's going to park the car you can put your finger on the pulse in her voice, the flutter and jump that says, "We shouldn't have come; I've made a mistake."

*I know no reason*
*Why gunpowder treason*
*Ever should be forgot.*

"Not much of a rhyme, is it?" Anna asks, but it's all right—she's found a place to put the car, even though there'll be a long, long walk down to where the parade will be. You put your hands up your sleeves—your gloves aren't halfway warm enough; you won't ask Anna to carry you on the way home, not even on the steep part; you're old enough to walk all the way by yourself, you'd rather die than ask to be carried home.

"Come on, Maeve, put on your coat. No arguments, please—you promised your mum you'd wear it—"

"But my costume. No one will see my—"

"Put it on, Maeve, let's do up the buttons, hold still, that's better. Now take my hand and hold tight—I don't want you getting lost tonight. If you get lost, go to the War Memorial and wait for me there—do you know where that is?"

"Halfway down the high street, Anna, of course I know." But you don't tell her that the street will be so filled with torches and bands and shouting that you'll never be able to see the angel on top of the War Memorial. Last time you came, you rode on your dad's shoulders—no one thinks you remember that, but you do. You'd seen the Christmas wreath the angel holds up—you'd seen it just above the heads of the people marching, and the crowds pushing against the sides of the road. Your dad's hands holding tight to your shoes, your hands tight in his hair, *Ouch, ouch, you're killing me* but he didn't mean it, he couldn't have. You can't ask your mum and you can't ask Anna—if you hold on too tight to Anna's hand, will you hurt her, will she slip her hand from yours and run away?

"Come on, Maeve. Let's follow those people up ahead—hold tight, and watch where you're going—oh look!"

A Catherine wheel, doing somersaults in somebody's garden, all the light breaking out and whirling over Anna's hair and eyes so she looks magic. You want to tell her how beautiful it makes her, but come on, Anna says, come on. "We'll miss the parade down below. You'll see better fireworks later, just come *on*."

So steep the hill, but you can't hurry, there are so many people, so many dark, woolly backs and so much laughing. Sharp, sweet fiery smells and a smash, and more laughing. Anna saying, "Watch out for the glass—would you like me to carry you?" "No, no—" and you hurl yourself faster and faster after the people so that your chest puffs up like a paper bag ready to burst, you can feel your ears pop, and your eyes—

"Here's a good spot. Let's go into the churchyard with the others." Anna tugging you and pulling you as though your arms are made of taffy. The churchyard crammed with stones and legs, hundreds and thousands of legs standing in and around and sometimes on top of the stones, when they make a tabletop. And it's still so cold, even with all the others pressing up against you. You can't see anything but it's so noisy Anna doesn't hear when you tell her, tugging at her hand, pressing your fingers hard. She's stamping her feet to keep warm and doesn't hear you, doesn't hear. You have to wait till she bends down beside you, putting her face against your cheek to see how cold you are, pressing both your hands in hers, "Shall I get you some cocoa—shall we see if there's somebody selling cocoa?" You shake your head and somehow you scream loud enough, "I—can't—seeeee!" and Anna's hoisting you up to her shoulders, but it doesn't help. Anna isn't tall, nothing like as tall as your dad. Now all you can see are people's shoulders instead of their bums and their backs, till Anna carries you over—lurching, swaying, so you think you'll fall like Humpty Dumpty—to a table tomb someone's cleared a space on; sets you down, holding on to your coat so you won't slip off. Nothing's happening yet, though there's pounding and blurting coming from somewhere down the street. You start to jump up and down, your shoes are that thin you can feel the letters carved into the tabletop and the scabby bits of lichen. Anna tries to get you to stay still but you can't, your toes and your feet are great lumps of ice, if you don't stamp and wriggle them they'll fall off, roll into the grass and be trampled by all the others.

"Here they come!"

The higher you jump, the more you can see—men in silly uniforms, they don't look like soldiers at all, and ladies with hoop skirts and spangly sleeves swollen up like your arm with the wasp bite in the summer—allergic, the doctor said, which means something magic: allergic, allergic, you'd like to draw the way it sounds, loops and fuzzy clouds with the side of the pencil, and the white horse galloping, galloping if you said it faster and faster, allergic—

"Look, Maeve—the torches!"

Dipping and swerving, scribbling with fire, the way you loop a torch through the dark on summer nights but theirs are looser and leap, leap—it's like water, too, running over the edges of the sticks and rushing out. Fire leaping across the black between the marchers, springing like the cat from the mantel to the carpet and bouncing up again. Smelling like fire, too, sharp and oily: puddles of blue and purple and green in the air, so cold and so black it pokes needles up your nose each time you breathe.

"Burmese Temple dancers?" Anna says—she's laughing, you can feel her laughing as she holds you tight against her, though it doesn't help, you're still freezing, your nose is ice, your eyes and your teeth are glass, breaking—

"Cowboys? Confederate soldiers?"

—and your fingers five icicles, look how they shatter when you make fists, tight, the way your dad showed you. Even with your coat on, coat thrown like a blanket over the beautiful flames at your elbows and shoulders and wrists. If you didn't have to wear the stupid coat you could flap your arms and make fire from the sleeves. If only you could reach out from over the railing and grab a torch, grab it right by its fiery hair, your hands going purple, glowing like the gas jets at home, burning your coat right off your shoulders, shooting up in the air—

"See the banners, Maeve. 'No Popery!'—No Popery?"

"I'm cold, Anna, I'm cold, I want to go now, I want to go home—" but Anna can't hear you because her ears are filled up with ice. When you came here with your dad that one time no one thinks you remember it was lovely and hot, just like summer, and you on his shoulders, higher than anyone. He clicked with his mouth and made neighing sounds and then galloped after the torches, you broke right away from the crowds on the kerb, swooping down, grabbing a torch still flaming in the gutter; he gives it to you, and you hold it high as high over your head, whooping down the streets and over the hills to the fire. *Throw in your torch, Maeve, throw it in* but the flames are a swarm of wasps, crimson and whirling the black *They won't hurt you, Daddy's got you* holding tight to your shoes and your hands in his hair, black like the air around you but so warm, so warm, as he tilts back just like a horse rearing up *Look at the sky, Maeve, look at the stars* cannons, thumps and roars, you hold tight so tight you can never fall off *you're killing me* with your head thrown back and the stars bursting into your eyes—

"Let's go, Maeve—we'll follow them up the hill."

"I have to pee."

"Oh—yes—I suppose you couldn't—? Well, then we'll just have to find a loo somewhere."

It takes ages and ages, everyone else is queuing up too, and when it's your turn Anna goes in with you, because it's such a big and dark place, and it smells the way Sally says the graveyard smells when you're lying under the earth. When it's your turn to go, you can't, not even a trickle. Anna sighs, but says nothing as you wash your hands, though there isn't any soap, she tells you to wipe your hands on your coat, because the towel's too dirty.

"Can we go home, now, Anna?"

"But Maeve, don't you want to see—"

"I want to go *home*, Anna." And this time she knows; there's nothing to argue about or buy for you that will make you want to stay, but she sighs all the same.

"All right, then, Maeve, if you want, we'll go."

You walk out of the loo and down the street but it's not the same street you came by, it's dark and narrow, and there are people running by, men making sucking and slurping noises as they run past you, whirling torches over their heads, and it smells of petrol everywhere. Anna grabs your hand so tight your fingers break off. She doesn't know she isn't holding your hand any more but your sleeve, that your hand's fallen into the gutter with the torch and its fire leaking out, souring the air.

"Don't worry, we'll find our way back to the High Street—they're just a bit excited with the lights and the band and everything, don't worry, Maeve, I'll get us home—"

But it's Anna who's crying—you don't even have to look up at her face to know, her voice all jaggedy as she turns the wrong way again, and you can't tell her because she's pulling you so fast the wrong way, the wrong way Anna, and sharp round this corner, sharp into a darker, narrower street, and a sign jutting out, a sign with a shepherd's crook and a man holding a lamb in his arms. "Wait here, Maeve, I'll just go in and ask directions. I can't take you in, it's a pub—I can't leave you, either, oh Maeve, just stand here inside the door. Don't move, don't speak to a soul, I'll be just—"

She's gone behind the smoke and the laughing and shouting, but it's warm here, warm enough that your face is turning back from glass into skin. You turn your back to warm it and you see, running down the road, you see them holding each other by the hand, except that she's trying to get away, she doesn't want him to hold her, and she breaks away. He's running after her, down and down, you leave the doorway so you can see what's happening, the two of them running, both of them split in two, black and white, down the middle, even their faces, even their hair, black and white, black and white, he's catching up with her, catching her—

"Maeve—I told you not to move!"

Anna grabs you, marches you off in the other direction. Anna doesn't want to hear about the two of them chasing each other, Anna leads you back the way you came, past the churchyard where you stood on top of the table tomb, up the steep, steep street, your legs stretching, straining, breaking like rubber bands, stop, just for a moment stop—

"Thank God. Get in, Maeve, I'll just warm up the engine, it'll take a while, it'll take all night before we can move an inch—oh *Christ*, I left the lights on— "

Anna leaping out of the car, slamming the door so it scrapes your ears. You get out and watch her standing with her hands in her pockets, she's trying to make holes right through the pockets, people coming and going past you, the car locked up with all the others, constables directing the traffic that isn't moving anywhere and on the hilltops all around bonfires spilling, leaping. Anna not moving, Anna not knowing what to do, like Mummy now, worrying, crying the bad way, inside, tears filling you up like a pool to soak you, drown you. Till Anna shakes herself and reaches for your hand. "We'll have to go down again, Maeve. There isn't a thing we can do. We'll have to see if we can get a room for the night—there won't be any rooms for the night—I don't know a single soul—oh God, oh God—not Simon?"

Mr. Jeffries from school, waving from the other side of the street with a torch he's picked up from the ditch. You stand between them, trying not to fall over as he talks with Anna, tired and so cold, you just want to curl into someone's pocket and go to sleep. But he's hoisting you onto his shoulders, Mr. Jeffries from school, and Anna's got the torch, the other kind, with its white, steady eye, and you're going a different way, along the overpass onto the Downs and home across the fields. You don't hold onto his hair, you're too big for that, you hold onto his hands that he's holding up for you—he's not wearing gloves, but his hands are large and warm, and you know he'll hold on to you tight, tight, even if you're falling into the dark ahead of you, the frozen ruts lit up by the torch that Anna's holding, the faintest pencil mark on a sheet of paper, the softest line you can draw and still see a line. Stopping, saying look, Maeve, look and over your head the stars are bursting. But your eyes are closing; your mouth and your hands are opening, opening—

*     *     *

"Watch out, she's falling."

"It's all right, I've got her. Can you see all right?"

"I'm fine. Is it much farther?"

"Take my jacket if you're cold—"

"I'm fine—"

But he stopped anyway, carefully wriggling his shoulders so that Maeve shouldn't slip off them. He held out the jacket and Anna put it round her, gripping the torch tighter, picking up cold gleams from upturned flints in the furrows. She could feel the night pressing down on all sides of them, as if they were walking through a tunnel with no warning of what was rushing towards them. Simon didn't say a word—he was whistling Bach chorales, oblivious to the muck glubbering at his boots. Anna had given up her shoes for dead and gone a long way back; every bone in her body seemed to be sticking out of her skin, her tiredness spreading the whole length and breadth of her. She felt herself taking on the darkness around her, even the whites of her eyes and the small crescent scar on her fingertip black, black. "Thank God," she kept saying to herself, "Thank God," and "What will I ever say to Fiona?"

As it turned out, she had to say nothing at all. Anna opened the Gibsons' door with the spare key Fiona had given her weeks ago; she didn't want to ring, in case Fiona had already gone to bed. Simon followed Anna up to Maeve's room; as he lay the child gently down and Anna pulled the coverlet round, leaving only her smudged face showing, it felt absurdly familiar, as if Maeve were their own child they were putting to bed for the night.

There was a light on in Fiona's bedroom—Anna knocked, but got no answer.

"She must be downstairs—perhaps she's fallen asleep on the sofa," Anna whispered, half hoping Simon would nod his head and go, half hoping he wouldn't. For she'd have to find Fiona and wake her up and tell her they were back, safe and sound. She didn't know how she'd explain Simon's presence—she didn't know what it would look like to Fiona. Though if Fiona were shut up in her study, cutting out pictures of the starving or dying or dead. . . . Simon should see that, he would know what to do, he would be able to help.

But Fiona was nowhere to be found. Not in her study, or in the kitchen—not asleep in front of the telly, nor in the dining room where her husband's paintings were hung. From room to room Anna and Simon walked, finding all the lamps lit, disclosing no one.

"You'd better go, Simon, you've got to teach tomorrow. Perhaps she's gone out for a walk—to a neighbour's, or just down the street to get some air. I'll wait here till she gets back, I'm sure it won't be long. Please, go—and thanks, Simon."

He waited for just a moment in the hallway, as if there were something he wanted to say to her, but Anna opened the door and waved him out. Then she flung herself down on the parlour sofa and within seconds fell asleep. So that she couldn't tell whether it were minutes or hours before she opened her eyes to find a ghost standing in front of her. Fiona, in a white bathrobe, drying her hair with a white towel and looking as though it were Anna who owed all the explanations.

When Anna said she'd returned with Maeve to find an empty house, Fiona shook her head, towelling her hair with short, rough strokes.

"I was in the shower—"

"But we looked in the bathroom—"

"The shower's in the basement. Did you go down there?"

"I didn't even know there was a basement—"

"Alun rigged up a studio there. We put in the windows ourselves. And a shower, so he could wash up after messing about with—It doesn't matter, it isn't important. You'd better go now, Anna."

It wasn't till she was home, turning off the lights in the parlour that Anna realized how she'd given herself away. In the tarnished mirror over the mantel she saw what Fiona would have seen: Anna dressed up in a man's jacket, much too large for her; a man's jacket with the sleeves patched and the cuffs eroded; a jacket that was as much a part of Simon Jeffries as his spectacles and baggy trousers. She stared at her reflection for a while, then switched off the parlour light. Pulling off the jacket, bundling it into as small a package as she could, she shoved it into a carrier bag, crept out the back door and dragged herself up the street, taking the roundabout way to Chantry Cottage. And on Simon's front step she abandoned the parcel, stealthily, as if she were committing a crime.

# XIV

# FORTUNA HOUSE

The envelope had slid through the letter box with such a determined thud—as if it were on a first-name basis with gravity—that Anna picked it up with special care. Though wonderfully creamy and heavy, it looked unfinished. You expected a ducal coronet, or some kind of embossing to tempt your fingertips. When Anna cut open the envelope, what came out was a bit of paper torn from a scratch pad:

*Fortuna House,*
*Pyeford, November 26.*

*Could you come to dinner Thursday evening? Seven o'clock—*
*quite informal. Nicholas tells me you're a writer, too.*
*I have an old schoolfriend staying.*
*Don't bother answering this note—we'll expect you anytime after seven.*
*Cressida Pryce-Jones.*

Anna, remembering the clutch of Mr. Pryce-Jones' hand at the wine and cheese; remembering, too, how eagerly she'd listened to all the gossip he'd had to spill, wrote back on her best double bond that unfortunately she had an important engagement in London on Thursday. She put the note into an envelope, sealed it, addressed it and steeled herself for an encounter with Mrs. Higley at the village shop.

On Thursday morning, getting ready to go up to London (she'd arranged to attend a matinée and take a first plunge into the British Museum) Anna found her polite refusal of Cressy's invitation still in her coat pocket. The post office had been closed for lunch the day she'd gone to mail the note—she had meant to return later, but must have forgotten. Fine, she would simply slip it under the Pryce-Joneses' door. Except that it was dated several days before. She could write another note, but on the very day of the dinner party? Wouldn't that be a little too offhand—too revealing? What had she to fear from Nicholas Pryce-Jones? That he would tell her something scurrilous about her neighbours, fill in the dots about Simon's divorce and Fiona's marriage and whatever it was he'd once had in common with Rosalind? Anna stepped back from the door and looked down at the gloves she'd just pulled on—looked at them as if all she had on her mind just now was the suitability of wearing black gloves with a brown coat. Slowly, she stepped back, shut the door, unpeeled her gloves and walked upstairs to examine the contents of her closet.

In the green silk jersey that Luke had christened her mermaid dress, Anna proceeded to Fortuna House at half-past seven that night. She told herself how glad she was she hadn't gone to London on this miserable day of stinging winds and sleety showers. Huddling under her umbrella, her skimpy leather shoes soaked through, she knocked at the door. After a long while it opened. A tall, black-haired girl in a blue velvet dress and soiled white tights stood frowning at her.

"I'm from next door—I've come for dinner," Anna began. The girl considered her carefully before she spoke:

"Then you'd better come in. I'm Angelica, I'm the oldest. They're in the sitting room. Mummy's still bathing Alyssum."

"I beg your pardon?"

"She's bathing the baby. The sitting room's that way. Aren't you going to give me your umbrella?"

Anna made her way in the direction Angelica had sketched out. The house was dimly lit—beams loomed in the oddest places. Dolls, stuffed toys, crayons, rag books, an abacus were scattered over the flagstones. Anna shivered—they felt so cold under her sodden shoes. She heard muffled voices and walked in their direction, managing not to get knocked down when a sheepdog came bounding out of the sitting room.

Nicholas did not rise to his feet, but merely gestured from the sofa.

"So you've come after all. Cressy couldn't remember whether or not she'd sent you the invitation. She's very bad at these things, I'm afraid. Scotch—or are you so craven you'll settle for sherry?"

Anna tried to answer brightly. "Perrier, if you've any."

"Oh, I imagine there's a bottle or two lying about somewhere. Anna?—right, English, Anna English, this is Priscilla Wilkinson, come down all the way from Cheshire. She and Cressy went to school together in—where was that bloody school?"

"You know perfectly well it's in Norfolk. How d'ye do." It was a statement, not a question. Anna returned the nod of the woman who'd made it, a woman primly dressed in a cardigan and pleated skirt, no pearls, but an oversized diamond on her finger. She kept fiddling with it and staring into the fire that was doing its best to sputter out. A small girl in tatty pyjamas was playing with a kitten before the fire screen, stroking the animal much too hard and heavily—Anna wanted to tell her not to, but didn't dare. The child was raven-haired with a face like blotting paper, a smaller replica of the girl who'd answered the door.

"Don't, Lily, you're hurting her. She'll scratch you." This from the woman with the diamond ring. Her face looked heavy, her features, congealed. She wore no makeup of any kind, which made the diamond all the more conspicuous on her hand. Lily gave a little cry and dropped the kitten, which screeched out the door.

"There—I told you. Come here and let me see."

But Lily would have nothing to do with Priscilla—she ran howling for her mother. They could hear the sound of something falling over in the hallway, something heavy, making a dull ringing noise. Lily began crying even louder, and a voice that belonged to a child a little older started in. "I'm telling on you. You're careless. Mummy says you're terribly careless." Lily was screaming now—the other child joined in, and then they heard Cressy's voice, light as a plume of smoke: "Angelica, darling—do see what's going on." But Angelica was well out of earshot.

"Damn—she's knocked over the planter. Don't know why Cressy keeps the poxy thing right in the middle of the hall."

"You'd better go out and do something, Nicholas."

"Oh, they'll fight it out between them. I never get mixed up in their quarrels. Now, Miss English, you wanted Pear William?"

"Perrier—"

But Nicholas had disappeared before she could correct him. The wailing of the children, the scuffling and shouting went on apace, with Cressy calling down every so often, "Angelica? *Do* something, won't you, darling?" Priscilla stared into the abortive fire, sighing. Anna decided to get up and poke the wood about—flames leapt up wildly. She put on another log, jostling the remains of the first, so that the fire wasn't totally smothered. Nicholas still hadn't reappeared, and there was no sign of Cressy. Suddenly the noise of children stopped, as if they'd all been packed into a soundproof trunk. Anna waited for it to start up again, the way you wait for a jack-in-the-box to burst from its tin, but nothing happened.

"It's worrying. There are so many burglaries these days," Priscilla suddenly announced.

"I beg your pardon?"

"The crime rate has fallen—the Home Secretary went on television last night and he was most reassuring. But the number of violent crimes has gone up. We've an alarm system, of course. I keep telling Cressy she ought to install one, but she'll never get round to it."

Anna refrained from observing that Cressy's children were a far more effective burglar-deterrent than any electronic alarm. Instead she asked, "You've been robbed?"

Priscilla looked up at her from under a fringe of rather dirty, dark hair. "Oh no," she said, as if displeased. "Never. You see, we pray to the Lord every night, to protect us. That's what counts. We put our faith in the Lord."

"I see." Anna's stomach began to growl—it was eight forty-five and she hadn't been offered so much as a bowl of peanuts. She wondered where her host could be; she was debating whether she could actually leave the room without seeming terribly rude. And decided that she couldn't care less—she simply couldn't bear another moment of Priscilla's company. But before she could move there was a sudden stream of laughter and Cressy appeared.

She was blissfully, flamboyantly pregnant. Like Niagara Falls she rushed onto the sofa where Priscilla was sitting, a sofa with stuffing coming out in random patches, as though it had mange. Anna stared at the sofa, and when she dared, at Cressy. She was wearing what looked like a Fortuny maternity smock in some impossibly gleaming, clingy fabric. The material strained over breasts like watermelons, a belly big as a harvest moon. But the most astonishing thing was that you could see odd rippling, thrusting movements under the dress—as if Cressy's belly were an aquarium with hammerhead sharks pounding its walls.

"I'm three days overdue. It could happen any day now—any moment."

All Anna could do was smile back and wonder, panic-stricken, where Nicholas had disappeared to. Priscilla didn't look as if she could deliver a letter, never mind a set of twins. Anna's stomach had begun to pinwheel, when suddenly Cressy clapped her hands. "How perfectly silly of me—I've forgotten all about supper. Let's go in to the dining room—everything should be ready. Oh, I *do* hope Ivy's kept the cat away from the aspic—"

It wasn't the worst meal Anna had ever eaten. Nothing was burned, though everything tasted supremely bland. Someone had put a vase on the table and filled it with water, but otherwise it was empty. Anna refused a second helping of veal blanquette but ate three rolls that were only slightly stale. An enormous carton of Flora margarine occupied most of the tablecloth: a stiff, lace cloth, unravelling in places, but, as Anna exclaimed, exquisite. "It's the veil from my great-grandmother's wedding dress," Cressy said. "She was married in the Anglican church at Buenos Aires. The nuns made the lace—poor things, I believe they all went blind. You sure you won't have any more navy beans?"

Nicholas was silent throughout the main course. Priscilla and Cressy reminisced about St. Elfrida's, about a gym mistress they'd both worshipped, and a girl with whom they'd roomed. "Did you know she's finally gone to Jesus?" Priscilla announced in a tone of voice that made Anna think of dim, dank basements.

"Oh dear, I *am* sorry. How is her husband coping with the children?" Cressy asked, helping herself to turnip purée.

"Oh no—you don't understand. I mean she's found Jesus—she's become a member of Our Church. Binny told me—I sat next to her at a lunch they gave at the Temple last week."

It was a moment before Anna realized Priscilla was talking about the law courts and not a tabernacle. She looked up at Nicholas who was smiling at her in an uncomfortably emphatic manner, and who, to her horror, began to draw her into the conversation. "Do tell us what you make of Pyeford, Miss English."

What else could she say? "It's charming."

"And England? Sorry, I should have said Great Britain, shouldn't I, Priss? Of course you'll know that we've put the Great back into Britain by shooting up the Argies. And God knows how many sheep, in the process. Not to mention—"

"Don't be a bore, Nicky." Cressy was busy picking the currants out of her pudding; Nicholas was filling wine glasses to the very brim. Anna's throat felt cracked—there was nothing approaching a water jug, and so she took a first, small sip of wine. She could feel it slipping down her throat the way silk stockings slide over your legs.

"I'm sure you must be impressed by the capacities of our very, very remarkable Leader. She's the one who's responsible for the enterprise revolution, of course—our George Washington, if you like, though minus the wooden teeth. She's made us pick ourselves up by the bootstraps. Revived the glory days of Empire by destroying heavy industry, pretending the Japanese don't really exist, and treating the Americans like some rich and senile uncle who's only nominally in charge of what anachronists like to call our independence."

Nicholas leaned over and topped up Anna's glass. Priscilla dropped her fork into a mess of custard.

"I won't have this, Nicholas. I simply *won't*. You're being blasphemous and unpatriotic and you're ruining my dinner."

"Oh, I'm not being critical, Prissy—you mistake me. My job is simply to observe and exploit. All for the glory of fiction and the greater good fortune of Nicholas Pryce-Jones, esquire, father of however many Pryce-Joneses can be pulled out of—"

"You are quite, *quite* disgusting." Priscilla pushed away her pudding. Anna hadn't touched hers. It was the name that put her off: Spotted Dick.

Nicholas had pushed back his chair and was using the custard bowl as an ashtray. "Shall I tell you what Priscilla's England is like, Miss English? It's exactly what you see for sale in those dinky little specialty shops. China replicas of Cotswold cottages and Regency terraces; standard issue country houses, tarted-up miners' rows. As for Our Glorious Imperial Past, it's a shrunken cosy keeping us warm just as long as profits can be poured out the old brown betty. But Priss doesn't like the word brown, does she? Nor does Priss's God. Remember your Blake, darling—didn't you learn that one in school? 'And I am black, but oh, my soul is white'—something like that. Miss English can correct me. But Priss's England—why, it's so small it can fit into the pocket of an Aquascutum.

"Yes, yes I know—why am I going on like this, singling out our poor, dear Priscilla? I mean, we're all in it together, aren't we? I make no bones about it, Miss English, I bare my soul to you. I vote for the present government. I've got to. Think of the wife and children I have to support. But do I write for the government? That's another question. What I write for is money, but in such a way that no one can tell whether I'm pander or parodist. My great accomplishment, you see, is to create in my readers an insidious sense of complicity, of having it both ways, and therefore, having to do nothing at all about anything—except making money, of course."

"What I cannot understand is why people like you are allowed to publish your filth at all. That's what it is, and you can't deny it. You can be very thankful you live in a democracy—"

"If I lived in a dictatorship, my dear Priss, I'd write exactly the same things in the same way. I'd just adjust the cloud of unknowing somewhat, so the powers that be wouldn't know whether I was shoring them up or shitting them down."

Nicholas leaned over and refilled Anna's glass. She covered the rim with her fingers, but he kept on pouring, the wine running over her knuckles and down her wrist, until she took her hand away and began to try and mop up the mess. Cressy looked on, beatifically, but Priscilla had pulled herself to her feet.

"I—will—not—listen—to—any—more—of—this." She was trembling, her face more than ever like a bowl of crusted porridge. Cressy gave another self-suffused, fertility-goddess smile, then turned to Nicholas. "Be an angel and run off to the study with Miss Irish. You can talk books and things while Priss and I have a chat by the fire." Heaving herself to her feet, Cressy propelled herself towards her friend and hung an arm like a coil of rope around her neck.

"Poor darling, I *have* neglected you, and you've been perfectly *sweet* to come all this way to visit us. Angelica is *so* helpful most of the time, but she *is* in a state tonight. I can't blame her—we're *all* on pins and needles with this *endless* waiting."

The two women walked arm in arm down the hall, Cressy like some great overblown duck, Priscilla an offended pigeon taking short, stiff hops beside her.

"Coming with me, love? Unless, of course, you, too, object to the fine flow of my conversation?"

What else could Anna have done, all unaccustomed as she was to the ways of the local gentry, and more than a little under the influence of the wine she should never so much have tasted? She didn't stop to consider whether it was indeed a good thing to closet herself with a man she hardly knew. But the man was, at least, someone she could talk with, or at least listen to, as opposed to all the others in this house and village. He wasn't vulnerable like Fiona, or even Simon; being someone who expected the worst of everyone, including himself, he was the exact opposite of Varti, whose invitations to spend a weekend at Greenham Common or in Leeds had become more and more pressing. Besides, he might tell her something about Rosalind, whose only communication to Anna, other than the postcard from Copenhagen, had been an aerogram mailed from Bologna and bearing the message, "We must get together when I get back from this BLOODY conference. At least the food's all right."

Nicholas's study lay through the kitchen, across a courtyard, and along a walk covered with a pergola through which dead branches writhed. It had stopped raining—the wind had blown away the clouds to leave a bulbous moon in full possession of the night. The lightbulb on the landing crackled and died as Nicholas flicked the switch; groping her way upstairs, Anna knew she ought to turn and run home. But Nicholas had already reached the upstairs door and turned on the lights. They weren't up to much, for the room remained crepuscular. Anna hesitated: it was only ten o'clock and despite the wine she didn't feel the least bit sleepy. If she went home all she'd have to do would be to stare at a blank computer screen. And if she stayed? What would happen to her other than an overdose of Nicholas Pryce-Jones's conversation?

Noticing a large lamp on a nearby table, Anna felt her way across to it and switched it on. Immediately, the room blanched before her, revealing a computer and printer on a large, mahogany dining table; enormous leather armchairs, and a semi-circular inlaid desk that might have belonged to Madame de Sévigné, but which was bare of anything resembling writing paper. "Loo's round the corner," Nicholas shouted— he was in the kitchenette, putting on coffee. She went round the corner, opened a door and found herself looking into a bedroom slightly larger than the room she'd just left. Hastily, she closed the door and opened another: here was the loo—twice as large as the bedroom, and taken up by an enormous whirlpool bath. Avoiding the mirror, Anna counted to twenty and returned to the sitting room. Settling herself in an armchair, she looked about her once more in a puzzled way. The room was like a drawing of a face in which the eyes or mouth had been left out. And then she understood. There were no bookshelves here: no books at all. In their place were a gigantic televison set and toppling stacks of video cassettes.

Nicholas was whistling—he came into the room with coffee and brandy on a heavy silver tray. "Thank God that's over. Thank the Lord," he said, mimicking Priscilla. "I cannot abide that woman. Cressy only asks her down to torture me. Nails driven through the forehead, large, bent, rusty nails, could not be worse than that woman's talk. Not that she chatters—far from it. She selects each word, each syllable, as an instrument of torture. Now do you see why I need this place?"

"'Shut the door of the Pope's chapel/ Keep those children out—'"

"Exactly. What a pleasure to have a literate person in this house. Even if you do come from"—and he screwed up his mouth like Priscilla's—"the colonies."

Anna drank her coffee greedily. The effects of the wine had suddenly begun to tell; she felt as though someone had dropped a blanket over her head.

"Well, dear girl, aren't you going to ask me all about my *oeuvre*?"

Anna merely held out her cup for more coffee. Nicholas handed her a snifter full of brandy, instead. She put it down on the table beside her. She would have been very glad, just then, of a cigarette: there were moments when the only possible response to a man was to blow smoke slowly and deliberately into his face. This was actually very funny—this had never happened to her before. She'd never believed Don Juans really existed, but here was one in the flesh before her, playing the same old songs. All it needed was etchings—surely he had some stored away under the VCR? Anna smiled—she hoped it wasn't her own giggling she heard. Nick was leaning towards her, so close that she could see balding places glisten under his hair.

Anna waited until his lips were an inch away from hers. "Doesn't it trouble you that your wife's going to have a baby any second? Two babies?" She didn't move so much as a finger, but sat perfectly straight, as though she were still at school, trying out for the crown of Posture Queen. To her great surprise, she hadn't blushed—if the truth be told, she was enjoying this, immensely. If only Luke could see her now—and Rosalind. She wanted to show off, she wanted to be outrageous, perverse, and unaccountable.

Nick sighed and took a sip of Anna's untouched brandy. He drew back in his armchair, curling his legs into a lotus position, so that he looked like a cross between a satyr and a buddha. "Oh—we've been through all this before. Seven times, to be precise. I could sit the midwifery exams without any trouble. And Priscilla's around to help with a prayer or two. She prays for my soul continually. I seduced her in the whirlpool—that's what led her to Jesus, she tells me. You have to sin greatly before you can enter into the kingdom, didn't you know?"

"Do you always seduce your wife's friends in the whirlpool?"

"Sometimes under the computer table. Once behind the cooker."

"I don't believe a word of it."

"She thought she'd lost an earring. . . Anyway, it's all in my novels." Nick took another gulp of Anna's brandy, his voice getting plummier than she'd heard it yet. "You see, my love, the way Cressy responds to my little flirtations and random involvements is to practise perfect fidelity, all the while hanging offspring round my neck like endless chains of office. Every bloody year she presents me with—what's the Dickensian phrase?—incontestable pledges of her affection. Seven daughters who all look exactly like her. Numbers eight and nine on the way—she exults in it. Fecundity, fertility, fidelity. It's enough to drive a man into the arms and far more interesting places of every woman he sees on the street. And I tell you, she started it. Not I. She literally throws women at me—she invited Priscilla for that express purpose, five years ago. When she was twelve months pregnant with Lily. They're all named after vegetation—you've noticed? Angelica, Rose, Jessamyn, Lily, Jasmine, Ivy, Alyssum. God knows what she'll call these—Crabtree and Evelyn, no doubt. And then it will start all over again. Impregnation, gestation, parturition. Good Christ. God help us."

"This is your novel?"

"This is my life. You have no sympathy for me?"

"Not a jot." Anna plucked at the skirt of her dress, gathering it up as if she were about to rise from her chair. "I really ought to be—"

"But it's early yet—they're still up talking, you're not going to throw me onto my own resources, are you? Where's your curiosity? I thought you were an academic, a critic. Here you have a chance to interview a prominent British writer, twice short-listed for the Booker prize, and bound to get it for *Bold Glen*."

"*Bold Glen*?" Anna let her hands fall back into her lap; she sat smiling and smoothing her skirt over her knees. Masterful, free, fearless. . . . She took a large sip from her brandy snifter. It didn't burn her throat at all—if the wine had been silk, this was peau de soie.

Nick poured himself another brandy and lifted his glass to her. "Just in case you may not yet have had a chance to sample the glories of British advertising, I should reassure you that *Bold Glen* is not a revisionist romance about the Scottish clearances. You might say it's—oh, let's call it a sociographic meta-ad. You see, the characters, setting, plot are taken entirely from a television commercial in which boy meets girl in W1. Whether they go to bed or not isn't the point—the point is to sell upmarket instant coffee. There's a sequence of ads, an interrupted narrative where action's endlessly deferred and meaning indeterminate or aporetic. In my novel, you see, the caffeine addicts are endlessly arranged to come together but keep mucking up because someone or something from another ad keeps breaking through at exactly the wrong moment. The cat from the Sheba commercial, or the woman who takes her congé from yuppiedom by divesting herself of ring, fur coat, credit cards—everything but the keys to her Volkswagen. It's all quite fiendishly cut and contrived—there isn't a single signifier that doesn't wink at the Saatchi brothers and their like. *Liaison Interruptus*, I could have called it. And it's bound to sell a billion copies. People want to read about what they know, after all, and what do they know best, nowadays? Material goods. Consumables. And how do they know? From their television screens. Think of the auction for movie rights: from telly to book to big screen to VCR. Ads will imitate art—you'll see them selling coffee by the book, my book—"

"You're pulling my leg, Nicholas. Both of them at once."

"And rather lovely legs, at that."

Anna was laughing. Or was this Anna, this woman in the mermaid dress, soft and shimmering under the lamplight, sipping brandy with a man who looked more and more like—who was that actor in *Out of Africa*—the one who played Baron Blixen? How could this woman be Anna, when Anna, who couldn't handle alcohol of any kind, has given out to all men but Luke, safe Luke, a scent like carbolic acid, a notice saying Sorry We Are Closed? Who was this woman sitting with her arms drawn back behind her head, her hair no longer tucked behind her ears but standing up in flames around her face? And who, when the bad baron got up from his chair, reaching down and shutting off the lamp, didn't cry out but let him run his hand over her shoulders and across her breasts, closing eyes which swam like golden fishes in a black night pond. . .

"Nicholas? Nicholas! You have to *hurry*. Her waters have broken and it's made a perfectly awful mess on the Wilton. I've rung the midwife—she really ought to be in hospital—not the midwife, *Cressy*. Hurry up, will you—we can't have the *children* helping."

The voice screeched up to them from the bottom of the stairwell. Quickly, delicately, Nicholas drew his fingers up from Anna's breasts and across her lips. Then he shouted something in Priscilla's direction, and left the room.

Anna—no longer anyone but Anna English—forced herself to count to a hundred before following him. The rain had started up again, not dribbling this time but smashing down. In the few minutes it took her to cross the courtyard, her hair and dress were drenched. Dripping down the endless corridor to the front door, she passed by the drawing room where she'd built up the fire only a few hours before. Cressy was lying propped up beside it. Her huge belly glistened with sweat, and Nicholas was crouching between her outspread legs. Suddenly she cried out, a shriek of laughter rather than pain. Her whole body heaved and a small shape, blue and compact as a plum, spurted into her husband's hands.

Anna felt as though a fist had hit her in the stomach. It was the wine, she thought, the wine and then the brandy and her stupid, unforgivable behaviour in the room upstairs. If Priscilla hadn't called just then—How could she, how could she have even thought of letting him—If she didn't hurry she'd be sick, she'd be sick right there by the front door where everyone could see her. Gathering up her skirts, clutching at her stomach, Anna rushed outside, nearly colliding with the midwife's car.

# XV

# SEASON'S GREETINGS

The arctic chill predicted as penance for an unusually mild November failed to happen. Instead, the skies over Sussex cleared and the weather grew steadily warmer, with roses beginning to bloom and trees to bud. Anna's radio announced it wouldn't last—meteorologists came on the air to predict dire consequences if it did: disruptions in the growing cycle, sheep birthing unseasonably early. Broadcasters and politicians routinely referred to the greenhouse effect; scientists casually discussed the possibility of London, New York and Paris sinking underwater in another forty years' time, along with the whole of Holland. They didn't, of course, mention the east coast of Canada, and Anna took what she knew to be an idiotic comfort in the fact. Sympathetic magic: if they didn't name it, it wouldn't happen. Besides, how could it be as serious as the scientists were saying? If it were, would they all just sit there talking?

Anna was sitting at the small kitchen table with a gross of Christmas cards and the Biro Mrs. Higley had sold her, one whose ink would be sure not to turn into a greyish wash on envelopes delivered in rain or sleet or snow. Purposefully, she opened her address book. There was a section at the back for people to whom she owed some annual sign of life—former students who had moved away; colleagues at the university. She tried to draft some formulaic phrases to fill the space between her name and the *Season's Greetings* in five languages, but however much she struggled, the words came out as though not she but Rosalind had authored them:

Greetings from the green and pleasant land. Except it isn't green any more, but the colour of toxic sludge. And as for pleasant, if you're not in hock to the loan sharks or defaulting on your mortgage because of the hike in interest rates then yes, things are absolutely spiffing here. My work's going well, and I've had the chance to dash up to London for some wonderful *theatre, concerts, exhibitions, dodging teenagers cut off the dole and sleeping rough, or the mentally ill with their bleeding heads and dormitory shifts in cardboard boxes.*

*All the Best in the New Year. If there is a New Year.*

In the end, she wrote just her name and a postscript, a duplicitous "All's well—will write a proper letter soon."

When she walked to the village shop to mail her cards—it was too late in the day to drive into town—Mrs. Higley refused to take them without a lecture.

"It's past the proper posting date. They'll never get there in time. You'll have to send them all first class, and they'll still arrive late. You can see for yourself in the folder. You ought to have obtained a folder months ago—if something's worth doing, it's worth doing right. Oh, go on, give them here. But there'll be no use complaining to me when people write back saying they've received their Christmas cards at Easter."

Anna had merely smiled the idiot smile which was her only means of mollifying Mrs. Higley. On her way back from the post office she stopped by Fiona's for a cup of tea. It was the first time she'd called since the Guy Fawkes disaster—Maeve had come down with a bad cold shortly afterwards, and was still convalescent. Fiona didn't seem to bear Anna any grudge, though, and Maeve was overjoyed to see her, making Anna read at least six chapters of *The Enchanted Castle* while Fiona prepared the supper she insisted on Anna sharing with them. If she remembered Anna's wearing Simon's jacket, she said nothing about it. Instead, she asked Anna to watch the news with her after Maeve had gone to bed. It was all about domestic issues: the latest trade figures and an update on the government's plans to privatise water in the new year.

"Next thing you know, they'll be fitting everyone's lungs with meters," Anna joked. "Britair, plc." It was neither a funny nor outrageous thing to say, given the current state of the nation's affairs. Fiona changed the channel to a documentary about the rising tide of crime against the elderly—several pensioners were calling for the return of capital punishment. Fiona switched off the program halfway through, saying she was tired; Anna insisted on helping with the washing-up.

"You're having company for Christmas?" Fiona had pulled the plug on the sink; the water made a heavy, sucking sound going down the drain.

"Company?"

"The man you live with. What's his name—Matthew? Didn't you say he was coming for Christmas?"

"Luke. Yes, he's flying over."

The whole room seemed to fill with Fiona's silence—Anna felt she'd drown in it if someone didn't speak. And she could think of only one thing to say.

"Look, Fiona, why don't you come too? For Christmas—you and Maeve. It will be like a house party. Do come. Unless, of course, you've got family to go to."

Fiona laughed as if she were coughing. "The last visit was a disaster, worse than all the others put together. You see, we don't get on together. Do you?"

"Get on? With my family, you mean. Yes—I suppose. No disasters, at any rate."

Fiona slipped her dishtowel through the handle of the cooker. "It's kind of you, Anna, but I don't think I'd be very festive company this Christmas."

"Please, Fiona. It would—be a pleasure. And Maeve would like it, I know she would."

"I don't know, Anna. I'll think about it. But please don't say anything to Maeve—not just yet." Fiona switched off the kitchen lights and went straight upstairs, as if she'd forgotten that Anna were there at all.

\*    \*    \*

Luke sent a telegram confirming his arrival on the twentieth of December. Anna considered phoning him to say they wouldn't be alone, and then decided against it. He wouldn't find it traumatic; his own children were nearly grown up, and besides, they were boys, so Maeve wouldn't remind him of any fatherly duties he was neglecting. And it would be much better to have company around to deflect Luke's immediate concerns—she'd just as soon he didn't walk in the door of Rest Harrow proposing marriage or interrogating her on the progress of her book. There'd be time enough for that on the Ivory Coast.

Anna plunged into preparations for the holidays, laying in provisions and sending out invitations for a small Christmas Eve party she'd decided to throw in Luke's honour. It was a reckless thing to do, given that she almost never entertained at home, and hadn't more than a handful of people to invite—Fiona, Maeve, Varti, Simon, who'd had her in for dinner all those months ago; Miss Molesworth, who'd come by the other day with half a dozen jars of homemade blackberry jam. Reckless, but irresistible. When she'd been a child, Christmas had meant only herself and her mother in the small apartment where no pets were permitted, not even a budgie in a cage. Now she had not just a house but also people to fill it, and she felt a surge of the abandon she'd experienced in much more dubious circumstances, that night in Nicholas's study. What she was abandoning, of course, was her worka-day, her homebody self, the Anna Luke knew as practical, prudent, supremely predictable. But this time there'd be no danger involved, and no possibility of betrayal. For what could be more innocent—more Dickensian—than a Christmas Eve party?

Anna spent the days immediately before Luke's arrival in the stores, coming home with her ears full of canned Christmas carols, and her arms full of turkey. She thought she'd haemorrhage if she saw another plastic sprig of mistletoe, or a Father Christmas ho-ho-ho-ing. Why did they always look so debauched? One she'd passed had reeked of hashish. Nevertheless, she twined cedar boughs through the bannisters, and stuck holly over the picture frames. Presents were easy, if unimagi-native—she'd simply gone into the first bookstore she could find and bought up three of the fattest novels on the Booker short list: one for Fiona, one for Luke, and one for herself, since Luke was apt to buy her a useful gift: computer diskettes or print cartridges. For Maeve, however, she'd made an exception. She'd found exactly what she needed in a small art shop run by Hungarian émigrés; they'd put together a package of paints and pastels, pencils and brushes and the very best drawing paper. It had turned out to be more expensive than all the Bookers put together, but for once, Anna couldn't have cared less.

On Luke's behalf she bought a dozen extra eggs—he made a spe-cial eggnog every Christmas, and she didn't want to deprive him of his one culinary tour de force. There had been some talk on the radio about salmonella poisoning due to infected eggs, but Anna was con-vinced it was scare-mongering. She had taken care, however, to buy eggs in boxes labelled "free-range"—she understood the problem applied to battery hens only. She'd also gone wild in the baked goods section of the supermarket. She was convinced that the only way to avoid deserts of silence at her party was to keep everyone's mouth crammed with shortbread and mince pies.

Everything seemed well under control until the twentieth, when Anna went to meet Luke at Gatwick. He did not emerge from any plane at the appointed time. Eventually she discovered that his charter had been diverted to Boston. She was told to phone tomorrow—a huge blizzard had broken out in Boston, and nothing would be taking off from there for at least another twenty-four hours. Dutifully, Anna returned to Pyeford, and spent much of the next three days phoning the airport from Fiona's house. Weather conditions were still abominable all over North America, or so she was informed. The last few times she'd tried to call, all lines had been engaged. She'd shrugged her shoulders and let herself get involved helping Maeve make paper chains for the Christmas tree. When she returned to Rest Harrow later that night, having accepted Fiona's invitation to stay on for supper, Anna found a bundle on her doorstep. It was Luke, half-dead and clinging to the door knocker.

Having tried to restore him with as hot a bath as she could muster—she'd had to keep pouring in kettlefuls off the stove, trying not to scald him—she next resorted to half a bottle of the brandy she'd bought to flame the Christmas pud. In between, Luke explained what had happened. He'd managed to get a train from Boston to Montréal and had jumped aboard a plane to Heathrow, at quite phenomenal expense. He'd spent the entire, protracted flight retching over his shoes—there hadn't been enough paper bags to go around, such had been what the pilot had announced as mere "turbulence." Then he'd taxied to Pyeford.

"You've grown a beard," Anna said. It made him look not younger, exactly, but rougher, hardier—handsomer, yes, that was it. He'd lost the tire round his middle, too.

"Is that all you can say? Do you have *any* idea how much that taxi cost me?"

Abashed, Anna steered Luke into her room, where he collapsed on the bed. She spent the night in the spare room, since she was sure he'd want to sleep for the next forty-eight hours, and she didn't want to disturb him. He woke up, in fact, just as Rosalind dropped by.

If you could call it dropping, in such regalia. Looking at her, Anna thought of double cream and emeralds and Spanish gold. Her dress was more like a costume: voluminous black taffeta, with lace at cuffs and collar, lace that looked like a finer version of Cressy's tablecloth. The neck was cut low enough to show her collar bones and the beginning of breasts so small and delicate they looked vestigial. Her long, beautiful hands appeared like fans at her wrists.

"I've come to crash your party, Annie—can you put up with me?"

"Lovely," Anna said, "perfectly lovely." But she stood frozen inside the hallway, even as Rosalind bent towards her, pressing her face against hers, nuzzling her cheek. This was the very moment that Luke chose to come down the stairs. He looked even worse than Anna felt. She made introductions, and explained about Luke's flight. "I know just the thing to pick you up—and throw you down again," Rosalind declared, tugging a litre bottle out of her overnight bag. "Line Aquavit."

An hour later the Aquavit bottle was three-quarters empty. Rosalind and Luke were sitting in easy chairs before the gas fire, getting on famously. They'd discovered they both had one thing in common—a loathing for England. It didn't seem to matter that Rosalind's venom was directed at what the government had made of her country in the past ten years, whereas Luke's was the product of the last few hours' air-borne misery. When Anna came by with a plate of pâté and crackers, Rosalind was explaining the inequities of the British electoral system, and Luke was vigorously nodding.

Anna returned to the kitchen, no longer flustered at Rosalind's presence, but furious: a Martha shown up by her slothful, disputacious sister. Deceiving sister. For why had Rosalind gone to all the trouble to dress up as the Duchess of Malfi in order to crash her piddling little party—how had she known about the party in the first place? And why bother to chat up Luke, who looked more and more to Anna's eyes like a stranger sitting there by her gas fire: a disruptive, unpredictable stranger.

Varti showed up next, in jeans and a handknit sweater. Rosalind, though perfectly polite, seemed to have little to say to her, and Luke, under the delayed impact of the Aquavit, had fallen silent. Luckily, Fiona and Maeve arrived soon after Varti. Maeve's cheeks were fever-red; she was wearing an elaborate party dress, all holly and ivy and golden ribbons, though Fiona was in her customary black. She looked right through the people in the room and took up a position in the farthest corner. Maeve had brought the cat along and a pad of draw-ing paper; she immediately sat down at the rickety table where the food was set out and started making sketches which she wouldn't let anyone see.

Simon arrived last of all, bearing Miss Molesworth's excuses. He couldn't stay long, he explained—he was on his way to Berkshire to spend Christmas with his father. "Really?" said Luke in a tone that alarmed Anna—it was baiting, nasty. For a moment she thought that Luke was jealous, that Rosalind had mentioned something to him—*Mind you don't break his heart, Annie*—but she convinced herself that Luke was simply recoiling from someone so helplessly a stage Englishman. She rushed over with a tray of mulled wine, which she'd made twice as potent as the recipe suggested.

Returning with more pâté, cheese and bread, Anna found Luke making loud, derogatory remarks on the English brand of Christmas tree: paralytically stunted, egregiously ugly, despite or because of all the frippery heaped upon it. Anna felt like striking him—it was Maeve who'd made the bulk of the ornaments. But then she realized that Luke was not only exhausted but half seas over, as well. She could have strangled Rosalind, or at least ordered her out of her house—Rosalind's house—then and there. Instead she crept over to Luke, putting her arm through his to draw him away, whispering that he ought to go upstairs and lie down. But before he could make out what she was saying, Nicholas barged in.

The room fell completely silent, either because Nicholas was so obviously drunk, ten times as drunk as Luke, or because Rosalind had risen from her chair and walked across to the bowl of mulled wine. Not walked, but made her progress, the way Elizabeth the First might have done through a string of shires. Her taffeta hissed as she crossed the floor; she ladled out a huge cup of wine, not seeming to care that the lace of her cuffs had drooped into the bowl and been stained a deep red. It was a performance, all right, and it seemed to be aimed at Nicholas, who was playing the courtier, bowing low to her, accepting the cup of wine she held out to him, and then breaking the church hush by announcing he'd come to borrow a cup of sugar.

"Sugar, sherry, anything to get out of that bloody house. It's bedlam over there," he explained. "Newborn twins—mewl and puke wherever you step."

Rosalind calmly ladled out another steaming cup and held it up to Nicholas, who stood rocking on his heels beside her, sloshing wine

down his white vicuña shirt. She gave a brilliant smile, an angel on top
of the Christmas tree smile, and addressed them all. "I propose we drink
a toast. To the peerless progenitor." But she put down her cup
untouched and made no attempt to join in the weak chorus of congrat-
ulations that fluttered through the room. Nicholas didn't seem to care;
he helped himself to another cup of wine and grabbed an empty chair,
close to the gas fire. Across from him, Luke, who'd disengaged himself
from Anna's arm, lay sprawled over the sofa. Fiona still sat stiffly in the
corner, with Maeve asleep on her lap, while Simon made conversation
with Varti about the quality of English drinking water. Anna turned
and fled into the kitchen.

Varti found her there a few moments later. She was due at the hospital, she explained—she'd be in touch later on. She'd like to have a
proper chance to meet Luke—perhaps they could come to dinner one
night during the holidays? Anna tried to make her stay just a quarter of
an hour longer—she was sure that with Varti there, nothing really disastrous could happen. But Varti left all the same, and Anna, trying not
to feel betrayed, turned her efforts to persuading Luke to come up the
stairs and be tucked into bed under a heavy comforter. Ten minutes
later he stumbled back into the kitchen where Anna was mulling up
another vat of wine. He pinioned her arms and started muttering something she couldn't quite make out—he wanted to tell her, he had to ask
her—"Later," she cried, fighting free of him at last. Luckily, she'd
smelled the cranberries burning.

When she next had a chance to turn round, Luke was slumped at the
table, snoring. She covered his head with a dishtowel, praying it would
keep out the light, and hurried back to the parlour with yet another tray
of drinks and mince pies. Maeve was gone—Simon had carried her
upstairs to the guest room, where she wouldn't be disturbed. Meanwhile,
the conversation had taken another precipitous turn. The mildness of
the weather had led them from the depletion of the ozone layer to the
greenhouse effect, through to the imminent flooding of London.

"What a lot of fuss and mischief over nothing," Simon was saying.
"Why, we've often had freakish winters—there's nothing new in this.
We've had primroses in December and snow in June long before aerosol
cans were invented." His eyes were fixed in the direction of the hallway, as if he were summoning up the energy to grab his overcoat from
the peg and be off, father-bound in the balmy night.

Nicholas prevented him. Putting his arm round Simon, he pressed on him another cup of wine, all the while speaking in a bluff and kindly tone of voice. "Did you know, Simon old bean, that the buds on that Grade A, Class One magnolia in front of our gate are actually open? Poking their null and spongy little heads out of the fuzzy sheaths, ready to erupt into the most voluptuous bloom?"

"Rubbish," Simon answered, gulping down wine as if that were the best way to keep from spilling it.

"God's truth, old boy. I'll take you to see them, right now, no trouble at all—I insist. Who's got a torch?"

"I do!" Anna shouted, far too eagerly—to get rid of Simon and Nicholas at one stroke was an opportunity not to be missed. She ran to fetch the torch, but by the time she got back, Nicholas was in full flood again.

"Cressy's got heaps of magnolia in the house—she's forcing them open. Vegetal rape, you might say. Do you know, Simon, it has these marvellous, creamy, cup-like blooms—awfully like female genitalia. Much more so than figs. I don't know why Lawrence went on so about figs. Especially that lovely streak of pink down the outside of the petal—purplish pink, the very shade of stroked and swelling—"

"Care for a mince pie? They're lovely and hot." This from Anna, who had practically rammed her tray into Nicholas's mouth. Miming indignation, he refused the pie, picked up what was left of his bottle of brandy, and made his way towards the door. Halfway there he stopped and stood upon his dignity:

"Ah, yes. There's the small matter of that cup of sherry—or was it sugar?"

Anna felt absurdly aggrieved. Nicholas had addressed not her but Rosalind with this request. Of course it was Rosalind's cottage—but it was *her* sugar being loaned. Why hadn't he thought to ask her, why had he barged in at all? And what had he said to upset Fiona so? For here she was, having jumped up from her chair and pushed into the middle of the room, as if her way were blocked by mounds of earth, or a flood-tide. Her silence was far more distressing than any shouting could have been. Over her face a stain was spreading, exactly the bruise-purple of magnolia blossoms.

"Right, then, I'll be off." But it was Simon rather than Nicholas who, springing up from the petit-point piano stool (there was no

piano), took his leave. Anna followed him into the hallway, feeling
she owed Simon some special courtesy for having carried up Maeve,
for having refused to take Nicholas's bait. She watched as Simon
reached for his coat and fought his way into it, looking about wildly
for the glove he'd lost. Finally he found it, crushed in a pocket and
strangely stained with something sticky, sharply scented. For a
moment Anna was filled with the wildest surmise—did Simon really
go about with used condoms in his coat pockets? What he eventually
succeeded in extricating, however, was nothing more compromising
than a branch of mistletoe.

"Sorry—I forgot to present it to you on arrival. It's rather the worse
for wear, but you'll accept the good intentions?" He looked as crushed
as his overcoat; not standing, but almost crouching in the hallway, ten-
dering the mangled, sticky sprig.

Anna gave way to impulse. She reached and took the spongy mess
from Simon's hands, held it up over his head, bent forward and kissed
him. She'd aimed for his cheek, but as if he'd foreseen, indeed arranged
her gesture, he flung his arms around her, kissing her on the mouth. His
tongue was warm, fragrant with cinnamon and cloves, and he was
pressing her so close to him in the drafty hall that it seemed the line
between their mouths, their clothes, their very bodies had been broken.

Then he pulled away and rushed out the door, leaving a glove
behind him. Just as Anna was bending down to pick it up, Luke came
in from the kitchen, carrying a pitcher of freshly made eggnog and a
motley assortment of glasses. He couldn't have seen, he mustn't have
seen. Anna stuffed the glove into her pocket, grabbed Luke's arm and
hauled him back into the parlour.

Which Nicholas still graced, rocking on his heels and examining
the contents of the mantelpiece. Luke poured out the eggnog into
glasses, and when no one made a move towards them, proceeded to
drain them, one by one. Rosalind and Fiona sat side by side, not saying
a word: with their cropped heads and long, thin bodies, they looked
like sisters, deaf-mute Siamese twins. Anna looked around her. On the
piano stool lay a toppled tray of mince pies—one of them had been
ground into the rug. Someone had spilled a cup of wine on the
mahogany table, making a thick white cloud under the polish. The
silence in the room was far more poisonous than any argument, yet no
one seemed prepared to break it off like the heel of a loaf and say

something, anything. . . . This was awful, this was utter disaster. Anna couldn't help herself—she put her hands up to her head and screamed, "Stop!"

No one looked in the least surprised.

"Please, everyone, it's Christmas Eve. Why don't we play a game? What about snapdragon, charades, blind man's buff?"

It was Rosalind who insisted on the latter. And she did so by turning to Fiona and filching her black silk scarf. "Here's our blindfold," she said, winding it round her hand as though it were a skein of wool. She walked up to Nicholas, slipping the scarf over his eyes, tying it so tight Anna winced. Nicholas said nothing, even as Rosalind took his hands and raised him from his chair; spun him round and around as Luke pushed all the furniture against the walls.

Nicholas lunging here and there like a dancing bear, snatching in this direction, grabbing in that. Or opening his arms wide, a hawk circling Rosalind whose taffeta whistled as she rushed across the room, while Anna and Luke jumped to get out of her way, and Fiona stood silently, defiantly in the doorway, keeping herself outside the game. Until Nicholas left off chasing Rosalind, whirled round and dove straight for Fiona. She stood there and watched him, as if she weren't inside her body at all, as if the arm by which he tugged her towards him was no more than a sleeve pinned to a dressmaker's dummy. Standing stock-still as he ripped off his blindfold, holding her fast with his free hand.

Afterwards, when they'd put the furniture back and tidied the cushions; when Nicholas had left without his cup of sugar and Luke had stumbled up to bed for good; while Rosalind and Fiona were busy doing the washing-up, Anna crept back into the sitting room. She picked up Fiona's scarf from the mantelpiece to which Nicholas had thrown it and drew it over her eyes, pulling it so tight it cut into her face. No, he couldn't have seen, there was no possible way he could have known which of them was standing in the doorway. Anna reached up and loosened the scarf till it slid down round her neck. Women's voices, muffled, indistinguishable floated in from the kitchen, obscuring the image in the mirror: a black ring, slicing Anna's head off from her shoulders.

# XVI

# COUNTRY PLEASURES

It was only after all the presents had been opened and the turkey bunged into the oven that Anna made the discovery. And that was only because, Rosalind having proposed a walk, Anna had been obliged to hunt out her wellies from behind the coat rack. Slipped into one of them was a plastic bag containing a clumsily wrapped package. Ripping it open, Anna called out excitedly about treasure hunts, the joys of surprise. *The Illustrated Glossary of Architecture, 850-1830.* There was no card, and so she turned to the flyleaf: *For Anna, with very best wishes, Simon.*

Luke was calling from upstairs. "I *said*, where the hell's my scarf?"

"We used it to stuff the turkey," Rosalind replied, coming into the hall just as Anna slipped Simon's book into her pocket. "Honestly, Annie, he sounds as though he's been married to you forever. Why should you know where his scarf is? Why do men always expect women to have some seventh sense about where they've mislaid their handkerchiefs and neckties?"

"Anna! Why aren't there any gloves in this Christ-bitten house!"

Rosalind pushed Anna outside.

"He's got an awful hangover," Anna explained. "He's never like this, he's a university administrator, for heaven's sake, he's—I don't know what's come over him. He probably caught a bug on the plane."

When they were halfway down the street, they heard a door slam. Luke caught up with them, gloveless, bootless, scarfless. He was wearing a pair of jeans Anna had never seen before—in fact, she had never known him to wear anything more casual than corduroys, and that under duress. And all he had on his feet was a pair of disintegrating sneakers.

"You'll get all muddy," Rosalind warned.

"Bugger the mud!"

"I'm afraid I haven't got the right equipment. But you're welcome to have a go."

"Rosalind, please—" Anna had meant to whisper, but found herself shouting so loudly she was sure Mrs. Higley would hear. She tried again. "Where shall we go?"

"To the pub," Luke growled. Neither woman paid him any attention.

"We'll go to Campsey Old Church," Rosalind announced. Luke groaned. "Not a bloody church."

"Why not, on Christmas Day? Besides, it's disaffected—redundant, what's the euphemism they use nowadays for 'dead'? Simon would know—right, Annie? Come on, there's a footpath that shouldn't be too hard on your trainers, Luke, though why you won't wear wellies I simply cannot fathom."

Rosalind wore the expensive kind with little straps on the side; Anna lubbered along in her Polish imports. She was wearing a tweed skirt and a handknit sweater she'd much rather have had as a present from Luke than as yet another self-indulgence. Or, come to think of it, as a gift from Rosalind. The only thing she'd left for Anna underneath the tree had been an envelope containing a filecard with a typed text: *I never in my life felt so entangled in politics as I do at this moment. I hang on the newspapers. I feel I dare not miss a speech. One begins to feel that it's one's duty to what remains of civilization to care for those things and that writers who do not are traitors.*

Unable to place the quotation, Anna had been a little offended by its belligerency. Rosalind hadn't ventured a word of explanation, not even after she'd unwrapped her Booker novel and kissed Anna thank-you. Anna had been as disappointed by this lapse as Maeve must have been by her art set. The child had looked at it for a long while, but hadn't touched any of the brushes or colours. When she'd caught her mother's eyes on her, she'd put away Anna's offering and reached instead for the face paints and costume Fiona had given her: a harlequin outfit, black down one half, pure white on the other.

Anna could hear Luke labouring behind them, slipping on the damp chalk. She didn't see why it was slippery. It hadn't rained for a week; it was, in fact, a distressingly warm day, nothing like what Luke had left behind—ice and blizzards and frozen pipes. This misty mildness was exactly the climate in which microbes flourish, she thought, hearing Luke cough behind her. She wished the lane weren't so narrow and that they could walk side by side, arm in arm. They hadn't yet had a minute alone together, except for the aborted embrace in the kitchen, which she'd begun to confuse with Simon's attack under the mistletoe.

There was a stile to negotiate. Rosalind practically jumped over it, her hair a brief, angry flash of red. Anna followed cautiously, laboriously—why had she chosen to wear a skirt? Or rather, why had Rosalind insisted on taking them through farmers' fields? Luke stumbled halfway up, and nearly went head over heels. Anna was suddenly furious with him. What was the matter, he was never this clumsy at home, why couldn't he negotiate a simple stile? He'd been acting much more strangely than jet lag or hangover could account for. It was almost as though he wanted to make the worst possible impression on everyone, including her. Anna waited for Luke, hands in her pockets, clutching Simon's book as though it could ward off all evils. If only they were on that beach along the Ivory Coast; if only they could hang on till they got to the sun—

On and on they walked, the women's boots glistening in the wet grass, Luke's canvas sneakers squelching. A listless, lackadaisical day, the weather dull, the light forlorn, yet Anna wanted to stretch out her arms and draw it all into her embrace: jasmine flowering in the hedge; ridges of flint and chalk inside the furrows; even the nettles and the cow patties underfoot—things that were what they were in spite of us, defying us. If Varti were here, she could have spoken this out loud—you could say anything to Varti—but Varti was on duty at the hospital, dealing with other things that were what they were: tumours, blood clots, embolisms. . . . And perhaps because Anna wanted too much to find someone she could tell things to, real things, true things, she fell behind the others, looking back to see another wanderer, an angular woman with a walking stick and a determined stride. "Look—" she called out, but no one seemed to hear. "Look, look behind you—" But by the time Rosalind turned her head only sheep were to be seen, browsing noiselessly in the mist.

"It really is ridiculously mild," Rosalind observed. "There'll be lambs before long, well out of season. And then a thick frost, and they'll freeze to death on the hillsides."

"Where is this bloody church, anyway?" Luke's voice was shaky; Anna rushed over to him in alarm. He was pale, sweating; his face had that bright green tinge you find on potatoes growing too near the surface of the soil.

Rosalind strode on, calling back, "Around this rise, and past the level crossing, through the farmyard and up the hill. Look, you can see the tower."

Half an hour later, they were walking round it. Anna could just discern the popped eyes and leering tongue of a gargoyle high over the church door. It was locked, and there were instructions to ask for the key at Breaky Bottom Farm. Anna was suggesting they go look for it when Luke interrupted.

"No way. Never. I refuse to go a step farther. These places are always more interesting outside than in. And this exterior—" he pointed to the shaky buttresses, the wind-chewed stone, "is definitely not worth a detour." And so while Rosalind walked back in the direction of the farm, Anna followed Luke to a fine growth of gravestones in the far corner of the churchyard. The slabs veered crazily, like teeth in an ancient jaw. Some had split in half. Anna put her arm through Luke's. He didn't seem to notice, but kept staring down at the carvings on a row of headstones—hourglasses, knobbly skulls, dulled scythes—till Rosalind came back empty-handed.

"The farmer and his wife are spending Christmas in Majorca. Besides, they don't keep the key any more. Sorry."

Luke went straight to bed when they got back. Anna was busy with the turkey, which she'd almost convinced herself would not give anyone botulism, though it had smelled undeniably pongy in its precooked state. Rosalind was wandering restlessly about the house, unable to sit down long enough to read even a page of a book. She'd given up trying to help Anna set the table—she kept dropping things and apologizing, then falling into fits of silence.

Yet dinner went without a hitch: the turkey was adequately worshipped, the pudding demolished, and Luke's leftover eggnog polished off—by Luke alone, since Anna touched nothing but Perrier, and Fiona and Rosalind preferred to stick to wine. Luke didn't seem to be offended—he looked much better for his nap, and his mood had turned as smooth and plush as the eggnog he was tossing back. Rosalind, too, was back to her usual self—she was in the middle of telling them what hell it had been growing up a bishop's daughter when Nicholas wandered in through the back door with a bottle of Sheep

Dip whiskey under his arm and the shreds of a fuschia-coloured, tissue-paper crown on his head.

This time Anna nearly wept. She wanted to tell him to go home, but here she was letting herself be nuzzled on the cheek, wished a Merry Christmas; here she was finding a chair for him, sitting him down opposite Rosalind, who hadn't acknowledged Nicholas's arrival, but was asking Luke when they were flying out for the Ivory Coast. Before he could answer, Nicholas, trying to be conciliatory, leapt in.

"You'll have to get to the airport a good six hours before you're meant to take off. The security will be especially tight after—"

"We'll phone and find out." Anna didn't want to get on to the subject of aerial terrorism, not with Maeve here. Anna made a point of passing her the plate of tangerines and nuts, which Maeve immediately tried to feed to the cat.

Luke was talking now. "Of course they knew. And of course they acted, just as always, to save their own skins. Diplomatic immunity is what it's called. Selective murder—"

Anna thumped her water glass on the table. "Let's drink a toast to—to being together at Christmas."

Nicholas, pouring out a tumblerful of whiskey and lifting his glass, put on a choir-boy singsong: "God bless us every—"

"To the worst of times." It was the first time Fiona had spoken since they'd sat down to table.

"Every generation thinks it's living in the worst of times," said Luke, almost kindly. Too kindly, for Fiona tore into him.

"It's only our generation which can flip a switch and kill itself a thousand times over, not to mention every living thing on earth. It's only our generation that can gas whole villages—whole countries—that can—"

"Come along, Maeve, let's see if there's anything good on. . ." Anna's voice trailed off. She'd remembered she had no telly. Resolute, she jumped up from the table and went to fetch a notepad and pencil from the study. She gave them to Maeve, but the child shook her head and wriggled closer to her mother, who had lapsed back into silence.

"Here we are," Rosalind was saying, "here we are living in the very worst of times, and yet I know people who think we're still in the forest of Arden, who curl up their whole thinking lives with the collected works of Trollope or the Silver Poets, or Virginia Woolf—"

"Or who slum it with the latest Pryce-Jones, the aesthetico-intellectual equivalent of soft porn," Nicholas declared, all joviality. "May they keep on slumming to their hearts' content, so long as it fattens the assets." Rosalind's reply could have scratched steel:

*Out in the street it's dark*
*and my conscience glitters ahead of me*
*like salt strewn on the pavement.*

Into the silence that followed, Anna rushed. "As we are a doomed race, chained to a sinking ship, as the whole thing is a bad joke, let us do our part; mitigate the sufferings of our fellow prisoners, be as decent as we possibly can." There was something she'd left out, something about flowers and air cushions—but what did it matter? For while Nicholas was clapping his hands, calling out, "Well done, Mrs. Dalloway, well done," Fiona had scraped back her chair and jumped up from the table.

"Go on talking, on and on until you choke yourselves." Each of her words was a small explosion, leaving holes behind. Everyone stared up at her, everyone but Maeve, who was scoring a line into the notepad Anna had brought her, driving her pencil violently back and forth. Luke left the table, but no one called after him. Everyone was watching Fiona, who kept on talking in a voice as contorted as her face.

"There's nothing but words for you. Everything is just words about words about words. Well, you're liars, all of you. Liars. Because there are things—real things—that no amount of words can shove away. Things that happen to people, things that are made to happen. I'm sick of you—sick of the lot of you. Don't you see anything outside of words and books and paper games? Everything's smashing up, blowing up—everything. Don't you know that? Can't you see?"

No one answered. The only sound was Fiona's harsh breathing, the silence her hands made, gripping the edge of the table. Until Nicholas poured out another glass of whiskey. "Of course we see," he said, gravely, attentively. "And when the world goes bang, the saving remnant won't be any pious souls chanting holy, holy, holy. From what I understand, it will be cockroach colonies. First the dinosaurs, then the mammals, then the insects inherit the earth. Why shouldn't they have their chance? Come, don't let's hold grudges—let's all lift a glass to the brilliant future of our six-legged friends."

Fiona stared at him for a moment; stared as though her eyes were a pair of opened scissors. And then, without a look at anyone who might have stopped her, she grabbed the tablecloth and tugged it out from under the dishes. They leapt and clattered and shook but not one fell off the table to shatter on the floor. Fiona began to laugh, a dry, clacking laugh. She stretched out her hand to Maeve, who jumped up and took it, walking with her mother out of the room and out of Rest Harrow, the cat following at their heels.

Nicholas had vanished by the time Anna got back to the table, having vainly tried to lure her neighbours back. There was only a rumpled paper crown to show he'd been there at all. Rosalind was folding the tablecloth into a neat square, ignoring the wine and gravy stains. And then she left the kitchen and came down ten minutes later, with her bag. She shook hands with Luke and hugged Anna tightly. Within moments they could hear her car drive off.

They sat and looked at one another across the ruins of the table till Luke pitched forward and threw up his Christmas dinner into the dish of cranberry sauce.

*       *       *

Luke spent most of the next twenty-four hours retching into the toilet. Food poisoning, Varti confirmed, and a nasty case of it at that. Luckily it wouldn't require hospitalization—he would simply have to spend several days in bed, recovering. What had he been into? Anna mentioned the eggnog, and Varti shrugged her shoulders. "After all the fuss in the papers, if people *will* insist on eating raw eggs—"

"He's from Canada," Anna temporized. Hadn't she warned him, Varti asked. Of course she had, Anna insisted. Or at least, she'd tried. He wouldn't have believed her, anyway—he still thought of the egg as nature's perfect food.

Anna spent the next few days in the kitchen, brewing up the endless pots of broth and weak tea which Varti had prescribed, and listening to reports about the earthquake in Armenia. What had happened there was beyond imagining, infinitely more important than the sufferings of poor Luke, staggering between bed and toilet bowl. She would send the money she'd have lounged away under the African sun to the earthquake victims, and in the meantime lavish tea and tenderness upon her ailing fiancé. For that was how she thought of him now, even though there'd been rather more of irritation than avowal between them since his arrival.

By the time New Year's Eve came round, Luke, though still shaky and many pounds thinner, pronounced himself well enough to go out to Varti's for dinner. By this point Anna had reconciled herself to the wreck of their holiday, declaring Luke's entire visit to have fallen into the category of an Act of God. They'd have another chance at Easter—perhaps they'd go off to Yugoslavia or Greece (someplace, at any rate, where there were no earthquakes) and take up where they'd left off in August. Anna watched Luke from the bathroom door; he was soaping his beard and didn't seem to have noticed his old razor, which she'd purposely left out for him. It didn't matter, she told herself; if anything, it was a good sign, a new beginning.

In the car she explained about Varti, or rather, she told a few fictions. She said that Varti was her doctor—which was true, since she'd gone to her once about a sinus infection. She didn't describe the lecture at the Meeting House, or their fortnightly dinners at the Station Café. He wouldn't understand, she told herself. He wouldn't see what drew her to Varti, what made Varti so necessary to her. And she knew she couldn't explain it, that it would sound infantile, self-serving—this need for what she could only call love, unconditional love, the kind a parent has for a child, and that, like energy itself, can never be lost or destroyed but only changed into other forms. That much she remembered from Grade Twelve physics—that much she knew about love.

Varti lived in a modern house on the edge of the county town—if it had been daylight there would have been a view clear up to the Downs. There would also have been a garden visible from the huge window at the end of the sitting room. Varti confessed to them that her one indulgence was a gardener. She'd always managed without a char, even when the children were small, but she simply could not abandon the garden. There followed an account of what kinds of bulbs and perennials she'd planted, with Varti conjuring iris and day lilies, phlox and begonias and rhododendrons out of the glistening dark before them.

"Don't you lose a lot of heat through the glass?" Luke finally asked, trying to switch the subject. "It must be expensive."

"It is. Especially when I have to replace it. Because of the rocks thrown through it. Though I mustn't dramatize—it only happened once."

"Rocks?"

"Oh, it's not bad at all in Sussex," Varti explained. "It's the housing estates in the Midlands or London that get worst hit. They've installed an emergency phone system there for Asian households—it's the women who really suffer, left alone all day, shut up inside and afraid to go out. Because of people throwing stones or setting fires. Or just shouting, calling names, writing things. I find what happened to me here rather difficult to understand. You see, I was born in this country, I have never had any other home, any other culture. My son tells me things are different in Canada."

"Not that different," Luke admitted. "It depends where you live. But on the other hand, in Canada nearly everyone's an immigrant."

"Visible minorities," Anna interjected, a phrase she'd heard used as often as "reduced for quick sale" or "trespassers will be prosecuted."

"Visible minority," repeated Varti, thoughtfully. "It's a nice name for nigger, is it?"

Luke jumped in this time. "When are we having dinner, Varti? It smells delicious. I'm sick of crackers and broth."

Varti had prepared grilled chicken and rice for him—bland and nourishing—and Mongolian hot pot for Anna and herself. But just as she was carrying out the pudding, she got a call from the hospital. "You two go ahead," she said. "I'll be back as soon as I can. Help yourself to coffee. Oh, and Luke—I'd stay away from the trifle if I were you. Stick to water biscuits, will you?"

An hour passed, and Varti showed no signs of returning. Anna cleared the table and washed up—Luke, after all, was still convalescent, though he'd flouted Varti's warnings, and polished off half the trifle. He sat leafing through a medical magazine, while Anna roamed about the house, which she'd never visited before. In spite of what Varti had told her, Anna really had expected some flash of exotica, anything to relieve the Standard British Décor. But there were no silks or beads, no Benares brass, no reproductions of Mughal paintings or Hindu deities. There were no paintings or prints, either, just a few posters taped to the kitchen walls: CND, Friends of the Earth, Greenpeace. Fixed to the refrigerator was a small postcard, an entirely black surface with a candle burning, and the caption *It's better to light a candle than to sit crying in the dark*.

"Stop prowling about, Anna—you should be ashamed of yourself. Look, why don't we go? It's getting late, she won't be back for hours, yet." But Anna didn't answer. She felt no guilt at examining the walls of Varti's house, gleaning clues as to what this woman was really like. Walls were public property, after all.

"Anna? We've really got to get going. I've a plane to catch tomorrow morning, remember?"

"Coming."

But she walked instead into a room that turned out to be Varti's study. Medical books were crammed onto the shelves which covered every wall but one. And there, on the wall behind Varti's desk was the only real picture in the house.

At first, Anna took in nothing but the background of black cloud, with rain like dark incisions slanting down. And then she saw the woman lying shrouded to the breasts, blue eyes rolling up, mouth slack with grief. Her golden hair coiled under her, except for one lock, pointing up like a unicorn's horn. Her hands were tightly clasped over her breasts, her head twisting from her neck. And above her a pack of clouds became white horses, stamping and straining into the dark.

A kneeling rider leaned out over the first horse. Anna couldn't tell if it were male or female, but with its golden horn of hair it seemed a twin to the dying woman below. The rider hung down its arms to pluck up a small, naked child that belonged to the woman and yet was leaving her, its arms beseeching the rider, *take me up, take me away, deliver me—*

"Please, Anna." Luke in the doorway, standing stock-still, his arms tightly crossed against his chest, as if his ribs had dissolved, and this were the only thing he could do to keep his heart in place. "Anna, please." In his voice the outstretched arms of the naked child, pleading. And Anna knew, with the clairvoyance that comes to those on the brink of chasms, that she ought to run to him, put out her arms and take him in. That to do so would be to repair everything that had gone wrong between them, to offer the one thing she had always refused him. And perhaps she would have gone to him if he'd stood there for only one moment more; if they hadn't, that very minute, heard Varti's key in the lock, heard her walking in the front door.

They left for Pyeford soon after—Varti was tired and distressed. A miscarriage, she explained; a woman who had lost two babies previously, and who'd nearly managed to carry this one to term. Luke looked terribly pale, and Anna bundled him out to the car with apologies to Varti. They drove back to Pyeford as quickly as Anna could manage, Luke racing for the loo as soon as Anna opened the door, then staggering back to bed, clutching his stomach. Without a word of reproach Anna cleaned up the mess, fetched cool cloths for his head, and proceeded to pack his case for him. She took special care with his razor, carefully padding it in plastic and stowing it in a side pocket of the valise.

That night Anna, anxious and unable to sleep, rose from the spare bed she'd been using ever since Luke had arrived. In the dark, she made her way to her own room, where Luke lay sleeping. The bed was too narrow for them both, but Anna gently pushed her way inside, pulling up the covers and burrowing as closely as she could against him. Luke woke, at last—he turned to her and after a moment, reached out his arms. He held her awkwardly, as though it were necessary, for the sake of her health, to keep some distance between them. They lay together a long while, without speaking. When Luke fell back to sleep again, Anna gently disengaged her arm, rubbing it to bring back some feeling as she made her way to the spare room across the corridor. She lay awake, thinking of horses stampeding across the dark; babies abandoned before they were ever born.

# XVII

# THE PAPERS

Alone again, the house set back to rights, Anna prepared to don the equivalent of diver's mask and oxygen tank and plunge into the matter of her long-neglected book on Virginia Woolf. What did it matter if she knew she couldn't write the only necessary book, the one that would conjure up the voices of the dead, transmute the silences they'd left behind them. She would simply do what everyone else in her situation had done before her: obscure, evade, ellide, telling her readers far more about her own chosen fictions than about Virginia Woolf's. *We are in the dark about writers; anybody can make a theory: the germ of a theory is almost always the wish to prove what the theorist wishes to believe.*

And so it was hardly auspicious that, having decided to go under, having made the day's first pot of tea and set out for the study, Anna should be interrupted by an unfamiliar thump coming from the direction of the front door. It turned out to be a newspaper, shoved through the letter slot. Either it had been disgorged by the Medusa head or else it had been delivered by mistake, but Anna wasn't about to call back the delivery girl, who was well up the road by now. She would simply lay the thing aside till someone knocked at the door to reclaim it.

An hour later, Anna found herself profoundly thankful that she did not subscribe to a newspaper. Not only had this morning's offerings plunged her into prophecies of planetary devastation and economic ruin, but she'd wasted precious time she should have spent in starting off her book. Wasted it reading column after column of interpretation and analysis; studying photographs that begged to be pasted on Fiona's walls. She kept thinking, as she read, of Fiona's outburst on Christmas day about everything smashing and blowing up; she recalled that first lecture she'd attended at the Friends' Meeting House with Varti— *Fatalism is fatal*. And as she read further and deeper into the paper, cataloguing the expressions of alarm and opposition in the Letters to the Editor, she became more and more disgusted. Words on paper, that's all it was. Just as the radio's announcement of yet another plane crash this morning had been so much undifferentiated noise in the air. Newspaper, rusepaper. She would stuff the whole thing into the rubbish bin or under the sink—use it to wrap up vegetable peelings, tea leaves. And go straight to her desk, her book—which would also be nothing but words on paper if not mere electronic pulses invisibly lodged between chip and screen.

Crumpling up the paper and thumping it into the bin, Anna resolved to have done with all further distractions. Yet as soon as she clicked on the computer, she was faced with the pattern Luke had set there all those months before: hearts and daggers. And all she could focus on was what had gone wrong, or hadn't gone anywhere at all, during Luke's visit.

They'd talked of nothing but the safest, most sensible things the morning of his departure. He'd seemed more like his old self on the drive to the airport, swearing he'd never eat another egg in all his life; declaring chickens to be far lower on the evolutionary scale than snails. They had laughed together, even when the traffic became horrendous and it seemed that Luke would surely miss his plane. At the airport there'd been time for only the briefest of hugs and then she'd found herself alone, bereft, watching Luke's suitcase disappear on a conveyor belt, and then Luke himself vanish. He hadn't turned to wave. There'd been simply too many people in the lobby, too many luggage trolleys, overexcited children, and security guards. Not that this was an omen; nothing was over except, thank God, the calamity of Christmas.

To clear her head, she broke another vow, shutting the computer down and taking a walk up the chalk road, to the very top of the Downs. The lack of rain, the absence of polar gales, the pale but persistent sun made her curiously happy, as if it all had been arranged for her private solace. Winter wheat sprang up in the fields below, a fresh and bladed green. She hadn't known how beautiful it could be, this continuity of grass, of growing things: midwinter spring. She wished she'd taken Luke up here instead of to that abandoned church—he would have liked this, he would have understood her attachment to this place if he'd gone walking with her on the Downs.

A train ploughed past in the valley below: four coaches, bound for the county town in which, even now, Varti would be listening for foetal heartbeats; encouraging, consoling, soothing, healing. The train disappeared, leaving a great green sea of quiet—you could hardly hear the mosquito whine of traffic from the motorway. Before she could stop herself, Anna remembered an article she'd read in that morning's paper about the danger to city children of lead poisoning from car exhaust. Lucky that Maeve lived here in the country—she'd be all right; Fiona didn't have to worry. As if worrying could stop these things, things she hadn't even known about until reading the paper today. But she wouldn't think of that right now. Her head was clear, her thoughts composed—the wind from the sea had done its work; it was time to get back to her book.

Coming downhill, Anna took the path through the ash glade. At the second stile the white horse was waiting for her, stretching up his long beautiful neck to be stroked. It startled her—she was afraid to climb over, afraid he might rear up—afraid, stupidly, that she might be forced to jump on his back and gallop away, like the girl in the nursery rhyme: *Sally tell my mother I shall never come back.*

Think, said Anna, closing her eyes: think him away. Think of his whiteness against the grass as the whiteness of cream, not of bones picked clean. But the charm refused to work; it wasn't until the horse, pricking up his ears at some disturbance far out of Anna's hearing, galloped off to the farthest corner of the field that she got up the courage to jump the stile and run towards home.

\*       \*       \*

The next day another paper appeared, and this time Anna did catch the delivery girl, who assured her there was no mistake. Indeed, the paper had been ordered on a gift-subscription basis. By whom, Anna demanded. The girl said she should phone the station bookseller's to find out. Anna did, and discovered that a year's subscription to Rest Harrow, Pyeford, Sussex had been paid for by a certain R. Oliver. No, it couldn't be cancelled, as the cheque had already been cashed, and they didn't give refunds. Anna hung up, deciding she would simply let the papers accumulate unread, then let the dustmen deal with them.

But in the end her good intentions came to nothing. She could no more have ignored the summons of the newspaper thumping on the hallway floor than she could have refused to pay a traffic fine, or her income tax. Perhaps it was an unshakeable deference to Authority and

Presence—the same deference that had obtained for her a doctorate and a place in the profession—that made her submit to the paper. Perhaps it was because of the bond it made between herself and Rosalind, who with the paper had given her this gift of her person, since all the editorials and leaders spoke in her voice, and with her politics. At any rate, it became a custom for Anna to collect the paper each morning and sit down at the breakfast table, drinking pots of tea and making discoveries about places and people whose existence she'd never before conceived of. They were real enough to her now, part of the only world of which she felt herself still to be a citizen—the world of paper and ink.

At first she assured herself she'd soon get tired of the news; learn to skim through the paper just for the weather or financial forecasts. She could look at the whole thing as a form of involuntary immunization: the sooner she got used to it, the better. The trouble was that once she got started, she couldn't stop—the problem some people have with tobacco or caffeine, she had with the news. Thus her morning sessions at the kitchen table leaked into early and then later afternoon. She found herself reading the paper from cover to cover, convinced that each sentence hooked into every other, that there was a pattern, a code to be registered, and that she would never make sense of the part unless she'd ingested the whole. And as she read, her head began to feel more and more like a map of the world, with pins—rusty, filth-tipped, tetanus-inducing pins—stuck into ever-extending trouble spots in which Iranian dissidents were executed (eighty thousand at the last count), or plutonium spilled into playgrounds and farmer's fields from cracked carbon-steel containers.

In what little was left of her working day, she turned to Virginia Woolf, not her fiction but the later journals. *Perceptible but ominous friction between public pain and private bliss.* An account of how the Woolfs find a destitute young woman fainting on their doorstep; bring her inside and feed her. *Never saw unhappiness, poverty, so tangible. And felt it's our fault. And she apologized. And what could we do?* Sometimes it seemed she heard Fiona being spoken to: *We pour to the very edge of a precipice. . . . & then?*

And then? The papers couldn't tell her, despite all the editorials and leaders and opinion pieces. For there was no help against the facts. Facts about sports and the weather; facts about hunger and disease and the oblique forms of genocide, mass murder—whatever you chose to call it. It was facts, Anna thought, which were the greatest mysteries. When they were brought to light, they simply went out again. They told you nothing you could understand; nothing you could bear to know.

Face the facts. Anna faced them—they were a mirror that threw back no reflection whatsoever, only shattered glass. She read and recorded one set of facts, which were then displaced by others; she connected one chain of facts with another and another till they were wound so tight she felt them inside her skin, clanking and chafing each time she made the simplest gesture—reaching for the teapot, closing the curtains. Brute facts, plain facts, that remained purely symbolic, like the language in which they were printed out each morning. Words that referred only to other words; words that never touched what they described: things that kept happening, being made to happen.

*       *       *

Famine in the Sudan. Child prostitution in Bogotá. Comparisons between New York's homeless and Calcutta's. Escalation of the civil war in Lebanon; renewed clashes between Palestinians and Israelis.

Anna closed the paper somewhere between lunch and tea. Ran the bath—she had been reading in her dressing gown and slippers; felt a scum on her face, her body leaking offensive and unnameable odours that must be scrubbed away in the always-tepid water. She worked at her skin with a nailbrush, as if to restore a sense of blood moving through her and not just welling in stagnant pools. Dried herself, dressed, and sat down at the vanity. Opened the wings of the mirror for the first time since moving into Rest Harrow; looked up to what had always been there. Three versions of the circle that was her face, and the nothing that outline contained. Three zeros; three open mouths with no sound coming out: three blanks, three holes.

*       *       *

The NATO countries were preparing a strategy to counter the Soviets' Peace Offensive. A whole family in a Midlands village was jailed for child sex-abuse. In Harlem, the Princess of Wales cuddled babies dying of AIDS. On the medical black market, a brisk business was reported in the sale of kidneys. A plane crashed in the Canadian north, killing forty-two passengers, but it wasn't a Boeing, and there were no terrorists involved. The report was only two inches long, and tucked in between the tail end of world news and the sports section.

\*        \*        \*

Four or five hours a night, two or three times a week, Anna babysat while Fiona went out to

1) lectures at the Women's Institute,
2) meetings of the local book club,
3) films in town.

A good thing, if it got her away from her scissors and paste and the pictures Anna had started to save for her, ripping them out till her hands were deep-dyed with printer's ink and would never come clean. But the study door was locked each time Fiona went out. Anna would shut herself up with Maeve, playing checkers or snap, but mostly watching her draw, something Maeve did very little of when Fiona was at home. Sometimes she'd fill a whole page with nothing but doors and windows, or circles whose edges never intersected. When she drew, her face went whiter than the paper, her eyes like the lead of her pencil. She'd bite on the very edge of her tongue, refusing Anna's few attempts at conversation. And though the gift of crayons and chalk pastels and watercolour paints had been given pride of place on her desk, Maeve used only black on white, the lines so strong and clear they seemed etched instead of drawn; indelible.

Later, Anna would read her to sleep from the favourite picture book, the dark and undefined form rising from the mud of the creek and Maeve chanting the words *who am I, who am I?* Until at last she'd fall asleep halfway through the fifteenth reading of the story, and Anna would put down the book and arrange the blankets gently, carefully. Making sure, before she turned out the lights, that the cat lying like a fur boa over Maeve's chest didn't impede the rise and fall of her breathing. Waiting in the kitchen where the electric clock buzzed each minute Fiona stayed out and out and wouldn't come home.

\*        \*        \*

*A sound of weeping wakes you, frightens you so that you run to your mother's room. And find a woman lying on the narrow bed, a woman you've never seen before. Her head presses so hard into the wall it must hurt her; that's why she's crying. Her book has fallen to the floor; all the pages are crushed. A strange woman with her hair down, long and black and terrible snakes coiling over her shoulders, spitting into the lakes of her eyes. This is what they mean when they say "crying your eyes out"—this woman has no eyes in her face, only holes. And from these holes come sounds, not words, but "ah, ah, ah," a sound soft as bleeding. The woman is wearing your mother's dressing gown, her crying shakes it open so her skin pours out like milk from the bottle you smashed on the steps: by accident, it was an accident, but she shouts at you all the same, then holds you so tight against her you can't breathe, your lungs are tissue paper, crushed. Your mother wears her hair coiled round her head; even at night she wears it in braids down her back but this woman's hair is loose and wild: it eats at her face, you can hear it licking and scraping. Why doesn't your mother come back to her room and make this stranger go away? Why doesn't she see you standing here, wanting the woman to go away, unable to stop this wanting, this watching? The weeping woman can't see you; she is trying to fill the holes in her face with the palms of her hands, they root inside her face but still the sound pours out, a hiss or a sigh—"ah, ah, ah."*

*You want to put out your hand and stroke this woman's hair, the way your mother comforts you when you've hurt yourself. But you can't, you can't, the woman can't see you, her hair will stab you and all you can hear is the sound of her tongue cut loose from her mouth, a sound like drowning.*

\*　　　\*　　　\*

"Now this kind of window is particularly interesting because—"

Anna, sitting in a Georgian box pew the colour of honey, was examining her rescuer. Back from his Berkshire Christmas, landing on her doorstep one Sunday afternoon, rattling the knocker till she'd been forced to open the door and let in the wind and the rain and Simon, apologizing for not having called earlier, renewing his invitation to come church-crawling. Finding Anna a good deal thinner than he saw her last, her eyes bleary, her hair uncombed, he didn't wait for a refusal but unhooked her mac from the peg, draped it round her shoulders, and took her off to a gross of country churches: Saxon and Norman, early English, Decorated, Perpendicular.

Simon, who had made his own salvation out of mullions and ogee arches, poppy-heads and predellae. Letting her sit in the choirstalls as he jotted down measurements and made notations. The sun had come out again: it poured through the glass in shapes of tears and knives, striking fires against the stone. He was telling her the names of the shapes: daggers and mouchettes making cusped circles, webs to trap the light.

"Look at the glass, Anna—it's there for you to look at, not through. It's a screen, not a window; it shows us what otherwise we'd never see. A witness, Anna, bearing witness to the light. The light that's here, now. Don't you see what a paradise this world could be if only we'd allow ourselves to see?"

Simon's stained glass, Fiona's photographs, the headings from the papers Anna has devoured. She shook her head, more in bewilderment than in refusal of what he offered her.

"Poor Anna—you must be frozen." Simon was walking over to the box pew, unfastening the latch, giving her his hand to help her out. The pew was slightly raised, the floor tiles uneven. Anna hesitated for only a moment, then gripped Simon's hand. The brief spell of sunlight was over: they had to feel their way out of the church. And though the puddles were all on the other side of the path, he wouldn't let go her hand until they'd reached the car.

# XVIII

# SWANS

Everyone agreed it was unseasonably warm. Snowdrops, having opened with indecent haste, curdled by early February, by which time daffodils had long been blowing trumpets. Succulently scented hyacinth were crowning well before the first of March. Miss Molesworth's black, stump-tailed cat took to sunning itself on the church lamp post, refusing all blandishments to come down. Wood pigeons croaked lust from every hedgerow; primrose shone like pale, damp pats of butter in the ditches; cherry trees burst into feverish bloom and lambs were cutting capers in the grass.

Pyeford shook its collective head, reluctant to unbutton jackets, unpeel gloves. As soon as the leaves unfurled, as soon as the fruit began to form, along would come a blast of winter to chop off their heads. At the village shop mutterings about the greenhouse effect were heard, and Mrs. Higley personally removed all cans of hairspray from the shelves, replacing them with cough mixture, catarrh remedies and assorted brands of decongestant. For the same soft air that coaxed buds into leaf and stroked open the petals' eyes seemed to be breeding microbes in their millions and tens of millions. England's surgeries were filled to overflowing; Varti herself had come down with a vicious form of 'flu—it had been weeks since Anna had seen her.

Anna, too, had been through a bad patch, as she described it to herself, but she was better now. The day after Simon took her church crawling she'd driven into town, to the chemist's, where she'd spent as much on cosmetics and hair grips and perfume as she'd done on the week's groceries. So that when she next sat down at the vanity table she could make a face for herself, mark it with powders and pencils, fix it with anchors in her hair and a name tag for her skin. She'd even gone to a photographic booth in the railway station and sat for her picture, celluloid strips she posted off to Luke, and fixed in each of the frames of the vanity mirror she now kept open at all times.

And she'd abandoned the news, going back to her book. She'd decided to begin with an extended discussion of *Between the Acts*, a novel that opened with a cesspool and closed with a lily pond in which a woman was supposed to have drowned herself. Much of the text was taken up with an estrangement between a couple whom Anna couldn't help likening to Luke and herself. They patched things up at the novel's end, a development from which she drew a certain consolation.

Despite the extraordinary mildness of the weather, Anna spent no time to speak of out of doors, except for her Sunday jaunts with Simon. She wasn't impressed any longer with England's pastoral beauties. From what the papers had told her, the air atop the Downs was only marginally less polluted than that of London, and the blue sea below was foul with discharged sewage, toxic waste, radioactivity. The cows grazing so contentedly in the fields would be over-injected with antibiotics and fed diseased offal, so that their milk might easily be infected with a rare, transmissible form of encephalitis.

And so she divided her time between her study and the various interiors of country churches, half-listening to Simon, half-wondering how things were going on at home, her real home. Her tenant had written to say that everything was fine. She loved the house—it would be difficult to leave, come August. She'd had to have the plumber in to fix some pump or other. The bill was enclosed—she hoped it wasn't extortionate. (It was.) She could have called in another plumber for a second opinion, but the toilet had been leaking pretty badly by then. She was going to paint the laundry room yellow, if Anna didn't mind. (She did.) And, she thought Anna might want to know, in case she heard anything from other sources: Frank was leaving. They'd decided they just couldn't make a go of things together. But she'd have no trouble in paying the rent, there was no problem about that. She was in good spirits, and her work was going well. She'd discovered she actually liked being on her own.

Anna had sent a cheque for the plumber's bill, thrown out Emma's letter, and then fished it from the bin. Re-reading it, she tried to remember what Emma looked like—she was a former student, upper B's, with an interest in the epistolary novel. Quiet, considerate, responsible—or she'd never have let her rent her house in the first place. More country than preppy in her tastes—faded jeans and loose cotton dresses: Woodstock redivivus, Luke had joked. As for Frank, he'd obviously found someone more to his taste. It was just as well—there'd be less wear and tear, all round.

*     *     *

On Sunday afternoon Simon picked her up slightly earlier than usual. They drove to a village on a stream—there was a church with a round tower, and a chantry window embellished by a rare form of plate tracery. This time, however, Anna wouldn't go inside but stood on a small wooden bridge, watching the water rush below. For once she wasn't thinking of dioxins or the devastation of the rainforests. Instead, she mused on Emma's brave remarks about living alone, then started wondering how Rosalind managed. Did she see love, even friendship as a deletion from her truest self, a diminution of her possibilities? Or was she simply too busy to have any private life at all, always travelling, lecturing, politicking? Hadn't Rosalind ever thought of marrying, of having children? She couldn't imagine her with anyone who would tie her down in any way. You could no more keep Rosalind in one place than you could grab hold of a flame, or a jet of water. Whereas she, Anna, couldn't have been more fixed. Like that twig caught against the river bank. The current was trying to dislodge it, but the twig stuck fast.

Everyone, everything else moved on. Fiona was always out these days. Even Nicholas wasn't to be seen—Anna knew because Cressy had mentioned it when they'd met at the village shop. A slender Cressy this time, her blue eyes a little vaguer, as if each pregnancy watered them down. The new babies were curled up in a kind of double-decker pouch against her chest. "Poor Nicky does get a bit fed up with all the children rushing about. Though of course, it's their house as much as his, they have a perfect right to be there—that's why he has the study. And he has such a lot of things to do right now, the new book's been terribly successful, you see. He's negotiating something or other with a film director in London, so he's always away. I'd like this package weighed, Mrs. Higley, it's going to New Zealand of all places."

A door swung shut—she heard Simon calling. "Really, Anna, you should have come inside. It's a magnificent specimen. I only hope the photos turn out. Oh look—just there, upstream!"

A pair of swans was gliding towards them, stopping a little ways from the bridge. Anna did take a good long look at them. Swans were supposed to be beautiful. But she found herself repulsed by the violence of black-and-orange beaks against the shock-white plumage, the muddy stains round their necks. She watched as they dove to feed on the river bottom, then rose up and shook themselves, spreading curiously constricted wings which they then flung back, jiggling their tail feathers. The male was larger, Anna observed—and foul-tempered, too. He kept jabbing at the female, stretching out and doubling back his long neck. Its sinuousness revolted Anna—the nakedness of muscle, the probing beak, the indifferent way in which the female submitted to the pokes and jabs.

"They're ugly. They're hateful. I loathe swans." She stalked away from the bridge, back to the car. Simon called after her, but she wouldn't answer him; they were silent for the first ten minutes or so of the drive back to Pyeford. And then Simon started to talk of Northumbria, where he'd grown up—spoke of how wild and bleak and free the countryside was. "Do you remember asking me once what I'd do if they built some horrible nuclear plant down the road from Pyeford? I said I'd move. Well, I think I'd go back to Northumbria. Somewhere along Hadrian's Wall. Or else on the coast. The only trouble there is the noise from all the planes."

"There's no airport on the Northumbrian coast," Anna said, more crossly than she intended.

"No. But there's an air base. American, I believe. They have all these war planes, they do what's called low-level flying. It drives people mad."

"Then why don't they move? Or make the bloody air base move?" Anna rubbed her hands across her eyes. "I'm sorry, Simon. I'm just feeling out of sorts today. It's this cold, I can't seem to shake it off."

"Ah, well, they do say that Sussex is the catarrh capital of Britain. You really ought to see a bit more of the country, you know. The north is quite remarkable—if you like I could draw up a list of places you should see, between oh, Durham and Lindisfarne. Or I'd gladly—"

"Thanks, Simon, but I'm far too busy to travel anywhere these days." She was afraid he was about to suggest they take the trip together, that he become her personal guide to the small parish churches of Northumbria.

"Ah, yes," he said at last. "Your book."
"My book."
They drove the rest of the way home in silence.

\*       \*       \*

Anna couldn't put it off any longer. She opened the block of writing paper, uncapped her pen, and pulled out all the stops.

> *Darling Luke,*

She stared for a long time at the salutation. It was like wrenching off her arm to write the words and let them lie exposed on the page.

> *I ought to have written this the day you left. I've been worried sick not hearing from you, not knowing what you could be thinking. In fact, I've been through a hellish few weeks, but I've thought it all through now, and I know you've been right all along. It's stupid to live apart—I want to share my life with you, my life and my house and everything else we could have together.*
>
> *Please write—you can't know how much I need to hear from you, love.*

And then, having already squandered her affection, she simply signed her name.

\*       \*       \*

If anyone had asked Anna why she was going up to London, she would have answered, "Pleasure," defiantly enough. She had booked for a matinée, after which she'd just have time to peek in at a gallery or two before an evening of Haydn sonatas. She might even have said she was attempting a shock-cure for what Varti would have diagnosed as " 'flu-like depression" and her Dean denoted as *accedia*, that sloth and melancholy attendant on the decay of the contemplative life.

And perhaps her Dean would have been right, for Anna was going off to London for the sole purpose of mailing her letter to Luke. Superstition, plain and flagrant. She couldn't rid herself of the belief that were she to post the thing from Pyeford or anywhere in the whole of Sussex, it would be as jinxed as Luke's visit had been. Whereas to release it into any one of a thousand London postboxes would be to take it out of the realm of disaster and into the pure air of possibility. Besides, she felt it was time to re-assert herself, her normal, independent self. She would leave the house well before the newspaper arrived; she would inform Fiona that she'd simply have to do without her baby-sitting service for that night. And once she got into Victoria she'd ring up Rosalind to see if they couldn't meet for dinner. Better still, she'd just drop in, the way Rosalind had done to her on Christmas Eve.

Willing herself into a state resembling competence, Anna arrived at the station with a quarter of an hour to spare, marching up to the wicket, slapping down her five pound notes, presenting her ticket to the man in the booth beyond the waiting room door. She found the right platform, she managed to open the compartment door and shut it tight behind her. Marvels, miracles. Perhaps she really was going to undo the damage of the last few weeks; work a counter spell to protect her from all harm. Just to make sure, she held her letter tightly in her hand throughout the trip, determined not to lose it to any lager lout she met along the way.

Yet once off the train, having dropped her letter deep inside the nearest pillar box, Anna knew she'd made a hopeless mistake. She should have kept the letter with her till the last possible moment, kept it as a crutch to get her through a day which suddenly seemed endlessly, appallingly open. She no longer felt any desire for theatre or art or music: all she wanted was to return as fast as possible to the shelter of Rest Harrow. A few yards on from the pillar box, Anna stopped and clutched her handbag closer. She couldn't remember where she was supposed to be going, what she had planned. Helplessly, she turned and turned about, until she found herself caught up in the crush and press of people going down into the Underground.

Hours later, moments later Anna was up and out. Horns were blaring, engines idling, heels slapping against the pavement. She had no idea where she was, but followed the crowd down a flight of stairs and across a stretch of pavement, to the river. From nowhere a man ran headlong into her, an old man, his hair fallen away in huge tufts, leaving an oozing pinkish-brown crust. He raised his hand not to steady himself, but to strike her. Anna backed away and was about to run when she caught sight of her: a slender woman in a shabby dress and broad-brimmed hat, her arms full of books. "If only I don't lose sight of her," Anna prayed, rehearsing some question she would ask, something about directions or the time of day—anything to hold the woman's attention. She was sure to have, if not the answer, then at least a question infinitely more important than any Anna could invent.

The woman walked quickly, purposefully, without a wasted motion. It was all Anna could do to run after her, to keep the edge of her dress, the line of her head in sight. And then, just as Anna thought to have caught up with her, the woman turned and vanished. Disconsolate, Anna walked on the length of a few more streets, until she found herself in front of a long, low building she recognized from her *London Guide*.

Once inside she let herself drift for a while among the Pre-Raphaelites and then the Whistlers, admiring Cicely Alexander and Battersea bridge. Degas' stubby dancers attracted her less—the decomposing skirt of the Little Dancer made her think of the scarf Fiona had worn on Christmas Eve, the one they'd used for playing blind man's buff. Anna reminded herself to buy a postcard of Cicely Alexander to give to Maeve; she checked her watch and decided it was time at last to go to Rosalind's.

On the way out she took a series of wrong turnings and stumbled on a canvas she'd never seen before yet which she recognized instantly as the twin of the painting she'd first seen at Simon's. A man and a woman: naked, unbeautiful. The man sat dejected, his head hanging limp as his penis, his knees splayed out. His skin was liverish and cold-looking despite the gas fire glowing behind him. The woman took up the entire foreground of the canvas. She too had surrendered to gravity—her breasts sagged, her belly flapped, her lids looked far too heavy for her eyes. Beside her was an uncooked leg of mutton, pinks and purples echoing the woman's nipples and lips and cheeks, the doused mop of her pubic hair.

Nothing was hidden: everything was foreground, and exposed. But it wasn't the show of testicle and breast that made Anna grip the railing in front of her with both hands, that kept her staring at the picture, oblivious to all the people on their way up or down the stairs. What she was seeing was a portrait of her parents as they must once have been. In the slouch of their skin, the unrelenting angularity of hip bones and shoulders, you could already see the borders and lakes and cities they would put between them. The woman in this painting looked nothing like Anna's mother; the man could be anyone at all. It didn't matter. These were her parents, penned together, forever, in all their apartness.

Anna shut her eyes. Slowly, she let go of the railing—she could smell iron in the sweat of her palms. She turned and walked away, out into the street.

*       *       *

When Anna got out of the cab she rang the wrong bell—a man she'd never seen before opened the door and let her inside. Coming up the stairs to Rosalind's flat she heard people talking: as soon as she entered under the cherub's wooden spoon she knew she'd made her second mistake of the day. Rosalind had someone in for tea, someone whose presence had turned the very air in the room as hard to breathe as smoke. It was the woman Anna had last seen bleeding on the bathroom tiles, the night of Rosalind's party.

"Annie—how lovely. I've just been telling Jinny all about you. Come on in, she won't bite—in fact she's just going, aren't you, Jinny."

It wasn't a question. Jinny had risen from the sofa, but stood with her hands in her pockets, digging deep down as if to root herself into the floor. She stared at Anna with a mixture of hostility and commiseration on her face, then turned and spoke to Rosalind.

"Will I see you tomorrow at Clare's?"

"No, I don't expect so."

"But we have to talk, you've got to explain—"

"Never explain. It's time you learned the rules, Jinny. Now you'd better go. I've got company, as you can see."

Only when they heard, far below, the sound of the front door being slammed, did Anna begin to speak, twisting her hands in her lap, looking at the carpet and not at Rosalind. "Isn't she the one—?"

Rosalind sat cross-legged on the sofa, cupping her knees. She looked as though she hadn't slept much since Anna had last seen her; even her voice was drawn. "She's had some bad luck, and I've done everything I can to help her. But I am not letting her move in with me. It's the one unbreakable rule of the house. 'Free, disentangled, separate'—"

"I don't understand—"

"No, Annie, I don't suppose you do. Never mind. Let me get you some tea—or scotch, if you'd prefer—that's what I've been drinking: Ballantines, instead of Twinings. No cream cakes, either. Now, what will you have?"

"She's one of your students?"

Rosalind rubbed her bare feet, as if to work out a cramp that had settled there. And then she looked up at Anna, with a smile so warm Anna couldn't help smiling back.

"Jinny's one of my lovers, Annie—at least, she used to be before she started getting territorial."

Anna laughed, a little too loudly. And then, as she watched Rosalind watching her, she understood it wasn't a joke.

"Now, Annie, what's it to be—unless, of course, you aren't particularly thirsty?" When Anna didn't answer, Rosalind went over to the trolley and poured herself a scotch. Then she flung herself down on the sofa again and shut her eyes. "There's a wonderful Henry IV on—shall we go to it tonight? It's rather clever: Hotspur's a skinhead and Gadshill a Mohawk-punk. Hal's meant to be a sort of British Springsteen, I suppose, and—"

"Jinny—" Anna began.

"Oh, give it a rest, Annie."

But Anna couldn't. She felt as though she were suffocating, as though if a window weren't flung open she'd choke to death. "What were you telling Jinny? You said you were telling her about me when I came in. Just what were you saying? Did you tell her I was her replacement? Did you? Did you?"

"Sit down, Annie—and please don't be dramatic. I've had enough drama for today and besides, this is none of your business."

"It is my business if I'm being used—it's entirely my business."

"Used? Ah, you mean the way you've been using Simon."

"I don't want—I don't know what—" But she did know. She knew that she didn't want what had happened to Jinny to happen to her: to find herself pushed one day from Rosalind's favour, that warm fall of light which had marked her out, coloured her in for the first time in her life. She knew that she wanted what she could never have, and she felt a sudden, unstoppable hurt that she couldn't contain.

"Sorry, Annie—tit for tat. If you don't mind, I'm tired of the whole business. You haven't told me what you'd like to drink."

Anna couldn't answer. Rosalind shrugged and walked over to the window, leaning her head against the glass.

"I'll tell you something, Annie, just in case you'd like to know. I thought it would be so much easier, loving women instead of men. That we'd none of us ever be stupid or jealous or cruel. Least of all me."

That was all she said. Anna knew she ought to switch on a light, put on a kettle or a record, anything to dispel the silence between them. But she did none of these things. Nor did she go over to Rosalind, who was staring out the steadily darkening glass. Instead, she grabbed her coat and rushed from the room, pausing on the steps outside the house to catch her breath, as if it were some huge, broken bird that had to be forced inside a cage.

# XIX

# CHANGE RINGING

Just after Anna returned from London, something came from Luke. Their letters must have crossed in the mail. She didn't open the envelope at once; she wanted to create the fiction that the letter was of no importance to her one way or the other; that it was about her tenant, and had to do with leaks in the roof. So she forced herself to read at least the first few pages of that morning's paper. Over a breakfast of hard-boiled eggs and only slightly mouldy toast, she caught up with the world: Moslem riots in Bradford. A catastrophic train crash in the Soviet Union. Food scares, one headline warned, were shaking public confidence.

Anna turned from the paper to Luke's letter with as much relief as apprehension. For a long moment she looked at his handwriting, thinking how much of Luke was in the exaggerated tilt of his t's, the generous loopings of his o's and a's. She decided that it was a good sign, an excellent sign that he should have written longhand, not with the cowardly impersonality of a computer.

She opened the letter. It wasn't very long.

> *Dear Anna,*
>
> *After the fiasco of my Christmas visit, this won't come as a surprise, I know. Emma has written you that she and Frank have parted ways. The reason for this is that Emma and I are in love, and have been, for some time. That was what I came at Christmas to tell you.*
>
> *I fully intended to break this gently. I'm sorry for the way things have worked out, Anna; I want us to remain friends. Emma's a very caring person. She's moved in with me here, though it's awfully cramped—she will, of course, continue to pay you rent, and we'll make sure everything's all right at the house. I'm looking to buy a place for us—we plan to be married in August.*

*You needn't worry about anything—Emma has kept the house as neat as a pin. In fact, the garden's never looked better.*

*I'm sorry Anna, I really am. But there's nothing for it, is there?*

*With all best wishes,*

*Luke.*

\*          \*          \*

When Simon called that Sunday, Anna didn't even ask him where he proposed for them to go. She just got into the car and let him drive. To the other side of the county, it turned out—a church with a Rhenish helm and several unusual features, including a primitive Ionic capital patterned like a pomegranate. Simon talked a good deal about pomegranates on the way down; Anna gave a good imitation of someone paying strict attention.

Afterwards, they had supper at an inn. She was unusually quiet, Simon remarked. He hoped she hadn't had bad news from home. "Oh no," Anna replied. It was something to do with her book, she told him—a chapter that simply wouldn't go right.

But all she could see on the drive back, in the soft darkness through which the car seemed to be feeling its way, was Luke's letter. Had they been lovers even before Christmas? Wasn't it Luke who had suggested Emma to her as a tenant? Or was she turning paranoid with hindsight? Emma and Luke sharing her bed, the bed in which she and Luke had never spent a whole night together, the bed she needed all to herself in order to get to sleep at all.

"Home again, home again. Is it jiggedy jig? Or joggedy jog? I can never remember which. I tell you what—why don't you come in for coffee? You look as though you could use a cup."

She'd thought she'd said, "No," but here she was, walking beside Simon on the path round the church to Chantry Cottage. Just as they were pushing open the lych gate the bells rang out, as if in some crazy parody of a wedding march. For as far as Anna could tell, there was no melody, nothing she could call music, just random and contradictory sounds tumbling down the stairs of her ears and crashing into that space inside her which had once enclosed her heart. Not heart, but something vestigial, unattached, like a floating rib, something that gave you pain if you ran too fast or too long; if you cried out without caring or warning.

"Change ringing," Simon said, standing halfway through the gate, his face glistening with a happiness which Anna could only describe as an immersion in joy, something at once both water and light. "The music of the spheres, of paradise—that's how I imagine it. None of your angel choirs, just the pure mathematics of sound—"

Anna pushed away from him, through the gate and into the churchyard. Overhead was a full moon, intersected by the hard, bare branches of the oaks; it looked like a fractured lamp, fractures just about to give way so that the glass showered into you, needles and slivers and razors of glass too small to reflect anything but themselves. It couldn't have been very late, yet there were no lights on anywhere, just a small yellow gleam from the tower window. Anna turned away from it, keeping her eyes on the ground, shutting out the moon. She could feel the warmth and softness of the earth below her, its obliterating darkness—if she kept her eyes down she seemed to be walking barefoot, wearing nothing but a magic cloak that made her invisible, as if the darkness had worked its way into every pore of her skin. When Simon came towards her, finding her hand and keeping hold of it, he seemed a mere extension of the strange, blind comfort of the night. They stood together, listening to the church bells, drawn into their changing convolutions as if into the spirals of a shell. And when they began to walk further into the dark, away from the church tower and the trees carving up the face of the moon, Anna could not have said which hand gripped tighter, hers or his. She could not have said where they were headed, but when they found themselves inside the clearing it was she who knew exactly where to go.

Inside the cave made by the roots of the fallen beech it was even warmer than outside, and so dark she could not see the man beside her, this man who no longer had a face or name, who was no one she could recognize. With Luke she had always kept the lights on so that she could assent to what was happening, confine it within boundaries drawn by what she knew, what she could put a name and face to. The whole time he was inside her, he would shut his eyes, while she would have to keep looking, looking and naming, keeping the outlines of their bodies sharp, distinct, so that nothing should blur or erase her, so that nothing should be taken from her. *Set yourself never to want anything, never to need anyone but yourself, your self.*

Yet now, in this dark, her hands, her mouth, the very skin of her eyes plunging into blind ways of knowing: surrender, not sight. For her whole being was holding up its hands, not to the man beside her, but to the panic locking her breath, the panic she'd pushed away from her after reading Luke's letter, keeping it like a coat thrown over her shoulders, something she could always shrug off. Panic shaking her bones now as if she were a carpet being beaten; panic, loss, and the drowning urgency to grab and hold, the way the change ringers heaved and pulled their ropes, freeing the sounds sealed up inside them. And so she grabbed and held with her hands and her mouth and her thighs, and the harder she held, the more of herself she seemed to abandon, as if their bodies were leaking, one into the other, drinking the warm salt dark of this sea they'd made between them. Their breathing harsh, strange as the pattern of the bell ringing; no words, no names, just cries sounding inward, as if their bodies were shells holding nothing but the movement of the sea.

And then there was nothing to be said, nothing to be done but a pulling apart; a parting, not of lovers, but of intimate strangers who would never meet again.

# XX

# SPYING

On her way back from the laundromat, staggering under a month's accumulated sheets and towels, Anna stopped dead on the High Street. Taped to a travel agent's window, a placard screamed **DEAL OF A LIFETIME**: two weeks in Crete for the price of one, and that in itself unbelievably low. The only snag, she discovered, ten minutes and much dropped laundry later, was that the price of one was meant to be paid twice. If she did wish to go on her own, she would have to finance an absent partner rather like the invisible friend she'd made up for herself in childhood. It didn't make sense, the agent agreed, but there it was.

Anna deliberated. She needed desperately to get away; since she couldn't afford to go on her own, she would simply have to find some-one to go with her. She took the agent's brochure and his warning that she'd better act soon before someone else snapped up the deal. It was a cancellation, she wouldn't get another chance like this. And Crete in the latter half of March would be paradise—no crowds, thousands of wildflowers, weather sunny enough for beach-wear, but no risk of burning.

Anna deposited her laundry in the car and drove up the hill to Varti's house. She was in luck; her friend was at home instead of leafletting somewhere. Anna was invited in for a cup of coffee and a half hour's chat, no more, since Varti had a lecture to attend. Unless Anna cared to come with her, in which case they could spend the afternoon together. From the poster on display in Varti's kitchen, Anna could see that the subject was toxic waste: **What Can We Do to Keep Britain From Becoming the Chemical Dump of Europe?** She gave Varti a few pounds for the fund-raising kitty, and drank another cup of coffee. And then, remarking on how tired Varti looked, how run-down and worn-out, Anna blurted out an invitation to holiday in Crete, practically for free.

Varti shook her head. On the contrary, it was Anna who was looking run-down. A week in Crete would be the perfect medicine. Varti had made her own travel plans months ago—she was flying off to Edmonton to visit her son and his wife. Besides, she was hardly the right company for such a vacation. And then she smiled at Anna. Surely this Cretan adventure was something that should be embarked upon with Luke? Providing he steered clear of raw eggs, of course. Anna smiled back. Luke wasn't able to get away from his administrative duties, she explained. Varti nodded sympathetically and changed the subject back to Easter in Edmonton. How much snow should she expect?

Anna left shortly afterwards, passing their conversation through a sieve, looking for traces of a cooling-off on Varti's part. Did she disapprove of her for not attending protest meetings, for having suggested Crete when she'd turned down Greenham Common? Or was it something else, something more private, personal. . . Someone honked a horn behind her—the light had been green for a good ten seconds. Anna shot across the intersection, her cheeks red as stoplights. She absolutely refused to think about Simon. Of course Varti wouldn't know—how could she? As far as Anna was concerned there was nothing to know at all.

Then why was she trying so hard to run away? Because Simon was due back any day from Berkshire, to which he'd rushed the day after that last bout of church-crawling. While queuing up at the post office with her reply to Luke's letter, Anna had overheard Mrs. Higley tell Miss Molesworth that Simon's father had had a stroke. And Anna, forgetting all about the butter and eggs she'd come in to buy, had rushed out of the shop before the women could see the relief on her face. A reprieve, she'd been granted a reprieve. What shouldn't have happened, couldn't have happened: when Simon came back she would make that clear. Yet only now, with his return looming over her, did she admit that she hadn't the least idea of how to go about it.

A sheaf of mail awaited her on her return from Varti's. Anna was reluctant to sit down with it—her mind was still on Crete. She was just about to surrender all hope of going when she had an inspiration. Of course—she'd ask Fiona to come with her. Fiona needed a holiday far more than she did—Anna had never seen her as haggard as she'd been the past few weeks. Re-reading the brochure, Anna discovered that for children under a certain age the holiday was free. Maeve was under a certain age. She would waft Maeve and Fiona away to Crete—how on earth could they refuse her?

Anna rushed next door. She let the electric buzzer ring and ring, but there was no reply. Of course, Fiona could be out. It was, after all, a Saturday afternoon. Yet it was so warm today—perhaps she was in the garden where she couldn't hear the buzzer. Perhaps it didn't work. Anna ran round to the back of the house. The garden was deserted. Undaunted, she examined the back door. Firmly shut. But what if Fiona weren't out, but, as seemed perfectly possible, ill—and Maeve, as well? In which case they'd surely need a warm and airy place to convalesce. . . .

Anna sat down on a gently rotting bench screened by Maeve's play house. She felt uneasy at her trespassing, but even more upset that Fiona wasn't here to help her. It had to be decided right away, so Anna could get back to the travel agent before anyone else did. The more she thought about it the more imperative it seemed that they all fly off together. But Fiona was out, and there was nothing to be done about it; the travel agent would be closed by five o'clock. She'd have to wait for Monday. She couldn't wait. Perhaps she hadn't rung hard enough, perhaps she should have knocked instead, perhaps there'd be a note inside saying where Fiona could be reached. And there was one door she hadn't tried, the door to the basement studio Fiona had told her about on the night of Guy Fawkes.

Anna walked up to a door at the side of the cottage; tried the handle and found it unlocked. She pushed it open into a small corridor hung with mildewed coats and jackets—men's clothes which couldn't possibly belong to Fiona. At the end of the corridor was an inner door, fronted by a sheet of glass obscured by cobwebs. She was about to open the door but didn't. She didn't open it because she could make out, through the glass, the shapes of two people on the other side.

They hadn't bothered to take off all their clothes, though the woman's shirt was pulled up over her shoulders. A black shirt—it looked like a noose around her neck. He was holding her pinned against the wall, yet she was clutching at him as if he were the only thing that could keep her from falling.

Anna could not look away, anymore than they could stop the jerking of their locked bodies. And then the woman's arms hung limp at her sides; as he moved away, she reached her arms across her breasts, shivering. He was buttoning up his trousers; he didn't look at the woman standing with her shirt looped round her neck. He didn't say a word, he didn't touch her face or hands or hair. She reached down for the puddle of her clothes on the gritty floor, her movements abrupt, impatient. Except for the shriek of cartoon music overhead, there was silence.

Anna crept back through the corridor and out the door. Once outside she started to run. Without caring where she went, whether the couple inside or the whole village saw her she blundered across the yard and through the gap in the hedge into the safety of Rest Harrow.

*          *          *

Later that afternoon there was a knocking at the door. Anna, slumped on a chair in the parlour, ignored it. Rosalind walked in.

"Don't look so shocked, Annie—I'm not staying long. I've been to a meeting in Brighton and thought I'd stop by. I know I look a mess; there's no need to stare. I've just got through three successive bouts of 'flu. I could use a cup of tea, in other words. Never mind, I'll make it." And she disapppeared into the kitchen.

Anna sat up stiffly in her chair. Her mail was still on the little table by the gas fire—she supposed she ought to open it, if only to give her an excuse not to talk to Rosalind when she came back into the room. Two of the letters were from Canada, one from the bank, inquiring whether she'd like her overdraft privileges extended, the other from the Dean, who inquired in the friendliest possible way as to the whereabouts of Anna's mid-term sabbatical report. Next came a leaflet from the Ouse Valley Environmental Watch Group. Free samples of a super-effective dishwashing powder. And a thick envelope, addressed in an unfamiliar hand, to Miss Anna English. A letter enclosed in a card. Anna put the card down without looking at it; unfolding the letter, she began to read:

> My dear, dear Anna,
>      I should be most distraught if you were to interpret my current absence as a sign that I look with any levity or presumption upon what has happened between us. You can be in no doubt about the state of my affections for you,

*and the seriousness of my intentions, just as I can no longer be in any doubt*
*about yours. Though I never imagined that I would ever again want to*
*marry—*

"Here—it's strong enough to stand a whole drawerful of spoons in.
Go on, it's only tea. That's better. And now, Annie—you little sneak!
Why didn't you tell me?"

"Tell you what?" Anna panicked, hiding Simon's letter inside her
copy of *The Waves*.

"That you were planning a getaway. It looks wonderful—I must say,
I abominate package deals, but Crete at this time of year would be
heaven. And for a song—I'm almost tempted to join you. It's years
since I was there. In fact—" Rosalind was skimming the sheet which
the travel agent had given to Anna, and which Anna had left in the
kitchen.

"It won't work," Anna protested. "Someone's sure to have snapped
it up by now—it was a cancellation."

"But it's still worth a try. Why don't I pop down the road and
phone? I can put the whole thing on my credit card—you can pay your
share later. Don't look so glum, Annie—don't you like doing good
deeds? You're saving my life, you know—you can't have any idea of
what the past three weeks have been. 'Flu was the best part of it. I'll go
and call now, it won't take a minute."

By the time Rosalind returned, Anna had hidden *The Waves* in the
study, rinsed her face with cold water, and prayed that the travel agent's
was closed. But Rosalind's smile was triumphant; she saluted with the
brochure, then tossed it to Anna. "Done. Aren't you pleased? Thank
God for plastic money—I believe I just made a substantial donation to
my favourite charity in the process. That will assuage our guilt when
motoring past starving Cretan peasants. Or have they all turned into
*hôteliers* by now? This is going to be such a relief. If you only knew—"

"I wasn't going to go."

"Oh, come now, Annie—of course you were. You'd even filled out
the form. Is it the prospect of my company that bothers you? I assure
you, you'll be in safe hands—that is, you won't be in anyone's hands at
all. What I need most, right now, is a holiday from entanglements of
any kind. Look, you needn't come if you don't want to, I'm quite prepared to constitute a couple on my own. I simply thought we might

spend some time together, Annie; I thought we might finally have a chance to talk together, really talk. Christ, woman—I've never in my life met anyone so frightened of herself."

Rosalind bent down to pick up the brochure from where Anna had let it fall. Slowly, precisely, she folded it and put it into her briefcase. "Thanks for the tea. I'm going straight back, I've got to cancel a couple of engagements. I'll meet you—or not—at the airport, in a week's time. You do just as you please. It really doesn't matter."

# XXI

# AGIA MARIA

Anna refused the stewardess's offer of a *Daily Telegraph*: she had said goodbye to all that for at least this fortnight away. Rosalind was too tired to read—she'd worked right up till the flight, getting a brief ready for a steering committee that was to meet during her absence. She slept most of the way from London to Heraklion, which was just as well, since it fell in perfectly with the strategy Anna had adopted for getting through this holiday. She'd simply pretend that Rosalind was someone she'd never met before, a perfect stranger. Though their seats were side by side, Anna sat with her body twisted towards the aisle, as far away as possible from the woman sleeping next to her.

Anna wasn't about to fall asleep. Not that she wasn't tired—she'd been up at four to catch this flight. It was just that her sleep had recently been full of dreams she'd rather do without, dreams involving Nicholas and Fiona coming together like scissor blades while Maeve looked on, sketching them as sharp black lines and broken circles. But it was precisely so that she'd stop thinking of Nicholas and Fiona and Maeve that she'd come on this trip, so she swallowed coffee and buried herself in the Greek phrasebook she'd picked up at the airport. *Kali mera, kali spera, kali nikhta.*

They landed safely. Anna had performed preventive magic again, reading the safety-precautions booklet inside-out, folding her hands together as the plane descended, praying to the God of Travellers to let them all come through unscathed. The sky looked overcast through the airplane windows; there were cacti planted in front of the airport building, bluish cacti that seemed to be shivering in the wind. Anna put on her raincoat before descending the ramp; Rosalind carried hers defiantly, baring her arms from the elbows down to air far colder than what they'd left behind.

"Ée-lee-os. That's the word for sun." Anna made no reply, but Rosalind was not about to give up. "Ée-lee-os. It's not so very difficult, is it?"

"Not difficult, just minimally useful."

They cleared customs and retrieved their bags, heavy with sinus remedies, since they both were nursing colds. An improbably blond girl named Edie greeted them at the door of the transfer bus with carnations for "the ladies," and doll-size bottles of Ouzo for "the gents." From her accent, she was a Lancashire girl, though she seemed to have no trouble bantering with the Greek-only driver. The bus jerked away as Edie took up the microphone and gave them a pocket tour of the island, telling them, as they passed mile after mile of concrete shells, brick piles, telephone poles and TV antennae, of the wonders of Knossos, and the picturesque villages where old ladies in black spent their days tilling the fields while their husbands kept the cafés in business. "Not a very liberated sort of place for the ladies," Edie observed. There was general headshaking among the carnations, and a satisfied grasping of bottles.

"It's a bit built up along the coast here," Edie continued, "but don't worry—Agia Maria's really beautiful. That's because it's next to a rocky bay that can't be adopted for touristic use. Many locals have private homes overlooking the rocky bay."

But as the bus turned off the highway down a winding road, all that lurched into view were scattered blocks of reinforced concrete, some painted white or mauve or watermelon-pink, others still raw-grey, with metal prongs sticking up, as if some mighty-feelered insect had been embalmed within. At a cluster of blocks encircled by bulldozers, cranes and a cement mixer, the bus pulled up and discharged its passengers. Edie was saying something into the microphone, but no one could hear her over the jack hammers.

*     *     *

Anna left Rosalind fast asleep in the bedroom, with the shutters closed—not to keep out the sun, but to stop them from banging in the strong wind that had started up out of nowhere. It was blowing grit into her eyes, tearing at her hair as she walked past a swimming pool brimming with leaves and dirt, and the plastic ribs of lounge chairs scattered like wishbones over the terrace. Picking her way over abandoned carpenters' tools, Anna struck out along the highway to the bay.

She hadn't bothered to ask for directions at the reception office: Edie had informed them that no one there spoke English. Before she'd left them that afternoon, Edie had suggested they hire a car, since it was usually ten degrees warmer on the other coast. Rosalind, half-somnambulist by then, had furnished her driver's licence and credit card; Edie had promised the car by that evening. Anna remained profoundly sceptical about the whole idea. As far as she was concerned, she and Rosalind would only survive the next two weeks if they saw and heard as little as possible of one another—the last thing they needed was to be shut up together in a rusting compact, breaking down in some forsaken valley.

About one thing the travel agent hadn't lied—the island was, indeed, covered with wildflowers. Walking along the rutted road Anna counted dozens of different kinds, only two of which she could name. Lupins, growing wild as they did in Nova Scotia; rock roses with petals like crumpled paper, their furred leaves twisting at the edges like the mouths of people who've had strokes. Anna banished the comparison. It made her think of Simon's father, of Simon receiving no answer to his letter, rushing back from Berkshire to find Rest Harrow empty and Anna gone for good for all he knew.

By now she'd left behind all the supermarkets, gift stores and RENT ROOMS signs. The noise of tearing down and building up gradually dimmed, until she reached a place from which she could hear only wind thrashing the leaves of the locust trees. Following a path which twisted down to the bay below, Anna found herself at a beachside villa. In the courtyard geraniums sprouted out of old tin cans. A hen came by, pecking the ground then lifting her head, listening, jerking one foot and then another before she began to feed again. Dead-looking branches convulsed over a trellis—it too reminded her of something she would rather forget: the little porch over the stairs leading up to Nicholas's study. Anna shook her head as if it were a book out of which she could shake scraps of paper marking compromising passages. Her legs were aching from the walk. She sank down at a wooden table under the trellis, too tired to care whether someone might shout at her for trespassing, or set a dog on her.

Nicholas and his brandy-snifter seductions. What technique had he used on Fiona—and when had it started? Fiona and Nicholas in the coach house together while she'd been reading *The Wizard of Oz* to Maeve. . . . Luke, taking up with Emma, who'd had no qualms about letting him stay the night his whole life long. . . *Why do you think people make such a fuss about marriage and copulation? . . . Certainly I find the climax immensely exaggerated.* Oh, why couldn't he have gone on play-ing Leonard to her Virginia? *Immensely exaggerated.* And yet that night of the change ringing—falling, turning, losing herself inside a warm, dark sea. . . .

A shutter creaked open, making Anna jump from her bench. A stray cat, half starved—it mewed sourly and sidled over to her, trying to rub against her ankles, but she wouldn't let it. Instead, she pushed back up the path and retraced her steps to Agia Maria, saying over and over again the few phrases she'd learned in Greek. This had a soothing effect, so that by the time she reached the apartment she felt her face to be perfectly opaque. She needn't have bothered. Rosalind was still sleeping, and looked as though she wouldn't wake till morning. Anna closed the bedroom door and took a blanket onto the couch in the sit-ting room. Eating a packet of biscuits and cheese she'd saved from the plane, she began to read a history of Crete. It took her till the Vene-tians to fall asleep.

*          *          *

They woke next morning to the sound of buzz saws, not birds. The hotel's proprietors were adding on a new wing, and work crews were drilling away, pouring concrete and hammering beams long before Ros-alind had boiled up the water for tea. She'd been up for hours, she explained to a still sleepy Anna—she'd even gone down to the super-market to buy some bread and jam. It was really too cold to breakfast on the balcony, but they did so anyway, trying to match the contours of their bodies with those prescribed by the plastic chairs. Rosalind wore a bikini under a short black kimono: Anna had a terry-cloth robe pulled tight over the cotton nightdress which for this weather should have been heavy-duty flannel. On the balcony across from them, in diaphanous babydolls, sat two enormous women playing Nat King Cole on a ghetto blaster.

"I'm going down to see about that car," Rosalind announced. "It should have been here last evening."

A few minutes later, Anna heard Rosalind arguing with Edie on the terrace below. Across the bay the sea was changing back and forth from lead to dirty turquoise. Cars and motor bikes roared along the road; more English couples appeared on the balconies, staring gloomily at the mist towelling the hills. Yellow hills, covered with what looked like gorse. It could, Anna admitted, it could very well have been England.

The apartment door opened and slammed shut. Rosalind flung herself into her chair, and gave an excellent imitation of Edie: "Your car will arrive first thing tomorrow morning. It's a lovely car, absolutely unspoiled. All the locals drive them."

Within an hour the rain had softened to a mere drizzle. Rosalind set out on a walk, grudgingly accompanied by Anna, who could not bear to spend another moment cooped up inside an apartment so damp that even the pages of her passport were starting to swell and curl. They went in no particular direction, taking dirt roads that turned into cul de sacs, and then backtracking along footpaths. The earth was crudely scarred where bulldozers had flattened the fields, smashing down bushes and small trees. They passed one building site after another, dodging the rocks, the Coke tins, the stray dogs that came up to sniff at them. You could hear the sea pounding in the distance. Anna was beginning to hope that Rosalind, too, had taken a vow of silence when the words "Ann Arbor" jumped into the air. "Ann Arbor," Rosalind repeated. "Do you know it?"

"It's near Detroit," Anna answered, as if the mere mention of that place would be enough to silence anyone.

Rosalind remarked that having lived in London for the past few years she'd be perfectly prepared for Detroit. And then she began rhyming off a great list of English academics who had, as she put it, Gone West. Gradually, Anna came to understand that Rosalind was not condemning the Diaspora, but proposing to join it.

"Don't be stupid. You'd hate living in America—you wouldn't last a week. You don't belong there."

"I certainly don't belong in England any more. The simple fact, Annie—and I've become a great one for simple facts—is that I'd be stupid not to go. They'll pay me twice what I'm getting here, and let me teach a third fewer courses. So that I can get on with my research. They're very big on research. They seem to like people flying off to as many conferences as possible. I could get back to London every summer. And to crown it all, they have a Comprehensive Dental Plan—they seem to think that's quite a drawing card."

"But what about the Charter work? What about civil liberties and freedom of expression and saving Brave Little Britain from Itself?"

Rosalind refused to be drawn. "As someone or other has said—a very convenient someone or other—if the survival of an organization depends on one individual, then it's doomed from the start."

Anna replied in something like the sing-song voice which children use in taunting one another. "Varti wouldn't put it like that. Varti—that friend of mine you met at Christmas—"

"The Friend of the Earth and All Its Works? She told me she was thinking of emigrating to Canada. Doesn't she have family there?"

"How would you know?" Anna snapped. Why should Varti have confided anything to Rosalind? Varti was her friend, not Rosalind's: it wasn't right—it wasn't fair. Anna began to walk a little faster. She was jealous, she might as well admit it: jealous, resentful—why not throw in selfish, too? What's more, she was taking a perverse delight in being all these things.

Rosalind, struggling to keep up, sounded apologetic. "I haven't committed myself one way or the other. I just thought I'd tell you. Things are getting—things are impossible, Annie. I can't—"

"We'll have to hurry before the rain gets any worse," Anna shouted, running on ahead until she could no longer hear Rosalind's footsteps behind her.

*         *         *

It was dark by the time they found the one taverna open for business. Although it was on an open terrace, with vine branches twisting through the iron railings, Anna didn't like the look of it. There were photographs of alarmingly glistening entrées over sample menus in five languages. As they stood reading, a fortyish man came down from the terrace and welcomed them. "*Guten Abend, meine Damen. Willkommen.*"

Rosalind swept past him, but Anna lingered a moment—"We're not German," she volunteered.

"You're the first of the season," the man replied in perfect English. He followed Anna to the table Rosalind had chosen. "Have an apéritif. It's on the house. You like flambé? We do first class flambé. Or maybe you'd prefer steak and chips?"

Rosalind ignored him, settling herself at the table, removing the ashtray and the plastic carnation. Once again, she'd put herself through a metamorphosis. Her skin had the kind of calculated glow you see in ads for posh cosmetics. And you could see a lot of her skin, given the tank top and more or less dispensable skirt she had put on despite the frigid weather. Yannis—for so their self-appointed host was called—returned to their table with three large glasses of ouzo, "absolutely one hundred per cent on the house." He proposed a toast to their happy stay in Crete, called a waiter to take the ladies' orders, then lit a cigarette and sat down with them. He told them he'd studied to be an engineer, but that the life hadn't appealed to him. He was a people-person. He'd been running the restaurant for five years now—he owned some apartments up the road, too.

"I can't abide the stink of cigarettes," was Rosalind's reply. Quickly, Yannis dropped his, grinding it out with his heel. He called to the waiter and ordered a bottle of wine—again, on the house, in honour of the ladies.

Yannis drew his chair closer to Rosalind's; before long he'd draped his arm over the back of her chair. He started talking again, with gestures and flourishes. Things were at a crisis in Greece right now. The corruption was terrible. And the economy—you wouldn't want to know the mess it was in. What Greece needed, Yannis continued, inching his fingers closer to Rosalind's bare shoulder, was a strong leader, someone tough and principled enough to say what he meant, and to do what he said. Someone like Britain's prime minister, for whom he had the greatest admiration and respect.

Rosalind remarked that the wine was corked.

Yannis apologized, effusively. He made excuses for the windy weather, too. "But I promise you a summer's day, tomorrow. Blue sky, sunshine. You'll be able to spend the whole day on the beach. In your bathing suits—or out of them, just as you please."

He paused for a moment, expecting some response. They carried on eating their squid.

"My mother, she's swum in the Nile—fully clothed, of course. She's very religious. If you're Greek Orthodox and you swim in the Nile you get to be something really special—very holy. I don't know, I don't believe in that stuff, myself. But all hell broke loose when we opened this place up to tourism. There's a monastery not far from here—you can just see it from the hilltop. It's God knows how many miles fom the beach, and you'd think the monks would have better things to do than spy on topless swimmers. They said either the nude beach went, or they did. The monastery's deserted now. There's a church with frescos—if you like that kind of thing you should go up, take a look. Ano Viannos, it's called. You need a car, though. I have a new Ford. I could take you round a bit if you like. Things are quiet these days—the season doesn't really start till after Easter." Yannis's arm was resting on Rosalind's shoulder blade, as light as a butterfly upon a leaf.

"We've already hired a car. Now bring us the bill." Each of Rosalind's words was an ice cube clinking in a glass. She was putting on an excellent performance, but for whose benefit, Anna couldn't tell. She told herself she didn't care.

Yannis rose from the table. "Ano Viannos," he repeated, and sent the waiter to present the bill. There was a clot of people down by the steps where the picture-menus were displayed. As Rosalind and Anna walked out onto the road they could hear Yannis clapping his hands and calling out—*Guten Abend, meine Damen und Herren. Willkommen.*

They headed up in the direction of the apartments, passing a shrine on the way, a little box fixed on a pole and lit by an electric bulb. An icon of the Virgin and child, a faded paper rose, and a toy car were carefully arranged inside the box. They stopped and looked for what seemed a long time. Long enough, at least, for Rosalind, pointing to the plastic Chevrolet, to attempt a joke.

"That must be the car they've promised us."

Anna knew that it was an appeal—for rescue, or a mere response; that if she were even to smile or nod her head, things would go back to the way they'd been between them. Or rather, would have changed in an alarming way, with Rosalind the one in need of definition now, making confession, turning to the Annie she'd invented. But Annie was all broken lines and vacant space; all Annie could do was stand and stare at the votive box, her tongue like a shard of glass inside her mouth.

The apartment felt like a freshly drained pond. Anna went to the bedroom and hastily undressed. When Rosalind came in, Anna had her face turned to the wall and was pretending to be asleep. Yet all the same, Rosalind crouched by the side of her bed, calling "Annie— Annie?" She could feel Rosalind close beside her, chill and damp and smelling of the sea. Anna shut her eyes even tighter, her body rigid under the thin blanket

They lay for a long time listening to each other's breathing in the dark.

# XXII

# ANO VIANNOS

Edie showed up with the car at noon the next day. An hour later they were on the main highway, heading down the coast. They had all the windows open and the radio on: bazouki rock. Anna was driving— she couldn't help tapping her fingers against the wheel for sheer relief. The handle didn't work on Rosalind's door, and the muffler made clanking sounds, but how could that matter? The car had materialized just in time. Anna was in exaggerated good spirits, overjoyed that they now had something perfectly safe to talk about: where they would go, what they would see. Talk that would fill up the silences without revealing anything.

Rosalind vetoed Knossos with her customary confidence, much to Anna's relief. "The reconstruction's hopelessly ugly, as well as inaccurate. Arthur Evans was an aesthetic terrorist." Anna, for her part, wouldn't hear of the Lassithi Plain—she had no interest whatsoever, she declared, in windmills. Nor did she care to go grubbing about in caves—and anyway, they hadn't the paraphernalia. Rosalind had to agree. So they compromised and drove inland, exchanging avenues of video clubs, computer outlets, porno emporiums for small roads on which peasant women rode donkeys burdened by olive branches.

They picnicked under a ruined bridge, watching a herd of goats cascade into the valley below. They stopped by dim, whitewashed churches to look at ancient frescos cheek by jowl with Hollywood Christs. Some of the new icons were slatted, like Venetian blinds— when you walked past, Jesus's face turned into Mary's. Rosalind said it gave her a queasy feeling, as though she were witnessing a celestial sex-change operation. "Let's find a café. I need a brandy after this."

They found one in the next small town. Each table had its plastic bucket of pink and yellow freesias, or cinnamon-scented phlox. The only other female presence in the place was Janis Joplin, braying from a juke box. The décor consisted of faded paintings of Japanese junks and illustrations from *Heidi,* except for one wall, which was blanketed with reproductions of the frescos at Knossos. Going up to look at them, Anna recognized dolphins, the blue boy who was really a monkey, bulls and snakes and wasp-waisted priestesses. Next to the profile of the Parisienne, however, was an image she didn't know. On a dirty-white fragment of fresco she could just make out a small pink star. She heard laughter behind her: the men at the corner table were watching her, making some kind of joke. She ignored them, turning to the last repro-duction, a large reconstruction of a group of priestesses. And there, like a jigsaw piece that had at last been fitted to complete a puzzle, Anna found the star again. It turned out to be a nipple, contained within a bodice that looked like the upper half of an hour glass. Anna decided she preferred it on its own: a small, separate, fleshy star.

All that night rain pounded on the roof tiles. Rosalind fell asleep at once, but Anna lay awake. She couldn't stop thinking about Maeve. Because of the frescos, she reasoned—they made her think of Maeve's drawings, though there really wasn't any resemblance between them. Anna punched at her pillow, trying to make it feel less like a rock, a small, wet rock. She wished that she hadn't cancelled that last Sunday dinner at the Gibsons'—that she'd offered to take Maeve away on hol-iday. But what would have happened to Fiona? Ought she have tried to warn her about Nicholas? And on what grounds? Besides, Fiona was old enough to know what she was doing. It was Maeve who needed protecting.

Towards morning Rosalind began to talk in her sleep—nothing intelligible, just moans and sometimes sharp exclamations, directed not at perceived assailants, but inward, as though she were punishing her-self. She stopped, at last, when the fog horn sounded: soft, low, strangely consoling. Anna lay back and listened, falling, before she knew it, into a sea of dreamless sleep.

\*       \*       \*

For the rest of the week they drove, and kept a more or less companion-able silence. Their expeditions took place in streaming rain, or in a sil-very light which seemed a distillation of the olive leaves. They climbed the hills, searching for dwarf iris and dittany. They stopped at deserted beaches, walking up and down the shore in what passed for perfect peace. Only in sleep did Rosalind cry out, and Anna open herself to doubts and fears—about Maeve and Fiona; about how she'd disentangle herself from Simon, and how she'd deal with Luke; about the book she'd failed so dismally to write.

Rosalind took masses of photographs, as if she could control the days by boxing up each moment, separating objects from one another with a click of the shutter. She would find a subject and exhaust a whole roll of film upon it, sometimes shooting from every possible angle, at other times firing the same shot over and over and over again. Black-eared sheep on stony hillsides, looking much less stupid than their English cousins; small, lost villages suspended like streaks of mist in the valleys.

By the last day of their first week it seemed they had already seen everything they could, given the unending rain. And then Anna remembered the deserted monastery nearby, the one whose frescos Yannis had mentioned. She didn't tell Rosalind they were going to Ano Viannos, but simply started driving. It was much farther than she'd thought, endless hairpin turns in rain so hard it blurred the windshield. Only as they climbed out of the last valley did the sun break through.

They had to park the car at the foot of a pathway marked with an arrow and a word in Greek—Anna's phrasebook was finally some use. At the end of the path they found a courtyard with a fountain and a pair of ancient plane trees, then an archway into another, smaller courtyard. There was a large whitewashed church inside, and they spent some time walking round it, admiring the small stone grille carved in the shape of a vine, with some strange animal underneath, its snout raised towards the grapes that hung above it. Anna waited while Rosalind took a photograph of the grille, then led the way into the church.

Beeswax and freesia perfumed the darkness. Groping towards the altar, Anna found a cardboard box full of enormous candles. She stuffed all the coins she could dredge from her pockets into a brass slot in the wall, lit a pair of candles and, calling to Rosalind to follow her, headed into the blackness of the side-chapels.

Moving the candles back and forth across the wall, she uncovered a nativity scene. The figures were drawn with the utmost tenderness, the faces seeming to bend and open in her candle's glow. Anna walked further along to a place where she could make out a jostle of dim shapes.

"Come here," she called back to Rosalind. And then, her voice rising sharply—"You've got to see this, Rosalind—come here."

A group of women, naked, trapped in a nest of snakes sucking their breasts, mounting their parted thighs, shoving heads like fists inside. The mouth and nipples of one woman daubed a vicious red, her womb cut open to reveal a pit of writhing snakes. Two of the figures hanging upside down, snakes roping their ankles, thrusting out their mouths and the holes between their thighs. One woman hugging a snake thick and long as a tree trunk, her legs drawn up so that her knees bruised her huge, sagging breasts. A snake head hatching from her anus.

Anna stared until the hot wax rolled over her hands. She blew out the candles, whispering "We'd better go." But Rosalind wasn't there to hear her.

Anna found her outside, in sunlight so harsh it seemed to have scraped a layer off her skin. She was leaning against one of the enormous plane trees—she'd been sick in the bushes behind it. Anna led her to the fountain and made her wash her face, then dried it with her own sleeve. There was no one to call for help, nobody but Anna, and all she could do was to make Rosalind sit down on the stone bench and lean against the broad trunk of the plane tree. After a few moments the colour came back to her face, and she stopped shuddering. And then, without looking at Anna, she grabbed her hand and pulled her so that she was sitting down on the bench beside her.

"You're lucky, did you know that, Annie? Do you know how lucky you are? You've kept yourself clean and separate: chaste, that's the word for you."

"Rosalind—"

"Nothing can ever touch you. And touching's bad, it makes messes, bruises, stains. You've been the cleverest of the lot of us, haven't you? No—don't move away—you're going to have to listen, Annie. You see, as the saying goes, I have something on my conscience, and there's no one I can tell but you."

Rosalind holding her hand so tight Anna could not move a finger, even to cover her ears.

"Something on my conscience—it's a suitable expression, don't you think? As though conscience were a white sheet held out to catch every gush and stain. And there've been so many, but I won't trouble you with that.

"I was braver than you think, Annie—coming down to you for Christmas. Or perhaps just brazen. Yes, that's it. But what else could I do? She'd been phoning me, she said she had to see me, that she needed my help. And I couldn't have her coming to London—surely you can see that? The whole reason I've kept away from Pyeford is that she's there, and I've needed to think that she never knew. We made sure of that. We didn't want to hurt her. Not that he hadn't had all sorts of affairs, before—she must have known about that, at least. But that's hardly the point. In this one case I'm the guilty party. He was an accessory. Something you use to set off—what? A fact? Your face? It was more than that.

"At first, I didn't even know who they were. They moved in quite a while after I bought Rest Harrow. And I was away so much. I think we were introduced at one of those wine and cheese parties Miss Molesworth organizes every year. God bless Miss Molesworth, I wonder if she knows how much harm she does in her fussy little way. At any rate, I came in late. I was bored instantly—the same faces, the same drivel being talked. I was tired of saying rude things about the govern-ment. That's how they were perceived, of course. Not as provocative but simply rude—a child misbehaving at a party. But it would have been worse to stay away. At least that's what I thought, then. Because if I hadn't come, I'd never have met Alun.

"No, don't say anything, this is the foolish part, the wrong part. I can't remember now—no, I'm lying, I remember perfectly. It was her I saw first. You can't imagine what she looked like then. Do you know that Mansfield story, where a woman goes to a window and sees a pear tree brimming over with blossom and for the first time in her life feels ravished, possessed by her own happiness? Fiona was that woman. She had her little girl by the hand, and he had his arm around her and they looked—they had whatever it was I've wanted and wanted and never been able to have.

"I couldn't have done anything else. I went over to them and said the stupid sort of thing you do at that kind of party. It turned out he'd heard me on the radio, and that I'd been to one of his exhibi-tions. Fiona was pulled away after a little while by one of those terri-ble W.I. women. We went on talking, Alun and I—about the awful wine, the rubber cheese, the whole impossible affair. He said it was good for drumming up trade—he'd got half a dozen commissions that evening. Mostly his wife's doing. She was wonderful at that, he said. It was the only thing of his he could count on selling—views of the Sussex Downs. Of course I said I'd love to see his other work, the things that didn't sell. I even promised I'd buy something, provided it wasn't a landscape or a holy family. He laughed, and said why didn't I come over one afternoon. It was about time—weren't we neighbours, after all?

"I came the next day. That was the only time I ever went inside their house. She was home, busy with the little girl. She's grown into a strange child, hasn't she? She frightens me—she looks so like him. I declined the offer of a cup of tea, and went down with him to his studio. He had all sorts of canvases—other than the bread-and-butter ones, I mean. There were some of Belfast in that meticulously detailed style he used for his landscapes. You could hardly bear to look at them, and yet you couldn't stop staring at what he'd given you to see. I was astonished by how good they were; he saw that at once. And I—well of course I built on that. I had to, to get what I wanted.

"It sounds so naked, so horribly assertive, doesn't it? I'd decided I wanted him, not all for my own, but just to stake some kind of claim. You can't reason with what you want: you want something and you get it or else you don't. And what I wanted was Fiona's happiness—not to take it from her, just to have a little of it for my own. Whatever it was he'd given her. Oh, I reasoned it all out, it fit perfectly. If she truly loved him it wouldn't matter—a neighbour's borrowing a cupful of sugar. When she already had more than she could possibly need.

"We next met in London. I had the use of a flat there. We met almost every week. Nothing ever happened in Pyeford, we were careful, except at the very end. They had had a quarrel. In an indirect way, and in this sort of affair there only are indirect ways, it was all my doing. I'd been at him, you see, from the first moment I saw his paintings, his real paintings. To forgo the pretty-pretty pastures, the pastel portraits of mother-and-child, and come back to London to work. It was her money, or rather her parents', that bought them the cottage. She wanted their children to grow up in the country; she wouldn't hear of them leaving, she loathed London. And so, after this particularly hopeless quarrel—she wouldn't budge an inch, he had to do as she saw fit, there was no other way about it—he walked out one night, just walked out the door and disappeared.

"He was careful to cover his tracks, going down to the pub for a pint, sticking to the back lane coming back, sneaking through a gap in the hedge to Rest Harrow. For the first time, he stayed the night. I was so happy—stupidly happy. I had all sorts of wild ideas—that we would go away together, that we would have our own child together. And I wanted a child so badly, I held him so long inside me that night. . . .

"He was gone when I woke up. He wasn't with her, either, though he must have stolen back to pick up the few things he needed. I kept waiting for him to get in touch from London—I went back and forth from Pyeford to the flat; I spent hours at his gallery. And do you know how I heard? From Mrs. Higley, of course, while I was queuing up one day to get my letters weighed. She was telling Miss Molesworth that he'd gone home to Belfast. He still had family there, you see. He'd told me that when the baby was born Fiona had made him promise never to go back. He didn't need to, he could have made his living, if that's what you want to call it, from the landscapes. They were fine, of course, but nothing like the others.

"I don't know what he told Fiona. I'm sure he wouldn't have told her about me—after all, I was just one of his other women, snake ladies, shall we say? He may have said he was leaving her for the sake of his painting. Or perhaps he went on about needing time to be alone, to work entirely on his own. He would have come back, I'm sure of it. Not to me perhaps, not even to her—but he could so easily have come back. You can get through your three score and ten in Belfast quite as easily as in Brighton, if you live in the right neighbourhood, if you're reasonably careful. More people die from traffic accidents there than from bombs and guns. He must have been a fool or blind drunk to get shot just weeks after he'd arrived. By his own side, if he even had one.

"I got the job in London shortly afterwards; I got the house there, too, after my mother died. I'd meant to sell Rest Harrow then, but I've never got round to it. I haven't been down to stay since Alun's death—not till this Christmas. I had to come—she'd been phoning me, saying she had to see me. And she kept mentioning you, Annie, saying what friends you were with her little girl, saying how you'd made it possible for her to get some time away from the child, opportunities—she didn't say for what. I hardly recognized her when I saw her. We talked over the washing-up, after that awful game of blind man's buff. She said she wanted to leave Pyeford—she had to leave Pyeford, and could I help her. Find her a place to stay, find her a job. So of course she knows, why else would she have asked me? I told her no, Annie: I said there'd be nothing in London that she could do—that it would be a mistake to take the child there, London wasn't safe for children. 'So you won't help me,' she said, and I said no, Annie.

"What else could I have done? I'll admit I'm to blame, but not for everything. He must have slept with fifty other women before me. And he might have gone back to Belfast, broken his promise to her, without my pushing him. You could even say that their marriage was finished the moment she made him promise such a thing. If he'd only gone to London, if he hadn't been such a fool. All I got from him in the end was one of his paintings, one of the last ones he'd done before running away. His dealer sold it to me at a price I wouldn't want to name. Fiona's held on to all the others—she won't sell them, and she won't show them—they're still in his studio, at the cottage.

"And she keeps phoning me, Annie, saying she needs my help and I don't know what to tell her. What can I do? Take her and the child into my happy home and expiate my sins? What would you do, Annie? What can anyone do?"

Rosalind loosened her grip on Anna's hand; she stood up and walked away from the bench where Anna was sitting slumped against the tree, her eyes like envelopes that had been torn open. But she wasn't seeing Rosalind, Rosalind sick with fear and guilt, like the painter of the snake women inside the church. All Anna could see now was the first fresco, the madonna and child, the folds of their garments no longer stiff but writhing, engulfing. Fiona holding Maeve too tight, bruising her, choking her; Maeve trying to run from her mother's clutch to the closest place of shelter. It was Maeve who needed her, Maeve, not Rosalind. That woman standing there with her arms wrapped tight around her, as if she were trying to warm herself in the thin, uncertain sun—she did not exist for Anna anymore. But Maeve, who had pleaded for help, who'd kept turning round to her, eyes full of the words she couldn't say: *stay with me, help me, I need you*. . . And she had run away from her, she had abandoned her, the way Maeve's father had abandoned her. She was as bad as Rosalind, there was nothing to choose between them, unless she could change what had happened, what would go on happening—

Rosalind was asking her something, but Anna heard only the wind shaking the leaves of the plane tree overhead, shaking and shaking as if rousing her from a state of shock. Suddenly, she knew exactly what she had to do, and when she spoke it was with a clarity that made her voice sound like a stranger's.

"I have to go back, I have to get home. To England, not Agia Maria—I have to leave right now, today."

If Rosalind made any protest, Anna didn't hear it, not even as the car raced down from Ano Viannos, careening along hairpin turns and jolting over roads so narrow that had another car approached them they would have been forced off the hillside onto the rocks below. She said nothing as Anna crushed papers, books, clothes into her suitcase, and pitched not only a sheaf of wildflowers but also the glass which held them, off the balcony into the empty swimming pool. All her actions had the recklessness of certainty, and though there was a good three hours to wait between the time Rosalind drove her to the airport and the time her plane was due to depart, Anna insisted on remaining in the small, glassed-in departure lounge, rather than lying out on the grass, ringed by the mountains that were suddenly visible in all directions. For just as suddenly, the weather had turned hot and dry, the air rasped by a sun brighter, larger than Anna remembered it from England. Perhaps that was why Rosalind decided to stay on the extra week, leaving Anna in the cramped and stuffy waiting room, a shimmer of urgency all round her like the whirr of a propeller. For she was no longer on the island of Crete, waiting to board a plane back to England: she was already in Pyeford, running up the path to the white cottage, knocking down the door and pulling Maeve to safety, as if from a house on fire.

# XXIII

# DISAPPEARING TRICKS

No lights anywhere except at Fortuna House, where a window bulged in the dark like a harvest moon. It was long past midnight, far too late to do anything but stagger up the steps to Rest Harrow. The cottage was exactly as she'd left it, except for an avalanche of newspapers in the front hall. She kicked them in the direction of the closet and lugged her suitcase upstairs to the guest room, deciding she preferred the innocent lumps of the mattress there to the compromised ones in Rosalind's bed. The air was close; Anna couldn't settle for the night until she'd wrenched open a window. Leaning into the cool, damp dark, she cast about for warning signals, messages, but the whole village seemed to be locked in sleep.

It was mid-morning before she woke—Maeve would already be at school. Anna decided to go and buy milk and bread at the village shop. As soon as she'd had breakfast she would go over to Fiona's; she would try to speak to her about Maeve, though she didn't know how on earth she'd begin. She was still searching for an opening line when Miss Molesworth, who'd come into the shop for half a pound of butter, rushed at her excitedly. "Hello, Miss English. Did you have a lovely time away? Have you heard the news? It's been the most terrible shock to us all. We don't know what could have become of them, running off like that. Why, your neighbours, of course."

For a moment, Anna didn't understand. And then she felt as if her heart had turned to a lump of lead. She kept seeing them as she had through the filthy glass of the basement door, Fiona and Nicholas—

"Of course it's most unpleasant, all the publicity—we're a very private village, you know, and we do have our pride. Some of the things written up in the local papers have been unspeakable."

"The little girl—what's happened to her, where is she?"

"Why, she's gone with her mother, of course. The family says they haven't seen hide nor hair of them. Nobody has. One knows it's been awful for her, no one could say she hasn't had the most dreadful time, although—"

"Come, come, Miss Molesworth," Mrs. Higley called from the counter. "You needn't get yourself worked up about it. There is nothing to be done—or said—until the police have finished their investigations. And I dare say there's an entirely innocent explanation for everything that's happened. If anything has happened."

For once, Anna was grateful to Mrs. Higley, though she couldn't help feeling bewildered. She'd assumed the postmistress would display a violent loyalty towards Cressy, and an equally violent animus against the lovers, if that's what they were to be called. Anna pushed the Mother's Pride, a pint of milk, and two pound coins across the counter. If Fiona and Nicholas had decided to take Maeve with them it meant they were gone for good, and if that was so there was nothing she could do. And yet Maeve was in trouble, she knew that, she had to try and help her. Anna smiled anxiously at Mrs. Higley, who seemed to look at her a little less banefully than usual.

"I don't suppose you would know anything, Miss English, but if you have noticed anything out of the ordinary at Mrs. Gibson's, you'd best report it to the constable."

Anna couldn't help herself; she so badly didn't want to hear what Mrs. Higley was saying. "But if she's simply run off with him, why need the police get involved at all?"

Mrs. Higley turned on her with an immense, majestic scorn. "No one has made any suggestion to the effect that Mrs. Gibson has run off on some romantic escapade. She disappeared with her daughter three nights ago, telling no one where she was going or why. And leaving her front door wide open. That's the worrying thing. It seems as though considerable damage was done to her late husband's paintings, as well. Hooligans, no doubt. We are talking of serious things, Miss English—it's not a pretty thought that vandals are loose in this village. If you do know anything, you had better get in touch with the police. Now Miss Molesworth, you're not to worry. I had a word with the chief constable himself this morning, and he told me things were well under control."

Anna turned on her heel, clutching her loaf of bread so hard it was the size of a fist by the time she got home. She made herself a phenomenally strong cup of tea, then let it get cold as she sat thinking. Ought she to go to the police? What did she know? That Fiona had been having an affair with Nicholas Pryce-Jones. Or at least, that they'd had sex once, to Anna's knowledge. That was it, "having" sex—like having a headache, or a nasty case of 'flu. Slowly, Anna got up from the table and forced herself to the parlour, to the mantelpiece. She examined the mirror as if expecting to find in some obscure and tarnished spot a reflection from Christmas Eve: Nicholas with Fiona's black scarf tied tight around his eyes, chasing Rosalind and then, as if he'd suddenly finished with the game, homing in to Fiona, searching her out, grabbing hold of her. And Maeve asleep upstairs, Maeve watching cartoons, turning the volume so loud she wouldn't have to hear them.

Anna slumped into the chair by the fireplace, her head in her hands. Should she go to see Cressy? Of course Cressy would know—hadn't Nicholas complained of how his wife revenged herself for all his infidelities by giving him the freest possible rein? At a price, of course. She wouldn't be surprised to hear that Cressy was pregnant again. She wouldn't be surprised at all.

But did it have to mean that they'd run off together? Couldn't Fiona simply have driven off one night, tired of Pyeford, sick of living with all those photographs glued to her study walls? Or—no longer satisfied with mere phone calls to London, had she taken Maeve and run off to Rosalind's? Not finding Rosalind at home, couldn't she have simply decided to go on running? Impossible to think anything else, there could be no other explanation. Anna held her head firmly between her hands. There was only one way to find out. She would go, not to the police but to Fortuna House and demand to know what was going on.

Cressy answered the door. She looked astonishingly well, positively blooming. The house was a wreck around her, but quiet—most of the children were off at school. Before Anna could say why she had come, Cressy asked her in, leading along a toy-bombarded corridor into the very room where the babies had been born. A harried-looking girl appeared—not Angelica, but a stubby, sullen au pair. Cressy asked her to bring some coffee, and then, reaching into a cradle beside her chair, she began to feed her baby.

Anna watched, torn between fascination and impatience. The baby fussed for a moment, then latched on to the nipple which Cressy had been manoeuvring into its mouth. It was nothing like the small pink star Anna had seen in the café; it looked instead like a huge, purple bag. Cressy looked up, saw Anna's eyes, and smiled.

"It's quite the most marvellous feeling in the world." Cressy sat gently rocking as the baby gulped at her breast. The au pair brought coffee, and poured out a cup for Anna. Cressy wasn't having any—she explained that it was bad for her milk. She pulled the baby gently away from her breast, patting the loose, pink bundle against her shoulder till she heard an enormous belch, then aimed her other nipple at the baby's soft, milky mouth.

"It's a shame Nicky isn't here—he'd so love to see you. He's been gone—oh, for ages, I haven't a clue when he'll be back. I don't understand these business arrangements, though I believe there's rather a lot of money involved in this one. Would you mind awfully handing me a tissue?"

Anna relaxed her grip on the armrests, latching onto a possibility as helplessly as the baby to its mother's breast. Mrs. Higley was wrong, and she'd been right all along. If Nicholas had been gone for days without giving Cressy any idea of when he'd be back, then he could easily have run off with Fiona. They were probably on their way right now to Italy or Spain, making a new start away from newspapers and contracts and paintings and babies. As for Maeve, she would have had no say in the matter, but at least she hadn't been left behind. Perhaps she'd taken the cat—she'd certainly have asked to take the cat. She would be all right—she would have to be. Of course she wouldn't have asked to stay behind, to stay with Anna—whatever had she been thinking? Maeve wasn't her child, she was Fiona's—had she really thought she could have taken her away from Fiona?

Angrily, Anna shoved the entire box of tissues over to Cressy, who didn't seem to want them now. She was gazing into her baby's eyes, and the baby was gazing up into hers as it fed. Anna noticed the baby's foot curling and uncurling in the most explicit pleasure. It made her think of the fresco at Ano Viannos—the tenderest of Cretan nativity scenes. She jumped up from her chair, desperate to leave the room.

"Ah, you'd like to hold her, would you?" Cressy detached the baby, holding it out to Anna, who stood stupidly before her, arms stiff at her sides. She had no desire to hold Cressy's baby, yet she didn't know what else to do. Reluctantly, Anna lifted her arms and accepted the child. "You'd better sit down here," Cressy said, motioning to the rocking chair she'd just vacated. "Do relax—anyone would think you'd never held a baby before. That's better. I'll just go and see how the other one's doing—I shan't be a moment. I'll bring her back for you to have a look. They're both such darlings—we've been so lucky."

Anna rocked jerkily back and forth. She didn't know what to do with anything this small. But Cressy's child seemed not to have the slightest idea that this body occupying its mother's chair was an utter, unaccommodating stranger. It gazed at Anna and smiled, regardless of the fact that Anna's lips stayed locked. And then the baby did a curious thing—it began rooting in Anna's jumper, searching out a nipple. Panicking, Anna jumped up, holding the baby as far from her as she possibly could, whereupon it started bellowing. Endless moments later Cressy returned to the sitting room, moving slowly, voluptuously, as though she were swimming through glycerine. In her arms she was carrying the other twin swathed in pink flannel. The au pair followed, like a nerve-wrecked dog on too short a leash.

"Agnès, take the baby from Miss English—she'd like to have her coffee. Ah, you've an appointment to attend? Never mind. You must come again—my husband will be so disappointed to have missed you."

"There, there," Anna heard Cressy crooning, as she made her way out. "There, there, my darling." As Fiona, Nicholas and Maeve jolted down some sunbaked road towards the open sea.

*     *     *

Over the next few days there was still no sign from the runaways. Too anxious to think about anything else, Anna ignored both the daily flood of newsprint and her blank computer screen, spending more and more time on the Downs. The skies had cleared, and it was still alarmingly warm. The first lambs had been born while she'd been away in Crete—the fields were full of bleating, udder-swollen sheep. Anna would stop along her way to look at them, noting the grizzled fleece, the shrivelled umbilici of the newborn lambs. And the indifference of the ewes as their young darted in under the filth-smeared fleece; tugged at the teats for a few seconds, tails spinning, till their mothers kicked them away.

On her way down the hillcrest she would see the white horse waiting for her. She'd stop and stare at it, certain that the animal's eyes were fixed on her own small shape, picking out the brown of her coat from the muck of the path. Why should it single her out, raise up its head and begin a high, hysterical whinnying? Anna would refuse to look at the horse all the time she was crossing the field to the ash glade. He would stop whinnying, but she would hear his hoofbeats as he cantered up and down the field, as if to frighten and bully her into acknowledging him. But she'd keep her eyes on the ivy raining down from the branches, the violets camped between the roots of the trees.

Once she had walked by Chantry Cottage, but the place was shut up, the garden parched. Simon must still be with his father—he must have taken extended leave from school. She was grateful for this new reprieve. It would be an awkward scene to have out, telling him that it had all been a mistake, nobody's fault, and couldn't they just forget it had ever happened, please? He would take off his glasses and pretend to polish them, and she would blush to the roots of her hair, and then each would turn and walk away. No harm intended, no hurt sustained.

*     *     *

When Anna came in from her walk one afternoon a police constable was waiting for her. She received him politely, brewed up a pot of tea, and answered his questions, agreeing with him that there were a few oddities in Fiona's house—the newspaper-wallpaper, for example. No, she didn't know about the slashed canvases in the dining room and studio. Yes, she was aware that most villagers found Mrs. Gibson somewhat unstable in temperament, but for her part—and living next door to Fiona Gibson, she could speak with some authority—she had no serious misgivings. She spoke of how conscientious a mother Fiona was, despite the lonely and constricted life she led. She mentioned that Fiona had begun to go out evenings, after Christmas—that she, Anna, had babysat for her, and had seen it all as a healthy, even encouraging sign. Did Miss English have any reason to think that Mrs. Gibson might have formed an attachment to someone, a romantic attachment? Dr. English answered that Fiona had told her nothing of where she went and whom she met, but that one couldn't overlook the fact that Fiona was, after all, a young and attractive woman, and that she had a right to some happiness after the terrible times she'd been through. The constable had left soon after, reassuring her that, as far as he could see, there was no cause for alarm, that doubtlessly the lady and her daughter would simply return that night or the next, as suddenly as they'd set out.

*   *   *

*Put out the light, I can't sleep with it on, you know that, darling, put out the bloody light.* Even out of the soundest sleep he'd wake if you switched on the lamp beside the bed, reaching down to pick up the baby, feed or soothe or change her, needing a light because you could never be too careful, and because you needed to see her, make sure she was real, alive in your arms after that long and silent sleep sealed up inside you, hidden safe inside you. Now she could never curl small enough for you to shield her, hold her so tight against you that she'd breathe with your lungs, fall asleep inside the soft, steady beating of your heart.

When she was newborn you lived in a fog of tiredness, your limbs heavy as sticks of furniture, only your ears and eyes alert for signs of danger: sparks from the fire, rain in the garden where you'd got her to sleep, at last, wishing you could lie down beside her, soak up sleep like a square of gauze dropped into a pail of water. Now you can never sleep, though you're forever tired you cannot keep your eyes closed, you've stopped undressing at night, even kicking off your shoes, you only lie down so that if she wakes she'll know where to find you. If you cannot sleep you might as well stay as you are, in an emergency you won't waste time pulling on your clothes. Stories your mother would tell about the war, the first raids, shivering in her nightdress till the all clear meant she could leave the shelter, crawl back into a bed that felt as cold and wet as the night outside. Some nights you think you'll take one of your mother's tablets, the little bottle she gave you the day you found out he was dead as well as gone, that he would never come back one day or night. That you would never again feel the rasp of his tongue against your thighs, your breasts, cat's tongue, the way he licked but never kissed. You liked that, you'd had enough of kisses from other men, kisses soft and sugary as lemon curd, you'd laughed together over them, you'd told him all about the others, though he'd never once mentioned his women: models, girlfriends, mistresses, but only you his wife, the mother of his child, as the saying goes, the saying came and went as he did, too. How many years did you have of him—the year before Maeve's birth, and three years after, and the year when you heard nothing, neither phone call nor letter nor even a card to mark her birthday, though she'd pretended not to mind, making drawings of the two of you, mother cat and kitten, long pink tongue licking, cleaning, taking care. You were always good at taking care of her, you'd wanted five at the very least, you had a knack for babies, calming them, feeding them, playing counting games and singing the nonsense rhymes Maeve was too big for now, though she'd pretend to want them. The way you'd pretend to be asleep when she came into your room before dawn, to warm you, you who were so cold from not sleeping, from lying with your hands like a mask over your face to stop you from seeing their faces, even when you'd locked up the room and left them to curl and yellow, falling like leaves from the walls.

Sleep, if you only could sleep, even for an hour, stone-dead sleep to put out the fire behind your eyes. The doctor could give you drops for that, put out a fire with an eyedropper, like taking a pill every night, you'd known right away it would be the whole bottle or nothing, you have the whole bottle, still, locked in your desk in that room you hate to enter now, because of their faces, because of the words, because no matter how hard you've tried to keep them from vanishing you could not make them into anything but ink to be rubbed away, paper to be used for lighting fires, bundles tied up for the dustman, week after week, as if they'd never been. Each of them demanding to be looked at, just looked at, until you can never not see, in that grainy field of images, dark and less dark, the soldier aiming his rifle at a mother holding a child. The moment before the shot is fired, that cannot end as long as you keep looking, that must not end because it once began, and to forget that, to stop seeing that, is to make it go on happening to all the others holding rifles, holding children in their arms.

He saw them once, when you were careless and hadn't locked the studio door. You'd told him no, Anna was busy that night so you had to stay home, you couldn't come to him. He'd made his way in and crept upstairs and found you here, at work. *Scissors and paste? Back to the schoolroom are we? But what are you doing, pasting pictures to the wall? It's been done before, you know—hardly original, my love, and making an awful mess, at that. Bad for the resale value—just goes to show you're cracking up, dear girl, but we can fix that, can't we? No need to stand on ceremony, in fact, no need to stand at all—*

And you'd let him, what else could you do to quiet him before he woke Maeve, he'd been shouting at the top of his lungs, he'd had too much to drink, as usual, as usual he'd needed too much to drink because the work was going badly, he was a fraud and he knew it. The same as with Alun, you had wanted someone as different as possible, someone who would never remind you, but they might have been brothers in this, if nothing else. Only this one had nowhere to run to, he'd told you once he'd take you away but you'd never believed him, you'd known from the start there was no such thing as away, only the coach house, or the studio downstairs, or here on a heap of newsprint, shoving and pushing against the papers scattered everywhere, so that they printed your very skin, and he kissed the ink from your back, running his hands over and over you, laughing, saying your bones were like blades under your skin; he was afraid every time that he'd walk away bleeding. *I can read you like a book, darling, read me a book, I can't get to sleep tonight unless you read to me.*

You cannot sleep this night, or any other night, and so you've come downstairs to this room you keep locked now, though nothing can keep them from leaking through the walls, printing themselves into the air you breathe, the light pushing through the windows, no matter how many curtains you pull. You unlock the desk and take out the dark, small bottle of sleeping pills that you will not take, but that you need to feel in your hands, solid as stones, a possibility, a precaution. And then you switch out the light, thinking you will go upstairs now, thinking you have heard a noise from your daughter's room, that she may need you, she who sleeps so fitfully, her breath like the tumble of leaves in autumn air, light and brittle as leaves falling. And just as you switch out the light you see it and smell it, for the first time: a dark haze, something acrid, like dust burning on a lightbulb. But it doesn't come from this room, you're sure of it—you walk out into the hallway and it's stronger there: a smell of burning.

You hear a sound like a flint being struck; you walk along the hallway and though no smoke curls up you can hear the fire, you wait for a moment, then throw open the door to the room where all his paintings hang. The frames are crackling on the walls; great tongues of heat prod and burst through each canvas, leaving red, open blisters. You have to shake yourself, you have to run, the balloons on the wallpaper over her bed will be turning to bulbs of molten glass, you have to run to her, carry her off to where it's safe.

Smoke—that's the real danger, not the flames: cram wet cloths beneath the doors while you wait to be rescued. But there's no time to wait, and no one to help you. Maeve's fast asleep, she's turning from you, fighting to get back under the blankets, her eyes plugged with sleep, like the mucous which sealed her inside you once, the way olives are sealed in earthenware jars. On your honeymoon you'd eaten jars full of salty, pungent olives, you with his child inside you; salty, pungent, the way his tongue inside you never rasped as it did on your face or breasts but was soft, soft, free as a fish in a stream, if only you couldn't remember, you had to remember the danger, though you could sleep now, you could crawl under the covers and curl yourself round your child; sleep inside the milky scent of her skin, the warmth of her fine, dark hair, his hair—

It's the smoke, making you drowsy, fogging everything so you can't tell, anymore, whether the fire is only behind your eyes or bursting through the locked door downstairs. Her eyes are open, now, and her whole body sprung like a pocket knife, stiff, sharp. She's thirsty, wants a drink of water; hungry, and you feel in your pockets for the bottle of pills, beautiful blue ones, indigo, lapis, wait, wait. You come back with a glass of water half-spilled on the bathroom tiles—come on, darling, take these with the water, they'll make you feel better. It's just for tonight, you must do what I say, it's an emergency. Wait, put on your slippers, there may be broken glass—no, don't run, you'll trip and fall, the stairs are dangerous in the dark. Shhh, don't cry, of course you can take the cat, but hold him tight, don't let him run away, and be quick, now, quick, outside—

You stand for a moment on the porch, looking for a light in Anna's windows, a sign that she's awake, that she understands the danger and will shelter you. But Anna's house is dark, Anna is gone, and besides, fire can jump from roof to roof; no house here is safe. There are no lights on, none, everyone has gone, everyone has heard the alarms and run away, leaving you alone, you and your child burying her face against you, holding on to your leg as if it were a ladder on which she could climb to someplace cool and safe and free. Let go, Maeve—I'll burn you, can't you feel how hot I am? My eyelids are singed, you can see right through my hands, look, they're like candles, darling, don't say anything, don't say a word, just get into the car, we're safe now, we're going where it's safe, strap yourself in, that's right. Don't let him scratch you, hold him tight. Don't look back, keep your eyes shut, it's easier that way, you won't be frightened, I won't let anything hurt you, so close your eyes and sleep now, darling, sleep—

Turning down the lane you see ashes like huge golden kites sailing out the shattered windows of your house, the very roof tiles melting, lead dripping from fiery pillars, fire leaping from house to house. Nowhere cool or dark or distant, even the trees are fiery parachutes, as the road bubbles under your wheels. You must get to the water, smoke smearing the windshield so you can't see, only guess the direction in which you are moving, on and on past hedgerows flaming, gorse on the hillside bursting fire. And somehow you're not driving, anymore; the car's wheels are locked, your hands and feet frozen. The road itself hurling you out of the flames and into the water, sea or river, anything to keep your child from flaring up like a twist of paper. She's sleeping now, but you can't hear her breathing, you call out Maeve, Maeve, but the heat is splitting your throat in two, you have no words to wake her, wake you from this hurtling dream where the whole world's on fire and only the water can save you, seal you, put out the smoke and the light, the light—

\*  \*  \*

The next day two bodies were found in a river some miles away. It would appear that Fiona had driven the car off a little-used bridge where the water ran unusually wide and deep. It was discovered that the child had been given sleeping tablets; most likely she hadn't been conscious when the car had plunged through the wooden rails, into the stream. A boy out fishing had seen the car roof peeking above the water—he'd thought at first it was an old cooker someone had junked. The deceased's parents had been contacted, and would be making all the necessary arrangements. Along with the bodies of woman and child, the corpse of a cat had been found in the car.

\*  \*  \*

Varti had office hours until six, but she gave Anna the key to her house, instructing her to wait there till she returned. Anna had watched the early news, but there'd been only a sentence or two in the local report, and a shot of the car being raised from the river. Anna walked over to the window, saw her face floating in the glass like a fat, full moon, and tugged the curtains shut. Maeve with her inky, narrow eyes, pushing up her face to be kissed. Scratching black lines in white paper. Afraid to go into Fiona's room, afraid of the pictures on the wall.

When Varti came home she took Anna into her study, sat her down in the chair across from the reproduction of Blake's *Pity* and explained that one could be just as devastated by a mental as by a physical shock. She refused to agree that Anna was to blame for anything. Blame, said Varti, did not strike her as a particularly useful notion in this context. Certainly, Anna had been involved. Each of one's actions had a myriad repercussions, the majority of them unforeseeable. It was quite likely that Anna would reproach herself for a long time to come with what she had or hadn't done. That was part of the process of grieving, and grief wasn't at all the self-indulgence some people assumed it to be. It hurt. It would pass, eventually, leaving some kind of scar. But then, Varti said, drawing closer to Anna, taking Anna's hands in her own, "Those scars become—what's it called on our passports? Distinguishing marks. They're how we know ourselves, how we identify our selves to ourselves. And to God. No one else is involved, now," Varti insisted. "Just you and God."

Anna gently disengaged her hands, looking down and examining her fingers one by one, finding a pale scar on her fingertip. She couldn't remember how she'd come by it.

"You're exhausted, Anna—you need to get some sleep. Look, I have lots of room. Why don't you stay the night?"

Anna shook her head. "I have to get back to Pyeford."

"You're sure you can manage the drive?"

"I can manage it." Anna had to fight to keep the irritation from her voice. She was furious at Varti, at her crosses and kindness and God; at her television set which had confirmed the deaths by showing the car, the broken bridge, the river.

"I'll be here or at the office all week, Anna. Call me, if you need anything. Or if you just want to talk."

Anna drove to Pyeford without seeing the road, or the clouds skimming the moon overhead. It was no surprise to her that she reached Rest Harrow all in one piece. For she was, she knew, the sort to whom nothing would ever happen, either for good or ill. She was perfectly safe, safe and sound and impermeable—like a macintosh. Lying in her bed that night, listening to the wind ripping leaves newly unfolded from the trees, she felt cold black waves of panic rising up in her, each one carrying her farther and farther from the neat, narrow bed. She could not weep or cry out; she lay naked, open, exposed to the dark that was washing over her.

If she wanted anything, it was to have someone she could grab and hold onto, someone who would keep her from dissolving into the night and the cold all around her. And there was no one to help her, no one at all.

# XXIV

# MONK'S HOUSE

Anna did not attend the funeral service in the village church. Nor did she call Varti, or attempt to get in touch with Nicholas or Rosalind or Simon.

The first thing she'd done after learning of what Pyeford had begun to call "the accident" was to get rid of her subscription to the paper. She'd called the station booksellers and told them to send her copies on to a local hospital or old age home—anywhere, so long as they didn't keep coming to her door. Next she'd unplugged the radio, wound the cord tightly round it, and shoved it back in the airing cupboard. And then she'd spent a good day clearing out the study, bundling the newspapers she'd accumulated over the past three months and dumping them in and around the rubbish bin. She trashed her various computer files, and threw out the contents of her desk— the letters Luke had sent, drafts of her replies to him, various notebooks detailing strategies for the book she was to write. Last of all she took her doctoral thesis with its leather covers and bravely embossed spine into the garden. There she'd dug a grave at the back of the rosemary bushes, and buried the thing as if it were of no more consequence than the bones of a bird or cat.

Inside again, she'd drawn all the curtains in the house, shut herself into the study and plunged into the space she'd freed. The text which poured onto her computer screen had nothing to do with scholarly exposition or theoretical fireworks. It was nothing but interrogation. Why and what and how to write in a world of sirens and alarms and step-by-step catastrophes. If death is the moment when illusion fails, how do we keep ourselves from not knowing what we do know? *Occupation is essential. And now with some pleasure I find that it's seven & must cook dinner. Haddock and sausage meat.*

Fiona, dressing up Maeve in costume; undressing herself for Nicholas, till she'd finally let go of all occupations and evasions, slashing her husband's paintings but leaving her study walls untouched as she'd run out into the night. She knew, she hadn't a single illusion left, least of all Maeve. So Anna understood it, now. And as Fiona's parents were scraping photographs of starved children, earthquake victims, dying refugees off their daughter's study walls, Anna read and reread Woolf's last diary, until she, too, heard the bombers on their way to London, stocked the garage with enough gasoline to induce asphyxiation, learned the amount of morphia needed to produce a fatal overdose.

*We live without a future. That's what's queer, with our noses pressed to a closed door. Now, to write.* Anna hunched over her keyboard, biting her fingernails to below the quick, tapping, tapping, refusing to go out for a walk or even to open the mail which dribbled through the letter box. Obsessed with getting down a text that grew like an infection or contagion in the space between Woolf's words and the newspapers Anna had devoured all winter; between Woolf's walk into the Ouse and Maeve and Fiona's nightward plunge.

She worked day and night, her only interruptions those moments when she was overwhelmed by the truth, the necessity of her text. Moments when she woke from dreams leaving jagged edges in her head. The car slowly arching to the water, Fiona's fingers clamped to the steering wheel; Maeve's eyes gummed with sleep. And the cat, springing from the child's lap, clawing at sealed windows.

*         *         *

It was the effect of driving herself so hard, shutting herself up for so long, Anna's fainting one afternoon. She was writing faster, more fluently than she'd ever done: hours at a stretch. Sometimes she'd go to bed at one and wake three hours later, words still streaming through her head. Dawn would find her facing the milky glow of her computer screen—or would have found her, had she ever opened the curtains. So it wasn't in the least surprising that one afternoon, when she'd been writing for five hours at a stretch, Anna should suddenly pull away from the keyboard and announce to no one in particular, "I'm going to faint."

Some time later she found herself on the floor, staring at the cracks webbing the ceiling. She sat up gingerly—it seemed she hadn't hurt herself. Slowly she got to her feet and pulled herself into the kitchen, where she made herself a cup of tea, stirring in three tablespoons of sugar. It was two-thirty, and she hadn't eaten since breakfast of the day before. Ransacking the cupboard and refrigerator, she came up with a boiled egg and a package of Rye-Vita. She ate both, then—still a little shaky—picked up a carrier bag and went down to the village shop.

It was beautiful outside. The sun blazed, and the grass over which she walked looked far less green and lush than usual. Inside the shop, people were talking about the possibilities of drought and water rationing. Miss Molesworth was there, hand-picking her half-dozen eggs—there was still a scare about salmonella. She was talking over the aisle to Mrs. Higley.

"It's such a shame. One hears he's very popular with the children."

"Ah, but his father's all alone up there. I think it's very natural for him to stay on with him. Commendable, in his circumstances. You don't often find men making sacrifices like that—they usually leave it to the women."

"He hasn't got a sister, then?"

"I shouldn't think so. We would know if he did, don't you think?"

Anna paid for her apples and cheese, and left the shop.

She stopped, on the way home, by the call box. Miraculously, it was working. She dialled the number of Varti's surgery and made an appointment for the following afternoon. Probably Varti would tell her to spend a day in bed or take a walk by the sea. Though it was just possible there was something under par with her blood—she'd been anaemic before; she really ought to check. And besides, she wanted to see Varti's calm, fine face again—apologize for how rude she'd been to her the last time they'd met. It was nothing, it was just her feeling slightly grey and shaky, but she wanted, just for a moment, for Varti to tell her everything would be all right.

That evening Anna forced herself out for a walk. Not up the Downs but only as far as the ash glade, walking along the now-hardened path, listening to bird song tumbling on either side of her. Making way for the person walking towards her, she discovered Mrs. Higley, with a dog on a lead. "Good evening," Anna called out, almost against her will—it had been so long since she'd actually spoken to another person, face to face. To disguise the fact that she'd nothing else to say, Anna bent down and caressed Mrs. Higley's companion—a stunted sheepdog, peculiarly tufted and far too long in the body for its stumpy legs.

The transformation of Mrs. Higley was immediate. Eagerly, she informed Anna as to the dog's name and breed, praising its virtues as a family dog, stressing its fidelity, the gentleness of its character. Next, she admitted its few foibles—how it loved to cut loose and run cross-country. How she'd often get phone calls from farmers living ten miles away, to the effect that her dog was in their field—could she please come and retrieve it? "She's very much a country dog—she would hate the city. That's something to take into account if you're thinking of getting one."

"But I do live in the country," Anna countered. "In Canada, I mean. Where I live would be perfect—it's right on the sea-coast, there are no major roads. I'd love a dog like this." And she turned to caress the dog again. "You're a lovely, lovely girl, you are." Remembering that the last time she'd held anything alive and warm had been at Fiona's house, reading stories to Maeve.

By the time they parted, Anna and Mrs. Higley were, if not fast friends, then allies of a kind. Letting herself into Rest Harrow Anna asked herself why she shouldn't buy a dog on returning to Canada. She didn't care what people said about childless people lavishing attention on small, hairy animals, she wouldn't listen to anything anyone said. Except Varti. She had an appointment for tomorrow morning. If only she could somehow get through the time between now and ten o'clock tomorrow morning.

The only help for it was to work, to try and finish the book in one last, running leap. Though she didn't feel hungry in the least, she made herself eat a slice of toasted cheese and half an apple. Then she hurried to the study and sat down to her desk as though what she had to deal with were a diving, not a keyboard; as though the element opening its arms to her below were either water still and deep as glass, or glass so dark it looked like water.

The reflection she saw below her, in what was either glass or water, undid all certainties and consolations. Nothing stayed, nothing held: neither stillness nor motion, building up or smashing down. Just floodwaters rising: over the child playing at the edge of the lake, the mother reading on a blanket in the sand, the father on his vanished horizon. And yet as long as she wrote, she was safe; as long as there were words, tangible, material as the keys she stroked. Guns rattling the windows, making her pen jump from her fingers; searchlights flooding the meadows. And an ageing woman, shutting her book, taking up her walking stick, and heading for the river.

Sometime just before morning, Anna felt the crazy joy that comes with risking everything and running blind. Her book was finished, as true as she could make it. She could shut down now, she could go home. And she could tell herself that by some miracle she had done what she came all this way to do. Whatever the losses and errors, however catastrophic, however irretrievable, she could at least do this: hold up her book in her hands. Look to it as to that small, pink, fleshy star: attached to nothing and pointing nowhere, but shining in its own way, all the same.

*       *       *

Varti listened to Anna's confession that she'd spent the past month in a delirium of writing, then made her describe her eating habits. She asked all the usual questions: did she suffer from headaches—no—were her periods normal—yes, she thought so, though she never really bothered to keep track. Varti got Anna to lie down on the examining table and tested her reflexes, palpated her abdomen, listened to her heartbeat, examined her eyes, ears, mouth and nose. She took blood and urine samples, explaining that it was very likely Anna was anaemic, though not seriously so. The test results would be back in a few days' time—Anna should call next week to see if there were a need for iron tablets or any other medication.

Once out of the surgery Anna had no idea what to do. It was too fine a day to drive straight back to Pyeford—besides, if she returned to Rest Harrow she'd be tempted to read what she'd written, and that would be ruinous. What was done was done; she mustn't alter a word lest she panic and throw the whole thing away. She ought to celebrate, to ride her euphoria as far as it would take her. At the very least, she could try a country drive. She pointed the car in a southerly direction, thinking she might make her way to the coast, even hop a boat for France. But then she saw the turnoff for Rodmell, and thought of Monk's House. It would be the perfect way to bring her book to its completion. She couldn't remember the opening times, or when the visitors' season began, but she knew she'd get in, she knew it as well as she knew her own name.

What did it matter that Rodmell wasn't anything like what she'd expected? Housing developments were going up at either end; the village was turning into a suburb. One of the posher houses had a seasoned-brick wall, and a tall, black-stained wooden gate. There was a plaque attached to the brick: the name of the house, and for heraldic emblem, two crossed tennis racquets. Savage barking came from a dog chained within—Anna hurried past. Overhead the sky was a bright, blank blue, with clouds pure as the white of a child's eyes. In the fields beyond a row of brick cottages she heard sheep fussing: the lambs, she noticed, no longer capered but spent all their time tearing up and digesting the grass.

Monk's House was open. Anna paid her way inside and found that she had the place completely to herself. She had to shake herself every now and again to register the fact that she was crossing the same floorboards, looking out through the same windows that Virginia Woolf had known. She wasn't prepared for the stillness of the rooms, nor could she rid herself of the feeling that the house, though occupied by strangers, was possessed by ghosts. And yet she felt no great rush of understanding as she looked dutifully at the Omega tiles, or the glass fish which the dead novelist's dead nephew had brought back to her from China. Every object in the house ought to have had a nimbus round it, and perhaps it did, but she couldn't perceive it, hard as she tried.

Entering Woolf's bedroom, she felt a disproportionate sense of space, so that she was most keenly aware not of bed or table or painted tiles, but of the room someone's absence had left behind. It puzzled and disappointed her; it was like looking at a painting of an interior in which the human figure—a woman reading or bathing or writing letters—had been excised, letting in opacity instead of light. And the longer Anna stayed in the room, the more the furnishings receded, so that all she was left with was this dull, hurtful sense of absence, abandonment. *They have all gone blackberrying in the sun.* And though you held out your arms to them and called, they would never hear you, never turn and come back again.

There was nothing for her in this house. She would faint again, she would fall straight down through the tube of her body and under the floor if she didn't push herself outdoors. Stumbling into the garden, Anna breathed in great gulps of sun and air, till her eyes stopped rocking in her head and her ears left off their yellow humming. Soon she'd recovered enough to consult her guide book. It told her that the elm under which Woolf's ashes were buried had succumbed to disease. She went into the garden house in which Woolf had written *Between the Acts*; glanced at the photographic exhibit arranged there. The printed text was judiciously concise: "On the afternoon of March 28, 1941, Virginia Woolf drowned herself in the Ouse River." There was nothing about it having taken them three weeks to recover the body.

Anna looked out the wavy glass of the windows at the mass of green and blue outside. The week before her death, Woolf had walked round and round this very garden, bumping blindly into trees; would come into a room on an errand and stand suspended, having forgotten whatever business she'd been about. Until that moment when, focussed, intent, she'd weighted her pockets with stones and walked down to the river.

What kind of stones, Anna wondered, retracing her steps from the garden hut. (Birds were singing, yet the rush of sound she heard wasn't birds, but water.) What kind of stones, and how many? It was important, it was suddenly necessary to know this. (The river flowed right through the garden, right up to and over her feet.) Virginia Woolf had lived to be sixty, not thirty; she hadn't crashed her car through a bridge; she hadn't taken anyone else along with her. (Water rising over the bulge of her knees, the blades of her hips, over her breasts and throat and lips.) Going to her death, Woolf had been perfectly composed: a lady in a marble effigy, ruff undinted, hands clasped upon an adamantine breast. (The river deeper, wider than she'd ever imagined.) Placing her walking stick upon the bank, easing herself down the sloping bank. Nothing like the speed, the violence of that leap taking woman, and child, into *complete submarine calm*.

*Floating on their backs along the bottom of the river, staring up at the shadow of a branch waving in a wind they cannot feel. Knowing nothing, hearing nothing but the flow of the river, lapping and stroking and combing their hair. Mouths open, eyes and ears, so that the water enters them and they become the water and their bones, white boats upon an open sea.*

One of the attendants came out to tell her, very gently, that the house and grounds were closing; she could perhaps come back another day. Anna thanked him, but shook her head. Only when the man offered her his pocket handkerchief did she discover that her face was wet; that the only rivers in this garden were her eyes.

# XXV

# BLUEBELLS

Anna telephoned the surgery first thing Monday morning.

"Yes, your tests have come back. Dr. Penrose would like you to start on some iron tablets. She's written out a prescription—you can pick it up this morning."

Anna drove straight over, rang the buzzer, and asked for the prescription. The receptionist said that Anna would have to wait and see the doctor, who wanted to speak with her. Instantly, Anna summoned thoughts of fatal or incapacitating illness. Since her visit to Monk's House, the euphoria of finishing her book had given way to anxiety and gloom. She was terrified some computer virus would attack her text, yet she couldn't bring herself to print it out, lest she reread what she'd written and find the whole thing to be ravings, rubbish. And she'd been unprepared for the news that Simon's cottage had just been sold. Queuing up at the village shop she'd heard Mrs. Higley informing Miss Molesworth that Simon had returned to finish up the school term, but was renting a room in town. Anna felt oddly bereft, as though she'd been robbed of something inconspicuous, yet absolutely necessary to her, like the laces of her shoes or the lining of a winter coat.

Less than an hour after her arrival at the clinic she was called into Varti's office. It was the extraordinary gentleness of her friend's expression that made Anna jump to the worst conclusion.

"What is it, what's wrong with me? Please don't hide anything—it's better if you tell me straight out."

"Sit down, Anna," Varti laughed. "There's nothing to worry about, it's nothing life-threatening."

"So there *is* something you haven't told me. Please, Varti, out with it. I've been imagining the worst—"

"Then stop. There's absolutely nothing wrong with you. You're nine weeks and a bit pregnant—that's all."

Anna's mouth gaped wide enough to swallow a full moon. And then she recovered herself, convinced that if only she could speak with enough force she could change Varti's diagnosis. "You've made a mistake—or a very bad joke. There's no way I can possibly—"

"My dear Anna, I'm not at all interested in who or how or why. My only concern is to make sure that you have a healthy baby. We've made a start—here's that prescription for iron tablets. What we'll have to do now is take some notes, find out a bit of family history. The nurse will take care of that. I just want you to promise me that you won't panic, and that you'll take things easy for the next little while. Give yourself time to adjust to the idea—though it's not an idea at all, it's a distinct physical presence, as I felt the other day on the examining table. Physical and spiritual presence, I might add. Now, I'd like you to go and see the nurse, and I'd also like you to join me for dinner at six o'clock tonight. I want to take you out somewhere special. This calls for a celebration, Anna. Don't look so dubious. Having a baby is the most natural thing in the world, and there's no reason at all that this pregnancy shouldn't go swimmingly. Now off you go—the nurse is in 3B, down the hall."

*       *       *

Coming out of the surgery, Anna squinted at the noontime dazzle of the street. The sun was a giant kettle spitting and scalding her skin and hair. You could imagine bees thrumming, all the windows bursting into flower. Turning down a side street, she found herself staring into a shop window, unable to register whether it were violins or toasters or calf brains displayed within. There was a snuffling sound behind her: a woman in a broad-brimmed hat, her dress held up by safety pins, her knickers puddled round her shoes, was going through a rubbish bin that had been left out on the street. She was putting the things she wanted—a bottle of soft drink with an inch of liquid at the bottom, a bashed tea canister, an odd sock—into a carrier bag, making no attempt to shove what she discarded back inside the bin. Before the woman could look up and notice her, Anna rushed away.

It was far too hot to be out for a stroll, and yet she kept on walking, up and down Castle Hill, around the public gardens, past grungy pubs and pastel cottages throttled with wisteria. Walking anywhere and nowhere, thinking of nothing but the need to place one foot before the other. When she could walk no more, she found a table at the Station Café and, leaving her plate of scones and jam untouched, rehearsed what she would say to Varti.

Anna arrived at the surgery at precisely six o'clock, her clothes hopelessly crumpled, her face streaked with dust and sweat. Varti took her into the washroom next to her office, bathing her face and brushing her hair for her. She straightened Anna's dress and smiled—"Perhaps we'll forgo the oysters and champagne tonight. Come home with me and I'll fix us something there."

"I'm not hungry, Varti. I'd rather just talk, if that's all right."

"If you like—"

"I don't like, Varti, I don't like any part of this. That's what I've come to tell you. I can't go through with this pregnancy—"

"This baby—"

"This pregnancy, Varti. I need your help."

"Anna—you can't decide what to do in a few hours, you need to take time, think things through—"

"I haven't got time, Varti. And I've *lived* things through—that's surely good enough. You said you needed my family history—shall I tell you what I didn't tell the nurse?"

"Let's go to my office, Anna."

"No—I can tell you here just as well."

Varti leaned against the white-tiled walls, folding her arms. "Go on, then, Anna. I'm listening." Her hair and her skin so soft, so dark against the carbolic white, and yet she looked to Anna far more tired than she was herself—tired and ill and her eyes so ruined Anna would have to read to her, spell things out beyond any possibility of misunderstanding.

"I never knew my father, Varti—have I told you that? But it wasn't his fault. Everyone thought he'd deserted her, but it isn't true. She told me, Varti, I've known this ever since I was old enough to know my name and address and telephone number—you know, in case of emergencies. My mother simply walked out of my father's life one day, with a suitcase full of books, and with me curled up inside her. I don't know whether she ever told him about me—I never had the courage to ask. Because I was afraid, if I did, that she'd do to me what she did to him—just disappear one day, walk out of my life, for no reason at all.

"It wasn't that he drank, or beat her or that he had someone else. He was a good man, she always said, as if somehow that made things all right. I could never tell her that that's what frightened me most—that even if I were perfectly good and never made any trouble for her at all, she could still just get up and walk out on me one day. Because that's what she'd done to my father—she decided she couldn't go on living with him, being his wife, and so she left, and she took him away from me. When I was small I used to think he was waiting for me somewhere, and that I ought to be able to find him; that he would walk into the schoolyard at recess or into our apartment one evening when she was out, and just let me look at him. I'd make up stories about being taken to see him, about running away on a bus or a train that would arrive at a station in an unknown city where he would be waiting for me on the platform, and I would know him—as soon as I saw him, I would know his face, and his name, and he would know mine. Do you know what it's like growing up with that kind of lack—not being able to put a face to the name of your father, not being able to mention just the word, father? It's like having only one eye or arm or leg, and living your whole life in terror that you'll do something stupid and lose the other one as well— something stupid that you'll never be clever enough to prevent, because it's all your fault of course, that's what you never understood, that I would know, know it was really all my fault, by having insisted on being born in the first place. So don't start in with 'At least I went through with it and had you, and would you rather you hadn't been born at all?' Because I've been thinking all day, walking round and around this horri- ble little town, I've been thinking that you should never have had me, that it's been the great mistake of both our lives. And that were I to go through with this baby, I'd simply be playing your life all over again. One mistake making another, that's what it would be—and I couldn't do what you did, I haven't got the will or the courage. I haven't got the ignorance either, to think I was doing the right thing, because I know what that child's life would be, the damage and hurt there'd be. I know, it's the one thing I'm still sure of, and I won't, I can't, I refuse."

"Anna—"

But Anna refused to take even half a step in the direction of Varti's outstretched arms. *Mother May I*—she wouldn't play that game any- more, and she turned her face away when Varti made a movement to stroke it. And so, instead, Varti reached up to the window sill behind

Anna's head, to a small basket of artificial violets which someone had put there, perhaps to soften the naked, functional nature of the room. Varti ran her fingers over the surface of the flowers: they came away streaked with dust. She shook her head.

Anna, speaking to Varti's image in the mirror across from her: "I need your help with this—there's no one else. You have to try and understand."

Varti, putting the violets back on the sill, brushing her hands against her stiff, white, doctor's coat. "I can't help you, Anna, not in the way you want. If I did, I'd be unmaking more than a human life; I'd be undoing the self that I've made, Anna, made for *me* ever since my husband died and I was free to think for myself, be someone other than the woman he wanted. I could say I understand your reasons, but that would be a lie—I don't understand anything but the fact that you don't want the only help that I can give you. If you change your mind, you know I'll be here for you, for as long as you like. Otherwise—" Varti took out a pad of paper and a pen, wrote down an address and handed it over to Anna with the gentlest expression on her face, pleading the opposite of what her words announced. "You should call them, Anna, as soon as possible."

But all Anna saw in the face of the woman turning away from her now was the face of the dying woman on the hospital bed, who had turned away from her then because she'd been unable to make Anna do the one thing for which she'd been preparing her all her life—to walk away from her, never to need her or anyone else. Except her own self, the self that refused, once again, to return her gaze, no matter how long or hard she stared into the mirror which no longer bore even a shadow of Varti's face.

*       *       *

Anna's appointment was scheduled for noon. At eight o'clock—she'd been awake since four—she decided she couldn't stand another minute alone in Rest Harrow. She got into her car and drove down The Street, along the leafy tunnel and out of Pyeford. She would take an especially long, circuitous route to Brighton.

When she found her hands shaking so violently that she couldn't grip the wheel, Anna pulled into a lay-by. Rolling down the window, she drew in great, shuddering breaths of air. Mayblossom, hawthorn—thick, musky scents. Wood doves were cooing, hoarse-throated, repetitious, like idiots playing penny-whistles.

It was no easier to wait in the car than in the cottage. Anna decided to get out and walk towards a field of bluebells she'd glimpsed from the road. Before long she found herself wading through waist-high grass into a stretch of woods. Everywhere, trees lay toppled: one trunk had been completely smashed, and yet a part of it pushed out green shoots, obscenely vigorous. It made her think of the only part of *War and Peace* she could recall with any vividness—Prince Andrei's drive to the Rostovs' country place. His carriage goes through an oak grove in which he sees an ancient tree, massive, misshapen, but putting forth a host of small, new leaves. And this perfectly anomalous, perfectly natural occurrence strikes him with the force of an annunciation. It is after this, it is because of this, that he falls in love with Natasha when she leans out of her window to look up at the stars. ·

Anna reminded herself that she was no Natasha. And that, after all, Prince Andrei dies in the novel, more or less by choice. She began to walk more quickly, tripping over fallen branches and losing all sense of direction till at last she found herself in a flood of flowers.

They weren't at all the same blue as Maeve's eyes. *Bluebells, cockleshells, easy, izy over.* If you could think of time as being like one of those chains of paper dolls joined at hands and feet, then perhaps the child she'd been could touch hands with a lost Maeve, skipping rope to the same rhyme. She couldn't stop herself thinking of Maeve, thinking how Maeve was dead, and this child alive, inside her. She wanted Maeve alive, and her own child dead. No, she only wanted them to change places; for neither that death nor this life ever to have been.

Anna went further and further into the woods, trying not to crush the flowers underfoot. It was so cool and still, it was like walking into a sea that could never rise higher than your knees, and yet that covered you, washed over you, sealed you with its scent. But when she bent closer to the bluebells, running her fingers over them, she found them sliced from their stalks, dying all around her. At first she thought some animal had tramped through, and then she understood—the cuts were so clean, the path so deliberate that someone must have come here with a knife and slit the heads off all the flowers.

She felt sick, at first, as though her stomach had turned into a snake and were rising up in her throat. And then she felt nothing but the fury that can make you act with clarity and force, and a kind of grace. Dropping to her knees, Anna began heaping the lopped flowers into her skirt. When it could hold no more she made her way back to the car, her laden skirt stretched out in front of her. She shook the bluebells onto the passenger's seat, turned the car round, and drove back to Pyeford. Once inside Rest Harrow she crammed the flowers into glasses, jam jars, carafes. In the end the cottage was dark with blue-bells, their scent invading all surfaces—plaster, tiles, floorboards, Anna's very skin.

When she next glanced at her watch it was half past noon. She would have to run down the road to the call box, lie to the receptionist at the clinic—say her car had stalled, or she'd had a flat tire. She would have to make a new appointment, though it was almost too late already. She would have to go up to London, or onto the continent, find someone who would take her at her word and her wallet and ask no questions. She would have to do so many things, though she was suddenly so tired she could barely hold the vase in her hands. It fell and shattered on the tiles, spraying up and soaking her skirt, her shoes; stranding her in a sea of flowers.

# XXVI

# UNDERWATER

After a glacial week, when three inches of snow (later identified as hail) fell in Kent, June turned torrid once again. In the gardens of Pyeford, bellflowers fried, snapdragons crackled and flabby roses dribbled scent into the curtain-heavy air. Water tables fell to the lowest level ever recorded; two-hundred-pound fines were slapped on anyone caught using a garden hose. Every afternoon helicopters hovered in the Sussex skies, searching out guiltily green lawns. For the money squandered on overhead surveillance they could, Miss Molesworth grumbled, have pumped water down from the Scottish lochs. From the pulpit of the post-office counter Mrs. Higley disagreed: if the law decreed the lawns must suffer, suffer they would. She had no qualms about informing on those who sneaked out at night to turn on their sprinkler systems.

The flower beds at Rest Harrow turned to bare, cracked clay. Aphids colonized the roses, which bloomed no longer white or red but green under the constant press of small, sucking bodies. Once Anna spent the better part of an evening watching a solitary ladybug feast on a tribe of aphids. It stayed light so long, these days—it would be the solstice in a week's time. But she had lost all sense of calendar time.

Anna slid into lassitude as if it were a wide, warm lake, through which she could barely look up, so green and hazy were its waters. She was insatiably sleepy and spent most of her time either in bed or on a chaise longue, dozing in the sun. She hadn't so much as looked at her computer; she hadn't left the village, even to buy groceries—thanks to her, Mrs. Higley was doing a roaring trade. No one had written except Rosalind, a postcard from the States, where she was being interviewed for a university post. It suited Anna very well for Rosalind to be off on the other side of the ocean; let her stay there forever, while Anna sank deeper and deeper into the stillness and silence of Rest Harrow.

Sometimes, to keep herself company, she'd listen to the radio she'd disinterred from the airing cupboard. News would float in and out the reeds over her head, sending back glassy echoes. Though disturbingly high levels of dioxin had been discovered in random samplings of breast milk, mothers were still encouraged to feed their babies as Nature intended. Strikes had paralysed buses, trains and the London Underground, though the weather continued so fine no one seemed to mind being crippled very much. And students were demonstrating for democracy in China, occupying a central square in Beijing, issuing statements and fashioning statues of liberty.

An apprehensive festivity seeped into the news from China, infecting on-the-spot reporters, radio announcers and commentators alike. These days Anna had no access to a television set and never looked at a paper, so she didn't see but only heard about the lone demonstrator dancing a duet with a tank. She pictured him empty-handed, bareheaded, bones as light as thistledown. But when the tanks stopped dancing and started smashing; when the reports came in of bodies being torched in the central square as old men watched from tortoise eyes, it was the same for Anna as if she were listening to Haydn or Handel from the sandy bottom of her lake. Whatever went on in the solid as opposed to the watery world could not concern her; nothing could be farther from her now than the panic of newsprint and static.

She might have gone on forever in this dim, damp drowse if it hadn't been for Rosalind showing up one afternoon. Finding Anna sunning herself in an improvised bathing suit and listening—or not— to a string quartet, Rosalind announced her arrival by switching off the radio.

"Hallo, Annie. Isn't that an unusual posture for you to take up— recumbent *en plein soleil*? Playing hookey, or have you bid adieu to academe?"

Anna sat up in shock, nearly toppling off her chaise longue. Pulling on the shirt she'd left lying on the grass beside her, she blurted out the first thing that came into her head: "You're supposed to be in the States. What are you doing here?"

"Spying on you, of course." Laughing, Rosalind kicked off her shoes, lay back in the matching chaise longue, and waggled her feet in the air.

Anna looked across at her. The sick, strained air Rosalind had worn in Crete had given way to buoyancy. She was wearing a sleeveless silk dress, ultramarine and cut so simply it had to have cost the earth. Her hair was longer and fuller round her face, and she was brilliantly made up—lipstick, rouge, nail and toe polish. "I don't suppose there's anything stronger than mineral water in this house?"

"There's some whiskey in the larder—it's left over from Christmas."

Rosalind vanished, appearing moments later with the last of the Scotch and two tumblers of water. They sat sipping their drinks in the blaring sun, Anna trying to beat down a wave of rage. The last thing she needed was Rosalind barging into her private limbo, tugging her back up by the roots of her hair into a world of facts she didn't want.

Rosalind, chattering on about the Proms, sunlight playing its own brass band upon her hair, hadn't said a word yet about what had happened in the village—hadn't even mentioned Fiona's name. What if, off in the States for interviews and manicures, she hadn't heard? Should Miss Molesworth be called in and asked to tell all, or was it up to Anna to sit back and give the news herself? Spinning ice cubes in her glass and whispering out loud, "What a shame about your ex-next-door neighbours. You haven't heard? Well, my dear, let me tell you—"

Rosalind ought to have heard, she ought to be made to know. But there she was, sitting back in her chair with her skirt rucked up, tanning her legs and talking about America. The ice water turned brackish in Anna's mouth; it hurt her to breathe. Why couldn't they all just leave her alone?

"Annie—?"

Anna had flung her glass away. Water arced through the sluggish air, spilling onto blistered grass. She couldn't tell what had angered her more—Rosalind's not knowing, or her having forced Anna to think again about all the things she'd tried to banish from her underwater world. And why should Rosalind get off scot-free? Anna started to say something about Maeve, about Fiona, but Rosalind cut her off.

"I don't think I can talk about it just yet—I don't think I have any right to talk about it." She reached into her purse and pulled on a pair of dark glasses. Taking a long sip of whiskey, she settled back on the chaise longue, and, as if taking up a dare, began to talk as breezily as if Anna had never interrupted her.

"I was wooed in the States, Annie—shamelessly wooed. They want me to set up a program in cultural politics. They've been extremely generous about course reductions. And there's no problem about my spending at least four months of every year in London."

Anna leaned over and switched on the radio, which happened to be reporting the five o'clock news. She turned up the volume as loud as it would go. The People's Army had got rid of all obstacles to order in Tiananmen Square; there were very few people left to be interviewed about the prospects of democracy in China. Britain was not expected to implement any retributive measures against the Chinese government.

Rosalind switched off the set. "And so we sell out once again— we can do business with them, after all. You can hear it in all the broadcasts now, however much the on-the-spot reporters strain to keep our attention. Sorry, dears, but the world's changed channels. We must move on to Wimbledon." She fell silent then, picking at a scab on her knee.

"When do you go?" Anna asked abruptly.

"Go where?"

"To the States, of course."

Rosalind took off her dark glasses and looked directly into Anna's eyes. "I never said I was actually going. I said they wanted me. I should have added that I'd be a fool not to go. But I am a fool, among other things. I've just left my own university, you see—given notice, thrown myself into the embrace of the Open Market. I'm going to do consulting work, freelance for special interest groups. Right now I've got something with a publishing house that's putting out broadsides on social issues by important dissenters—subversives, I suppose our government would call them. It's quite exciting, Annie—it means there's some hope of change, of people waking up at last. In the most tepid and tentative way of course. But still—"

Rosalind waited, as if for some gesture of interest or approval on Anna's part.

"But that's not why I've come down. You see, Annie—I'm afraid it's not I but you who've got to be going. I hope you understand—I've had to sell the cottage." Again, there was no response. Rosalind leaned forward in her chair and lightly pressed on Anna's wrist. "I've sold Rest Harrow."

Anna drew back her hand and rubbed at the spot which Rosalind had touched, as if it were a bruise or a puncture mark. What was she supposed to say? Where was she supposed to go? She had a lease, of course, but she knew she wouldn't use it in any way. Let Rosalind evict her—she would be better off someplace else, where no one she knew would ever find her.

"Naturally you're more than welcome to come to London for the rest of your stay. There's lots of room, you can have the whole top floor if you like. I'm sorry about the cottage, Annie, really I am. But I couldn't afford to keep it on any more—after all that's happened—someone approached me and—you do understand?" Rosalind got up from her chair and crouched by Anna's side. "Don't worry, there's no great rush. You'll have all the time you need to pack yourself up and say your goodbyes. Don't be cross. You'll flourish in London—you've been cooped up here far too long. It's all right, isn't it Annie?"

Anna waited for a moment, eking out her silence as though it were water dripping slowly, maddeningly from a tap. And then the words came out, different from anything she'd intended.

"I'm not Annie. That isn't my name. I'm Anna."

"Anna?" Rosalind looked puzzled, as though the title of some obscure dynasty had been introduced into the conversation.

"My name is Anna."

Rosalind stared at her for a moment, then walked over to the end of the garden and retrieved Anna's glass from the lawn. After a moment she returned, picking up her own empty glass and smiling the way a hostess might at an awkward, unanticipated guest. "I've brought some things for tea. I've even brought a cream cake—we'd better eat it right away. If it sits around any longer in this heat we're sure to come down with botulism. Or is it listeria? Probably both, these days. Oh well, it doesn't really hurt you, they say. As long as you're not pregnant or elderly. Or both."

"Or both," Anna repeated, to the Downs, to a blackbird which had suddenly careened into song, to the shirt-tail she was twisting in her hands.

*     *     *

Later that night, Rosalind went out—she said she had some business in the village. She'd be back late—Anna needn't wait up for her. Anna replied that she'd be staying up late anyway; she'd have to get started with her packing.

But she didn't so much as drag out a suitcase from the cupboard. Instead, she ran herself a long bath and washed her hair—things that didn't require any effort, any thinking at all. With her robe wrapped tight around her, a towel turbanning her hair, she was halfway down the hallway to her room, the spare room, when she changed her mind and entered Rosalind's.

It looked the same as usual—Rosalind's things were heaped on the bed, but the vanity table with its threefold mirror stood in the corner, expectant, unencumbered. Anna went across to it and sat down before the mirror, turning on the lamps at either side. In their light her reflection looked bleached-out, as though the features had been printed in and then erased, leaving only a web of indentations. Around the eyes, at the corners of the mouth, across the throat. She reached up and gently touched these lines she had never seen before. Undoing the towel from her hair, she leaned as close to the glass as she could. No grey hairs. And yet she felt suddenly old, old—she who had always thought of herself as the youngest of any group; the baby, the child. This wasn't Anna in the mirror; this face didn't own her any more than did the others she had worn. Where was her true self, the one which would fit inside the outlines of her skin and stay, so she'd know at last who she was; what she still might be?

Anna pulled back from the mirror; loosened her robe so that it fell around her waist. Her breasts looked fuller; the nipples darker, wider. Her belly glistened, like dough that had been kneaded and kneaded. She put her hand to her throat, and let it slide down to her breasts. She might have been touching lambswool or cotton instead of her own skin. She put her hand between her breasts as if to catch the beat of her heart, the way, as a child, she'd caught grasshoppers in the long grass by the lake. But there was nothing there. She spread her hands over her breasts to take some warmth, some fullness from them. Nothing again; nothing. And then her hands dropped to her belly; she pressed so hard it hurt and then let go. The skin leapt back into the space her hands had made. Whatever was inside her, whatever insisted on rounding and filling her, she couldn't feel at all.

\*     \*     \*

Rosalind stayed on for the week, taking down pictures, packing up crockery, while Anna accomplished her own acts of dispossession. Despite the heat she worked methodically, with surprising spurts of energy. She threw almost everything away. The clothes she'd worn that fall and winter went into bin liners to be given to Miss Molesworth for the next church jumble sale. The only things she would take with her would be her computer, the diskettes which contained her book, her copies of Woolf's novels and journals, and a small suitcase of the clothes into which she'd still be able to fit over the next month or so. For her session at the mirror had made it clear that there were changes going on over which she had no control. Changes she'd have to accommodate, accede to, however little she could feel them working inside her.

Once she'd packed up her belongings, Anna sat at her desk, facing the empty space where her computer had been; confronting the shore on which she'd been stranded. She could hardly go back to Canada in her present condition; she could never go back with a baby. She would have to speak with Simon, as soon as possible. She'd write to him care of the school and ask for a meeting. He would have to be told; they would have to do what was called the decent thing, just as if they were characters in the novels her mother had loved to read, novels in which the lovers retire beyond the line drawn by the book's last page, under the sentence of marriage.

Going over to the box that contained her books, Anna found her copy of *The Waves*. She shook it till the envelope with Simon's letter fell out, the letter she'd received the day it had been decided that she and Rosalind would go to Crete. She read it over several times; found it a direct declaration of love and open proposal of marriage, one which had deserved the courtesy of a reply just as honest and open. Folding the letter carefully she looked for the first time at the card in which it had been enclosed.

It was a reproduction of a painting called *The Resurrection: Cookham*. On it an entire village seemed to be waking out of the grave. No Lazarus, just ordinary people in their own familiar flesh, unperturbed at finding themselves at home, in Paradise. In the porch of a church rather like the one at Pyeford sat a huge bolster of a woman, her children on her lap. Above her leaned a ghostly man, fingering her thick, dark hair. Two naked men erupted from the middle ground, one lit sharply, all his limbs contorted, the other shadowed, his genitals hidden by the tip of a cypress tree. Tugged up from the clay, a red-haired woman in a dress of daisies. Across from her, a wife brushing lint from her husband's coat. And off in the background, almost too small to see, pleasure boats sailing under golden skies.

The theological equivalent of a village fête, thought Anna. But her heart was beating uncomfortably fast. Surely the inclusion of the card was a good omen, proof that Simon's affection for her could withstand the meanness and coldness of her lengthy silence. Even if she couldn't bring herself to believe in the paradise the images revealed, at least she needn't worry as to whether Simon might have changed his mind. Someone like Simon didn't change, she told herself. He was what he was—that was his mark, his unmistakable sign. Then wasn't Simon exactly what she needed; she who could never fix herself in place, who was always being turned and rearranged by everyone she met, like the pebbled glass in a kaleidoscope?

Anna sat there for a long time, gazing at the picture in her hand. Envisioning Simon not as a ragged-haired, unravelling schoolmaster but as the softly slouching nude in the Cookham resurrection. Black-haired, unabashed, his head turned in a direction outside the painting, as though he were searching for someone who hadn't yet arrived within the boundaries of the canvas.

# XXVII

# DEMOISELLES DE LIBERTÉ

Soon after Rosalind's return to Pyeford, Miss Molesworth had come round with posters for the village fête, which was to take place at the solstice. Rosalind bought two tickets, though Anna insisted she wouldn't go. But in the end she had no excuse strong enough to hold out against Rosalind's insistence that they join the celebrations. Besides, she'd decided it would be the perfect chance—her only chance—to get hold of Simon. The letter she'd tried to write to him was still in her desk drawer. She'd found herself unable to get beyond the salutation, frightened as she was that she'd scare him off by saying too much, or baffle him by saying too little.

The fête was to be a costume affair, in honour of the bicentennial being celebrated across the channel. Most of the villagers were dressing up in costumes of the *Ancien Régime,* and Rosalind had set her heart on a counter-coup. She raided the nearest Oxfam shop and came back with the raw materials for fancy dress: she and Anna would be radical women of the streets, wearing Grecian robes and Phrygian caps. Anna was afraid the costume would give her away, but the material turned out to be light and loose as a nightdress around her.

The weather was perfect on the twenty-first, but then there'd been months of perfect summer days already. The village green was the colour of scorched pastry. This year the number of floral displays was significantly down, and no one seemed willing to purchase the pound and fruit cakes burdening the trestle tables. It was too hot to think of eating anything, even the congealed coconut oil dispensed from a Mr. Whippy van drawn up behind the marquee. Too hot for any plot to the day—no pageants or concerts, just a sauntering back and forth, a sipping of watery lemonade, an ogling of costumes.

There were several Madame Récamiers, half a dozen Sydney Cartons, one teenaged Danton, and a gross of Scarlet Pimpernels. Miss Molesworth had got herself up as a cross between Old Mother Hubbard and Little Bo-Peep. With a fine disregard for period, Mrs. Higley had turned herself into the Iron Duke. As for the vicar, he'd accepted a lucrative dare to impersonate Robespierre, thus earning fifty pounds for the Reshingling of the Steeple Fund.

Nicholas's dare, of course. With a patched and powdered Cressy at his side, a train of black-haired, beribboned children at his heels, he'd made himself into a most convincing Louis Seize. Striking lascivious poses in white Lurex tights, he appeared not merely debauched but positively syphilitic. When he attempted to put an arm round each of the citoyennes, Anna twisted out of his embrace, running off without a word to the coconut shy. Rosalind stayed behind: from across the green, Anna watched the pair of them walking in the direction of the marquee and earnestly discussing something. She refused to think about what they could possibly have to say to one another. It wasn't her business, anymore. Her business was to find Simon.

It was mid-afternoon before she did so. He was lodged behind the school's second-hand bookstall, sorting out small change, making sure no one disarranged a thirty-year's collection of Reader's Digest donated by some village wit. At first he seemed not to recognize her—perhaps it was the red cap, which made her look, she felt, more like a rooster than a demoiselle de liberté. But when she took off the cap and held out to him a book she'd randomly picked off the stall, he beamed at her. She waited till the other buyers had wandered off, then, plucking up her courage, asked whether they mightn't have a few moments' conversation together. Five minutes later, Simon had begged off counter duty and was walking with Anna to a hiding-place she'd discovered between the tents.

Knowing how bedraggled she must look, how precipitous her appeal would seem, Anna was floundering for the words with which to begin when Simon pre-empted her. Simon, not the naked torso in the Cookham Resurrection; Simon wearing a pair of sagging woollen trousers, a sodden string vest under his shirt. His hair wanted cutting; his glasses were spectacularly smudged. But the look on his face was as gentle, as guileless as any she could ever hope to see.

Only gradually did his words make any sense to her. He was wishing her something—bonheur? No, bon voyage. Rosalind came into it somehow—Rosalind had come by to see him, had mentioned that Anna was leaving Pyeford, spending the rest of her stay in London before heading back to Canada. He wanted to take this opportunity to apologize—and to thank her. He'd come to the conclusion that she'd been perfectly right not to respond to the letter he'd sent. It would have been pure selfishness on his part to have burdened her with the kind of life he'd be leading from now on. For he wasn't on his own any longer. He had his father to look after—there'd been an unexpected improvement in his condition; he would be able to come out of the nursing home and live in the terraced house Simon had bought on the outskirts of Durham—though of course they'd need to have a home help during the day. He was grateful, truly grateful to Anna for having so tactfully ignored his foolishness. Worse than foolishness. He would always think of her—and here Simon's voice went into italics—with the greatest respect. And he wished her all possible happiness on her return to the wonderful country which was, as he now had the good sense to recognize, the only place she would ever want to call home.

Anna felt her face go numb as Simon spoke. Her lips and eyes seemed needled with ice, though she kept on smiling, nodding. She was watching his face for a sign of the man who had offered her mistletoe; gone with her into the clearing, listening to change ringing. He was holding out his hand to shake hers and be gone, and there wasn't a thing she could do to stop him. She grasped his hand, but instead of shaking it she closed her own hands over it, holding tight, trying to tell him with the pressure of her fingers what she couldn't say. "Goodbye then, Anna," he said at last, gently pulling himself free. He turned from her and walked away.

Moments later Rosalind came up to Anna with a cup of tea. "Isn't this heat *awful*—I thought it would cool down towards evening. Here, drink it, go on. I've been trapped in conversation at the tombola with Miss Molesworth for the past half hour. She'd heard that I was selling the cottage, and wanted to know all about the new owner. I was tempted to say that he's a Rastafarian anarchist. You don't look at all well, Anna—I think we ought to get back. By the way, I'm finally making progress with the village prodigal—the great Pryce-Jones, of course. I think I've persuaded him that the winds are slowly changing—that it might be politic for him to write for us as well as Sky TV. It's the only condition on which I'd sell, of course—he's been wanting the cottage for years. Anna—didn't you hear—are you all right?"

"Perfectly all right." But all the same she leaned on Rosalind's arm as they walked away from the green. As soon as they reached Rest Harrow, Anna sank into a chaise longue in the garden. Rosalind reappeared a moment later with a large bottle of white wine, several jugs of iced water, and a pair of silver tumblers. Silently, they lay back on their chairs, sipping at the wine. It was too hot to think of eating, or sleeping, or even talking; too late to have anything to say. It didn't matter to her anymore what Rosalind did, or Nick, or anyone else, for that matter. Too hot, too late, too still. Languor, Anna thought. The whole world had become that one word: languor.

Then Rosalind got up from her chair and reached for one of the jugs. She walked with it into the middle of the garden, where she lifted it over her head, so that the water gushed down, washing off the dust and sweat that had glued her hair to her face, her dress to her skin. And then she walked back to where Anna was lying. She held out her hand and pulled Anna to her feet—she picked up the other water jug and led her into the garden. Anna looked at her and nodded. There was no longer anything to watch out for, lose control of. She was perfectly free. Slowly, Rosalind poured the water over her, till her hair and the flimsy cotton of her dress were drenched. While Anna stood savouring the coolness of the water on her skin, Rosalind went back to the chaises longues, took off the mattresses and threw them down, side by side, onto the grass.

"We'll sleep out here tonight—it's still an oven inside."

Anna collapsed on a mattress, lying back and looking up at the fingernail moon.

"What will you do, Anna?"

"Do?"

"With the baby."

"Oh."

"That isn't an answer." Rosalind came and sat down beside her. Gently, she lifted her hand to Anna's belly, where the nightgown clung to the round, full skin. Rosalind's hand was stroking Anna's belly in little fluttering motions. "*Effleurage*," she said. "It's a lovely word, isn't it?"

"How did you know?"

"Effleurage? I read about it once."

"I meant about the—" She couldn't say the word; she merely touched Rosalind's hand as it stroked her belly.

After a moment, Rosalind answered. "I was pregnant once, a long, long time ago. And it was at just about this stage—"

"Yes?"

"That I lost the baby. Or it lost me. That doesn't matter. Are you going to have her here, or back home? What does Luke say?"

"How do you know it's a her?"

"I just know. What does Luke say, Anna?"

"Luke doesn't know." Anna, too, waited for a moment, and then, with the same insouciance with which she'd let Rosalind shower her in the garden, she spoke again. "It's not his baby."

"Oh."

"I haven't thought of where I'll have it yet."

Rosalind kept fluttering her fingers round and round the small, still globe of Anna's lap. "You could always stay on with me in London, you know. Till the baby's born. And for as long as you want, afterwards. There's plenty of space. I'd like that, Anna, I really would. You could have the baby at home—I'd make sure you did all the exercises, the breathing and panting, all of that. You don't have to tell me right away. But I'd like you to stay, Anna—I'd like to be with you, if that will help at all."

Rosalind lay her head against Anna's breast, still stroking the roundness of her belly, her fingertips light as moths circling a lamp. And Anna had the oddest feeling, as if her body were humming a tune she couldn't hear but felt so strongly she knew she could dance to it, were she only to try. She didn't get up—she simply lay there stroking Rosalind's hair, her hand taking on the colour of that rich, red flame in which, for the first time, she saw strands transparent as glass. She stroked Rosalind's hair all the more gently, now. The humming went on and on inside her, and she began to feel something curious, both gravity and lightness, as if for the first time she were attached to her body and what it carried; as if she were relieved of a burden she'd carried so long it had grown into her very skin.

*     *     *

Anna woke to the sound of a moth bashing at the study windows—the light was on inside, making a milky sun behind the glass. Half of her was still in the shallows of sleep, trying to shut out the beating of the moth's wings; the other half was afraid the noise might wake the entire village, or at least Rosalind, who was lying next to her, her body cradling her own. Gently, slowly, Anna pulled away. Rosalind was still sleeping, her breath rising and falling so softly Anna had to listen hard to hear it.

The churchbell rang—it was half past one. She was wide awake, now. The heat was still intense and she felt terribly thirsty. She managed to get to her feet and to turn off the study light without disturbing Rosalind. But she didn't go back out into the garden; instead she felt her way up the stairs to her room in a darkness heavy with the day's accumulated heat. She turned on the lamp by her bedside table and found her suitcase, already packed for the trip to London. At the bottom was her copy of The Waves, marked by Simon's card and letter. She tore the letter into small, indecipherable pieces, and fluttered them into the wastepaper bin. But she kept the Cookham card, poring over it in the small pool of light.

She tried to read the painting as she would a text, left to right, looking for some pattern of meaning she could fix. But the images kept tilting this way and that; she was forever finding new scenes and combinations. No sooner did she focus one detail than it altered her perception of another, and another. Till there was no image that did not change and yet continue, as if the whole were some unending country dance where the music beat a silent measure of its own.

She put the card back in the book and took some clothes from her suitcase. She dressed quickly, noiselessly, carrying her shoes in her hands, waiting until she reached the carpeted hall downstairs to put them on. From the study she fetched her computer and another suitcase full of books, and loaded up the car. When she was done, she closed the door of Rest Harrow softly behind her, putting her hand like a blindfold over the Medusa knocker.

# XXVIII

# PEACHAM HOUSE

Anna drove off in the general direction of the airport, determined to board the first plane to Canada, whatever the cost might be, wherever the destination. If she didn't leave now, if she didn't act on pure impulse she knew she'd never get going at all. And she had to go, she knew that, in spite of everything that Rosalind had said. She would have liked to have taken her leave as graciously as Simon had—she would have liked to have spoken to Varti, too. But she had to keep moving, she had to get home. Nearly at Heathrow, Anna felt her eyelids flickering, her head lolling down onto her chest. Biting her lips to keep herself awake, she turned off the motorway and pulled up into a field on the outskirts of a small town.

There was a churchyard at the very edge of the field; a breeze was blowing from it, inviting her to leave the car and walk a little way into the night. And so she got out and made her way toward the church, the wind lifting the edges of her dress, lengthening and fluting it round her, moonlight bleaching it to a fine, porous white.

They were expecting her, the people gathered in the churchyard. The woman blanketed in ivy on top of the table tomb—she was Anna's mother. Simon was the oddly dressed man—a judge, a trecento physician?—hoisting himself out of a floral bunker. In the church porch, cradling a mass of babies, Varti sat. Nicholas, naked, blackhaired, leaned his elbows on a pair of gravestones. Off in the distance Anna saw Luke and Emma, he standing patiently while she brushed the lint from his lapels. And that woman draped over a tombstone white as icing-sugar, a woman in black, wearily but defiantly *louche*, was Rosalind.

Only she, Anna, wasn't there. Nowhere was she to be found among the newly hatched, the blithely re-assembled. She went from group to group, in and out the gravestones, past the Elders lined up against the church wall, through the stile beside a gate on the other side of which

not a woman in white, not even an angel but a white horse waited, tossing his head so that his mane stung her face like sleet. She got up on his
back, her hands digging into the mane which was not hair but shards of
glass, so that her fingers were pouring blood as she galloped towards the
river. There were no pleasure boats on the water, no waiting crowds,
only two black figures on the bank below: Fiona. Maeve. They too had
no place among the resurrected. And they looked right through her, as if
reproaching her for having forgotten them. But she couldn't stop, she
couldn't even lift a hand to wave for fear of falling off the horse which
was taking her faster and faster away from them all, down the bank and
through the water rising higher and higher up the horse's flanks, white
as lump sugar, melting like sugar in a pot of boiling water—

Sun pouring through the windshield woke her. It was only six
o'clock. Anna got out of the car and stretched, rubbing her back and
her legs, then making her way to a stream cutting through the field.
Though the rocks which had once been on the river bed showed
parched and white, there was water enough for her to wash her face and
arms. She got back into the car and crawled down the road, looking for
a call box from which she could phone the airport. She found one outside a restaurant: to her astonishment, it was in order. The woman at
Air Canada told her there was a seat available on the afternoon flight
to Halifax. Anna gave her credit card number and hung up before she
could be told to have a nice day.

In a Happy Eater restaurant, over something that was either mush-
room soup or coffee, Anna tried to possess her soul in patience. She had
some eight hours to kill. The waitress brought her scrambled eggs, toast,
sausages, and she devoured them all. She read the menu backwards and
forwards; she even leafed through a copy of *Woman's Own* that she'd
found in the loo. Articles on the glories of motherhood, the bliss of dec-
orating your first home, the rewards of being the perfect helpmeet to
your husband in a world as sweet and clean as a line of laundry washed
in Ivory Snow. The model on the cover looked something like Fiona,
Fiona as her husband had once painted her. Something sour rose in
Anna's throat; she felt the lightness, the ease of the last few hours leak
away from her, leaving a hard, obstinate edge of knowing.

She paid her bill, returned to her car and started down a road that
looked as if it would take her back to the motorway. A few miles on
she knew she'd taken the wrong turning. The only clue to where she

might be was a hand-painted sign for something called Peacham House. *Illustrated Guide Book. Café. Cream Teas.* Anna turned down the wide, leafy drive. No one was behind her, no one ahead: she might as well pay a quick visit, since it seemed she'd have the place to herself. No doubt it would be awful, the house attached like a withered appendix to the main attraction: a safari park, or motorbike museum. Coke tins would clot the flower beds: they'd be selling T-shirts of Mickey and Minny Mouse in feudal dress, like a couple on a funeral brass, but in living colour.

On the day the Nazis occupied Paris, Virginia and Leonard Woolf had visited Penshurst. Was anything of equal significance going on as Anna walked towards the lichen-mottled front of Peacham House? While sun warmed the ancient oaks, their leaves already bitten to green lace, peasants with no great desire to starve their children were destroying the Amazonian forest. As water played from a stone dolphin by the entranceway, real dolphins, their blood riddled with toxins, were expiring off the Welsh coast. One day—perhaps when this child inside her reached her present age—there would only be stone dolphins left. A stranger whom she could not even imagine as her own might walk up this drive in thirty-seven years' time and see—what? See if the drive remained, if the house still stood, if it hadn't been converted into a luxury housing estate, or sunk beneath thawed polar ice.

Anna leaned against the balustrade, watching water spout from the dolphin's mouth into a lily-clogged basin. She knew that what was here, now, existed only because of some wrinkle in the map of Enterprise. She knew that there were many more important things being destroyed while Peacham House stood firm, among them the lives of countless children. Thanks to Rosalind's Christmas gift she knew how many thousand died each minute, for want of a few pennies' worth of sugar and clean water. Knowing all this she still walked into the house, through the hall with its copper bowls of lupins and poppies, past a woman who sold her a ticket and guidebook, assuring her that all proceeds went to the needy. Which needy? Distressed gentlefolk? London's beggars? It didn't matter. She was quitting this intractably foreign country, she wanted only to enjoy one last morning in the pages of a fiction she had once called England.

Peacham had been built in Tudor times. There was an Elizabethan great hall, a Regency parlour, a Victorian nursery and an Edwardian library; the full complement of pewter and stained glass, mahogany and rosewood, rocking horses, dolls and gilt-edged morocco. Everything was perfect of its kind, beautifully arranged, a monument to stability and order and the considerable redeeming qualities of wealth. There was a plethora of family portraits: husbands adoring obedient wives worshipped by impossibly beautiful children. Even the dogs were docile, the skies as blandly beatific as today's.

Fanning herself with her guidebook, Anna walked out into the gardens, between borders of roses and lilies, intricately planted beds of aromatic herbs. A haze like powdered sugar thickened the air. She bought herself morning coffee in the pavilion at the end of the garden and sat there staring out at the yellowed lawn, but thinking of home. Herons would be nesting in the pines by the inlet; milkweed ripening. There would be boats out on the bay, netting herring and mackerel. And across the bay, the nuclear power plant she never liked to think about, the one with picnic tables planted round it, making it look as benign an interruption of the landscape as a primary school or children's playground. Whole crews of scientists and engineers and experts had declared it safe as houses—safer, better, brighter.

Leaving the pavilion, Anna began to shiver in spite of the heat. In less than twelve hours she would find herself at home, without husband or friend or lover, and thrown on the riskiest of resources: a job dependent on a book she'd probably never get published; an isolated house too close to a sea as polluted as any in Europe. And before the year was out she would be alone with a baby, a baby brought into a world no longer blue and green and beautiful. Not a world so much as a ruined house, a house on fire, a persistent smell of burning.

Anna knew she ought to hurry back to the parking lot and head for the airport, but instead she sat down on a sunny bench by a shrunken pond. Carp, sluggish in the heat, broke the water's skin. She stared at them, past them, into the black below. Slowly, she stopped shivering. Or at least, only her belly went on shivering, while the rest of her stayed still. It was the merest flutter, a transitory quickening. Anna bit down on her lip, hard enough to draw a bead of blood. Her head seemed to ring, like crystal flicked by a finger. It made her think of Rosalind's effleurage last night, but this time it had happened of itself, had come from deep inside her.

One fat, red carp turned slowly in the pond, appeared to shrug, and sank below the surface of the water. Anna stared at where it had disappeared—her lips were moving, but no sound came out. The water started to shiver, but this time it wasn't a fish rising, nor was it the wind stirring gently overhead. It was a reflection forming at the farthest edge of the pond, a reflection wished for so long and so hopelessly that now it had appeared she dared not look up to prove to herself that the woman was indeed standing just across from her. That the face which floated so mockingly, yet hauntingly across the pond, belonged to the figure she'd glimpsed only a handful of times, here and there and nowhere at all.

If she could only reach out and seize some smallest proof, some talisman. But the moment she did so, she knew the woman would vanish. So she looked, instead, at the face in the pond, how it seemed to float just below the surface of the water: white and strangely bare, as if washed of all inessentials. It wasn't the face of anyone she'd ever known, and yet it was more familiar to her than her mother's, or Varti's or Rosalind's. And the more she stared at it, the more it seemed to her that this face she could not name was somehow so close to her own that she might at last be looking at her very image in the water.

And now the great carp leaps, breaking the surface of the pool. Anna feels something like a shock or seizure which both roots her and flings her harder, farther than she can measure. It's as if she were a pane of glass; she can feel herself split, jagged as lightning; feel fractures race across her surface; feel, too, the heaviness with which the shards of glass still hang inside the frame, hang and then painfully give way. And last of all, how the air whirls in, unravelling, scattering what remains of the face she's glimpsed, her one true face.

From the branches above, a tumult of notes, cutting a message into her ears. But what is it saying, what does it mean? The heroes of fairy tales learn the language of animals, of birds and fish and serpents. There are charms to be disclosed, charms without which certain death would come; irreversible catastrophe. What is the bird speaking— warning or encouragement? That she is right or wrong to be doing what she is? And is it speaking to her, or to the child curled up inside her blood and bones?

How can Anna tell what the bird is saying? Fictions again—nothing she can be sure of. She rises from the bench, glancing, one last time, at the blankness of the water, the perfect emptiness across from her. She doesn't know any longer who she's been or what she will become. She can only be sure of this: that there will be a plane waiting for her at the airport; that she will claim her ticket and make her way on board. That on the flight home she will accept the newspaper the steward offers her, knowing that from the solid, menaced world lies no escape to any free and open water. And that she and the child she's carrying will step out at last onto a different continent, where they'll breathe in the same half-poisoned, yet sustaining air.